OCTAVIA'S BROOD:
SCIENCE FICTION STORIES FROM SOCIAL JUSTICE MOVEMENTS

edited by
Walidah Imarisha and adrienne maree brown

OCTAVIA'S BROOD:
SCIENCE FICTION STORIES FROM SOCIAL JUSTICE MOVEMENTS

edited by
Walidah Imarisha and adrienne maree brown

foreword by
Sheree Renée Thomas

Advance praise for OCTAVIA'S BROOD:

"Never has one book so thoroughly realized the dream of its namesake. *Octavia's Brood* is the progeny of two lovers of Octavia Butler and their belief in her dream that science fiction is for everybody. In these pages, we witness the power of sci-fi to map our visions of worlds we want, or don't, through the imaginations of some of our favorite activists and artists. We hope this is the first of many generations of *Octavia's Brood*, midwifed to life by such attentive editors. Butler could not wish for better evidence of her touch changing our literary and living landscapes. Play with these children, read these works, and find the children in you waiting to take root under the stars!" —**Moya Bailey and Ayana Jamieson, Octavia E. Butler Legacy**

"'All social justice work is science fiction. We are imagining a world free of injustice, a world that doesn't yet exist.' The first time I heard adrienne maree brown provide that frame, I was changed. A longtime devotee to Octavia Butler, my ideas about love and community and family, and of course, the future have been shaped by her fiction. But brown offered a new and utterly useful prompt, a way to integrate all of my selves (for I'd long viewed my "activist" self as some separate person). In this provocative collection of fiction, Walida Imarisha and adrienne maree brown provide boundless space for their writers—changemakers, teachers, organizers, and leaders—to untether from this realm their struggles for justice. Most of these stories are written by people who are new to fiction. Political prisoner Mumia Abu Jamal literally writes from behind walls. Yet he writes with abandon, giving us new, imaginative analyses of an American classic. Like Butler's fiction, this collection is cartography, a map to freedom." —**dream hampton, filmmaker and Visiting Artist at Stanford University's Institute for Diversity in the Arts**

"Those concerned with justice and liberation must always persuade the mass of people that a better world is possible. Our job begins with speculative fictions that fire society's imagination and its desire for change. In adrienne maree brown and Walidah Imarisha's visionary conception, and by its activist-artists' often stunning acts of creative inception, *Octavia's Brood* makes for great thinking and damn good reading. The rest will be up to us."—**Jeff Chang,** *Who We Be: The Colorization of America*

"Octavia once told me that two things worried her about the future of humanity: The tendency to think hierarchically, and the tendency to place ourselves higher on the hierarchy than others. I think she would be humbled beyond words that the fine, thoughtful writers in this volume have honored her with their hearts and minds. And that in calling for us to consider that hierarchical structure, they are not walking in her shadow, nor standing on her shoulders, but marching at her side." —**Steven Barnes, author of *Lion's Blood***

"Conventional exclamatory phrases don't come close to capturing the essence of what we have here in *Octavia's Brood*. One part *sacred text*, one part *social movement manual*, one part *diary of our future selves* telling us, 'It's going to be okay, keep working, keep loving.' Our radical imaginations are under siege and this text is the rescue mission. It is the new cornerstone of every class I teach on inequality, justice, and social change. It is my new reference for how to think across fabricated boundaries—organizers vs. artists, academy vs. community, real world vs. utopia, doing vs. envisioning. It should take pride of place on our nightstands, within reach any time we become weary with the world as it is. [*Octavia's Brood* is] a portal, a gateway, a glimpse in to an alternate reality where the answer to the perennial question, *What Do We Owe Each Other?*, turns out to be 'Everything, Everything…' This is the text we've been waiting for." —**Ruha Benjamin, professor of African American Studies at Princeton University and author of *People's Science: Bodies and Rights on the Stem Cell Frontier***

Octavia's Brood: Science Fiction Stories from Social Justice Movements
edited by Walidah Imarisha and adrienne maree brown

ISBN 978-1-84935-209-3 | Ebook ISBN: 978-1-84935-210-9
Library of Congress Number: 2014958844

Cover design and chapter opener illustrations: John Jennings
Melanie Hardy illustrated the map on page 56 to accompany "The Long Memory"
Alixa Garcia supplied illustrations for "In Spite of Darkness"

Interior Design by Margaret Killjoy (birdsbeforethestorm.net)

Printed in the USA on recycled, acid-free paper.

AK Press
674-A 23rd Street
Oakland, CA 94612
www.akpress.org
akpress@akpress.org
510.208.1700

AK Press UK
P.O. Box 12766
Edinburgh EH8 9YE
www.akuk.com
ak@akedin.demon.co.uk
0131.555.5165

Institute for Anarchist Studies
www.anarchiststudies.org
anarchiststudies@gmail.com

To Octavia E. Butler, who serves as a north star for so many of us. She told us what would happen—"all that you touch you change"   and then she touched us, fearlessly, brave enough to change us. We dedicate this collection to her, coming out with our own fierce longing to have our writing change everyone and everything we touch.

"I am not going to
die, I'm going home like a
shooting star."

—Sojourner Truth

CONTENTS

Foreword 1
Sheree Renée Thomas

Introduction 3
Walidah Imarisha

Revolution Shuffle 7
Bao Phi

The Token Superhero 15
David F. Walker

the river 23
adrienne maree brown

Evidence 33
Alexis Pauline Gumbs

Black Angel 43
Walidah Imarisha

The Long Memory 57
Morrigan Phillips

Small and Bright 79
Autumn Brown

In Spite of Darkness 89
Alixa Garcia

Hollow 109
Mia Mingus

Lalibela 123
Gabriel Teodros

Little Brown Mouse 135
Tunde Olaniran

Sanford and Sun 145
Dawolu Jabari Anderson

Runway Blackout 167
Tara Betts

Kafka's Last Laugh 177
Vagabond

22XX: One-Shot 187
Jelani Wilson

Manhunters 197
Kalamu ya Salaam

Aftermath 215
LeVar Burton

Fire on the Mountain 225
Terry Bisson

Homing Instinct 239
Dani McClain

children who fly 249
Leah Lakshmi Piepzna-Samarasinha

***Star Wars* and the American Imagination . . . 255**
Mumia Abu-Jamal

The Only Lasting Truth 259
Tananarive Due

Outro 279
adrienne maree brown

Acknowledgments 283

Bios 287

FOREWORD

BIRTH OF A REVOLUTION

SHEREE RENÉE THOMAS

"We believe it is our right and responsibility to write
ourselves into the future."
—*Walidah Imarisha and adrienne maree brown*

IN 1963 MARTIN LUTHER KING JR. CAUTIONED US ABOUT ADDING
"deeper darkness to a night already devoid of stars."[1] He wrote that
darkness cannot drive out darkness, that hate cannot drive out hate,
and he reminded us that only love can do that. Thirty years later, Octavia E. Butler wrote in her novel *Parable of the Sower* that our "destiny
is to take root among the stars."[2] The activist and the artist seem at
first to have been engaged in markedly different lifework, yet they embraced a shared dream for the future. Their work is linked by faith and
a fusion of spiritual teachings and social consciousness, a futuristic
social gospel. In its essence, social justice work, which King embodied
and Butler expressed so skillfully in her novels and stories, is about
love—a love that has the best hopes and wishes for humanity at heart.

Today social justice represents one of the most serious challenges
to the conscience of our world. New technology and corporate political policies make it possible to accumulate wealth and power in

---

1   Martin Luther King, Jr., *Strength to Love* (Minneapolis, MN: Fortress Press,
    2010), p. 47.
2   Octavia E. Butler, *Parable of the Sower* (New York: Four Walls, Eight Windows,
    1993), 77.

startling, fantastic ways, while widening the gulf between those who have and those who don't. In America and in the big beautiful world beyond, the gulf widens perversely, making a mockery of freedom, justice, democracy, and even mercy. James Baldwin said that we are not born knowing what these concepts mean, that they are neither common nor well defined. If we "individuals must make an enormous effort to arrive at the respect for other people that these words imply," as he wrote, then our communities must make a sustained and concentrated effort to create societies that reflect that same sense of respect and meaning.[3]

The stories in *Octavia's Brood: Science Fiction Stories from Social Justice Movements* represent a global quest for social transformation, for justice. They are about people from different backgrounds and worlds, expanding the notions of solidarity and community, redefining service, and exploring and rediscovering the human spirit in baffling times, under challenging circumstances. The writers collected here offer stories that explore a broad range of social justice issues, from urban gentrification, bioterrorism, racism, and militarism to motherhood, environmentalism, spiritual journeys, and psychological quests. Culled from artists who in their other lives work tirelessly as community activists, educators, and organizers, these stories incite, inspire, engage. If the purpose of a writer, as Toni Cade Bambara said, "is to make revolution irresistible," these writers, these stories *represent*.[4] With incisive imagination and a spirited sense of wonder, the contributors bridge the gap between speculative fiction and social justice, boldly writing new voices and communities into the future.

A trickster, teacher, chaos, and clay, God, as described by Octavia E. Butler in her Parable novels, is change, and *Octavia's Brood* is an important resource in our journey toward positive cultural and institutional change. May it spawn new conversations in classrooms, inspire vigorous discussion in coffeehouses and book clubs, and create new organizing tools and "case studies" for strategizing in our community organizations.[5]

---

3   James Baldwin, *The Price of the Ticket* (New York: St. Martin's Press, 1985), 156.

4   Toni Cade Bamabara, interview with Kate Bonetti (Columbia, MO: American Audio Prose Library, 1982).

5   For more information, see *Octavia's Brood*, http://www.octaviasbrood.com/.

INTRODUCTION

WALIDAH IMARISHA

WHENEVER WE TRY TO ENVISION A WORLD WITHOUT WAR, WITHOUT violence, without prisons, without capitalism, we are engaging in speculative fiction. All organizing is science fiction. Organizers and activists dedicate their lives to creating and envisioning another world, or many other worlds—so what better venue for organizers to explore their work than science fiction stories? That is the premise behind the book you hold in your hands.

In the years we have been working on this book, many folks have asked us what science fiction could possibly have to do with social justice organizing. And every time, we have responded, "Everything. *Everything.*" We want organizers and movement builders to be able to claim the vast space of possibility, to be birthing visionary stories. Using their everyday realities and experiences of changing the world, they can form the foundation for the fantastic and, we hope, build a future where the fantastic liberates the mundane.

We titled this collection in honor of Black science fiction writer Octavia E. Butler. Butler explored the intersections of identity and imagination, the gray areas of race, class, gender, sexuality, love, militarism, inequality, oppression, resistance, and—most important—hope. Her work has taught us so much about the principles of visionary fiction, inspiring us. The title plays on Butler's three novel collection, *Lilith's Brood*, which is about adaptation as a necessity for survival. Changes will occur that we cannot even begin to imagine, and the next generation will be both utterly familiar and wholly alien to their parents. We believe this is what it means to carry on Butler's legacy of writing visionary fiction.

"Visionary fiction" is a term we developed to distinguish science fiction that has relevance toward building new, freer worlds from the mainstream strain of science fiction, which most often reinforces dominant narratives of power. Visionary fiction encompasses all of the fantastic, with the arc always bending toward justice. We believe this space is vital for any process of decolonization, because the decolonization of the imagination is the most dangerous and subversive form there is: for it is where all other forms of decolonization are born. Once the imagination is unshackled, liberation is limitless.

This anthology of visionary fiction contains short stories from people who have dedicated their lives to making change. It also includes pieces from well-known science fiction writers Tananarive Due, Terry Bisson, LeVar Burton, and Kalamu ya Salaam, and from award-winning journalist and political prisoner Mumia Abu-Jamal (who writes here about *Star Wars* and imperialism).

The process for creating this anthology was unlike any either of us editors had been involved with before, one that was both very intensive and highly collaborative. We worked with contributors over the course of many rounds of edits to pull out the visionary aspects of their incredible stories, as well as to ensure that the writing and storytelling captivated and inspired. We appreciate immensely the countless hours each writer poured into this creation of love. And we both feel lucky beyond words that we had the support and advice of the incredible Sheree Renée Thomas, who edited the groundbreaking anthology *Dark Matter: 100 Years of Speculative Fiction From the African Diaspora.*

Many of the contributors to *Octavia's Brood* had never written fiction before, let alone science fiction. When we approached folks, most were hesitant to commit, feeling like they weren't qualified. But overwhelmingly, they all came back a few weeks later, enthusiastically, with incredible ideas and some with dozens of pages already written. Because all organizing is science fiction, we are dreaming new worlds every time we think about the changes we want to make in the world. The writers in this collection just needed a little space, and perhaps permission to immerse themselves fully in their visionary selves.

We especially wanted to make space for people whose identities are marginalized and oppressed within mainstream society. Art and culture themselves are time-traveling, planes of existence where the past, present, and future shift seamlessly in and out. And for those of us from communities with historic collective trauma, we must understand that each of us is already science fiction walking around on two legs. Our ancestors dreamed us up and then bent reality to create us. For adrienne and myself, as two Black women, we think of our ancestors in chains dreaming about a day when their children's children's children would be free. They had no reason to believe this was likely, but together they dreamed of freedom, and they brought us into being. We are responsible for interpreting their regrets and realizing their imaginings. We wish to continue the work of moving forward with their visionary legacy.

At a retreat for women writers in 1988, Octavia E. Butler said that she never wanted the title of being the solitary Black female sci-fi writer. She wanted to be one of *many* Black female sci-fi writers. She wanted to be one of thousands of folks writing themselves into the present and into the future. We believe in that right Butler claimed for each of us—the right to dream as ourselves, individually and collectively. But we also think it is a responsibility she handed down: are we brave enough to imagine beyond the boundaries of "the real" and then do the hard work of sculpting reality from our dreams?

REVOLUTION SHUFFLE

BAO PHI

She got to the top of the high hill first. She sat in the grass, dropping her pack down beside her, and drummed her fingers on the machine pistol holstered at her hip. As he caught up and stood beside her, she looked up, cocking her head, and flashed a crooked grin. The moon was out, lighting wispy bare clouds in the sky. "Old man hair clouds," she quipped.

After a moment of silence, she asked him, "What do you miss right now?"

This game again. "A messy plate of nachos," he said with a sigh. "You?"

"Phở," she replied, pronouncing it the way only a Vietnamese American whose best language skills revolved around a menu could. He heard it the way a Vietnamese American who understood Vietnamese best when it was coming from his parents would. He smiled. Phở was always her answer.

"How about that lady with the shack out by that camp," he asked softly, craning his neck, peering up at stars. "You remember, that camp just outside the remains of Kansas City?"

She let out a dismissive puff of air through her lips. "Dingy beef water and spaghetti noodles do not a phở make, buddy," she laughed. "You of all people should feel me on that one."

"Certainly wasn't as good as my mom's, that's for sure," he deadpanned.

She laughed loud and sudden, her smile cornering deep into her cheeks. They were about the same height and roughly the same age, so most assumed that they were brother and sister, though they could not look any more different. While both had black hair, hers cascaded down her back, a river in the dark. His was ragged and short like a burnt field. Her small long eyes slanted, like two dark swans, beaks dipping in to kiss above her nose. His eyes were deep, difficult. She was beautiful, magnetic, even if she did not want to be. His appearance was forgettable at best; for better or worse, he was always the background.

In the distance, the rough silhouettes of nine giant metal pistons rose into the night sky, temporarily blotting out their view of the moon and stars. The hydraulic arms lifting the pistons repetitively jackknifed and then stretched with a low bellowing groan. The drums of steel hung suspended in the air for a moment like the hammers of gods poised to strike, then dropped dully to the earth, thumping the ground, the noise and impact felt and heard for miles. Though they were used to tremors from the machinery, the two companions started slightly and looked down the hill at the prison camp surrounding the gigantic ground-shaking devices.

The dim light emanating from the interior complexes barely illuminated the pacing guards and nesting snipers on top of the tall walls. The guards' heads constantly turned on their necks as the guards vigilantly watched the two populations, one on either side of the barbed wire and thick concrete. On one side were the throngs of shuffling zombies attracted by the sound of the giant pistons, groaning listlessly against the slanting thick concrete base of the wall. And inside the work camp were the Asian Americans and Arabs forcibly interned there. Officially, the incarcerated were doing a service for their country by maintaining the rhythmic dance of the giant pistons, keeping them fueled, repairing them, as the sound and impact of the giant tamping devices lured the shambling hungry masses. Less officially, the smell of the inmate's flesh, tantalizingly out of reach of the zombies on the other side of the wall, kept the undead there, fresh meat outside of the lion's cage.

Zombies. Brown people. On any given day, the armed guards were prepared to shoot either.

He looked over and saw that she had closed her eyes and leaned her head slightly back. She smiled softly, every breath full and deep. She felt the night air on her, pretending she was somewhere else, in some other time. She often did this before she did something reckless. Her hope was that, if she died, her soul would travel to the last beautiful place she imagined.

He never asked her what her soul's place looked like; it was none of his business.

She opened her eyes and sighed, then smiled at him. She pulled off her boots, took a moment to curl her toes in the grass.

"I see you chose red," he remarked, looking at her toenails. It was one of the small things she did to feel normal. Her tiny way to hang on to what used to be, before the world around her went to shit.

She nodded, smiling. "I did them myself this time," she said, looking down at the grass between her toes.

"You didn't let me do it?" he asked dryly. "You took a job away from a fellow Vietnamese person."

She smirked and reached into her bag. She sat, cross-legged in the grass, and began to load bullets into spare magazines for her AK-47. He noticed one or two zombies at the bottom of the hill, slowly shambling in their direction, lured away from the thumping pistons of the tamping machines and smell of mass-incarcerated human flesh. Without taking his eyes from them he rolled his G36 carbine off his shoulder and twirled the silencer onto the muzzle, silently berating himself for not having done that earlier.

"Bad television," she said suddenly with a nod, biting her lip slightly. "I miss bad television."

He readied his rifle and looked through its scope for the wandering zombies. "I miss reading trashy magazines at the dentist's office," he said.

The zombie that was ambling closest to them was wearing a dirty trucker's cap. He put Trucker Cap Zombie in his crosshairs.

"Think they caught a whiff of us?" she asked, not looking up, still clacking bullets into a mag.

"Shouldn't have," he answered. "We're downwind."

She nodded. Her eyes darted up and tracked Trucker Cap, watching it shamble. Her fingers didn't miss a beat, still loading bullets.

The zombies did not seem to head deliberately toward the two of them, but he kept his scope on them, just in case. She looked over at him and contemplated him quietly. Her best friend. They had only known each other five months.

Five months in this new America seemed like an eternity.

"You sure you want to go down there with me?" she asked quietly.

He did not take his sights from the walking dead, nor did he reply.

She gave a resigned smile in his general direction, shrugged her shoulders, and reached for another empty magazine. She watched her own fingers as they plucked the long pointy 7.62mm cartridges from her pack and methodically stabbed them down into the clip.

"One of these days, I'm going to get both of us killed," she quipped.

"Better than being locked up in a prison camp like a fucking sardine," he answered softly.

When the epidemic hit America, everyone had a theory about who started it. Seventy percent of the American population eventually turned zombie, and those that didn't had to blame someone. Because many of the people who were taken by the wasting disease happened to be white, God was not a viable culprit. The field was wide open for the survivors in America to pick a suspect, a villain, an origin for this nameless evil. And so the government classified it as a terrorist act, without evidence, without even an idea of what caused it. And the American people duly picked the enemy to be vilified—China, North Korea, and the nebulous ever-shifting region known as the Middle East.

After what was left of the U.S. government and civilization regrouped on the East Coast, they started to construct the giant devices that shook the earth. They built fortified complexes in the middle of America to house the machinery. The noise and the force of the giant pistons drew the throngs of zombies to the isolated machines away from the coasts, giving the majority of survivors precious time to regroup. However, the complexes needed humans to operate and maintain the giant machines, a job no one wanted. It was like living under house arrest in a log cabin continuously surrounded by rabid wolves.

Eventually some enterprising politician suggested that surviving Americans of Asian and Arab descent be interned as laborers in these camps, an idea that caught on as quickly as the plague itself. *For their own protection*, the politicians insisted. Hordes of survivors had formed lynch mobs after the disease was classified as a terrorist act, attacking and brutalizing yellow and brown people. There were not enough police to protect them, not enough infrastructure left to respond to this racialized violence—or so the politicians said. Instead they argued that it would be in the best interest of the "targeted communities" to be guarded in these work camps away from the other survivors. No one explained how herding up Asian and Arab Americans based on the color of their skin, seizing their property, and then forcibly incarcerating them without trial in work camps could be in their best interest. But then again, history had shown conclusively that the American public didn't need a complicated explanation as much as they needed a clear enemy to blame.

Tragic times do not beg for complexity. After the emergency legislation was passed, police and military, deputized armed civilians, and new private military contractors began rounding up and transporting Asian Americans, Arab Americans, and any person in that particular color spectrum into their new work camps. It didn't matter if a person actually had ancestry from North Korea, China, or the Middle East. It became all too apparent that was not the point. There were Pacific Islanders, Native Americans, Chicanos, and Black people thrown into the camps for protesting, for daring to raise their voices in opposition, for choosing the wrong side. Close enough. And thus people learned not to speak out against the camps. In the wake of disaster, America became even less subtle.

Less than two years ago, the camps like the one below them were not even finished. Now this one sat thumping and belching smoke, crawling with the undead outside and the living entombed within.

She finished loading her last spare clip and dropped her hands down to the grass, looking down at the internment complex, listening to the pistons groan as they began their upward arc into the night sky.

She remembered those early days. One man and his battered, dirty driver's license. He had struggled against the officers at first, desperate and terrified. One of his wild swings hit a police officer on the side of the head, making the cop's cap fall off his sweaty blond hair. Seeing the cop enraged, the man wept, dropped to his knees, pulled out his wallet. He held up his ID like a shield. He apologized, crying, saying he was scared, he had a family. He swore he was Indian, not Arab. She was sure they believed him. They shot him anyway. His driver's license flipped face down into the dirt next to his body.

"You know, even if we succeed, some of them aren't going to want to come with us," he murmured, finally letting his rifle rest against his shoulder as Trucker Cap shambled off in another random direction away from them.

"I know," she replied, pulling on her boots and standing up slowly.

"You're getting three square meals a day and you're living in a camp protected from zombies by the U.S. military," he sighed.

"Armed private militarized contractors," she corrected him, cocking an eyebrow at him. They both knew how dismal life was in the camps. The cramped, stifled quarters. The lousy food. Sixteen-hour shifts. How everything smelled like oil and hot metal. The flat screen mounted on the wall in the cafeteria would sometimes broadcast a message from out east, declaring how important their work maintaining the pistons was. As if they had a choice—the shadows of men with guns, always, long on the floor. How hard it was to sleep with the constant drone of zombies hungry for you, how you could almost feel the tips of their rotting fingers digging into your flesh at all times. How turning down the sexual advances of a guard could get you thrown off the wall. How easy they made it to betray one another even in there.

Try as she might, she couldn't blame the prisoners. She had met a couple of activists who could not understand why the incarcerated were so, to their eyes, submissive. Obedient. But she knew that the truth was complicated. If not the camps, where could they go?

A week ago, many miles from where they stood, they had sat at a campfire splitting a cup of instant ramen with some strips of beef jerky thrown in. White trash phở, they called it. This was when she told him her plan. The light of the fire flickered high in the canopy of trees above as she watched him carefully to see his reaction.

"For the ones that follow us, where do we take them?" he asked quietly. "Alaska?"

She laughed at the mention of the largest American territory completely free of the epidemic, because it had had the good fortune of being far enough away when the epidemic hit to shore up its defenses before it got to them.

"We'd have better odds of creating a time machine and going back to try to prevent all this from happening."

"Hawai'i?" he asked.

"No way they'd let us in. We're like dogs with rabies to them."

He paused. Before he could continue, she shook her head, looking into the distance with a slight smile as if she was trying to visualize a place for them in the world. "East Coast, no way. They might be the most racially mixed region left, but a group of Asians and Arabs walking out of the middle? They'd shoot us before we'd get within sight of that ridiculous wall of theirs—or ship us back to one of these prison camps. I don't want to get into that fight between Mexico and the new nation-state of Texas in the South. Southwest is New Aztlan and the other united Native folks, they've got their hands full shoring up against raiders and zombies." She paused for a moment. "Maybe they'd let in one or two of us. But an entire group of Asian and Arab refugees recently busted out of a federal labor camp? They'd probably get threatened with drone bombing for agreeing to help any of us."

She chuckled and shook her head sadly, biting her lip, her eyes distant as she continued. "And the North, where all the white hunters and survivalists have dug in? Deer have got a better chance of going into those woods and surviving than we do."

"Don't mess with Wisconsin," he quipped. He waited for a moment, then asked, "How about back to the homeland? Somewhere in Asia?"

She laughed, long and hard.

He turned his head back to see she had been watching him silently, contemplating him. She often did not have to hear words to know what a person was thinking— intuition was her gift.

"No, buddy," she winked. "It's right in the middle of the box for our people, or nothing."

The middle of America, infested with zombies. Ruled by small warlords and thug fiefdoms, many of them made up of the remains of the Minutemen and other batshit-crazy racist militias. The most dangerous place in the world. The place no one wanted to be.

"And it's just one camp," he said.

"The first one," she corrected with a slight nod and a smile.

He looked over at her, shaking his head slowly in bemused disbelief. As the days got more grim, she somehow grew stronger, as if she lived to be the opposite of the dim future that seemed all but certain.

He turned to look back down at the camp, pondering their chances. "How many more camps are there just like that one? We can't save everyone."

"Doesn't mean we can't try," she countered. She waited a moment, crossing her arms in front of her in the slightly chill night air, before reminding him, "You don't have to go with me."

"You wouldn't be much of a leader if you didn't have at least one follower," he smirked, and she laughed her unbreakable laugh, shaking her head. Her smile broke clear across her face—her smile had become his horizon. But he did not say this out loud.

He turned and looked her solemnly in the eyes. "Is it too much to ask for a happy ending?"

She smiled sadly. "I don't think there are any happy endings left."

After a moment, she said, "I miss hotel rooms. I used to love to travel, you know? Before all of this. Sure, hotel rooms were never yours. But I loved that you came back to a place that wasn't yours, and someone made the bed for you." She shook her head, then smiled her radiant, breathtakingly beautiful smile for him. It got even wider when she saw his rare, small smile finally break across his face, a hairline fracture on an egg.

She put a hand on his shoulder, and they stood in silence for a moment, the giant pistons' blocky silhouettes swallowing them from the moon's light, their bodies becoming one with shadow before thumping down to the earth once again.

Then they strode down the hill together, rifles in hand, straight for the prison camp. Toward a war that just might turn into something like a revolution.

THE TOKEN SUPERHERO

DAVID F. WALKER

ALONZO RAMEY WAS BORN TO BE A SUPERHERO. AT THE TIME OF HIS birth, he tested positive for Kurtzberg-24 Syndrome, the genetic anomaly responsible for giving superpowers to people. All babies with K-24 were identified and monitored, with cautious eyes keeping track of the powers that developed. The vast majority of K-24 kids developed a power set that usually included superhuman strength, endurance, speed, and bulletproof skin—the "Standards" is what such powers were called by the doctors and experts who tracked such things. Some of the kids developed unique powers   anything from pyro telekinesis to the ability to breathe underwater. Alonzo's parents prayed that his powers would be limited to the Standards. With the Standards, there was always the chance of having a life that could at least pass for being normal. The more unusual the powers, however, the more difficult life could become. With some powers, there simply wasn't any chance of leading a normal life. Everyone knew about the Flamer, who could make fire but couldn't control it. The Flamer had to walk around in a specially designed suit to keep from burning everything and everyone around him whenever fire would randomly shoot from his body. And then there was Elasticene, who could stretch her body like it was made out of rubber, but it took days to return to its original shape.

"Them white folks ain't gonna take too kindly to a colored boy with superpowers," said Kelvin Ramey, Alonzo's father.

Kelvin had grown up in rural Mississippi, back when being black meant a second-class life. Alonzo was born into a better world, after the marching and the demonstrations and the water hoses and the police dogs, but his father remembered it all, and he worried for his son. They'd killed Martin, Malcolm, Medgar, and so many others, and none of them even had any superpowers. There was no telling what might happen to Alonzo if some crazed redneck decided a super-powered Negro was a threat to the possibility of the South rising up. That was, after all, what every southern redneck claimed was going to happen. Time and time again, the South had failed to rise again, but the fear and hatred of black people remained. And it wasn't just the South: black people were feared and hated all over the country. And where they weren't feared or hated, they were misunderstood.

Fortunately, Alonzo being born with K-24 Syndrome meant a ticket out of Mississippi for his parents and his older sister. Some clinic up north—the Kurtzberg Metahuman Research and Training Center—wanted to test Alonzo regularly, and as his powers mani-fested, they wanted to make sure he'd get the proper training. Proper training, of course, meant that he'd be trained to use his powers to fight for truth, justice, and all that other stuff they talked about in the comic books, movies, and television shows that recounted the adven-tures of superheroes and crime fighters.

By the time Alonzo turned sixteen, his powers had fully developed. Much to the delight of his father, Alonzo only had the Standards—although his strength levels tested right up there with some of the strongest superheroes. Kelvin Ramey's relief that his son only had the Standards was short-lived, however, when Alonzo was asked to join the newly formed Teen Justice Force, which was started by Super Jus-tice Force in a stroke of marketing genius to appeal to the younger crowd. Superheroes in their twenties and thirties were popular, but tended to trend low with teenagers. It all had to do with hostility to-ward adults—older superheroes made teenagers think of their parents and teachers. Teen Justice Force was created to bridge the gap between the younger demographic and the crucial adult demo, to make sure that valuable consumers didn't lose interest in Super Justice Force, their exploits, or, most important, the multibillion-dollar entertain-ment industry that kept the entire operation running.

"I don't know how I feel about you joining this Kiddy Justice Force outfit," Kelvin Ramey told his son.

"They're called Teen Justice Force, not Kiddy Justice Force," said Alonzo.

"Teen, Kiddy, it's all the same. You're too young to be running around playing being a superhero."

"I'm not playing, dad. I am a superhero," said Alonzo. "And these powers that I have are a gift. It's my responsibility to use them to help my fellow man."

"See, I told your mother, they brainwashed you," Kelvin said. He'd been convinced that his son would be turned into a pawn of the Man—even though he couldn't actually identify the Man or his agenda.

"I'm not brainwashed! I'm thinking for myself, just like you and Mom taught me to do."

The conversation went on like that, but in the end, Kelvin knew his son was going to be a superhero, and nothing could stop it from happening. He wanted to be angry, but his wife Voncetta—the pragmatic one in the family—helped calm him down. "Daddy K, are you really going to be angry that our son was blessed with wings and has decided to use them to fly?" she asked.

Even though Voncetta calmed him down, Kelvin could not bring himself to sign the parental release form required for Alonzo to join Teen Justice Force. Instead, Voncetta signed the release. "It's not that your daddy doesn't want you being a superhero, it's just that he worries about you," said Voncetta. "You know that, son?"

"Yes, ma'am," said Alonzo.

With the written consent of his mother, Alonzo Ramey became one of the first members of Teen Justice Force, and the only member of color—unless you counted Neptuna, who had bluish skin and could breathe underwater. Neptuna had been given a terrible name, and when it became the object of public ridicule, it was quickly changed. Alonzo didn't have the same luck. He had been given the superhero name Black Fist, which made absolutely no sense to him. It wasn't like he had unusually large fists, or fists made of anvils—like the supervillain Anvil Fist—or that his powers were solely based in his fists. No, he was stuck with the name Black Fist because, when push came to shove, no one wanted to think that hard when it came time to give the token black guy on Teen Justice Force his name.

Alonzo's career in Teen Justice Force was perfectly fine, although he was the only member without his own solo comic book or an endorsement deal. Even Neptuna got some choice deals—although these came after her name was changed to Princess Oceana. And when the Teen Justice Force animated series proved popular enough to see a line of action figures produced, the only member to not have a figure made was Black Fist.

If it had been just a case of not having his own comic, action figure, or endorsement deals, the degradation of being a black superhero with "black" in his name might have been bearable. But all of that stuff was minor compared to the fact that neither Black Fist nor his alter ego got much respect from the press. In private, Black Fist was pretty much the leader of Teen Justice Force. In a fight, the other members all turned to him for decisions, and on multiple occasions he'd saved each of them from certain death. But every article about the force's exploits always seemed to downplay his involvement, saying, "Black Fist was also present" (if he was even mentioned at all).

Things didn't get better when Alonzo aged out of Teen Justice Force, which is when Captain Freedom, the leader of Super Justice Force, offered him a position on the team. But at the age of twenty, Alonzo was already bitter, cynical, and tired of being a token. He tried to reinvent himself, with a new costume and a new name, but none of it took. Twice he'd been attacked by other superheroes who'd mistaken him for a supervillain, and then there was the time he'd been shot by cops. Fortunately the bullets had bounced off. Disgusted and depressed, Alonzo Ramey decided to retire from the superhero business.

Despite his original misgivings, no one was more disappointed by the retirement of Black Fist than Kelvin Ramey. He had come to see that his son was a great superhero. In the barbershop where Kelvin worked, the exploits of Black Fist were a regular topic of conversation, along with relevant issues such as police brutality in the community, gentrification, and how music was so much better "back in the day." The autographed picture of Black Fist hanging on the wall at the shop got more comments than the photos of famous rappers and athletes.

"You sure you want to do this?" Kelvin asked his son.

"I thought you of all people would be happy to see me give it up," Alonzo said.

"I just want to make sure you're giving it up for the right reasons," Kelvin said. He took great care not to explain what the "right reasons" were, because he knew that was something only Alonzo could determine for himself.

So Black Fist officially retired, and Alonzo tried to adjust to his new life, but it wasn't easy. He got a regular job and enrolled in college, with no plans other than leading a normal life. After a few months, however, he started missing the action and excitement of being a superhero—even when it came with little respect or acknowledgment. And one day, while riding the subway home from his boring job in the non-superhero world, he saw something that changed his life.

A group of rowdy teens, not much younger than Alonzo, had been terrorizing passengers on the train headed uptown. His years as a superhero kicked in, and Alonzo started to intervene, but before he could, another group of teens entered the subway car. These kids, a motley group of three boys and two girls—of various backgrounds—rushed the rowdy teens. For a moment it looked like things would turn violent.

The punks who had been terrorizing the other passengers were bigger, but the other kids stood their ground. And after a few heated words laced with profanity, the confrontation ended. That's when Alonzo noticed that the kids who stood up to the punks were all wearing T-shirts with an image of Black Fist. In all his time as Black Fist, there had never been any officially licensed merchandise—no T-shirts, pajamas, or anything like that.

"Excuse me," Alonzo said to the group of teenagers. "Where'd you get those shirts?"

"We made 'em," said one of the girls. She flashed a huge grin, revealing the braces that covered her teeth.

"You made your own Black Fist T-shirts?" Alonzo asked. "Why?"

All at once, the kids launched into an explanation of how Black Fist had not only been the coolest member of Teen Justice Force but was also the coolest superhero around.

"He does what he does because he can do it," said one of the boys. "It ain't all about the business with him."

"He just made me feel good about myself because, you know, he's black and all," said the other girl.

"I just wish he hadn't retired," said the first girl.

In that moment, it struck Alonzo Ramey that being a superhero meant more than endorsement deals, your own comic book series, and whatever fame and fortune might come your way for fighting the good fight. He had gone through years of training, been on countless missions, and saved hundreds of lives, but it was that moment on the subway that he understood what it was all about.

Yes, he'd been a token black superhero in a world made up mostly of white heroes. Yes, his name was ridiculous, and he hated that it was a constant reminder that others felt the need to state the obvious when it came to defining who he was as a hero. And yes, it sucked that he didn't get credit where credit was due. But that wasn't how those kids on the subway saw him. To them he was simply a superhero they admired enough to make their own T-shirts emblazoned with his image. And that was enough to make Alonzo Ramey rethink everything.

Shortly after that, Alonzo asked Captain Freedom about returning to Super Justice Force. He'd been apprehensive at first, recalling how his father used to say, "If you ask a white man for anything, you best be prepared to beg." But there was no begging. He didn't even have to "tooth it up" by putting on a fake smile—something his father told him never to do. Instead, Alonzo and Captain Freedom talked man to man.

"There's very little about this line of work that is easy," said Captain Freedom. "If I could make the world a better place—the kind of place where you could be who you are, without any of the crap that the world puts on you—then I'd do it. But in that world, there'd be no need for superheroes."

And so Alonzo Ramey went back to being a superhero. He once again donned his Black Fist costume and took to the streets fighting crime. But this time around, he changed his personal definition of what it meant to be a superhero. Yes, he still spent time slugging it out with supercriminals and engaging in what amounted to a ridiculous carnival sideshow, but that was only part of what he did. Instead of patrolling the streets of the inner city and busting gangbangers, he spent much of his time reaching out to the youth that most people saw as a threat. He became known as much for being a community organizer superhero as he did for being a superhero. With the money from his first real endorsement deal, he bankrolled his own comic book series, which was geared toward promoting literacy. The series became so popular that it launched an entire line of comics that helped teach kids of all colors how to read.

Over the years, Black Fist felt the bitterness rise up inside of him from time to time, as well as the cynicism. He hated his name, didn't care much for the costume, and when he finally got his own action figure, they'd made his lips look way bigger than they were in real life. But whenever these things got to him, Alonzo Ramey remembered that at the end of the day none of these things mattered. For him, his life would always be defined by a group of boys and girls, no more than fourteen or fifteen years old, wearing T-shirts with hand-drawn designs inspired by Black Fist. His life would not be defined as much by his adventures as by the adventures recounted in comic books that helped young people learn to read. That's what defined Alonzo Ramey. That's what let him know that, despite it all, he really was a superhero.

THE RIVER

adrienne maree brown

1.

something in the river haunted the island between the city and the border. she felt it, when she was on the waves in the little boat. she didn't say anything, because what could be said, and to whom?

but she felt it. and she felt it growing.

made a sort of sense to her that something would grow there. nuf things went in for something to have created itself down there.

she was a water woman, had learned to boat as she learned to walk, and felt rooted in the river. she'd learned from her grandfather, who'd told her his life lessons on the water. he'd said, "black people come from a big spacious place, under a great big sky. this little country here, we have to fight for any inches we get. but the water has always helped us get free one way or another."

sunny days, she took paying passengers over by the belle isle bridge to see the cars in the water. mostly, you couldn't see anything. but sometimes, you'd catch a glimpse of something shiny, metal, not of the river—something big and swallowed, that had a color of cherry red, of 1964 american-made dream.

these days, the river felt like it had back then, a little too swollen, too active, too attentive.

too many days, she sat behind the wheel of the little boat, dialing down her apprehension. she felt a restlessness in the weeds and shadows that held detroit together. belle isle, an overgrown island, housed the ruins of a zoo, an aquarium, a conservatory, and the old yacht club. down the way were the abandoned, squatted towers of the renaissance center, the tallest ode to economic crisis in the world.

she had been born not too far from the river, in chalmers, on the east side. as a child she played along the river banks. she could remember when a black person could only dock a boat at one black-owned harbor. she remembered it because all she'd ever wanted was to be on that river, especially after her grandfather passed. when she was old enough, she'd purchased the little boat, motor awkward on its backside, and named her *bessie* after her mama. her mama had taught her important things: how to love detroit, that gardening in their backyard was not a hobby but a strategy, and to never trust a man for the long haul.

mostly, she'd listened to her mama. and when she'd gone astray, she'd always been able to return to the river.

now she was 43, and the river was freedom. in that boat she felt liberated all day. she loved to anchor near the underground railroad memorial and imagine runaway slaves standing on one bank and how good—terrifying, but good—that water must have felt, under the boat, or all over the skin, or frozen under the feet.

this was a good river for boating. you wouldn't jump in for any money. no one would.

she felt the same way about eating out of the river, but it was a hungry time. that morning she'd watched a fisherman reel in something, slow, like he didn't care at all. what he pulled up, a long slender fish, had an oily sheen on its scales. she'd tried to catch his eye with her disgust, offer a side eye warning to this stranger, but he turned with his catch, headed for the ice box.

she was aware of herself as a kind of outsider. she loved the city desperately and the people in it. but she mostly loved them from her boat. lately she wore her overalls, kept her graying hair short and natural, her sentences brief. her routine didn't involve too many humans. when she tried to speak, even small talk, there was so much sadness and grief in her mouth for the city disappearing before her eyes that it got hard to breathe.

next time she was out on the water, on a stretch just east of chene park, she watched two babies on the rocks by the river, daring each other to get closer. the mothers were in deep and focused gossip, while also minding a grill that uttered a gorgeous smell over the river waves. the waves were moving aggressive today, and she wanted to yell to the babies or the mamas but couldn't get the words together.

you can't yell just any old thing in detroit. you have to get it right. folks remember.

as she watched, one baby touched his bare toe in, his trembling ashy mocha body stretched out into the rippling nuclear aquamarine green surface. then suddenly he jumped up and backed away from the river, spooked in every limb. he took off running past his friend, all the way to his mama's thighs, which he grabbed and buried himself in, babbling incoherent confessions to her flesh.

the mother didn't skip a beat or a word, just brushed him aside, ignoring his warning.

she didn't judge, though, that mama. times were beyond tough in detroit. a moment to pause, to vent, to sit by the river and just talk, that was a rare and precious thing.

• • •

off the river, out of the water, she found herself in an old friend's music studio, singing her prettiest sounds into his machines. he was as odd and solitary as she was, known for his madness, his intimate marrow-deep knowledge of the city, and his musical genius.

she asked him: *what's up with the river?*

he laughed first. she didn't ask why.

here is what he said: *your river? man, detroit is in that river. the whole river and the parts of the river. certain parts, it's like a ancestral burying ground. it's like a holy vortex of energy.*

like past the island? in the deep shits where them barges plow through? that was the hiding place, that was where you went if you loose tongued about the wrong thing or the wrong people. man, all kinds of sparkling souls been weighted down all the way into the mud in there. s'why some folks won't anchor with the city in view. might hook someone before they ghost! takes a while to become a proper ghost.

he left it at that.

she didn't agree with his theory. didn't feel dead, what she felt in the river. felt other. felt alive and other.

• • •

peak of the summer was scorch that year. the city could barely get dressed. the few people with jobs sat in icy offices watching the world waver outside. people without jobs survived in a variety of ways that all felt like punishment in the heat.

seemed like every morning there'd be bodies, folks who'd lost darwinian struggles during the sweaty night. bodies by the only overnight shelter, bodies in the fake downtown garden sponsored by coca-cola, bodies in potholes on streets strung with christmas lights because the broke city turned off the streetlights.

late one sunday afternoon, after three weddings took place on the island, she heard a message come over the river radio: four pale bodies found floating in the surrounding river, on the far side. she tracked the story throughout the day. upon being dragged out of the water and onto the soil by gloved official hands, it was clear that the bodies, of two adults and two teenagers, were recently dead, hardly bloated, each one bruised as if they'd been in a massive struggle before the toxic river filled their lungs.

they were from pennsylvania.

on monday she motored past the spot she'd heard the coast guard going on about over the radio. the water was moving about itself, swirling without reason. she shook her head, knowing truths that couldn't be spoken aloud were getting out of hand.

she tried for years to keep an open heart to the new folks, most of them white. the city needed people to live in it and job creation, right? and some of these new folk seemed to really care.

but it could harden her heart a little each day, to see people showing up all the time with jobs, or making new work for themselves and their friends, while folks born and raised here couldn't make a living, couldn't get investors for business. she heard entrepreneurs on the news speak of detroit as this exciting new blank canvas. she wondered if the new folks just couldn't see all the people there, the signs everywhere that there was history and there was a people still living all over that canvas.

• • •

the next tragedy came tuesday, when a passel of new local hipsters were out at the island's un-secret swimming spot on an inner waterway of belle isle. this tragedy didn't start with screams, but that was the first thing she heard—a wild cacophony of screaming through the thick reeds.

by the time she doubled back to the sliver entrance of the waterway and made it to the place of the screaming sounds, there was just a whimper, just one whimpering white kid and an island patrol, staring into the water.

she called out: *what happened?*

the patrol, a white kid himself, looked up, terrified and incredulous and trying to be in control. *well, some kids were swimming out here. now they're missing, and this one says a wave ate them!*

the kid turned away from the river briefly to look up at the patrol, slack-mouthed and betrayed. then the damp confused face turned to her and pointed at the water: *it took them.*

she looked over the side of the boat then, down into the shallows and seaweed. the water and weeds moved innocently enough, but there were telltale signs of guilt: a mangled pair of aviator glasses, three strips of natty red board shorts, the back half of a navy striped tom's shoe, a tangle of bikini, and an unlikely pile of clean new bones of various lengths and origins.

she gathered these troubled spoils with her net, clamping her mouth down against the lie "I told you so," cause who had she told? and even now, as more kinds of police and coast guard showed up, what was there to say?

something impossible was happening.

she felt bad for these hipsters. she knew some of their kind from her favorite bars in the city and had never had a bad experience with any of them. she had taken boatloads of them on her river tours over the years. it wasn't their fault there were so many of them. hipsters and entrepreneurs were complicated locusts. they ate up everything in sight, but they meant well.

they should have shut down the island then, but these island bodies were only a small percentage of the bodies of summer, most of them stabbed, shot, strangled, stomped, starved. authorities half-heartedly posted ambiguous warning flyers around the island as swimmers, couples strolling on the river walk paths, and riverside picnickers went missing without explanation.

no one else seemed to notice that the bodies the river was taking that summer were not the bodies of detroiters. perhaps because it was a diverse body of people, all ages, all races. all folks who had come more recently, drawn by the promise of empty land and easy business, the opportunity available among the ruins of other peoples' lives.

she wasn't much on politics, but she hated the shifts in the city, the way it was fading as it filled with people who didn't know how to see it. she knew what was coming, what always came with pioneers: strip malls and sameness. she'd seen it nuff times.

so even though the river was getting dangerous, she didn't take it personally.

she hated strip malls too.

then something happened that got folks' attention.

• • •

the mayor's house was a mansion with a massive yard and covered dock on the river, overlooking the midwestern jungle of belle isle, and farther on, the shore of gentle canada.

this was the third consecutive white mayor of the great black city, this one born in grand rapids, raised in new york, and appointed by the governor. he'd entered office with economic promises on his lips, as usual, but so far he had just closed a few schools and added a third incinerator tower to expand detroit's growing industry as leading trash processor of north america.

the mayor had to entertain at home a few times a year, and his wife's job was to orchestrate elegance using the mansion as the backdrop. people came, oohed and aahed, and then left the big empty place to the couple. based on the light patterns she observed through the windows on her evening boat rides, she suspected the two spent most of their time out of the public eye happily withdrawn to opposite wings.

she brought the boat past the yard and covered dock every time she was out circling the island looking for sunset. as the summer had gone on, island disappearances had put the spook in her completely, and she circled farther and farther from the island's shores, closer and closer to the city.

which meant that on the evening of the mayor's august cocktail party, she was close to his yard. close enough to see it happen.

dozens of people coated the yard with false laughter, posing for cameras they each assumed were pointed in their direction. members of the press were there, marking themselves with cameras and tablets and smartphones, with the air of journalists covering something relevant. the mayor was aiming for dapper, a rose in his lapel.

as she drifted through the water, leaving no wake, the waves started to swell erratically. in just a few moments, the water began thrashing wildly, bucking her. it deluged the front of her little boat as she tried to find an angle to cut through. looking around, she saw no clear source of disruption, just a single line of waves moving out from the island behind her, clear as a moonbeam on a midnight sea.

she doubled the boat around until she was out of the waves, marveling at how the water could be smooth just twenty feet east. she looked back and saw that the waves continued to rise and roll, smacking against the wall that lined the mayor's yard.

the guests, oblivious to the phenomenon, shouted stories at each other and heimlich-maneuvered belly laughter over the sound of an elevator jazz ensemble.

again she felt the urge to warn them, and again she couldn't think of what to say. could anyone else even see the clean line of rising waves? maybe all this time alone on the boat was warping her mind.

as she turned to move along with her boat, feeling the quiet edge of sanity, the elevator music stopped, and she heard the thumping of a microphone being tested. there he was, slick, flushed, wide and smiling. he stood on a little platform with his back to the river, his guests and their champagne flutes all turned toward him. the media elbowed each other half-heartedly, trying to manifest an interesting shot.

that's when it happened.

first thing was a shudder, just a bit bigger than the quake of summer 2010 which had shut down work on both sides of the river. and then one solitary and massive wave, a sickly bright green whip up out of the blue river, headed toward the mayor's back.

words were coming out her mouth, incredulous screams twisted with a certain glee: *the island's coming! the river is going to eat all you carpetbaggers right up!*

when she heard what she was saying she slapped her hand over her mouth, ashamed, but no one even looked in her direction. and if they had they would have seen naught but a black water woman, alone in a boat.

the wave was over the yard before the guests noticed it, looking up with grins frozen on their faces. it looked like a trick, an illusion. the mayor laughed at their faces before realizing with an animated double take that there was something behind him.

as she watched, the wave crashed over the fence, the covered dock, the mayor, the guests, and the press, hitting the house with its full force. with a start, a gasp of awe, she saw that the wave was no wider than the house.

nothing else was even wet.

the wave receded as fast as it had come. guests sprawled in all manner of positions, river water dripping down their supine bodies, some tossed through windows of the house, a few in the pear tree down the yard.

frantically, as humans do after an incident, they started checking themselves and telling the story of what had just happened. press people lamented over their soaked equipment, guests straightened their business casual attire into wet order, and security detail blew their cover as they desperately looked for the mayor.

she felt the buoys on the side of her boat gently bump up against the river wall and realized that her jaw had dropped and her hands fallen from the wheel. the water now was utterly calm in every direction.

still shocked, she gunned the engine gently back toward the mansion.

the mayor was nowhere to be seen. nor was his wife. and others were missing. she could see the smallness of the remaining guests. all along the fence was party detritus, similar to that left by the swallowed hipsters. heeled shoes, pieces of dresses and slacks. on the surface of the water near the mansion, phones and cameras floated.

on the podium, the rose from the mayor's lapel lay, looking as if it had just bloomed.

. . .

the city tried to contain the story, but too many journalists had been knocked about in the wave, felt the strange all-powerful nature of it, saw the post-tsunami yard full of only people like themselves, from detroit.

plus the mayor was gone.

the crazy, impossible story made it to the public, and the public panicked.

she watched the island harbor empty out, the island officially closed with cement blockades across the only bridge linking it to the city. the newly sworn-in mayor was a local who had been involved in local gardening work, one of the only people willing to step up into the role. he said this was an opportunity, wrapped in a crisis, to take the city back.

she felt the population of the city diminish as investors and pioneers packed up, looking for fertile new ground.

and she noticed who stayed, and it was the same people who had always been there. a little unsure of the future maybe, but too deeply rooted to move anywhere quickly. for the first time in a long time, she knew what to say.

it never did touch us y'know. maybe, maybe it's a funny way to do it, but maybe it's a good thing we got our city back?

and folks listened, shaking their heads as they tried to understand, while their mouths agreed: *it ain't how I'd have done it, but the thing is done.*

she still went out in her boat, looking over the edges near the island, searching inside the river, which was her most constant companion, for some clue, some explanation. and every now and then, squinting against the sun's reflection, she'd see through the blue, something swallowed, caught, held down so the city could survive. something that never died.

something alive.

EVIDENCE

ALEXIS PAULINE GUMBS

By reading past this point you agree that you are accountable to the council. You affirm our collective agreement that in the time of accountability, the time past law and order, the story is the storehouse of justice. You remember that justice is no longer punishment. You affirm that the time of crime was an era of refused understanding and stunted evolution. We believe now in the experience of brilliance on the scale of the intergalactic tribe.

Today the evidence we need is legacy. May the public record show and celebrate that Alandrix consciously exists in an ancestral context. May this living textual copy of her digital compilation and all its future amendments be a resource for Alandrix, her mentors, her loved ones and partners, her descendents, and her detractors to use in the ongoing process of supporting her just intentions.

We are grateful that you are reading this. Thank you for remembering.

With love and what our ancestors called "faith,"
the intergenerational council of possible elders

Exhibit A
Excerpt from Drix's Lecture Capsule: "The Black Feminist Time Travel of Self in the Twenty-First Century BSB [Before Silence Broke] Era"

"Therefore self should be understood as a vessel open to time and fueled by presence, where presence is as multiple as it is singular. This is what black feminist scientists called 'integrity,' a standard for affirming the resonance of presence across time, where action was equal to vision embodied through variables. Our ancestors reflect this reality in the self-inscribing letter process evidenced in algorithmic email retrievals from a twenty-first-century palimpsest called google. It is unclear, however, whether the authors of emails wrote them in order to remember or in order to not have to remember. Can you hear me?"

Exhibit B
Be Is for Brilliant

Letter from Alandrix, age twelve, sent via skytablet during dream upload, third cycle of the facing moon, receipt unknown:

Ancestor Alexis,
I've heard about you. I've even read some of your writing. Everyone says I have an old soul, and I'm really interested in what it was like back when you lived. It seems like people were afraid a lot. Maybe every day? It's hard to imagine, but it seems that way from the writing. I have to remember that no one knew that things would get better, and that even people who were working to make it happen had to live with oppression every day. I read your writing and the writing of your other comrades from that time and I feel grateful. It seems like maybe you knew about us. It feels like you loved us already. Thank you for being brave.
I'm twelve and last year I did a project for our community about your time, the time of silence-breaking. I made a poster and everything and an interactive dance. A friend of mine did one on the second abbreviated ice age instigated by oil on fire, but I thought writing about the time of

silence-breaking would be harder. The ice conti-
nents were in your imaginations, the limits of your
memory melted, you spoke about the hard things
and you could see your own voices. It must feel
almost like a force of nature when you live. I'm
12 and you would have thought of me as part of
your family, even though now we do family differently; we have chosen family now, so maybe we
would just be comrades if you lived here in this
generation. Who knows? But I think that if you
met me, you would feel like we have some things
in common. I'm a poet and I use interactive dance
so maybe you would choose me as family. I know
I would choose you. You could have been at my
wow kapow ritual that happened recently. In our
community, 12 is an important accountability age.
We named this ritual for how it feels in our bodies
around now. Wow kapow. I think you used to call it
the pituitary gland.

  We are here five generations after you and a lot
has happened. A lot of the things that used to exist when you were 12 and even when you were 28
don't exist anymore. People broke a lot of things
other than silence during your lifetime. And
people learned how to grow new things and in
new ways. Now we are very good at growing. I'm
growing a lot right now and everyone is supportive of growing time, which includes daydreams,
deep breaths, and quiet walks. No one is impatient
while anyone else is growing. It seems like people
are growing all the time in different ways. It was
great to learn about you and a time when whole
communities decided to grow past silence. It is
hard to read about the fact that sexual abuse, what
we would now call the deepest violation of someone else's growing, used to happen all the time. It
is hard to imagine what it felt like for people to

walk around with all that hurt from harming and being harmed. But I can tell from the writing that people were afraid so much. History was so close. But the amazing thing is how people spoke and wrote and danced anyway. Imagine being afraid to speak.

Anyway. I wanted to say thank you. Now in the 5th generation since the time of the silence breaking we are called hope holders and healers. There are still people doing a lot of healing, but it seems like generation after generation people got less and less afraid. People took those writings and started to recite them and then another generation hummed their melodies and then another generation clicked their rhythms and then another generation just walked them with their feet and now we just breathe it, what you were saying before about how love is the most powerful thing. About how everything and everyone is sacred.

I read a really old story where the character believed that time travel was dangerous because if you change one thing in the past the whole future changes and then you might never get born. I am still here writing this though so I think it's okay to tell you that everything works out. That it's okay. And it's not easy all the time, not even here, because so much has been broken, besides silence, but it is possible, it does feel possible. My friends and I feel possible all the time. So when you get afraid to speak, remember that you all were part of us all learning how to just do it. And most . . . take it for granted. Except poets like me. I remember you. I feel it. Wow. Kapow.

love,
alandrix

Exhibit C

Notes from Drix (age twenty-five), dissertation research notebooks on the time that silence broke:

found as a zoomed-in image of a stained subway cave:
a.k.a.
the writing on the wall

"Wait for the time when blood is all we have left to write with," they said, first in a blog post, then in circulated emails, then on scraps of cloth, then scrawled on the remaining walls, then in dirt when they could find it at the end. "Wait for the time ... when a woman must eat her own sorcery to bleed the ink of her existence. Let her write it and leave it. Let her call it future."

So I waited. And when I couldn't wait any more I waited twenty-eight more days. If you can read this, I am evidence. We had been wrong all along. Blood is not money. Money is not food. The anonymous prophets were right. We cannot afford our own blood.

As I write this, the air is thick with our failure. And I am alone.

Remember us and heal.

Note: Archaeologists say that this engraving came slightly earlier than the other markings all over the planet in small mostly unrecorded places spelled: love love love love love love love love.

Note: According to quantum archaeologists with bone echo data there was more than one person who thought she was the last person on earth. It seems to me that this one had the right timing cycle and materials to write on the wall.

Note: Clearly many aboveground people didn't know about the underground people at this point. This cave writer may have had an inkling because she moved toward a cave that had an entrance to the underground system of root communication embedded deeply.

Note: The historians of the underground people in the transitional time refer to the time the silence broke as their vindication for going underground, but may it not have been that their retreat also caused the silence to break the people who were left?

Note: Unless we find another record, this is our only witness account of the time that the silence broke, but recent historiographic interventions have begun to refer to something they call the "long broke open" which includes the oceanlogging of the digital infrastructure, the shrinking of populatable land and many other factors that they would argue have a causal relationship to the silence breaking.

Questions: What if I can never find evidence of what the people did to break the silence? Am I looking to the past in vain? Am I depending on evidence to confirm what my soul has evidence enough for?

Exhibit D
Found on Drix's wall at sixteen, rare paper artifact of a printed poem duplicate by Alexis Pauline Gumbs circa twenty-first-century BSB:

in my dream
my ancestors are written on the walls
lipstick leavings
gold pen graffiti
strips of magazine paper
wheatpasted faces

these must be the ventricles
wind blows through
shifting and caressing
the slapstick lovings
the glitter leftovers
the mimeographed urgency
the necessary flyness

i must be standing
inside my own heart
tagged with the evidence

of life living itself
i must be walking
through the back alley truth
the criminalized place where love is
where we all end up if we're lucky
or at least move through for a bit

Exhibit E

Letter from Alexis after capitalism to Alexis during capitalism, retrieved from email residue algorithm, received in inbox alexispauline@gmail.com on 9/13/10, send date category echo, referenced and archived in Drix's lecture capsule:

Dear Lexi,

Breathe deep, baby girl, we won. Now life, though not exactly easier, is life all the time. Not chopped down into billable minutes, not narrowed into excuses to hurt and forget each other. I am writing you from the future to remind you to act on your belief, to live your life as a tribute to our victory and not as a stifling reaction to the past. I am here with so many people that you love and their children and we are eating together and we are tired from full days of working and loving but never too tired to remember where we come from. Never exhausted past passion and writing. So I am writing you now.

Here in the future we have no money. We have only the resources that we in our capitalist phase did not plunder to work with, but we have no scarcity. You can reassure Julia we have plenty technology; technology is the brilliance of making something out of anything, of making what we need out of what we had, of aligning our spirits so everyone is on point so much of the time that when one of us falls off, gets scared, or caught up, the harmony of *yes yes yes, we are priceless* brings them right back

into tune with where they need to be. We have the
world we deserve and we acknowledge everyday
that we make it what it is.

Everybody eats. Everybody knows how to grow
agriculturally, spiritually, physically, and intellec-
tually. No one owns anything or anybody or even
uses anything like a tool. Each everything is an
opportunity and we are artists singing it into being
with faith, compassion, confusion, breakthroughs,
and support. It is on everyone's mind and heart
how to best support the genius that surrounds us
all. How to shepherd each of us into the brilliance
we come from even though our experience breaking
each other apart through capitalism has left much
healing to be done. We are more patient than we
have ever been. And now that our time is divine
and connected with everything, we have developed
skills for how to recenter ourselves. We walk. We
drink tea. We are still when we need to be. No one
is impatient with someone else's stillness. No one
feels guilty for sitting still. Everybody is always
learning how to grow.

Your heart sings everyday because your ancestors
are thrilled with themselves, a.k.a. all of us. Just
breathing is like a choir. And I have the presence
of mind and the generosity of spirit to even be
proud of the you that I was when you are reading
this, back in capitalism with all of our fear, and all
of our scarcity-driven behavior contradicting and
cutting down our visionary words. Counterpoet-
ics right? I am proud of you for being queer. I am
proud of you for staying present to the meaning of
your beliefs and to the consequences of your actions
even when they were crashing into each other every
day. I am proud of you for letting the tide of your
revolutionary heritage grind your fear of failure and
lack to sand. I love you. The me that I was.

But breathe this deep because this is the message. We did it. We shifted the paradigm. We rewrote the meaning of life with our living. And this is how we did it. We let go. And then we got scared and held on and then we let go again. Of everything that would shackle us to sameness. Of our deeply held belief that our lives could be measured or disconnected from anything. We let go and re-taught ourselves to breathe the presence of the energy that we are that cannot be destroyed, but only transformed and transforming everything.

Breathe deep, beloved young and frightened self, and then let go. And you will hold on. So then let go again.

> With all the love and the sky and the land and
> the water,
> Lex

BLACK ANGEL

WALIDAH IMARISHA

UNDER FLICKERING STREETLIGHTS, A. WALKED ALONE FOR THE FIRST time since she saved Tamee. For the first time, he was not waiting across the street for her when she began her nightly sojourn. He wouldn't admit he was upset, but she knew he was. Tamee had gone to stay over at his mother's for a holiday. A religious one. A. couldn't remember which one; she could never keep these humans' divisions straight. They thought following some book would open the barrier between Heaven and earth for them. It would be laughable if it hadn't been the cause of so much horrific violence down there.

Down here, she reminded herself. She had been cast out of Heaven, for trying to help these warring humans. She lived down here with them, and she knew as little about how to ascend as they did.

A. remembered when she first saw Tamee; surrounded by a gang of racist skinheads, him a beaten, bloody mess in the middle. They attacked him for being Palestinian, for being in New York, for being an antiracist skinhead— take your pick. One thing was sure, they didn't mean for him to walk away that night.

A. hadn't meant to get involved. But Tamee's eyes trapped hers. His desperate, terrified eyes. She had seen that look so many times before. That look had cost her everything. She would have nothing to do with that look.

But the neo-Nazis took her moment of reflection for defiance. Three of them peeled off. Menaced toward her. Circled her like jackals. One pulled a knife.

"You shoulda left when you had the chance, Black bitch."

She locked her eyes on them. She knew they couldn't seriously injure her. They didn't have the power. But they could hurt her. And she'd felt enough pain for three lifetimes.

And she just really, really hated boneheads.

With one fluid motion, A. whipped her trench coat off. Her remaining wing wrapped across her shoulder like a shawl. Tied down by a cord wrapped firmly around her waist. She ripped the cord free, and her wing, black as the night's sky, snapped back and out with a ten-foot span. Reaching for the lost Heavens.

"What the fuck?" The closest neo-Nazi to her scrambled backward.

"Man, it's some kind of costume or something. Don't be fucking stupid!" the leader Joker yelled. "Fuck her up!"

The racist nodded and charged A. She jumped in the air, flapping her wing.

The neo-Nazi ran right under her, carried by his own momentum. As he passed, she kicked him with a boot to the back of his head. He sprawled on the concrete like spilled milk, unconscious. She lowered herself to the ground slowly, a little off balance. Damn, she grimaced, I really miss my other wing.

She made short work of the two who bellowed and ran at her, enraged. An elbow to the face. Flurry of punches. Broken nose. Blood. Silence.

Joker stared at her. Fear and loathing mixed in his eyes. He looked about to rush her. But he must have calculated his odds because instead he turned to run. A. leaped forward. Wrapped her wing around him. Squeezed. Squeezed until he stopped struggling and slumped to the ground, breathing shallowly.

She surveyed the five men sprawled on the ground, the neo-Nazis and Tamee, who had uncurled himself but otherwise had not moved during the fight. Frozen with amazement and awe. He showed absolutely no fear. He looked as if he was in the presence of something incredible. Exalted. Divine.

She looked down at Joker. She should just leave them all here for the cops to find and be done with it. This wasn't her problem. She wouldn't have gotten involved if they hadn't pulled her into it.

A. sighed. She had lived in Harlem long enough to know that sending people into the criminal justice system did nothing but make them more damaged and desperate. She hid in the shadows, saw the police patrolling the streets. Not patrolling. Hunting. There was no mercy behind those shining badges. She watched this scene play out over and over like a flickering film projected onto the city. And she had done nothing each time before. Just waited for the reel to end.

She kneeled down next to Joker. Like this, he looked so fragile. So breakable. She could end this right now. Do to him what he had planned to do to Tamee. She was an Angel, after all, even if she was fallen—she would be merciful.

A small voice in the recesses of her mind asked, *Should I use the Voice?* She stared down at this manchild she knew to be a killer. She could smell it on him; this was not his first attempt at taking a life, nor would it be his last if something wasn't done. She shook her head, trying to clear the thought out, but it clung like a burr.

When she was an Angel, A. had used her Voice to change hearts, sing humans clean. There were no repercussions as an Angel, with a sanction from the Almighty. It had actually been a joyous communion, and the glow she felt had filled her with even more warmth and peace than she thought possible.

But God took that, along with everything else. He left her the Voice. But if she used it, she took on these humans' pain. She tried it only once, when she was first exiled. It was flames licking at her flesh again when she broke through the barrier between Heaven and earth, biting and tearing until she could not take it. She had collapsed; it took days to recover fully. One of the many reasons she avoided interacting with humans when at all possible. She'd already suffered enough pain for them.

But now that she was faced with this situation, she found she could not just walk away. Even though everything inside her screamed to. She could not shake the look in Tamee's eyes, the plea for help. Mercy. Grace. It had been a long time since she remembered not only the horror of humans, but the vulnerability.

A. opened her mouth. She began to sing. It was the most incredible sound Tamee had ever heard. Cool clean waterfalls cascading down into cool green valleys, his mother's hands cool on his hot forehead, the beauty of a grove of olive trees bright in the sunshine, his whole family, even the ones murdered and lost, gathered arm in arm. Complete peace.

Golden light shone in A.'s mouth, illuminating through her flesh.

She leaned over Joker. The light cracked and rained down on his face. Soaked into his skin. At the same time, a murky darkness crept up the stream of light. Climbed into A. through her mouth. Darkened the glow emanating from her chest. She grimaced and her voice faltered but continued singing.

Joker's face, twisted with hate and rage even when unconscious, began to relax. The lines of anger smoothed out. His face became serene. A child curled up in the arms of its mother, protected and safe.

A. turned and did the same to the others, the light in her chest almost entirely eclipsed by the smoky darkness from their mouths. She could barely reach the one farthest away, had to drag herself over, still singing, but now her voice sounded like that of a small wounded animal.

When she finished with the last one, she leaned backward. Wavered like a candle in a strong wind. Her head hit the ground with a sickening thud.

Tamee dragged himself toward her. Reached out toward her slowly, with reverence.

Her eyes slowly opened, focused on Tamee. A. jerked away, tried to stand up. She failed and only accomplished rolling away onto her side.

"Are you all right?" Tamee stared down into her face. The color of coffee beans dusted with rose petals. Flawless like glass. Eyes like galaxies.

"Get off." Her voice, though thin, was infused with steel. Reached out her hand to try to lift herself up.

"I—I can't believe you're here. You exist. I never thought I would see something—someone like you," Tamee sputtered.

A. gave up trying to stand. Lay there breathing shallowly for a while. Reached into her trench coat pocket. Pulled out a cigarette.

"So you think you know what I am." The snap of the lighter.

"Of course I know what you are." A touch of awe in his voice. "It's been a minute since I touched the Qu'ran. Years since I went to masjid. But I would know you anywhere. You're an angel."

She paused, and the look of pain on her face had nothing to do with her injuries.

After a long minute, she growled, "I used to be an Angel. Now I'm just like all of you. Scraping away on the face of this cesspool called a planet until you fucking die."

"Wow—um, okay," Tamee stuttered.

Silence. Her ragged exhale.

"Well, thanks. For saving me. I mean. I really appreciate it. Really," he babbled.

"Don't thank me." Her tone stung more than a slap to the face. "If I'd had my way, I wouldn't have done shit."

Tamee was a little taken aback by her callousness. She didn't sound much like an angel. For one thing, he had not imagined that an angel would curse. He thought there would be more love and compassion. She wasn't really at all how he imagined an angel.

She was a million times better.

A. reached into her pocket and pulled out some more black cord. She propped herself up against the brick of a building. Gingerly folded her wing forward across her shoulder. Began wrapping the cord around and around, until the wing was strapped down securely.

"So, what's your name?" Tamee asked after a minute.

"Don't have one."

"Well, what did they call you back there? In, you know, in heaven?"

"Nothing. Angels don't have names. We know each other. We can—"

A. had no words to describe the flow of energy. The connected contentment that linked all of the Angels. God. Heaven itself. They were all one. Separate and one. There was a me, but there was no you. No one was separate. Everything was felt. A continuous feedback loop of perfect joy. There were no human words to describe it, because they could not even fathom the depths of beauty that come from being part of God. It made her angry to try to find words to explain the most painful loss she would or could ever have.

A. barked, "We just feel each other, okay."

"Okay, can I just call you Angel then?"

"No." She threw her trench coat over her shoulders as she staggered to her feet. She began dragging herself away. Tamee sat, frozen, wanting to yell for her to wait, wanting to say something, anything, that would make her stay. Make her turn around so he could see her face one more time. But he could think of nothing. His heart contracted in his chest as he watched her limp away.

She stopped, hand on the dirty brick beside her. She turned her head slightly to the right. Enough for him to see her face in profile.

"You can call me A. Ain't no Angels in Harlem."

• • •

A. shook her head to clear it as she continued her nightly wanderings through a dark city. Tamee always said she saved him that night. But is it really saving someone if you didn't mean to? If you didn't want to?

A. sighed. Tamee wanted so little. He didn't even ask for her to love him. Just to treat him … gently. Like the blind sick kitten she found, lifted up by the scruff of the neck and cradled under her trench coat until they got home. Tamee wanted A. to invite him in rather than just leaving the door unlocked as she walked up the stairs, never looking back.

The kitten died. Despite everything she tried.

"I couldn't even save a fucking cat," she muttered to herself, a sudden pang in her chest.

She looked up and realized she had walked much farther than she usually did. The Black neighborhood of Harlem had blended into an immigrant one, with bodega signs in at least three different languages, ads for international calling cards plastered on every surface.

Just as she started to think about turning back, she heard a huge tumult, like a thousand hearts being ripped apart at once. Screams. No matter what language, she knew the sound of desperate prayers hurtled toward an impassive sky.

Without thinking, A. sprinted towards the noise. She turned the corner to see pure horror. People poured out of a tenement building like a river of tears: families, children, elders. All immigrants. They were shoved, driven, beaten by men in bulletproof vests carrying automatic weapons, the kind usually reserved for military war. The stomp of boots like bombshells exploding. A line of industrial-sized trucks, each branded "Immigration and Customs Enforcement." ICE. Windows of the trucks like angry slitted eyes on a face full of rage. The trucks engines growled, doors bared like teeth.

The agents threw people on top of each other into the trucks until they were full, then started on the next. Bodies packed in, shackled together. For the forced passage south to the border. Weeks choking on stagnant and feculent air. Darkness, cries, gasps dying on lips.

A. had heard about this. Once it had made its arrest quota set for it by Congress, ICE had no use for the undocumented immigrants

it snared. Since the economy had bottomed out, all new prison construction ceased, as politicians tried to do triage on the budget. What
prisons there were already overflowed with bodies, too often Black
and brown. But the ingenious and insidious "waste not, want not"
ideology of this system kicked in. After scanning everyone, ICE loaded them into trucks and drove them just across the Mexican border.
They sold other humans to the U.S. corporations' giant factories, *ma-
quiladoras*, a stone's throw from the border. The corporations bought
these "workers" by the truckload.

Most didn't last a year toiling in the unventilated, hundred-de-
gree plus heat of the dangerous and toxic production lines. Forced
to work, night and day. Given food you wouldn't feed a hog. Each
person expendable. Those who ran the sweatshops, the death shops,
knew there were always more where they came from.

A.'s heart sank. This was the embodiment of the evil humans do
to one other. Even animals don't turn on each other unless they have
to. Humans do it at the drop of a hat. The slip of a dollar. She shook
her head, disgusted.

ICE must have been at this a while because there were only two
dozen or so folks left. *How many hours has it taken them to clear this
building of hundreds?* A. thought desperately. *Why hasn't anyone done
something? What about all the people in these surrounding buildings?
Why haven't they called the authorities?*

A reflection of light caught her eye—the luminescence of street
light bouncing off the badge of a New York cop. *Courtesy Professional-
ism Respect*: the NYPD's motto.

The authorities were already here. Watching ICE round up people
and send them to their deaths.

No one was coming to help.

Out of the corner of A.'s eye, she saw a group of people, in ragged arrowhead formation, charge the NYPD's perimeter line. As they
moved, A. could see eight children protected in the middle, all under
the age of ten. One girl, maybe seven, stared back at A. The girl's
smallness emphasized her large eyes, brimming with fear.

The arrowhead of immigrant bodies hit the police line, which
gave a little but did not break. The formation backed up slightly, then
plowed forward quickly before the officers could draw their guns. This

time a fissure opened as two cops were shoved apart. The men and women grappled with the police, fighting with all their might. It all happened in less than a minute.

What are they going to do? A. wondered. The hole was not large enough for them to go through, and it would close up soon. The cops were already adjusting. It was not until she saw the quick movements on the other side of the line that it dawned on her: *The children! The adults had never intended to get out—they broke open enough space for their children to escape.* The small bodies poured through now, running swiftly and disappearing into the dark before ICE and the NYPD even knew they were gone.

A. had seen so many horrific scenes since she had been cast out, so much violence and hatred and ugliness. She had almost forgotten what else she saw when she gazed down from Heaven; self-sacrifice, immense acts of love. Bravery beyond words. Like now.

A.'s attention was drawn back to the formation, which had by this time disintegrated. One of the children hadn't made it through before the opening closed, the little girl with the big eyes. The child clung to the leg of one of the women fighting. A. assumed it was her mother.

By this time, agents from the other side ran over. They could not fire into the crowd without risking hitting their fellow officers. So they pulled out batons and began smashing people from all sides. There was no escape. Just the sickening impact of wood on tender flesh, on bones.

A.'s stomach tightened. There will always be those humans so twisted, so hungry for power, they will devour all in their way, even the weak, the sick. The children.

And she also thought, *But not all. There will always be those who fight against that, who push the forces of destruction back.* A. thought of the times since her expulsion that she had walked past a mugging, a beating. Times she'd heard screams through the walls. Seen fresh blood in the stairway. Heard whimpers in the dark. For the first time, she was ashamed of herself.

No, she shook her head, that's not true. She had been ashamed of herself since the first time she let her fear of pain, of having something else taken from her, stop her from doing what she knew was right.

This was just the first time she had allowed herself to admit it.

When A. was in Heaven, she was an Angel of mercy, never an Angel of vengeance. Never wielded a fiery sword and wrought terror on those who had done wrong. But no one who saw her this day would have ever guessed that. She threw off her trench coat like a dark storm cloud and unleashed her remaining black wing. It unfurled until it blotted out the glow of the streetlights. Her face twisted almost beyond recognition with rage, and she was more terrible than anyone could ever imagine.

Her wing sliced through two agents in front of her as she ran toward the trucks. Angels of vengeance have steel for wings, and her remaining wing had become razor sharp. She could not tell if the agents she hit were alive or dead. She did not care.

A. fought her way through dozens of agents, every part of her acting independently as a fighting instrument. Fists threw blows that crunched noses and broke jaws. Elbows cracked ribs, shoved the jagged edges up into lungs. Feet crushed larynxes of any unfortunate enough to fall. And always her deadly razor wing sliced furiously, shimmering with blood.

She broke through, leaving behind moans, the sound of bodies dropping. She saw only the agent holding the mother and the little girl—all of the other immigrants had been loaded into the truck. The mother began scratching and biting the agent with all her might, twisting and attacking until he dropped his hold on the girl to defend himself. The little girl ran to a dumpster nearby and hid.

A. raced toward them at top speed, but while her wing was able to deflect some of the bullets a dozen guns were shooting at her, it couldn't stop them all. A. felt the searing pain as hot metal entered her body, breached vital organs. Two in the heart, one in a lung, intestines shredded. She tried to keep moving toward the truck, but the pain was too much. She stumbled, fell. She could only watch helplessly as the mother was thrown on the top of a mass of writhing bodies.

A. pushed herself to get up, only to collapse back to the hard concrete. She could save no one, possibly not even herself.

The mother's eyes met A.'s as the agents swung the door shut. The mother's screams echoed through the metal: "Save her!"

A. forced herself up, ignored the agonizing pain, and as the truck revved and sped off, she dashed forward. She took half a dozen more bullets, but this time she felt nothing. She sprinted toward the dumpster, scooped up the child, and kept running, this time away from the agents. They continued firing but her wing blocked most of the incoming fire.

If I'd had both wings, I would have never gotten hit, A. thought bitterly. *Of course, if I had both wings, I wouldn't be here in the first place.*

She turned down an alley, then another. Another. She could hear the shouts of pursuit. But she was in familiar territory. She had haunted these streets for over a year now. They would not catch her.

A. continued stumbling ahead through the predawn darkness long after she could no longer hear the cries of the pursuers. It was only as daylight leaked out that A. collapsed in a dead end alley between two boarded-up buildings. Her arms could no longer hold the girl, who rolled roughly into a pile of foul-smelling refuse.

A.'s head hit the concrete, and then she was gone.

• • •

As A. regained consciousness, she had no idea how long she had been out. She opened her eyes, turned her head in the direction of the motion she sensed. The girl, balled up between two rusting dumpsters, knees pulled up and arms crossed on top so only her giant liquid eyes were visible. The girl stared without blinking.

A. avoided those eyes, slowly began to wind the black cord around her waist until her wing was secured again. She would have to make it home without the trench coat—she'd left it back at the tenement building. Unfortunately it was daytime, and her wing would be conspicuous. Fortunately, this was New York, so A. was pretty sure she wouldn't be the strangest sight on the street.

She felt a tap on the side of her thigh. She turned down to see the girl holding out the dirty trench coat. She had no idea when the girl had picked it up. The kid had been able to keep her wits about her even in the midst of the most horrible thing that would probably ever happen to her.

A. felt a knife stab deep into her heart, and still she would not meet the girl's eyes.

In a burst of motion, the little girl threw herself forward and grabbed onto A.'s leg. "Thank you," she mumbled into A's pants.

A. did not know what to say to this tiny girl, so delicate. Thank me? For what? For waiting so long to act? For allowing your mother and everyone you know to be shipped and sold like cattle for slaughter?

Her self-disgust threatened to overpower her. "Okay," she said gruffly and moved away from the girl's touch.

The girl let go but did not move away. She continued to stare up at A. in a way that completely unnerved the fallen angel.

"Did God send you?" the girl finally asked.

A. snorted. "You could say that."

The girl just stared, unblinking and silent.

A. sighed. She never imagined telling anyone the story—it was so much worse telling this kid than Tamee. "I—I was kicked out. I went against God's will."

The child remembered her brief time going to Sunday school and shrank back a little. "Are you—are you the devil?"

A. pulled a cigarette out of a pack using only her mouth and simultaneously lit it with the lighter burning in her hand. Exhaled as she snapped the Zippo shut.

"The only way I'm like Lucifer is we were both cast out. Him into hell. Me into Harlem." She shrugged. "Same difference."

"But why?" A. knew what the girl was asking. Of all the whys, she knew exactly which one the kid wanted to hear. She had never told Tamee the exact story of her fall. Never told anyone. Never imagined she would.

But she knew she owed this little girl. If anyone could understand loss, it was this kid.

A. leaned against the dirty wall and closed her eyes. "You are too young to remember this, but two decades or so ago—humans' time is so imprecise—there was a war. No," she corrected herself, "Not a war. Genocide."

"Genocide." The word sounded wrong in the mouth of one so young. "What's that?"

"It's when you hate not just one person but their mother and their grandmothers and their children and everyone like them. You hate them so much, you try to destroy all of them."

A. looked at the girl's face, drawn tight with too much knowledge too young.

A. did not have any comfort to offer other than the truth. A truth she had never spoken aloud.

"I could not watch it one more time. Especially since this conflict was not even caused by either of the two groups involved—it was outsiders who came in. They came to exploit, to plunder the country of its resources and the people of their hope. They used one group against another, egging them on, spreading lies and misinformation, until the entire region nearly washed away in blood."

She took a drag from her cigarette and looked up toward the cloudy sky. She wasn't even sure she was talking to the little girl anymore. But if she wasn't, she sure as hell didn't know who was listening. "I couldn't watch it happen again. I went to God and asked him to stop it. Send a sign, a prophet, a messenger. Throw a lightning bolt. Anything to remind them there was something bigger in this world than their rage."

The little girl's voice was so quiet it was almost inaudible. "And what did God do?"

A.'s laughter echoed hollow. "Nothing. He said it was not my place to tell him how to run His worlds. That I could not possibly comprehend the intricacies of His divine plan. He told me instead to gaze upon the infinite beauty surrounding me, contemplate His awesome majesty. He told me to forget."

"And then what?"

A. looked at the girl out of the corner of her eye. "Then this."

A. flicked what was left of the cigarette up into the air, and, as it fell, it burned brighter, glowing red and angry. It landed in a shallow puddle of spilled motor oil, instantly sparking a flame. The smell of burning gasoline filled their noses.

"That was how I got here."

The girl heard the rustle of A.'s remaining wing under her trench coat, but she couldn't take her eyes off the burning puddle, its rainbow colors and black smoke.

"What's going to happen to my mother?" The whisper felt like an indictment screamed in A.'s face. *I wish the kid would scream. Hit me. Tell me it's my fault. Because she'd be right.*

But A. wouldn't lie to this girl any more than she would lie to herself. She would have to live with her failure today for the rest of her life.

"You already know the answer. Do you really want me to say it out loud?"

A. watched as tears filled the girl's large eyes, pooled on her lashes, splashed down her cheeks until they stained her dirty collar. Wave after wave of silent tears.

A. looked away. If she could have used the Voice to ease the child's suffering, she would have gladly done it, even if it meant taking her pain on herself. But the Voice only worked to take away the negative. And she had sensed from the minute she saw her that goodness radiated from this child. There was nothing she could do for her. Absolutely nothing.

Except to vow to herself and this child that she would never allow this to happen again. This place, this earth, was pain, but it was also beauty and love. She would think of this little girl's mother, her community, any time she doubted that. Next time A. would not walk away. She would do exactly what she was kicked out of Heaven for doing she would help these flawed precious creatures called humans.

A.'s eyes slid upward. But would she be allowed to intervene? Or would that only arouse more of God's wrath? If so, what plague would He send to express His rage this time upon those she tried to help?

A. turned her back on the girl and began walking down the alley toward the street. The child's face overflowed with sadness, loss, fear.

A. walked a few steps, then stopped.

"C'mon, kid," A. barked. The girl started, her eyes wide as saucers again, but it only took a split second for her to be by A.'s side.

"Name?" A. didn't look down as she asked it.

The response almost inaudible: "Angelica."

A.'s body shivered involuntarily. *I guess that was my answer.*

They walked side by side out onto the street.

"Well," A. sighed as she slid another cigarette into her mouth, "Tamee better know what the fuck to do with you, because I sure as hell don't."

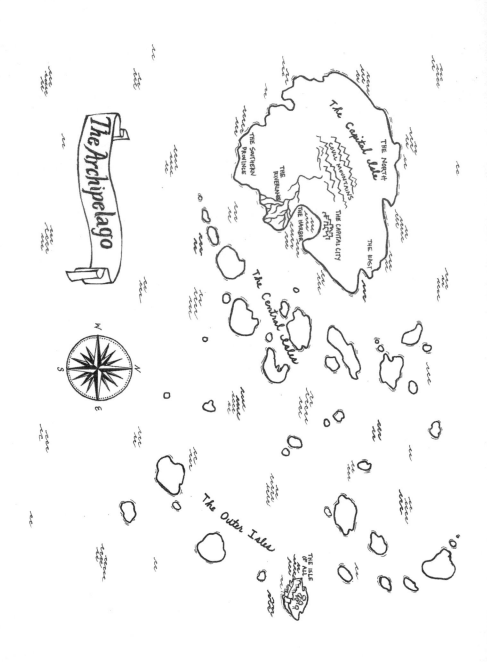

The Archipelago

The Capital Isle

THE NORTH

The Southern Province

GULL MOUNTAINS

THE RIVERLANDS

THE HARBOR

THE CAPITAL CITY

THE EAST

The Central Isles

The Outer Isles

THE ISLE OF ALL ENDS

W

N

S

E

THE LONG MEMORY

MORRIGAN PHILLIPS

CROWDED AND NOISY, THE FLOOR OF THE LARGE COUNCIL RESEMbled the bustle of a marketplace more than a place of governance. Anticipation had brought out all of the council plus other notables. But one voice cut through the din of scraping chairs, shuffling paper, and chattering voices.

"The Long Memory is the most dangerous idea threatening our peace, prosperity, and security today!" Councilman Holt, a prominent and wealthy merchant, thundered at the crowd.

"Any reverence for the Long Memory, for the long done past, holds us back as a civilization! Those among us who call for this continued reverence are jeopardizing the security of our children's future. We cannot be held hostage by memory. We cannot let memory keep us from forging our future. We owe this to our children. We owe this to our present, in which we see our peace, prosperity, and security threatened by bands of armed thugs in the north."

Shouts of disagreement met this statement but were soon drowned out by the shouts of Holt's supporters.

Among the dozen or so observers in the gallery sat Cy and her close friend Ban. They wore the dark green cloaks marking them as Memorials, keepers of the Long Memory. The very people Holt railed against. Cy and Ban were not full Memorials yet. They had yet to finish their final year of apprenticeship at the capital's Central Library. There they learned to delve into streams of memories stretching far outside their lives. They were both apprenticed to the same elder, Hammon, considered to be one of the most skilled Memorials.

Ban sat, fidgety and impatient. She muttered under her breath a steady stream of expletives directed at Holt. Cy sat quite still, eyes fixed on the scene below.

Cy came to the Capital from the north as a nine-year-old after her family was killed in a battle in the foothills of the Coull Mountains. All of her family members were prominent regional Memorials. After the dust of the battle settled, Memorials from a nearby library searched for survivors. They found Cy holed up in a root cellar not far from her family's now-decimated home. Cy was taken to the Central Library, where Hammon took her on as a pupil, and now as an apprentice. When Ban arrived from the Riverlands west of the Capital some nine years ago, it had been like gaining a sister in her and Hammon's odd little family.

Cy examined Holt from her seat in the gallery. He was a large, bellowing man with muttonchops. His clothes always looked uncomfortably tight. In recent years, Holt had cast the status of the Memorials into debate. In times past, Memorials were positioned near power. The kings and queens of old kept Memorials near to guide them in their ruling. Memorials held positions of honor in towns and villages. From such places the Memorials had been instrumental in the rule of the Archipelago.

Over time, the royal houses diminished under the growing power of the merchant class. Kings and queens ceased to be meaningful rulers, and what had always been the Royal Court became the Large Council, from which all authority now came. But the reverence for memory remained. It was a part of the identity of the Archipelago that the record of the past should guide the governance of the present and the building of the future. Memorials, by law and custom, were part of any lawmaking, and approval of the Memorials was always required before actions such as mobilizing the provincial armies. Any new proclamation or law was sent to the libraries for review. This process frustrated a growing number of council members who saw it as slow, cumbersome, and unnecessary.

"The plodding methods of the Memorials hold us back as a civilization!" was a common refrain of Councilman Holt.

The resentment of the Memorials and their libraries reached a fevered pitch when the Central Library sent a proclamation back to the council. The council planned to mobilize all provincial armies to march on the north and quell rebellion and ethnic violence. The Memorials' findings cautioned against acting in a region where much of the current situation was due to the past actions of the council itself, a historical fact the council seemed most eager to erase.

Among the most outraged, Holt traveled from province to province condemning the Memorials for holding back necessary action. He was adamant that the actions of past councils were inconsequential and not germane. Without the support of the Memorials, the council could not move forward. Holt had spent years leading a movement to weaken the rules granting the Memorials sway over the work of the council. As the violence in the north increased, fewer and fewer council members spoke out to challenge him. Then, six months ago, a band of Orm Mountain rebels had barricaded a northern provincial government hall and set it on fire, killing 120 people. Meanwhile, the Coullish were moving down from the mountains, sacking villages and seizing back ancestral lands.

Now the debate taking place on the council floor below Cy and Ban would rule on a proposal by Holt and his allies that called for the containment of what he called threats to the peace of the Archipelago. This included elimination of the role of Memorials in governance, strict regulation of libraries, and abolition of the registry of new Memorials. Holt used the recent deaths to push forth his proposal at Large Council, bypassing public debate.

Cy let out an impatient sigh. She knew Holt had many interests in the north, none of which had anything to do with the peace, prosperity, and security of the Archipelago.

Cy let her focus shift inward, letting the scene before her blur, blending from one image to another. New voices sounded and others went silent. Her body relaxed, her heart slowed. Her eyes took on a glassy, unfocused look, their pupils dilated to large dark pools. Such was the demeanor and practice of a Memorial shifting from the present to the channels of Long Memory.

A past memory overlaid the present—ghost images superimposed on flesh. Cy felt the weight of the memory, knew it hailed from before her birth. Older memories felt heavier, the pressure behind her eyes increasing the further she reached back. In the beginning Cy felt like she was being crushed from the inside out by any memory before her time. But after years of training, in her final year of apprenticeship, she barely noticed the weight of this memory.

The phantom voices of a long gone council rose and fell: "The settlement must take place. We can no longer allow the Northernlings to continue wandering across all the lands with their herds."

"Yes, they claim all the lands their stock grazes on. They use too much given their size. That land is profitable and can be used for the benefit of all."

The gold coins clinked together. Cy knew these were the voices of the merchants. They said they wanted the settlement project for the good of the Northernlings. The memory had the sharp taste of falsehood. The land of the north was rich and good for growing grain and raising herds of livestock. Many of the wealthier merchant houses saw the settlement project as a means to gain access to production of goods in the north.

A green-cloaked figure finally stepped forward to speak. "The Northernlings are not of one people but of many, many identities," he said in a voice soft but firm. "The Northernlings of the mountains are not the same as those who roam the plains. They are the oldest people of this land, having been here before the boats of the Archipelago landed many of our ancestors on these shores. They are a proud and diverse people. We must seek a Memorial from the north to confer with before taking action."

Cy felt the figure's presence through the memory and knew it instantly. She had spent countless hours with this presence guiding her through the streams of memory—it was a much younger Hammon.

Cy would have known it was Hammon even if she had not felt his presence. In lessons at the Central Library, he had made reference to this memory often, a pivotal turning point in their history.

Ultimately, in what was one of the most divisive actions in the Archipelago's history, a northern Memorial was not sought, and the settlement project was enacted. Many were uneasy with the move to act without a blessing from the Central Library. It also precipitated the decline in the stability of the north, bringing on more violence and poverty. Ever since the settlement project, the north had been mired in conflict, with no small role played by the various armies of the governing provincial houses. One house would arm one faction while another would arm another. The factions then fought each other and the provincial armies, and the north saw the rise of petty rulers fighting for what limited power they could hold.

Jumping at a sharp jab to the ribs, Cy was yanked back to the present, back into the council chambers.

"Get back here!" Ban hissed in her ear.

Cy's pupils contracted and her face flushed as her heart sped up. Back in the present, Cy glanced around the gallery. A group of men sitting nearby looked at them with barely concealed contempt, while a cluster of women gave Cy and Ban uneasy glances. Looking down at the floor of the council, she sensed that there were far more speaking in support of Holt than in opposition. Cy stood sorrowfully, and left the gallery with Ban.

The air hung heavy from a recent rainstorm, the kind that frequented the coast. The humidity made the air fragrant with flowers and earth. Beneath a fig tree in the Central Library gardens Ban paced nervously, while Cy lay on the grass trying to stay cool.

Cy wore her thick dark hair long, as was the custom in the north for both men and women. She liked to lie on the grass, hair fanned out around her like a cape, the cool of the earth on her neck and scalp. In the heat and humidity of the Capital, Ban could never understand why Cy wouldn't just cut it all off. For her part, Cy couldn't understand how Ban could stand to be barefoot all the time. Coming from the Riverlands, Ban had grown up on boats and docks where most everyone went shoeless.

Ban flopped down at the base of the tree and began to eat one of the ripe figs.

"What will we do, Cy?"

Cy turned her head to look at her friend. "Prepare for the worst, I suppose. What else can we do?"

• • •

"She is a Coull and a Memorial," said the paunchy, balding man standing in the middle of Holt's chambers. "Her family were all Memorials, killed in some tribal dispute years back. She was at the hearing today, with another Memorial. She even had the audacity to use the Memory while you were speaking."

Holt only grunted. He did not turn to look at the four others in his chamber. He stared at the window, not out at the rolling seas but rather at his reflection. He wanted to see himself in this moment of victory.

"Yes," continued the speaker. "She is powerful, though—apprenticed to Hammon the elder."

Holt interrupted, breaking his gaze at his own reflection. "I do not care about the old man. But the girl I would like removed." He moved to sit in an armchair. "When we take the libraries, make sure you get the girl. Gather what men you need. Use plain blades, no house markings, and no uniforms. Take the libraries, starting with Central. Quickly. The momentum must be sustained. We can't allow anything to go wrong, not when we are so close to victory."

The men around Holt nodded acknowledgment and departed. The man who had spoken, Timmon, remained. Timmon had known Holt for years, watching and helping him build to this momentous achievement. Timmon could sense there was something more on Holt's mind.

Holt poured two glasses of wine. "You know the legend of the binding, Timmon?"

"Of course. Doesn't every child learn of it in school? It is the story of how the Long Memory was bound to a line of people charged with seeing our memories safeguarded."

"Yes, the great story of the binding," Holt spoke mockingly as he took a seat beside the closest person he had to a friend.

"Do you know, Timmon, in some circles it is said it was the Coullish who first told the story of the binding? I have been to the north many times and have heard the story of the binding told very differently than how we learned it in school. In the far north it is said that powerful story makers feared the loss of history, and they used the letters of the making found only on the scrolls in the caves of the Coull Mountains to write a story. A story that would bind memory to a line of people. The Memorials."

Holt paused to sip his wine, and silence ensued. Timmon was unsure if he should speak, and he was about to when Holt finally continued.

"In Coull and other obscure parts of the north, it is also said that these story makers wrote a story of unbinding."

"A story of the unbinding?" Timmon started. "I confess, I have no knowledge of such a thing."

"I am not surprised. I believe it is even little known among the Northernlings themselves. And among the Memorials it is an esoteric study."

"But would not the unbinding of memory be a means of reaching our end? To stamp out the Long Memory?" Timmon sat forward, looking at Holt.

Holt shook his head. "No, I think not. To unbind memory would be to free it. The Memorials are meddlesome, but they do serve a useful purpose in containing memory. Now the people remember only what they need to in order to go about their lives. To unbind memory would mean to restore full memory to all the people. It would mark our end. What we need only do is control memory through containing the Memorials."

"This Coullish Memorial, you think she—" Timmon lifted his eyebrows.

"If the legend is true, I believe the story of the unbinding might be held somewhere within her endless memory. She comes from a strong line of Memorials and from the very lands of the binding. Indeed, had a Memorial been sought prior to the enacting of the Settlement Act, it would have very likely been her mother."

"You have known of her for some time, then," said Timmon.

"Oh yes. She may not know it. But we have history between us, she and I."

• • •

Preparing for the worst does not make it hurt any less. Two days after the vote, they came to the library in the middle of the night. The smell of smoke woke Cy first. Within minutes, hands seized her in the dark and dragged her from bed. They thrust a burlap sack over her head, bound her hands behind her back. She heard shouting and the clanging of metal—the clash of swords.

It was hard to breathe under the sack. Her capturers half shoved, half dragged her. She stumbled and became entangled with the legs of one of the intruders. Both fell hard. A boot kicked her in the gut.

"Get up! Get up, damn you!"

Arms jerked Cy to her feet, and she struggled to stay alert, clinging to reality. It was no use. Feeling nauseated, she threw up and lost consciousness.

Over what seemed like days Cy flitted in and out of consciousness. She had been on a ship, that she knew. She had felt the rolling of the sea, the dampness and saltiness of sea travel. There had been bodies, many bodies, tightly packed in the hold below the ship's deck. She remembered groans mixing with the creaking of the wooden hull. No one had cried out, though. Cy herself had kept silent as a tomb.

But now there was nothing. No bodies, no sounds. Cy felt cold, sore. She lay face down on a smooth stone floor. Lifting her head, Cy could see a wooden cot. With a heave, she lifted herself onto all fours and crawled toward the cot. Lights popped behind her eyes.

Now she raked her hands through her hair, felt the knots and dried vomit. Cy's stomach clenched; she felt disgusting on top of broken. Cy slumped onto the cot and her face landed in something wet. It was a bowl of turnip stew beside a piece of flat bread and a small cup of water on a tray.

Cy cursed. Half the soup had spilled but the water cup was still full. She resisted the urge to down the water and the soup in a few gulps. Instead she sat and slowly sipped about a third of each, then waited to let it settle before downing another third.

The meals came twice a day, pushed through a slot in the cell door. Beyond their hands Cy saw nothing of her captors. After several days, she felt some strength and clarity return. She began to save a small amount of water from each meal until she had a full cup. Tearing a scrap from her tunic she dipped the cloth in the water, using it to clean her wounds and wash the filth from her body as best she could.

Cy scrubbed her toes and thought of Ban. She and Ban loved to go to the seawall in the Capital harbor to soak their feet in the cool water. Ban had grown up on boats. Her father owned a fleet of barges used to ship inland crops and other goods to the Capital. Cy hoped Ban had escaped the raid on the library and fled to her family's home in the Riverlands. She could easily have found passage, smuggled upriver on one of her father's ships if she had made it to the harbor.

"If Ban had been on the ship with me, I imagine she would have called out to me," Cy thought. She smiled a little at this, thinking about how her friend, continuously chattering, could not have kept her mouth shut, not even if threatened with death.

The days were monotonous. Cy spent her time watching her bruises turn from deep purple to yellow until the day she finally felt strong enough to dive into the streams of the Long Memory so she could understand where she was being held. Images layered upon one another to form a sort of moving diorama of the fortresses's history. Some were sharp and clear, some faded and blurred. All around her the memories of people imprinted in time. It was a cacophony of yells, sobs, and scraping of shackles. So many people had suffered here. Died here. It almost overwhelmed Cy. She swayed where she stood. With great effort, Cy cleared many of the memories, allowing those remaining to come into sharper focus. They confirmed Cy's hunch about where she was being held. The eastern edge of the central Archipelago was dotted with dozens of small stone islands turned defensive outposts and then abandoned. Some of the forts had dreadful histories, places where refugees or slaves would be held without recourse, until they withered to dust.

Cy spent hours swimming through the channels of memory, for as long as she could stand. Some of these memories were so old that they pressed down on her, making it difficult to breathe. It took time, but she allowed the images to layer and fade until she could clearly distinguish one memory from another. In this clarity Cy could almost walk through the memories as she paced her cell. She listened to a mother sing a lullaby to her child, both fresh from a slaver's ship. Cy sat in on a whispered conversation between ten former slaves turned captives. They huddled in the cell planning escape.

"The guards will have to open the door if they cannot open the slot for our food. We can be on either side of the door, ready."

Cy stood and let the memory fade. The practice made her feel sad and drained. It was the exploration of the past, not merely the facts of history but the stories of the past, that made the Memorials so important. A Memorial did not simply know that this fortress had been used to cage refugees, a Memorial smelled the death in the air, heard the sound of screams, sensed hope draining from bodies like spilled blood. With Memorials remembering the pain and devastation, their role was to ensure that things like these prison forts would never be used again. But here was Cy sitting in this cell, drowning in the pain of the past mixed with her own.

The sound of her door being thrown open ripped Cy back from the Long Memory. Then three guards were upon her, wrestling a burlap sack over her head and shackles on her wrists. In the moment before the sack went over her head Cy saw her guards' faces. Young, so young, she thought, and a little uncertain. Cy's heart pounded.

The guards marched Cy out of her cell, up several short flights of stairs. Trying to contain racing thoughts of being thrown off a cliff into the sea, Cy struggled, but her guards just dragged her with more force. Cy began to panic. She was going to start screaming, she thought.

A door scraped open and fresh air brushed over Cy. In an instant someone yanked the sack off Cy's head and shoved her forward. Hands still shackled, she landed hard, face down. Without a word, the guards uncuffed her and left, sealing a door behind them.

It took several minutes for Cy to gain her vision. She was in a tiny courtyard of sorts, completely surrounded by high stone walls. Gravel, grass, and some flowering bushes. Most welcome was the brilliant blue sky. Cy rolled onto her back, staring up at it.

After some time, the scraping of a door jarred her peace. Cy sat up quickly and looked around. Across the courtyard, a mere ten feet or so away, a slender man seemingly unfolded himself through a small wooden door. As he straightened, Cy saw that he carried a canvas bag and wore a broad woven hat. She moved to stand, and the man jumped at the sound of her body on gravel. He dropped the bag with a clatter, and an assortment of gardening tools spilled out. Taking a square of cloth from his back pocket, the man wiped his brow, cleared his throat, and bent down to collect his tools.

Cy watched cautiously. "Hello?"

The man finished picking up his tools with the air of a person focused on ignoring something obvious. He took up some clippers, setting to work on a hedge.

"Hello," Cy said again.

The man's clippers worked faster.

"My name is Cy. Are you the gardener here?"

The man stopped and wiped his brow again. "Yes, and they cannot be bothered to tell me when there will be someone here and when there will not be someone here, it seems. So please stay over there while I work." A slight accent flavored his soft voice, almost covered by the nervous tremor.

"Of course," she said, "I would not harm you. Please, do your work."

The man worked meticulously and seemed to enjoy the challenge of making everything symmetrical. After a while, he packed up his tools and went to the door.

As he stepped through, he looked back at Cy. "My name is Makati."

And so it began that every other day Cy would be removed from her cell, taken to this little courtyard and left for about an hour.

It was with no predictability that Makati worked in the courtyard. At first he would only acknowledge Cy with a nod. But over time and after many promptings, Makati began to respond. Mostly he would only answer questions about the garden. He told Cy the names of all its plants. Eventually he told Cy about the gardens in other parts of the fortress. Cy learned from Makati that there were about one hundred other prisoners. Makati said new prisoners arrived every now and then on ships, usually no more than two to three at a time.

One afternoon Cy sat in the shade of the wall and studied Makati as he worked. His deep red-brown skin was much darker than her own. It marked him as someone from the Outer Isles. He worked barefoot, dressed in plain linen pants and a soft woven shirt.

After a time, Makati asked, "You are a Memorial?"

Cy nodded yes and stretched her legs out in front of her.

"Is that special?"

"I don't know. Some people certainly think so."

"It wasn't until I reached the west that I heard of Memorials," Makati said, continuing to weed. "Where I am from, on the Island of All in the Outer Isles, we do not have Memorials. We used to have what we called Holders. Those raised to be keepers of the stories that made us. But they passed from existence some time ago."

Cy, curiosity peaked, asked, "How is it that the Holders stopped being?"

"Oh, it was many years ago now. Long before my day of birth. It is an old story." Makati sat back on his heels.

"The story says the Holders' tongues became heavy and clumsy. They couldn't tell the stories anymore without mixing up the details. The people thought the Holders were going mad; some thought a great illness had come. The Holders themselves became frustrated and angry. Some threw themselves from the cliffs into the ocean. Others sank into general village life to become herders or farmers. My family once had a strong line of Holders."

"What happened to the stories?"

"Oh, well, we have stories—legends and tales that mostly serve to warn the young to not act rashly, or to scold the unscrupulous trader. But very little is told anymore of the making of All. My people are very absentminded, it would seem. We forget so easily! Everyone in the Outer Isles knows this about All." Makati chuckled. "But they are no better, I can tell you that."

Makati stood with his canvas bag of tools, his hand above his eyes to shield them from the sun. "I am done now and must be going. It was good to talk to you."

Cy smiled. "Thank you for the story, Makati."

Back in her cell, Cy wondered at Makati's story. It had made her think of the story of the binding. She hummed a short tune as she fingered the frayed hem of her tunic. The tune was that of an old verse, one she and the other children would shout during a game of chase. It took a few minutes before Cy remembered all the words:

Papa yelled, *Do you know what you did?*
No Papa, no memories do we hold.
Mamma scolds, *Do as you're told!*
We children run, we don't know what we're told
For we have no memories of our own
The Memorial took them all to hold.

She ran through the little song a few times before letting out a laugh. "Well, that certainly does take on a new meaning now," she said aloud, thinking of Makati's story.

The object of the chase game was to pull little pieces of colored cloth from the waists of other children. The idea was that the cloth scraps were memories a Memorial had taken, and without the memories the children would always be in trouble with their parents for forgetting what they were told.

Cy thought of Makati and his story from the Isle of All. How could it be that the Holders of All had lost their stories? Why was it that on All there were no Memorials? It was troubling to Cy that on All, and perhaps elsewhere in the Outer Isles, the people would have no way to recall the stories of their own making. Cy whispered the last line of the rhyme, "The Memorial took them all to hold."

Cy lay back on her cot. The binding did not stop the people from remembering things on their own, of course. She certainly remembered things from her past. But without the collective memories of the Memorials, the past was utterly lost. Cy wondered if the stories of All could be found in the Long Memory. If so, what did it mean that she could find them but not the people of All, the people they rightly belonged to?

Had other places lost their memories and stories as well? Not in the north. The whole of the uprising was based on remembering past wrongs. Cy paused. Or was it? Were the people truly remembering or were they just reacting to immediate wrongs, based on which house armed them? Cy thought of the settlement project, the fighting in the north, Holt's most recent actions against the Long Memory. The Memorials were powerless to stop this repression from happening against themselves and their own, and the people did not rally to the cause. Some complained, muttered angrily against the actions of the council, but there was no fire behind their words. None outside the Memorials seemed called to action.

"Where are the people in all of this? Why do they stand by and let this happen?" Cy remembered Ban saying as Ban had stomped around their favorite fig tree in the Central Library garden. Her friend had received a letter from her father saying that the Riverland shipping guild would not cease transporting Holt's goods. Ban lobbied her father, vice chair of the guild, for months, but it was to no avail.

"It's like everyone has forgotten how important the binding was, how momentous. It is meant to protect and safeguard the Archipelago. But they allow it to be stripped away and replaced with Holt's preposterous Act for the Containment of Threats to the Archipelago."

At the time, Cy had laughed at the mocking tone in Ban's voice as she spoke of Holt's act. But now, in light of Makati's story and her own capture, Cy now saw nothing amusing. In fact, a creeping realization began to fill her. The people don't remember the importance of the binding. It is not their memory.

"The Memorial took them all to hold," she whispered.

Cy shifted on the cot, covered her eyes with an arm for a moment. Then a sharp rap on her cell door startled her, and a harsh voice shouted, "Prisoner, clear away from the door!"

A guard entered, followed by three others dressed in uniforms of the Provincial army. Moving quickly toward Cy, they lifted her, and before the familiar burlap sack came down around her head Cy saw the crest of House Holt embroidered the soldiers' coats. Cy's heart pounded.

Out of the cell, the guards went left instead of the usual right to the courtyard. After ascending several flights of stairs, her guards pushed Cy roughly into a room, forced her to sit. She heard an ominous click as cold metal touched her wrists.

A moment later, light flooded her vision. The room came into focus in bits and pieces. Walls of large stone like the rest of the prison, but the floor of this room was a deep polished amber wood. She sat on a small wooden stool at a large table, hands shackled together and chained to the floor. Across from her sat another person—it was Councilman Holt himself.

"Do you know how long you have been here in this castle, Cy?"

"This prison, you mean?" Cy met Holt's eyes.

Holt pursed his lips. "Four months."

Cy spoke again, fear making her mouth dry. "After all these months, I cannot imagine what there could be between us that needs discussing."

"What is between us?" Holt gave a snort. "Your existence! That is what remains between us. Your existence and that of the other Memorials held here."

"Held here?" *Anything to avoid the word imprisoned,* thought Cy.

"The war in the north moves apace," he continued. "The people are aligned with this progress. But so long as you and the others are here—"

Holt stood and moved toward an open window. "Well, then there is always the threat of the question *Why?*"

"You fear the people remembering," Cy said. She tried to make Holt look at her, but his eyes would not leave his view out the window.

"That they will remember you took me and the others away. That you killed many and burned the libraries, and they will ask why. And you will have to answer."

"Oh, shut up!" Holt snapped, finally stepping away from the window. "Only the nostalgic will truly question your absence and care. The Long Memory fades, and soon enough memories will be what they should be—myth and legend."

"You cannot render memory powerless, Holt," Cy said. "You could round up each and every Memorial in the Archipelago and let us rot in these cells. You could ensure that each newly born Memorial never has their skill fostered. In that you could most definitely end our line. But you will not eradicate memory."

Even as she said it, though, Cy wondered about the Isle of All and doubted.

The binding, Makati's story, her own memories—it all meant something.

Whispering to herself, Cy mused, "A people who remember will not be exploited again. A people who remember will take action."

A horrible realization began to take form in Cy's mind. People were not remembering. They could not remember those things of the past that shape the present.

"Memories are supposed to be shared. It is what gives them power." She said this loudly, though it was directed as much to herself as to Holt. "Perhaps it is time the people remember for themselves."

Cy looked directly at Holt.

Holt peered back at Cy, leaning closer. "What?" He forced the question through gritted teeth.

"Do your worst, Holt. But without the Memorials, memories will have to go somewhere. Each person holds her own memory of what she has lived through and seen. You cannot take that or destroy that, for it is human."

Holt's face purpled. In a few strides he rounded the table and then drew a short sword from his belt. He yanked Cy's head, exposing her neck. Cy's heart beat erratically and her face flushed. Her eyes traveled down to the blade and its hilt, on which the crest of House Holt was inlaid in gold. In an instant Cy wasn't in the room with Holt. She was far away in a moment of her past life, lying on hard-packed dirt, screaming as a man pulled her away from the prone dead body of her father. There was a flash of swords, one very nearly cutting Cy in the stomach. In this long-buried memory, Cy saw the glint of light off the hilt, the flash of a crest.

Just as suddenly Cy was back in the room with Holt. With the sword at her throat, Cy's chest heaved. She felt bile rising in her throat and thought she would be sick. Why had she not been able to put it together before now? The memory of the council hearing, the one she had always struggled to see through. She always lost it as Holt rose to speak, under his house crest.

"It was you," she gasped. "Your armies killed my people. It was House Holt."

Cy strained forward, pulling on her restraints.

"Oh, ho! She remembers. She remembers what truly remains between us." Holt smiled wickedly.

Cy struggled hard against her shackles. She wanted to leap at Holt. To hurt and maim him. Cy could only see the crest, and it filled her with a panic and rage she had never known.

Cy screamed, "I don't need the Long Memory to know what you and your wealth have done to my people! I lived it! Others will remember too!"

Holt struck Cy across the cheek with the hilt of his sword, knocking her to the floor. "Your people are weak!" he spat. "They remember nothing of who they once were. Only that they are now lawless barbarians."

He commanded his guards: "Remove her!" Then he stood with his back to Cy as she was hoisted up, dazed from the blow. "As a Memorial, Cy, you should know it is easier to control what people do with their memories than one might think."

. . .

Several days later Cy was given time outside in the small courtyard. She was anxious since her meeting with Holt, sensing that his anger would have repercussions. She had formulated a plan, and when Makati came to garden, Cy wasted no time.

"Makati."

His eyes grew wide as they fell on the large and swollen bruise on Cy's cheek.

"I need a favor. I do not think I will be given time outside again. I am sorry to have to ask. I do not wish to risk your safety or overstep any bounds of our friendship, but I need this from you."

Nodding, Makati stood up straight. "What do you need?"

"I need you to send a message for me, to the west. To the Riverlands."

Cy chewed her lip. This next favor carried more risk. "I also need some way to send a message among the other prisoners. Makati, do you . . . are you friendly with any of the guards or the cooks?"

Makati stammered for a moment. "A letter to the Capitol Isle I can send. I have a friend I write to sometimes. It will not look suspicious. But to communicate with the other prisoners?"

"A few days back, I was taken to Holt. He is angry and I fear he has plans. If I can get word to a friend in the Riverlands, I think the other prisoners and I can at least buy some time until—" Cy broke off, frustrated. She could only hope Ban was in the Riverlands.

"I know a few of the guards. We play cards together. They too are from the Outer Isles. And, like me, many of them do not agree with what is being done here. I can ask." Makati trailed off nervously.

Cy reached out and held Makati's shoulders. "Friend. Thank you!"

"I have some paper here. I can take the message and leave you with the rest and with my pencil."

Cy quickly wrote the note to Ban telling her friend where she was and what she planned.

Then Cy wrote a message on the other piece of paper:

My name is Cy. I am a prisoner here also. I believe Holt means to act soon. There is an old tradition among the Archipelago: in a conflict, wronged people will plant themselves outside of the home of the aggressor and refuse to eat until the other agrees to share a meal. It has been used in this very fortress a very long time ago. I am sure you have seen it in the Long Memory. I am sending word outside to trusted Memorials. They will ensure the people know. Would others join a hunger strike?

Cy handed Makati the bit of paper. He did not read it but rolled it up and placed it in his gardening bag.

"Thank you, Makati," Cy said, her voice heavy with emotion.

Makati nodded and left through the small door.

Cy was right in predicting that her trips to the courtyard would end. Five days went by during which she had not been taken out once. She paced her cell, her new daily routine, waiting for food.

Then one day, when her first meal of the day arrived, there was a small message tucked under her bowl, scribbled in haste on the same piece of paper as her original:

> *My name is Je, I am an Easternling from a library on the coast. I have already started refusing my meals. This tradition you write of is particularly strong amongst my people. If enough of us went on hunger strike and if you can truly get word to the outside then we could pose a challenge to Holt.*

Cy ignored her meal and just sat holding the note. She felt a tingling in her fingers. That undeniable feeling of something big beginning. Cy wrote back and left the note in the same spot under her bowl. She had to trust that, however the note had made it to her, it would make it back.

In time a reply arrived but not from just Je. Notes from other captive Memorials crowded the paper, creating a conversation. All supported a hunger strike. Cy got down on her belly and squeezed under the cot. There she pried loose a small stone behind which she had stowed Makati's pencil. Retracting it and pulling herself out from under the cot, Cy bent over and began to write. She was hardly able to contain her anxious excitement:

> *There are nearly one hundred of us being held here. Eighty of us on hunger strike would be enough. When you receive this note, mark your name and find a way to pass it to another Memorial.*

Cy also retrieved a small square of paper from under her mattress and wrote a letter to Ban explaining more of the emerging plan.

That night, Cy sat at the door waiting for the guard to arrive to take her untouched bowl and plate. It was risky, she knew, but she had to make sure the guard knew to get the message to Makati.

Cy sat so long that she fell asleep, but she awoke with a start when the guard came. She pressed the notes into the guard's hand.

"Please, Makati needs to get this."

The guard recoiled, but after a moment he took the papers.

• • •

One week later Cy's door was thrown open by four soldiers, not guards, who grabbed Cy and dragged her down a corridor. She heard the shouts of more soldiers, the sound of others being taken out of their cells. All Cy could think was that the day of execution had finally come. Perhaps Holt had intercepted the letters. She thought of Makati, and a panic built in her like that she felt the first time she was taken to the courtyard. An acrid bile taste filled her mouth. She fervently hoped Makati's part in this remained undiscovered. Her stomach clenched and her heart raced. Then she felt gravel beneath her feet and blinding sun above.

A soldier shoved Cy, and she hit the ground hard. Around her, others were made to kneel.

He means to execute us all at once, Cy thought, fear flowing wildly.

But after a time all went quiet, and nothing more happened. They had all just been left kneeling in the hot sun. At first perplexing, it became torturous. With the burlap sacks over their heads, the bound Memorials were suffocating. Cy's knees went numb. She sucked in air, but it was devoid of oxygen. Her head swam, and she thought she would vomit.

Hours passed. At the brink of losing consciousness, Cy finally heard footsteps and then a great commotion as soldiers yelled at everyone to get up. She stumbled, then was accosted and dragged back inside to her cell.

No message came with the meager evening meal. Cy could not imagine eating anyway, and just sipped the water. Thirst burned her throat. Her head ached. Once the water was gone she lay on the cool stone floor and fell asleep.

This became the everyday routine: pulled from her cell with others and dragged outside midday, then hours spent hooded and kneeling in the hot sun. Cy felt her strength waning both physically and mentally as weeks dragged on. The few times Cy tried to reach the Long Memory she nearly passed out. This more than anything made hope seem fleeting.

Some weeks into this torture, they knelt in the yard one day not baked by sun but soaked by rain. Not a refreshing rain but a thick soup. Unless Cy kept her head bowed, the burlap over her head stuck to her mouth, suffocating her even more. Cy was so fixated on how sore her neck and shoulders felt in this position that she almost cried out in surprise when she felt the shackled hands of the person to her left nudging her own hands. Then she felt a small roll of paper between fingers. Cy carefully accepted the scroll and held it so tightly that her nails dug painfully into her palms.

Back in her cell Cy lay on the floor. She was so tired, so thirsty. Her body ached all over and she felt hot, unable to cool off even on the cold stone floor. Slowly she unclenched her hand, fingers stiff, to pluck out the note.

It consisted of all the past notes and a collection of names. Some she recognized from the Central Library. Others were unknown to her. Seeing so many names, Cy suddenly felt much less alone. She counted the names and then counted again. Eighty-six.

Cy retrieved the larger square of paper Makati had left her with. She tore off a small piece and wrote a note to Ban, copying the names of all the Memorial hunger strikers. She beseeched her friend, "Compel the free Memorials and anyone sympathetic to our plight to honor the tradition we invoke and to think of us who are locked away for the crime of remembering."

. . .

"Search the cells!" Holt thundered. "Confiscate anything that could be used for writing! We have to cut them off from the world!" His hands gripped a dozen or so posters brought to him by Timmon.

Timmon had found the posters at a Riverlands inn, but they quickly spread all over the Eastern Isles. Sailors had left them, the innkeeper said. The names of each of the captive Memorials blazed in commanding letters. Underneath were excerpts from their letters. The posters gave information about the hunger strike and a plea that those on the outside take immediate action.

The people were taking notice of these posters. Rumbles of rebellion met Holt across the Archipelago, and what had been irritating setbacks grew into outright challenges to his authority. It was in the east that the most discontent brewed. Holt had needed to find a new way to transport weapons and goods to the north after his caravans were barred from the eastern road by one town council. He had tried to turn to the rivers for transport, but could not find enough captains and barges to carry his goods. In fact, the seas seemed to carry defiance faster. The hunger strike served as a beacon, uniting resistance in all parts of the land.

"Guards!" Holt bellowed from his office. "Are the prisoners in the yard?"

"Sir, yes, Master Holt. They were brought out two hours ago."

In the yard Holt saw rows of kneeling prisoners, a hundred in all. Each nearly identical in ragged clothes and burlap hoods.

When the soldiers saw Holt, they snapped to attention. The most senior among them came to Holt's side.

"Master Holt, this is a surprise."

Cy's stomach clenched. He was here. He must know of the letters.

Holt stood before the kneeling Memorials. "You think it matters to people if you all starve to death?" he bellowed. "It does not matter! No one cares that you starve and no one expects me to share a meal with you as some sort of pathetic penance."

Despite her fear, excitement coursed through Cy. This meant their letters had been received! And he wouldn't be here in such a rage if they hadn't been effective.

"I tell you now," Holt continued, "Give up this hunger strike and perhaps in time you will gain your freedom."

The initial responding silence was shattered by a shout. "Freedom will come from death before it comes at your hands, Holt!"

This shout unleashed a torrent of agreement, and the Memorials cursed Holt.

"Who said that?" Holt stomped across the gravel.

Cy heard a grunt, sounds of a struggle. Holt was pulling a hood off a head.

"You are Je from the East. You started this, did you not? You were the first to stop eating!"

Cy then heard the sound of spitting. Holt's scream of fury confirmed that Je had spit in his face.

"Kill her!"

Cy struggled up and pulled at her shackles. Adrenalin overcame thought and understanding. She just wanted to stop what was happening. But her efforts were fruitless, and after a few moments there was no sound of struggle. Perhaps Je was unconscious or maybe she just would not give Holt the satisfaction of seeing her afraid.

Back in her cell, Cy lay in utter exhaustion. Tears coursed down her cheeks, tears of sadness and horror at Je's death. But also tears of relief. She knew that the letters were getting out and people were acting enough to threaten Holt's power. No future was certain, but that was all right. Cy felt confident that the unbinding was upon the world, being shared by the many, as memories should be.

SMALL AND BRIGHT

AUTUMN BROWN

Orion lies on the horizon in winter.
Like a warrior rising from slumber
She raises first her chin
Then her heavy belt,
Heavy with skulls.
Orion rises early to guide us.

The Surfacing

I DREAM AGAIN THAT I AM LOST IN THE TUNNELS OF OUR CITIES. THE fires extinguished, but still a cool blue glow lights my way. The faster I run, the higher I ascend in the city toward the surface, and the light becomes brighter and burns my skin. I fill with knowing, knowing the place where I am going. More and more light fills each room. My skin burns and then becomes darker somehow. And then I am there at the door in the surface, and if I climb through, death and freedom await me. I stand there looking up. Up.

I stand there looking up. And then I wake.

Early. It is the morning of my surfacing. The fires are not yet lit, and the only light is the phosphorescent lichen growing down the walls of the tunnel just outside my cell. In the faint glow, I can make out the simple contours of this room, featureless except for the low bench on which I lie shivering as my body struggles to maintain core temperature. Everything has become a struggle. But this cell, this prison, feels so familiar that for the first time I sense in myself a buried attachment to the place. This may be the last place in which I ever feel any sensation of comfort.

There is no barrier between my cell and the tunnel beyond, but none is needed. The listening guards, chosen and trained from childhood for their advanced aural sensitivity, are undoubtedly already aware that I am awake because of the change in my breathing. Soon they will position themselves near the entrance and await orders from the elder midwives to retrieve me.

I will myself to move. I feel a gnawing hunger, and even as I wonder if I will receive a last meal before being surfaced, not knowing the protocol for exiles, I try to adjust my expectations, convincing myself that I may not eat a full meal again for many days, if ever, and that I am mentally and physically prepared for the task. I gently touch my belly. The lichen growing outward from my cord cut, usually groomed to fine detail, is now wild, wet, and fecund, reaching up to my ribs and down to my vulval hair. For the first time in my adult life I can truly value the belly lichen for its original purpose: a survival strategy in the early days of our community, when there were so many tunnel collapses and a person might have had to endure for many days on what leaked between boulders and what grew or lived on the body. Now we cultivate fungi and algae on the body from birth, but it is more for beauty than for use. Throughout the trial, I have let mine grow free. I hope this uncultivated wild space on my body will provide some sustenance on the other side.

If not, I hope death comes quickly.

I sit up and pull a loose shirt over my head. It falls easily around my swollen, sore breasts and my midsection, fleshy and alive. Over my legs I draw long pants. There is no way to tell what is appropriate dress for the surface, but I hope that one of my parents will provide alternatives. Things are such now that I must rely entirely on the ability and willingness of my family to advocate for me within the tight confines of the law.

Surfacing happens so rarely in our community that there is comparatively little ritual associated with it. This morning I am to spend in prayer with my vaginal parent, Geminii, until the guards come for me. I hear light, quick footsteps, and she enters my cell.

"You are the cavernous womb," I bow my head in formal greeting.

"And you are the diamond cut from within." She responds, touching my forehead with her thumb and forefinger. She offers me mushrooms and plump seeds, which I eat quickly. We sit in taut silence for some time, pretending to pray. Finally I ask her the only question I can.

"Where is Vega?"

"He is with Cassiopeia, in the sands."

The sands, the place in our community where we bring inconsolable, sleepless babes. Nothing more than a small cave, really, only it is very deep in the earth, closer to the molten core, and it houses the softest sands in all the underground. For years our people have brought their babies there to lay their bodies in the sands. We hold their little legs and drag them slowly in circles through the sand until they fall asleep. If he is there, it can only mean that the reality of his parentlessness is setting in.

I think of Vega, the immediacy of his world. He has no way to understand the complexity of my absence. He has only my absence. Another woman feeds him from her breast now, and surely she tastes and smells and feels different to him. I touch my own breasts gingerly, engorged as they are with useless milk. I try to stifle my fear, my regret, my unspeakable sadness. Even as I jealously hate her, I thank the unseen stars for Cass, my greatest ally and friend. Both of us warriors and also child-bearers, we trained together, we carried our children at the same time, and we birthed only days apart. During the gestations of our children, we made a pact that should one of us die in combat, the other would mother both children as her own.

"He will forget me." I feel the rage building in my throat, threatening to suffocate me. What kind of people would separate vaginal parent and child?

"We will keep your naming song alive," says Geminii. I pull up a wall around myself as my despair bears down on me. All of the things I will lose today sharpen into focus: sound, touch, language, song, my parents, my son. I cannot take comfort in my naming song. I will never hear it. I want my vaginal parent to keep speaking, to never stop. But I cannot ask her this senseless thing.

I shake my thoughts away. "I have no hope, Geminii."

"There is hope, Orion." She hesitates, glancing behind her. "Orion, I must speak with you openly." Her tone has changed, and there is a strange look in her eyes. Shifting. Nervous. Geminii is typically guarded and observant, but I have never seen her afraid. Until now.

"There are those who wish to help you." Her eyes slide towards the doorway, and I understand that she means to tell me something dangerous, and that she has reason to believe the listening guards can be trusted with the information.

"This surfacing has bitterly divided our community, Orion. And it is not just the fact that surfacing as an ultimate punishment is controversial. There are many who believe what you did was right, who would help you if they could. There are even those who refuse to call you an abomination."

I hang my head. "It does not matter now. They cannot save me with their beliefs."

"Listen to me, Orion!" Geminii commands me with such urgency that I force myself to meet her intense gaze.

"There is not much time. Listen. In the early days of the community, when we were still becoming the people who are buried, there were—expeditions to the surface. Not one returned, of the three groups. Not one. And never any word of what happened to them. And so the last stores of surface survival supplies were never used. They were hidden. There was a feeling then, because we were so few, on the brink of extinction ourselves, that we could not risk any more loss of life."

She waits a moment for what she is saying to sink in. Lost in this new information, it does not hit me immediately. "There is one more set of survival packs. I have taken one of them for your use. It might keep you alive. I have hidden it on the platform where you will be surfaced. You will have only seconds, when the surfacing begins, to get a hold of it. You should make your move just as the light begins to flood the antechamber, when the witnesses shield their eyes. You will be disoriented, but you must fight through it and take possession of the pack before the platform rises so high that you cannot reach it."

I am floored. I begin to panic. "You should not tell me this here."

"It does not matter if they hear me, Orion. Everyone will know soon enough. It is a risk I take willingly and for a purpose, the defense of which and punishment for which I will bear in your absence. Listen to me. You must locate the pack as soon as you step onto the platform.

There are maps and warm clothing and many other things I do not know the use of. I hope that you can figure it out."

"But—why are you doing this?" I cannot help but ask, although the answer may seem obvious to her, who could never wish my death no matter what my crime.

"You are my child, Orion, that would be reason enough. But ... it is something else too. There is a belief among some of us that there are other survivors, possibly other communities that grew up after the Felaket. You may know them as the people of color. Believers call them the people of the plastic. Rumors, rumors. We do not know for sure if they exist, but what we do know is that when our community went underground, there were other communities forming, trying to survive."

"What?" I demand. I have heard nothing like this before. Questions form messily in my mind. "There are no surface survivors and so there are no people of color left! We lost our color within five generations of becoming the people who are buried. Geminii, that is what you have always told me. What does this mean, the people of the plastic? What is plastic?"

"I cannot say for certain," Geminii shakes her head. "There are some who believe the word refers to a feature of the physical body. But more recent interpretations hold that the phrase refers to a place on the surface where some may have survived. On the surface there are great bodies of water, and in them, surfaces, maybe even cities, made of a substance called plastic. It may be in one of these cities that the people of the plastic exist. You must try to find them, Orion. I believe the maps may help you."

"How can I use a map? I have never seen the surface. I will be completely disoriented!"

"Orion, finding your way aboveground must be the same as finding your way below. Only there is more space, more to see. You must have faith in your abilities. You must have faith in the prophecy."

The prophecy. Many hundred years ago there was a child in our community who had terrible visions about the end of time. Some of these were dreams that clearly recalled events from the Felaket, which took place before the founding of our community. Some visions were not familiar at all. The child said that she believed that one of our people, the people who are buried, will join with her brothers, the people of color. There are many reasons to distrust this prophecy, not the least of which is that there are no more people of color. Not here, not anywhere among the people who are buried. Also suspicious is that the community we are to join with is comprised only of men: brothers. In any case, I had thought there were no more believers. But I am learning today that there is much I do not know.

"Our community is dying. Children are born, yes, but not enough. We have become too isolated. We must find our brothers. Orion, you must do this for all of us." Geminii raises her head, hearing the faint sound of footsteps in the corridor moments before I notice it. "They are coming."

I shake my head helplessly, frustrated by all of the questions I will not have the chance to ask. "How will I survive? I cannot even hear as you can."

She grasps my shoulders firmly. "You will learn to quiet your inner thoughts. You are strong. You will survive. Perhaps you will even find that what is a deficit to you here is an advantage on the surface. And who knows, Orion? Maybe I will follow you shortly." She turns to leave.

"Mother!" the word slips through my lips before I can stop it. She stops at hearing the intimate name spoken aloud. Such a name passes between vaginal parent and child only a few times in their shared life. "Thank you, Mother." She looks at me long and hard, and she then leaves as silently as she arrived.

• • •

The caverns of our community closest to the surface are also the oldest. Built more than two millennia ago by people seeking refuge from persecution and death, they are simple rooms with domed ceilings and cracking walls. It is a punishment to have to go up to these rooms to repair the cracks and buttress the ceilings. Stories of accidental exposure are used to instill fear and discipline in our children. But as with everything in our community, there is a contradiction, for it is also a test of bravery to go so close to the surface, so close to the light. Before now, I've only been to the upper rooms twice, once as a punishment and once on a dare. That all feels very far away from me as the guards escort me to the antechamber.

My people have never seen the sky and the stars. But we sing of them as though they are the last thing we see before sleeping and the first upon waking, like the cave dwellers of old. There is a deeply held belief among us that we will surface one day, not as a punishment but as a choice, and live again in the sun. The surfacing platform and the antechamber seem to have been built with this auspicious occasion in mind, for together they make up the only place in our community outside of the warrior's training caverns that is expansive and ornate. The ceiling of the antechamber is crisscrossed with designs, and upon a close inspection you can see that each is a unique picture of a living thing that crawled or crept or ran or flew on the surface of our dead world. All of them rising upward in the vaulted gloom, frozen in a moment of rebirth, bursting from nothing, from the place they were buried.

The surfacing platform has been used only once in my lifetime, and I was not yet old enough to attend. Surfacing is extremely rare in our community, primarily because the willing destruction of life, especially of those capable of bearing children, poses an extreme risk to sustaining the population level. It is also considered a hallmark of the Felaket and the time that came before it.

I have seen the antechamber, though. At the far end of the domed room is a gate and beyond that a tunnel that leads to the surfacing platform. Next to the gate is an ancient, heavy glass window covering almost the entire wall. The glass, warped with age, distorts whatever stands on the other side. In the antechamber is the single lever that opens the doors to the surface and, at the same time, raises the platform through the doors. My phallic parent, one of the city's season keepers, often said that when the surface was in its winter, you could hear the singing of the wind from there.

As we near the surface, I can hear it. The sound of the wind. I can see that the walls are cracked with cold. I feel dread pooling at the base of my stomach. *It is winter,* I think. *I will freeze to death before I take three steps.*

I try to imagine what the survival kit Geminii has hidden contains, and that is when the absurdity of it hits me. That she should try to save my life with a thousand-year-old survival pack. That I might be able to make sense of anything stored inside it. That there is any chance at all that I will survive more than an hour on the surface. Tears start streaming from my eyes before I even realize I am on the verge of crying. Something inside of me begins to collapse, and I claw for the edge of my sanity.

And then I am in the antechamber, and surrounding me are a hundred solemn faces, many distraught. I feel panic overtaking me, a scream forming in my throat. I search the crowd for Geminii's face. I find her standing beside the elder midwives. Her eyes bore into me, and I try to remember what she has told me. I know that if I lose my will to live, I will lose the hope she holds for me.

The elder midwives are withered and silent women, all of them warriors. From childhood, like me, they were trained as fighters, seasoned by combat with giant and vicious vermin that stalk our underground world. From middle age they apprentice in the birthing of children and in the esoteric art of reading our star maps. I may have become one myself, but it seems the people who are buried had other plans for me. The elder midwives stare at me without remorse for what they are about to do, but also, curiously, without judgment. It is not vacancy but something else. Anticipation?

The antechamber is wide, high-ceilinged, and, with only a few fires lit, oppressively dark. The witnesses in attendance seem to glow in their ceremonial white robes. The color of death. *Like a warrior. Heavy with skulls.* Fragments of my naming song find their way into my thoughts. I struggle to remain grounded, to master my trembling. I breathe deeply and direct my attention to the elder midwives.

"Death begets death." The words of the surfacing. "In return for the life you stole and the vow you have broken, one life you must give." First one, and then each in turn, raise their right arms and point to the gate. Beyond it are the tunnel, the platform, and the doors to the surface. Breath leaves my body.

Violence begets violence, and the violence I have known in my life derived from something ugly, vile, and jealous: a man filled with hatred, supported by a community so intent on reproduction and survival that it is blind to other ways of loving. He hated me because of who I loved. He hated me because I did not love him. I killed the man who nearly killed me. But now I will die anyway.

I move forward through the gate. I have no choice. It happens so quickly, acted out in silence. In moments, I am through the tunnel, looking at the distorted figures of my community through the glass. It is so surprisingly cold here I almost forget to identify the location of the survival pack. My eyes cast about for a moment, and there it is, directly to the right of the window, tucked in a nook between the edge of the glass and the ornate frame surrounding the tunnel entrance. The pack seems to glow with its own light because the fabric covering the bag is dyed with colors I have never seen before. It is the color I have always imagined the sunset to be. I suppose now I will have a chance to confirm this—if I can survive that long.

I am just beginning to calculate how much time it will take me to reach the pack when the ground heaves beneath me and the platform begins to tremble. The ceiling above me splits in two, and I am blinded, trying to breathe, trying to sense where the window is. I rush forward and slam against the glass, sending shooting pains through my chest. The wind howls through me as I use the window to guide my body along the edge of the platform until I trip over the pack. I pull at it and it jams as the platform begins to rise. I jimmy the pack and yank hard, pulling it free and throwing myself back onto the platform. I struggle to open my eyes and can manage only a flickering of sight. Through the glass, I register movement that I can only interpret as commotion. I try to stand and manage to gain my knees, grasping the heavy survival pack, whipped by wind and light and small rocks that dance in the air around me. The platform is groaning, rising. I open my eyes again, for moments this time, and through the window I glimpse a figure I believe to be Geminii, her hands splayed, mouthing something. I cannot make out what she is saying. She disappears beneath the platform's edge, and I am alone. A single guttural cry, and I force my body onto my feet, positioning the pack between my legs, assume a warrior stance. In moments, my head will clear the surface doors and I will know what awaits me.

I open my eyes. I stand there looking up.

Technician's Log A.C. 1019. jun. 35. 20:19

There is a life form moving south through the upper Mideast quadrant. Something different, something with intellect and purpose.

It moves with determination more reminiscent of nomadic and migratory patterns of pre–A.C. 650, the point being arrival at any cost, not the aberrant, reactionary motion of the newer life forms. I have tracked its course and used the infraction positioning program to predict its path. Whatever it is, it is coming for me.

IN SPITE OF DARKNESS

ALIXA GARCIA

Seven Years Ago

Mikra was born on the first day of the war. Ó screamed from simultaneous heartbreak and joy that cracked the sky above her. Unprecedented lightning fractured the heavens to deliver Mikra. What saved their lives that night was not luck but the thunder that roared louder than the guns; and like any movement toward an unfolding future, so thundered down the unknown hand of destiny.

Present

The heat of the fire danced against Ó's face, while the cold night pressed against her back. Mikra looked up from her seven-year-old hands toward her mother, her question still rattling the air. Ó's shoulders dropped in defeat. Mikra looked curious. She had never seen her mother slouch. It was as if the weight of something invisible had fallen heavily to either side of her neck and now pulled Ó toward the ground.

"Mama? Why do you keep saying 'where are our sons?' when you are sleeping? You have other sons, Mama?" Mikra asked once more.

Ó looked up, feeling suffocated by the blanketed night. This endless night had begun eight years before. Darkness was all they now knew. "What *were* the Suns is a better question, my child." Her body shivered. It had been eight years since Ó last felt their warmth over Kempúa, and in all this time she had never talked about the Suns like this, in the past, like a dead memory scraping at the surface of now.

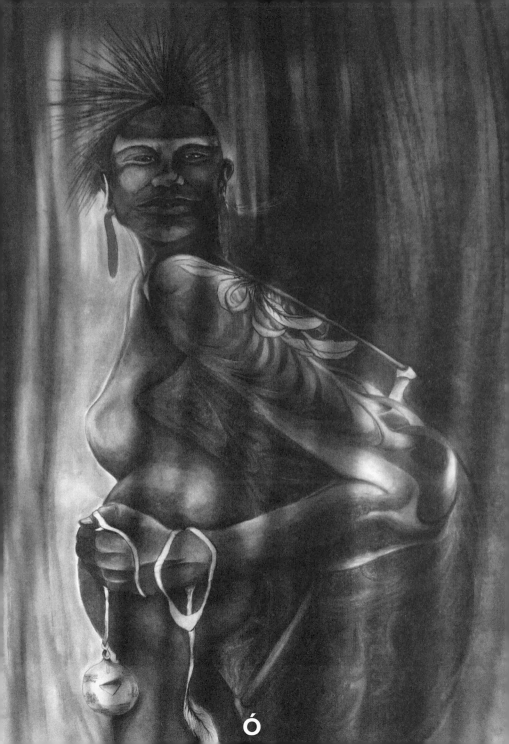

Ó

• • •

"Jaiku! Jaiku! Where are you? We need to get these Sol Gatherers out of here now! The humans are near, they will see our light!" The urgent panic could be felt in Tet's voice as he stumbled around in the dark. He had stepped outside of the light that emanated from the young Sol Gatherers' skin.

"Jaiku! Jaiku!" He whispered loudly, squinting, trying to see better.

"Aaaah!" Tet jumped in fear when he felt a hand on his head.

"It's me," Jaiku giggled.

"Jaiku! We have to get the young Gatherers out of here now!" he said panting, holding a hand to his chest.

"What's happening?" Jaiku's voice turned urgent.

"The humans are near, we've spotted their red light cutting through the forest. If we don't do something soon, the young ones will give our location away. We have them covered with leaves and shrubs, but their fear is making their skin luminous and the light of their Guide is growing brighter. I'm afraid that if we don't move soon, they won't be able to contain it!" He urgently walked back toward the glowing mound. The Sol Gatherers were affected by mood—fear and love being the strongest emotions that could make their firelike skin radiate. Jaiku could see his best friend's silhouette swaying to and fro as if he moved to a slow melody. Tet was Jaiku's age but half his size and half as fast. He could camouflage himself to any background and become virtually invisible—a trick not so impressive in the dark, but, when the days were long, his tribe, the Okanike, was the most mischievous and playful because of it. Legend has it that they are part Cominó, which gives them their ability and humor. However, few had ever seen a Cominó, and most still considered them myth.

The Okanike had taken it upon themselves to care for the young Sol Gatherers when their parents and elders never returned. Now they looked down at the last hundred surviving Gatherers and the future of Kempúa. Fear rustled the leaves that covered their large bodies. Jaiku could see the red light of the humans coming toward them. If the humans reached the mound there would be a massacre, and the last remaining Sol Gatherers would be captured and disappeared forever.

"Listen!" Jaiku said urgently, "Do you think that you can lie on top of them and camouflage the night? Or will you camouflage the light instead?" The crowd murmured. Some said yes, some no.

"We have to be in agreement if we are to hold this stance long enough to confuse the humans," one of them whispered loudly.

"But how can we? We always camouflage what we stand against; we would be leaning on them. How will we be able to mirror the night?" another one whispered.

"If we lay our bodies on them so that our backs are to the night and we picture only darkness, we might be able to pull this off," Tet interrupted. "We have no choice but to try!"

"It's suicide!" came a voice from the crowd.

"And so is standing here and doing nothing!" Tet rebutted. They could have argued all night, but Jaiku interrupted, "We have no choice, they are upon us!" Realizing that the red lasers were starting to cut through the last bit of forest that stood between them, they took the chance, and Tet's tribe began to lay their bodies one on top of the other until every inch was covered and, like a trick of the eye, they were gone. Jaiku smiled, quickly climbing a tree above them. He positioned his bow to the ground.

Leaves rustled and twigs broke. The humans were not skilled at being in the dark and often tripped and moaned when they went out like this—in large numbers, on foot, with no large machines in front of them to clear the path with fire and force. Soon Jaiku and Tet's tribe could hear the army around them—their heavy boots crushing life, their red light pointing in every direction, their dense armor glistening against one another's lasers. Jaiku could see that the armor was hard and appeared heavy, which was probably why they moved so slowly. They were big, clumsy, moving targets, Jaiku thought. If it weren't for their weaponry—if it weren't for their machinery and their numbers—they would have been destroyed long ago. Since the first day of the invasion, they came killing. They killed everything in sight, everything that moved, everything that breathed, everything that felt—except the Sol Gatherers. The humans wanted them.

Jaiku's heart pounded. He could feel his pulse against the bow. The humans neared, cracking twigs right below the branch he sat on. Sweat formed on Jaiku's brow. As they were about to trip over the mound,

Jaiku

Cominó

the humans' armor started to make an alarming sound that pierced the silent night. Red lights flashed inside their headgear. Jaiku looked on as the ghostly faces of roughly two hundred soldiers were washed in red. They made angry and disappointed expressions through the little glass window that allowed them to see. Their appearance, haunting and vacant, created an illusion of floating heads whose missing bodies littered the forest as far as Jaiku could see. In the distance, he heard birds take flight. The alarm was letting the humans know that their machines would soon run out of oxygen, forcing them to return to the darkness from which they came.

. . .

The fire danced against Ó's body, creating shadows along the hard round contours of the turtle-like shell that covered her back. The birds that lived inside the shell shifted with her unfamiliar slouch. Ó's heart ached as if it were the first time feeling a wound. How could she begin to explain where the Suns had gone? The question ricocheted inside of her like none other in hundreds of years. Mikra, on the other hand, couldn't find the reason why such a simple question could bend such a tall woman.

"Mikra, it is not sons I mention, it is suns," she said, picking up a nearby stick and scratching the subtle difference into the frozen ground. Ó stopped and stared into the fire, lost in thought for a brief moment. Mikra knew to wait if she had any hope of getting her questions answered.

"The youngest Sol Gatherers were still too young to fly when their elders were last seen," Ó began steadily—before the hesitation could creep in. Mikra looked intensely at her mother. "The elders, three thousand of them, took flight into outer space after a long rest of several months. They planned to return after our largest moon had come to the same place in the sky. But, unlike the moon, they never returned. They haven't yet, at least. It has been about eight years."

The faith that, for so long, she held like a mirror against the face of crouching maybes, began to crack that night. It was a small opening that allowed just enough doubt to seep into her heart. She began to consider that maybe the Sol Gatherers were now lost in the expansiveness of the universe and with them, she worried, the back-bone of liberation. Ó knew in her heart that only the Sol Gather-ers were strong enough in numbers to defeat the humans and bring peace, light, and regeneration back to Kempúa. But where were they? It was too much to bear. She swung her shoulders back just to keep from crying.

"You had just been conceived," Ó said steadily. "I could feel your presence inside of me like I had felt your brother Jaiku's. It was every-where. Your life was an open doorway to my beloved, Jaggúa."

Mikra furrowed her brow. She had never heard of Jaggúa and tried to picture her. Though she could be impatient at times, she was an intelligent seven-year-old, the second of her kind: a mixture of Sol Gatherer and Pattern Keeper.

"I was in love with you. During that time my heart held the hand of joy." Ó rubbed her hands together. "Jaggúa is a Sol Gatherer. You are half of her and so is Jaiku." Mikra looked puzzled; she had never seen a Sol Gatherer before.

"For as long as anyone can remember, the Sol Gatherers have gone up into that blackness as one and have come back with light for us all—pieces of sunlight which look much like the fire here, though a thousand times bigger. Jaggúa was preparing to go with them." Mikra looked up. She couldn't imagine any light coming from the vastness, not any that could closely resemble the fire that now danced before her and disappeared against the endless night.

"It was planned that, once the Sol Gatherers returned from this last journey to the Sun, festivities would commence and preparation for the following journey would consume us all, for it was this next jour-ney when the young Sol Gatherers would be shown the path to the star closest to Kempúa." Her voice dropped. Ó looked up at a pitch-black sky. Billions of little silver holes poked through the darkness but never threatened to break the fabric.

When she began again, she spoke in a low voice. "It was a happi-er time. The Sol Gatherers would show the map of the sky to their young, would speak the prophecy of their lineage, and their young would experience it for themselves. The magic that has maintained this world in balance for as long as time has been kept would be passed down once again to a new generation of Sol Gatherers. A vital

Sol Gatherer

initiation." Mikra looked at her mother, her gaze not veering for fear of missing too much.

"Sol Gatherers go together everywhere as a tribe and only leave behind their young for the first seven years of their lives here in Kempúa, because they are still too small to fly. Sol Gatherers only give birth every hundred years, and so it is a big celebration when the time comes for the new generation to soar beyond the sky and learn the secrets of their tribe."

Mikra rubbed her thumb and forefinger together as she often did when excited or anxious. Her large head of curls fell over her sculpted face. Ó continued, "Sol Gatherers fly beyond our galaxy and into another dimension in search of sunlight. The young ones fly with their elders after the initiation ceremony has concluded, and they continue to do so for the next hundred years. Once the young become elders themselves, on that hundred-and-eighth year, they will see their souls move toward ancestry and be reborn in the bodies of a new generation. The Sol Gatherers are an ongoing cycle that never stops." Ó's voice trailed off.

Mikra leaned forward. "Where do they find the sunlight? Isn't it so dark up there? Is Jaggúa up there?" Mikra looked up, letting her eyes focus on the brightest star.

"The Sol Gatherers have a Guide right here," Ó said, pointing between her eyes, postponing Mikra's last question. Mikra quickly looked down. "It's like a map," Ó continued. "With it, they can feel their way through the darkness until they reach the closest star."

It was rare to hear her mother speak like this. Often she was instructed on how to do this or that, always with a long explanation, but never had the information related to things beyond their survival been relayed to Mikra.

"Like my Guide, mama?"

"Yes, like your Guide."

"But I can't see any stars."

"But you can find your way through the most impenetrable darkness, and it lights up just like yours does, except much brighter once they get close to the Sun."

The fire was dying down. Mikra got up and walked to the edge of the darkness and was immediately hit by the cold. She wrapped the colorful blanket her mother had made for her around her neck and reached for the ground. She collected a handful of wood and hurried back. The darkness did not scare her—it never did—she simply couldn't wait for her mother's story to continue. Once the fire blazed again, she sat next to Ó, gazing at the flames.

After a short silence Ó continued, "The Sol Gatherers also move very fast once they leave our world and enter the infinite darkness beyond. They move so fast that they barely look or feel like what we know them to be. "Jaggúa," she paused only for a second, "our beloved, told me once that it is as if the speed stretches them out until they are no longer a body but rather circulating energy that feeds off itself, propelling them forward. Jaggúa also said that if it weren't for the Guide during these journeys, they would be lost to themselves and to each other in the expansiveness of the universe. Because only this map—this reminder of Kempúa—can bridge them between home and that which they were put on this world to do."

Mikra tried to comprehend all of the information she was being told. She had never gathered information from so many unknowns, except for the war. But even that was now a familiar unknown: the fear and the loud explosions, the screams that sometimes would wake them, set them running. Even in the unknown, her fear had a place and her feet touched the ground with intention. The bullets and explosions were often a part of the background, and they only sometimes came to the forefront, engulfing them with their decibels. This new unfamiliar had her heart racing and her imagination jumping in an attempt to picture such creatures.

Their beloved was one of them, and Mikra smiled at the idea of sharing someone so intimately with her mother, even if she had never met her before. "But why haven't they returned yet? I've never seen light in the sky, mama." Ó didn't know how to respond to the question. Questions like this were the reason why she had kept silent for so long.

"I sit and gaze into those stars, hoping to catch the moment when one of them slowly becomes larger and larger until all three thousand Gatherers can be seen across our sky, like our own dangling constellation of Suns," Ó said in a low voice. She shifted her body, turning the fire with a stick; the night became brighter. "But I am growing weary of these skies and the explosions that replace hope with frustration. How many times have I thought that it was the Sol Gatherers returning, only to find the disappointing fade-to-black that only an explosion can provide? The fear that follows is maddening. Mikra, I know it is nothing you have ever seen before, but close your eyes and try to imagine."

Mikra closed her eyes. "Imagine three thousand sleeping Sol Gatherers scattered across our sky with large pieces of burning Sun on their chests. This is how they rest. While they sleep floating in the sky, they are reenergized after their long journey by the Suns' magnetic field."

• • •

"Ooooh! Ooooh! Can you believe that worked?" Jaiku exclaimed after a long time had passed.

He jumped from the tree limb, making a big thud when he landed. The Okanike tribe slowly became light, then quickly began to morph back into themselves. Tet raised his hands into the air triumphantly when he rose from the pile. The young Sol Gatherers stood slowly, their massive wings unfurling as pieces of dirt, leaves, and twigs fell from them. The joy of the tribe calmed them down, leaving everyone in the dark.

"I can't believe that worked!" Tet came running to Jaiku and tried to wrap his arms around his large frame before darkness took hold. "I mean, I guess I had to believe it was gonna work if it worked!" He let out a shriek and rolled on the ground in laughter.

"What a great idea, Jaiku!" another one said, slapping him loudly on the upper arm. "If we can do this every time, we just might be able to save them—and ourselves." The Sol Gatherers, though only fourteen years old, were already taller than Jaiku. They towered over the tribe. It had been no easy feat saving the last hundred Gatherers. Their size, the natural glow of their skin, and their constant need to feed made them all vulnerable. The Okanike tribe regularly had to make large fires to simulate the sun and quench their endless hunger. It was in this manner that they had lost a hundred in the last two years. Prior to that, it was the sheer numbers that made them vulnerable—too many to protect.

Jaiku was sent by Ó to keep from harm the last of the Sol Gatherers. He was also part Sol Gatherer, and though he didn't inherit their large wings or the Guide like his sister Mikra had, he could glide between tree limb, rock, dirt, and mountain like the air currents themselves. His body was low to the ground, unlike his mother's. He could match any Sol Gatherer in brute force. Aside from these two characteristics, his physical attributes took more from Ó than anyone else. In her womb, his skin mixed with her deep browns and Jaggúa's shades of yellow and red, giving him a warm color to match his heart. He moved the wind as he pleased, a master messenger by trade and talent. Before the war began, one would generally see him etching out the bamboo-like wood of the forest with small vertical carvings varying in depth. To this day, he etches the message he intends to deliver, and with a single pull of his bow his communication is precisely shot near the ear of the recipient. The gouged arrow, as it travels, fills with wind in such a manner that the wood whispers the message effortlessly. Once the message is delivered, the arrow falls to the ground as if hit by an invisible hand and disappears into the forest floor. After the war started, no one trusted any message to arrive safely nor messenger to arrive safely, for that matter. Jaiku, with his rare offering, became essential to Kempúa's survival. This gift was perfected through the guidance of his mother. Ó had spent her childhood obsessively training the birds who now live inside of her shell, and she became a revered master messenger. She taught Jaiku the art of delivery.

Two Years Ago

Thirteen hundred young Sol Gatherers had been kidnapped or killed by the time Jaiku found the remaining Gatherers huddled with the Okanike tribe—scared, smaller, and skinnier than they should have been. Tet was the first to greet him; their brotherhood formed immediately. Tet briefed Jaiku over a small fire and told him that members of his tribe had slowly begun to understand the humans. They sat between two large boulders where the tribe and young Sol Gatherers had been hiding for a few weeks now.

"Our tribe started making themselves invisible against the bodies of dead soldiers," Tet began that night. "They picked up the soldiers' guns and studied them until they could mimic the materials they were made from. Eventually, some got bold enough to stand next to the large machines that the humans used in battles. They studied every detail until they could become invisible against them." Tet's face turned into a big grin. "Once they mastered this, they entered the ships themselves, sneaked right past the soldiers, entered their head-quarters, their sleeping quarters, their bathrooms, and learned the true reason for their invasion and the targeting of the Sol Gatherers!" Tet's hands moved like a hummingbird as he spoke. He suddenly leapt to his feet, stepping toward the fire, then turning back to face Jaiku. He put both hands up in front of his chest as if he were stopping some-thing. "They are so asleep to their senses, these humans! We could never come so close to anyone in our world without being noticed, even if we were invisible!"

Jaiku was amazed at what he was hearing. "What did they find?" he asked.

"When members of my tribe first entered the main ship, they found one large room in the center of the vessel. It had drawings sprawled on long tables with a series of rings inside of rings inside of rings. The rings got tighter in three different locations, marking the three Sacred Peaks!"

"How do you know these were symbols for the Sacred Peaks?" Jai-ku interrupted.

"Zaza, who was the one to see it first, thought that maybe they were maps of Kempúa because one large half circle, unlike all the other concentric circles, sat between the first and second Peaks." Tet picked up a stick and drew what he was describing on the ground. "Just like the half-shaped circle of our largest body of water—right between Mandip and Manisha." Tet pointed to the mountaintops he had drawn.

Jaiku interrupted again. "Do you think they know of the temples on top of our mountains?" The light of the fire moved against his face. Tet memorized his features as he spoke.

"We don't think they have made it that far. They move slow." Tet mimicked them. "At the same time, we don't understand how they would know about our sacred mountains at all or the spring of our water. They also have large drawings on the walls of the Sol Gath-erers." Tet spun in a circle re-creating the walls. "The young ones,

—we don't think they know about the elders—but the young ones are illustrated in vivid color, from skin all the way down to bone." Jaiku shivered. "Illustrations of how they move, how they fly, their wingspan, their facial expressions, and how they've grown in the last five years fill the main cabin. She said you could barely see the walls!" Tet's eyes became wide.

"But why the Sol Gatherers?"

"Well," Tet said after taking a long sip of his warm drink, "This was the puzzling question for a long time, and a much longer answer I'm too tired now to begin, but I will tell you this: Zaza and her younger brother Triik have committed to finding out the answer." Tet pointed them out by nodding in their direction. "They've spent most of their time in the main vessels stationed on the western side of Kempúa for the past five years, walking among them, decoding their language." Tet took another sip of his drink, "Zaza and Triik just got back a few days ago." Jaiku looked over at Zaza who ate quietly, staring at the fire. Triik was already asleep beside her.

"I'll introduce you tomorrow. They never speak for the first four sleeping cycles after they return. They say it helps them to not forget what they have learned or confuse the human's language and energy with ours. I think it's very hard for them to be among the humans for such long periods. Once we've all rested, they will tell you what they've learned and share their theories on why this war started."

• • •

Jaiku was woken up by Zaza, who nudged him gently on the arm. He could hear the tossing of wood into the fire and was startled by the large dancing figures between the boulders. For a second, in this sleep state, he thought the humans had finally trapped them. It wasn't until he saw Zaza's smile that his heart began to slow.

"Hi. I'm Zaza," she said in a low voice.

"Zaza, I'm Jaiku." They put their foreheads together and greeted.

"I know, we were expecting you," she said as they pulled back.

"You knew I was on my way?" He sounded surprised.

"Yes, we had heard word from your mother. One day, when things seemed all a mess, about a hundred of her magical birds appeared.

The tribe heard them coming swiftly through the forest and were terrified at first that it might be the humans with some new weaponry.
But when they descended, the light of the winded creatures sprinkled
down onto us from the treetops!" She threw her arms into the air and
drew circles above her. "We looked up in awe, knowing they were
the sacred messengers we had been told about as young ones but had
never seen or had the privilege to hear from." Her voice was hurried.
"We immediately broke into laughter as we generally do after fear has
subsided. Our laughter scared the creatures, sending them flying up as
one, and landing back down as another." She let out a chuckle. Jaiku
smiled at her riddle. "They told us that you were on your way and to
wait for you here."

"Well, here I am! Fill me in, I've barely slept from the anticipation."

Zaza sat next to him. "It turns out that the humans have destroyed
their world. They have created something called 'pollution.'"

"What is it?"

"I'm not sure. All I know is that it has completely engulfed their
planet and is now in orbit with Earth."

"What's Earth?" he interrupted.

"It's what they call their world. This pollution is orbiting with
them and it's as thick as a blanket. I heard one of them shout once in
desperation. It's preventing their sun from reaching them and maintaining life there. They are close enough to a sun that they've never
needed Sol Gatherers until now."

"Until now?"

"Well, somehow this tribe, by the name of NASA, saw our Sol
Gatherers harvesting sunlight—they have moving images of them
coming in and out of Sun. I believe we share Sun with them! I'm
not sure how, but we do. Either way, they found them and figured
out how to find Kempúa. The humans are trying to use the young
Sol Gatherers. They think it's the only way to save their planet." Zaza
paused. "It's obsessive the way they do things. It's almost like the rep-
etition allows them to finally understand. It can be maddening being
in those rooms with them, but it's then that they talk the most about
us and we gain new information. In these meetings, they develop tac-
tics for how to kill us off, suppress us, and get what they need from
us more efficiently!" She was disgusted and spat on the ground by her

feet. "They are desperate! The man who I heard shouting began to leak water from his eyes because his daughter wouldn't live much longer if they didn't figure out how to use the Sol Gatherers! They barely understand them or us or themselves, for that matter! They're mad with desperation! Many of the Sol Gatherers they have kidnapped have either killed themselves in an attempt to escape or as a result of trying to obey their rules. Our young Gatherers don't know anything about finding and gathering sunlight. They haven't been initiated!" Her voice quieted. "Unfortunately, not even enough to save their own lives." She shifted to face him. He could see she was agitated now. Bringing her knees to her chest, she began to tap her right knee with her fingers. It felt like she was somewhere else.

"They have invaded our world and killed so many of us in an at tempt to kidnap our Sol Gatherers and save themselves." Zaza looked down. It had been five years since the invasion. Her tribe, the Okan-ike, had managed to save a mere two hundred young Sol Gatherers from the fifteen hundred that had been left behind by the elders. She was ashamed. Jaiku put one hand on her knee and with the other lifted her chin up.

"You have done the best you can. You all have, and I hope to do as much as you have already done while I am with you."

"Jaiku, it's not easy. If the elders don't return, I don't know how our world will survive. So much has already died without our Suns and, to be truly honest, I don't think we can destroy the humans without them. We should have fought back in the beginning when we still had fifteen hundred young Gatherers with us. Instead we ran. What has running done?" She said in a harsh whisper. She stood up suddenly— her back to the fire—and looked at the eternal darkness around her. "I'll tell you what it has done! It has kept us in fear and diminished our numbers. Even though they are young, the Gatherers are strong. We should have made a wall of fire. But instead we ran, and now that's all we do."

Present

"Maybe it was the darkness that scared them," Ó said looking down at Mikra. What kind of answer could she give her daughter for why this war had begun?

"It seemed at first like the humans just threw fire into everything to catch a glimpse." Ó looked away from the fire and paused. "The first three years were the most confusing and terrifying—there was always smoke and loud noises that shook the ground. Tribes of all kinds were scattered by the fourth year, and most now travel in small numbers to avoid the killing raids." It pained her to know that her daughter so young knew what a killing raid was, for that was exactly what happened the last time they tried to live in a community and barely escaped alive. She hoped that Mikra didn't remember the details of that night. "By the fifth year, it became clear that the humans were after the young Sol Gatherers, since their numbers had diminished to less than two hundred. All who witnessed and escaped testified that everything and everyone was destroyed or killed, yet the young Sol Gatherers were left physically unharmed—at least amid the chaos. They were shot with a liquid that forced them to follow the human's voice and willingly get into large vessels, never to be seen again.

Mikra looked around but couldn't see beyond the small fire. "Did the elder Sol Gatherers also get kidnapped by the humans, Mama?" Mikra's mother could see the fear alive in her daughter now.

"Mikra," she said soothingly, "Come here." Mikra got up from the ground and placed her head on her mother's heart. She could hear the cooing of the birds inside the shell through the hollow of Ó's chest. She sunk deeper into her embrace.

• • •

Many sleeping cycles had passed with no incident, when Mikra began to toss and turn in her sleep, and for seven days she didn't wake. Her arms became stiff trunks. Her palms became wide-open branches. Her teeth clenched. Her forehead collected small droplets of sweat that glistened against her Guide, illuminating the makeshift home she and her mother had built. Her high temperature eventually heated their dwelling, so much so that after a while the snow and ice that had collected around the structure began to melt. After a couple of days, it became clear that Mikra had entered a vision far greater than her years. Ó took to collecting the herbs her tribe used in times of initiation and vision-seeking, doing her best to keep her daughter alive. When Mikra finally awoke, all she could feel was Ó's heavy arm, limp across her chest.

"Mama?" Her whisper entered Ó's dream with urgency. Ó shifted her body and pressed her arm around Mikra. The birds in her shell cooed and shifted with her.

"Mama?"

"Yes, I'm here," she responded into the night. Mikra's Guide had faded completely, along with her fever. The small fire had burned out hours ago, and their makeshift home was now as cold as the outside world. "It is good to have you back, Mikra. You frightened me. It has been seven days that you haven't responded at all. You merely tossed and turned or lay so still—barely breathing. I thought I might lose you to the world of visions."

"I'm sorry, mama."

"What did you see?" Ó said, gently touching Mikra's forehead.

"I'm thirsty, mama." Ó rose to her feet, stirring all the birds within her shell. She went outside and gathered snow in a cup. When she came back inside, she pulled over her head the small pouch she always carried around her neck. Mikra loved that pouch and dreamed of the day she would inherit it. Mikra's hands reached out to touch it without thinking. Ó poured a handful of stardust particles between her palms, rubbing vigorously and setting off the first spark. Mikra could see a tiny light between her mother's hands slowly getting brighter. She took the small flame and with it lit a pile of sticks and dried grass. Mikra immediately felt the heat—the shivering of her body subsided as the snow melted in the cup.

"Here you go, Mikra." Mikra took a long sip and then rested her head back down. "Mikra, what did you see?" Her mother was anxious, curious. She had never known anyone entering—or for that matter surviving—a vision at such a young age. She herself had been a woman when she had first experienced clairvoyance of such magnitude, and that had been in the company of all her elders after a long ceremony held to induce the visions.

"I first saw the three Sacred Peaks from afar in a cloud of fire. I heard screams in every direction, as if all of Kempúa was crying out at once. Everything became so loud that I thought it might drive me insane. Then silence, a deep unshakable silence that stopped the wind itself. I looked up toward the burning sky and from the smoke appeared Jaiku. He was fa-a-a-a-a-r away from me, flying on a half-opened seed.

"Did the seed look like this?" Ó drew the shape of a canoe with a tall sail protruding from the middle of it.

"Yes, mama! Just like that! This part was a beautiful color, blue but—" She tried to think what to compare it to. She had only known color by the light of fire, so all color had a warmth to it that her dreams sometimes did not possess.

"Was the blue softer?"

"It was a strong blue. Cooler, I guess. And this part was white but much brighter," she said pointing to the sail.

"Was there anything else?"

"When Jaiku appeared, the ground began to shake, a silent shaking that stirred the spirits within. I saw thousands of them lift upward and all at once come for me."

"Sleep now, Mikra, you will need your strength. We have a long journey ahead of us."

That very night Ó prepared her birds for flight. She opened the turtle-like shell that rested on her back and hundreds of birds flew out, leaving behind a trail of glittering light that cut through the darkness. She opened her arms and threw white powder up into the heavens as they flew in circles above her. She spoke with thunder in her voice.

"Tell Jaiku to come."

HOLLOW

MIA MINGUS

WEST WAS ALMOST DONE WITH HER SHIFT WHEN SHE HEARD THE loud sound of the long buzzer. Walking out into the hall with her cane, she could see the flashing orange lights, signaling a new Arrival was in the hatch. It had been almost fifty years since West first started working at the hatch and still, each time the buzzer rang, she could feel her heart beat a little faster. Her steps quickened, and she hurriedly entered the receiving room. Counting down the seconds, she leaned her cane against the shelf behind her and stood waiting for the small light next to the opening handle to turn from red to green.

After a few minutes, the light changed colors, and West firmly grabbed the handle on the large door and turned it with one quick motion, releasing it and sliding it upward. Inside she could see the large oval vessel just beyond the door. Slowly she unlatched the bottom of the hatch and pulled, sliding it out, so that the vessel sat directly waist-high in front of her. Locking it in place, she retrieved a key from the wall and inserted it into the hole at the top of the vessel. Then she returned the key to its place as circular lights lit up around the keyhole, and a moment later the top half of the vessel slid open, revealing its contents.

West reached in and pulled out a thick bundle of white blankets showing only the tiny face of the sleeping baby inside. West smiled down at the infant, gently pulling back the blankets and softly touching the infant's cheeks. West breathed a deep sigh of relief. This one had made the long journey from Earth. It was still alive and breathing peacefully. She hugged the baby close to her, rocking it slightly from side to side.

A new Arrival.

The door opened behind her and West turned to see Seva greet her with a smile.

"A new one?" Seva asked.

"Just came in." West opened her arms so Seva could see the baby. Seva peered in quietly at the sleeping face and sighed.

"Here," West offered. "You take the little one. I'll clean up in here. I was about to leave anyway." She handed Seva the baby and opened the door for her. As she turned to begin cleaning up, she could hear Seva softly singing to the infant as she made her way down the hall, her small voice echoing as the door closed. West smiled to herself. Seva had such a sweet spot in her heart for the Arrivals.

West began to gather the extra blankets that had fallen to the floor. Leaning on her cane, she pulled them up before she noticed the envelope sticking out from between the cloth. She froze as her breath caught in her chest. Putting the blankets down, she picked up the envelope, a cautious look on her face. They had never, in all their time here, received a communication in any of the vessels.

She sharply examined the envelope, flipping it over in her hands. It was from Earth, addressed to the General. After glancing back at the closed door, West quickly opened the envelope, pulled out a letter, and read it, then reread it.

"No, it can't be," she whispered. Her mind raced as she tucked the letter in her pocket and quickly finished cleaning up.

• • •

Ona ran her hands under the warm water of the faucet, trying to wash the dirt off. Her arms and hands were sore from working in the garden all day, and she knew it would only get worse later that night. Al Dwhin was still bringing in the day's harvest, buckets of vegetables to be used for the week. Prolt wasn't far behind him, pulling a small wagon of tools and supplies behind his chair. Al Dwhin grunted as he bent down to unhook the wagon with his big hand.

"You need something for the pain?" Ona asked, wiping her hands on a nearby towel.

"Nah, I'm okay. I just need to soak later tonight. I tell you, my muscles aren't what they used to be." Al Dwhin stretched his tall body and rubbed his lower back with his big hand, scratching his forehead with his little arm.

Ona wet a washcloth with warm water and brought it over to Prolt, helping him wipe off the dirt from his hands and arms. Ona searched for places where dirt had mixed with his drool and hardened to form a crust. When he was done, she looked down at him. "Knee and hip?" she asked.

He nodded and smiled, "Knee and hip."

Ona bent down and adjusted his knee, picking it up and pushing to the left. "Better? She asked. "Better. Much better," he answered, relieved.

"You know you should have told me when we were in the garden and I could have done it there," she reminded him for the millionth time.

"Yeah, but I didn't want to make you get up from your new method. Plus, you'd get my knee all dirty with your muddy hands." Prolt looked at her sharply with a half smile and laughed, catching some of his drool with his wrist. Ona smiled at him, shaking her head, knowing he had probably been in pain for the last hour although he had not said anything.

"Ha ha," she said, lightly elbowing his shoulder. He laughed.

"So did it work out better today?" Al Dwhin called over from the sink where he was finishing up. "Less pain?"

"A little," Ona answered. "My legs don't hurt anymore, but it's too hard holding myself up with my arms all day. Maybe I could ask Wild if she could build me a kind of little bench or something? Something similar to the one she made for Rex?"

"Mm-hmm, let's ask her tonight at dinner. I think she could get you one by tomorrow afternoon." Al Dwhin raised his eyebrows knowingly at Ona and Prolt. "*If* she's in a good mood."

Ona laughed quietly and shook her head. "At that rate, I'll be waiting forever."

Prolt expertly backed his chair up to the large metal wagon filled with the food and some flowers. Al Dwhin secured the full baskets and crates so they wouldn't topple over on their ride back while Ona connected the wagon to the hitch on the back of Prolt's chair. Once finished, she carefully maneuvered herself onto the small empty space that had been left for her on the wagon. She reached over and held the bucket of flowers on her lap as Prolt began to pull out of the shed, with Al Dwhin walking ahead to open the large doors of the biosphere.

• • •

Rex sat still, staring down at the letter after having read it. West watched her, patiently waiting. Rex felt like the earth beneath her feet had fallen out from under her.

"Have you shown this to anyone else?" Rex's rough hands carefully folded the piece of paper back along its creases, laying it on the table between them.

"No, I came straight here. Seva was with me, but she didn't see it. She's still back at the receiving center. Do you think it's real? Do you think they're coming?"

"It's real. It was with an Arrival. It can't be anything else." Rex ran her hands over her hair and thought for a moment. "It says they sent word through the system. I wonder how long ago that was."

"There's no way to tell. Holdan broke the system soon after the last one of them died. There's no fixing it or getting it back. He made sure of it."

"Damn, Holdan," Rex sighed. "Can we get one of the Arrivals to work on it and try to fix it? Maybe they could also find out if there have been other messages sent."

West paused. "I can ask, but what would we tell them it is? Won't they ask? We can't tell them the truth."

"I don't know. We can tell them whatever we have to. We just need it done. It's our only way to find out more about this letter. If there are messages there, we need to know what they say."

West nodded her head and paused. "But why would they come here? And why now, after all this time? What could they want?"

Rex lowered her eyes, shook her head, and spoke slowly, almost as if she were talking to herself. "I don't know. I just don't know. Once the Arrivals started to come, I just assumed that was the end of it. But maybe it was just the beginning."

West was quiet. When she spoke next, her words were almost a whisper. "They think we're dead—or worse. This message was clearly meant for the General. They have no idea we're alive and the rest of them are gone. When they find out what has happened," she leaned forward, "They will kill us."

"We can't think about that now. We don't know why they are coming, but we have to be prepared, and our only hope is to try and retrieve the messages they sent from the system. There's got to be a way."

West raised her head, pulling herself out of the whirlpool of thoughts racing through her mind. Exhaling deeply, she said, "Okay. I can ask tomorrow."

"Good. And for now, we don't say a word to anyone." Rex looked at West.

West held Rex's gaze and nodded. Steadying herself on her cane, West rose from her chair and began to limp away. At the door, she stopped and turned her head toward Rex.

"When we do decide to tell the rest of them, you have to be the one to tell Wild." West paused for a moment, before leaving.

Letting out a long breath in the dim light, Rex sighed, now alone. "I know."

• • •

"In the beginning, it was supposed to be a punishment," Rex began slowly. "It was the best solution the Perfects could come up with: send the cripples away. They couldn't bear to look at us, but they couldn't bring themselves to continue killing us. UnPerfects, they used to call us—U.P.s." She trailed off, staring into the fire, not moving, breathing slowly. "I don't know. Must've been something in their souls. Call it guilt, call it instinct, call it morals, but they couldn't do it. Believe me, they tried. They killed most of us, but something didn't sit well with them about it. I think it was the children that finally did them in. They couldn't keep killing their own, but they couldn't keep or raise them either. So they came up with this," she motioned with her arm. "They sent us here to die."

"Wasn't no children, it was Jay Lu," Wild interjected gruffly from her chair. "If it wasn't for him, we'd all be dead, like we should. Was his daddy that put a stop to it. Those men would've kept on shooting and injecting us and dragging us out to the Fields for the birds to finish us off if his darlin' little baby boy hadn't been born. I was waiting for my turn and that damned baby had to come spilling out of his mother like a goddamned alarm."

"Wild." Al Dwhin's voice was disapproving as he furrowed his brow.

"What?" Wild challenged, looking squarely at Al Dwhin. "I was ready. We was *all* ready. We was all prepared and ready, goddamn it. If it hadn't been for him, it all would have ended then and there like it should have, and we never would have ended up here in this mess about to lose everything again, everything we've worked so hard for. We all know it was Jay Lu and his high-powered daddy."

Wild paused, shaking her head and frowning. "Jean shouldn't have been there." She trailed off, slowly curling in on herself. The room fell silent.

Ona turned back to Rex.

Rex kept her eyes on the fire. She hadn't heard Wild talk about Jean in a very long time. No one had. It was like being pulled back into another time. Suddenly, clear as day, Rex could see Jean throwing her arms around Wild, the two of them smiling and laughing, gazing at each other. She could see Jean passionately hunched over the dining room table late into the night, mapping strategies and plans with markers and pens. She could hear Jean yelling, refusing to leave the rest of the U.P.s, defiantly resisting the surrounding soldiers, and Wild looking up at her, pleading with her to go. The air had been thick with smoke and screams, as thousands of soldiers carted U.P.s away by the truckload to the camps to be burned, tortured, killed. No one knew at that time, but they were certain they weren't coming back.

Jean was one of the hundred or so Perfects who didn't run. There had been thousands of Perfects there that night who had fled once the trucks showed up, but not Jean. She stayed and was taken to the camps alongside Wild and the rest of them. Beaten and raped like everyone else, she endured the camps for the three weeks they were all there. She was shot and taken out to the Fields minutes before the order came down to halt the killings.

Wild was set to die that day as well, but it never happened. She screamed for them to kill her too, all day and into the nights that wore on as they all sat in agonizing anticipation of what was going to come next. Right up until they loaded her onto the rocket bound for Hollow, Wild tried to die.

The orders had been swift and firm, from the head of the New Regime himself: everyone in the camps was to be shipped off to Hollow. Two hundred soldiers would accompany them. For what, no one knew.

Rex had only ever heard of Hollow as an experiment, as a new planet they were hoping to make inhabitable. There had been talk at one point that the regime would send all the criminals there to be quarantined and die, but everyone knew the regime needed the free labor in the prisons too much to send their criminals away.

In those days, none of the U.P.s knew what was to come. Would they be unloaded and killed there? Would they be tortured? Experimented on? Or simply left to starve and die in their own filth?

The six of them in that room had organized together for years, heading up much of the leadership of the U.P.s before they were taken to the camps. And their bonds remained strong, as many of the other U.P.s on Hollow looked to them for answers and guidance. They had all met working to free U.P.s from violent institutions to join the mass movements that were happening, laid down strategy and plans for their communities, and provided shelter and support to more U.P.s than they could name, who were being abandoned and hunted by the Perfects. They had lost many on their team, hard blows to their spirits, but they knew they had to keep moving on. They owed it to their departed teammates and to each other to keep moving toward the world they believed was possible.

The sound of Ona's voice stopped Rex's thoughts. "Who is Jay Lu?" she asked.

West interrupted loudly. "Well, we should head to bed. It's getting late and we have a long day tomorrow. Come on," she urged, nudging Ona's shoulder from above. Ona sighed and got up slowly, leveraging her weight from side to side until she was steadily on her feet.

"You too," West ordered the other Arrivals who had been quietly listening.

The Arrivals offered good-nights to the room and left. West followed them to the door and closed it behind them, turning quickly on her cane.

"What are you all doing?" she demanded. "Telling them everything? Telling them now will only make it harder when we have to leave."

"What are you talking about? They asked, and they deserve to know. They *need* to know," Prolt responded.

"It's true," Al Dwhin began. "After all, they came to us. They're old enough to hear about it all. It's where they came from. Plus, we don't know what's going to happen. We may not be here that much longer."

West was firm. "The letter said we had six months. That's plenty of time to—"

"We don't know if that's true," Rex interrupted. "The Perfects can change their minds anytime and do what they please, as we've all seen. They could send more tomorrow, and we wouldn't be able to stop them. Shit, we don't even know where we are. We don't have any more time. We have to move fast, and that includes getting the Arrivals ready. We need them. We're not as young as we used to be, and we can't do this on our own."

West softened and looked with defeat from Rex to Al Dwhin to Prolt. "But they are so young. I just—I ... I just don't want them to get hurt," she said as she sank into a nearby chair, letting her cane drop to the floor.

"They don't know what it was like. And how do we tell them? Even if we do, there's no way to get them to understand. How do you teach a history of hate in the name of love? How can we warn them of what kind of monsters they might have to face? How do we tell them what the camps were like? Do we tell them of it all? Jean screaming in the next cell over, Ashlin begging for his life, still alive after the injection to see the birds eating his flesh? The way they just disposed of us and piled us dead in the Fields. Like we were some kind of garbage, like human waste. Sometimes I can still hear the sound of those damn crows, and it haunts me." West hung her head, her face buried in shadow.

The room was heavy with silence, everyone drenched in memories of another world.

Al Dwhin was the first to move slowly across the circle, coming to kneel next to West, dropping his tall body to the floor. "I know," he said in a soft, knowing voice, filled with all the weight of their past. He gently moved his little arm under hers and she caressed it as she collapsed against him.

"We have to tell them," Prolt said, wheeling closer, lowering his voice. "We have to tell them all of it, even if it is hard. It's the only way for us to be able to save Southing if that letter is true."

"But where will we go? We haven't come up with anything yet. And the thought of starting all over again—" West trailed off.

Wild spoke up in her deep scratchy voice. "We will go towards the edge of the red sky to look for Holdan, Nuroh, Elda, and the rest of the U.P.s. It's our only hope. If we can find them, we might be able to come back and fight."

"Leave? You can't be serious." Prolt looked at Wild incredulously. "Southing is our home. We built it into what it is. We transformed it and poured our hearts into this city. We can't just abandon it. We have to stay and fight for it. And what about the rest of the U.P.s? We tell them they have to leave too?" Prolt snorted, shaking his head as he continued. "And besides, Holdan left years ago. I thought we were done with him. Even if he's alive, he doesn't deserve to be found. And if Nuroh and Elda's team had found him or any of the U.P.s that went with him, they would have come back and let us know. We don't even know what is beyond the red sky. There may not even be vegetation. How will we survive without the biospheres? You're going to lead a whole city of cripples across an unknown planet? There's no way. I'm not going to just give up my home to those bastards."

Wild had moved closer to the circle, and she held steady. "We can send a team out to go and look. We don't all have to leave. Some of us can stay here and guard Southing. The Arrivals are stronger and younger, far more mobile than most of us. They can scout the land and come back. We've dealt with the soldiers before, we can do it again."

"Separate?" West shook her head. "That is certain death. We can't separate. The only way we will make it is to stay together. The Arrivals are too young to go out alone with no water and food."

"Of course we will give them food and water to travel with. We will prepare them," Wild sternly pushed back.

"Nuroh, Elda, and the rest of them left five years ago. What's to say that the Arrivals will be able to come back in the next handful of months?" Prolt countered.

"And *we*? What do you mean, *we*? *We* haven't decided on anything yet." West turned to Rex, demanding answers.

"No one's decided anything yet," Rex said, raising her hands, looking directly at Wild, who was sitting up defiantly in her chair now. "But I haven't heard another suggestion of what we should do."

Everyone knew she was right. No one knew what to do, and even though Wild's idea was extreme, it was the only viable option they had heard. They all remembered the massacres and the camps. They all remembered Hollow before Southing. No one wanted to relive that, and it felt like an imminent future that none of them wanted to admit, let alone face. Rex was right: no one knew how long they had, and if the soldiers came before they were ready it would be too late.

Southing had become a home for so many of them, after such horror, that no one had thought it would end. After the initial batch of soldiers had been killed off, it felt like they were finally free from the Perfects. Finally able to live again. The work of transforming the stations they had been brought to into places they could inhabit with pride and ease felt like a way to heal from all they had suffered through. They built new adaptations for their chairs, lifts, canes, crutches, braces, and their UnPerfect bodies, without thought to what was allowed or having to rely on the Perfects to do so. They experimented with their wildest dreams and ideas, making pulleys and slides and inventing new tools. No one could imagine leaving.

• • •

Seva sat quietly on the couch, sadness running through her like a slow, steady river. Her heart hurt. She loved Southing, and the thought of leaving was enough to make her consider searching for Holdan. She had never had a home like this, never lived somewhere with people who loved her. She could still remember her childhood spent at institutions after her parents had committed her and never returned. Being shuffled back and forth with no say, the beatings, the punishments, the meds, and the terrorizing silence. She had wanted something so much better for their kind—they all had—and now it seemed so hopeless.

She was the youngest of three, born to Perfects, the only U.P. in her family. Her parents had tried to raise her for three years before finally giving up. After what seemed a lifetime of hoping they would visit, days spent sitting at the east-facing windows looking for any sign of them, she had reluctantly given up. They weren't coming back for her, and she would never see them again.

She didn't know where they were now and didn't care. Sometimes she thought about her sisters and wondered what her parents must have told them when they came home from school to find her gone. And the next days and weeks and years—what did they say?

The night she first met Al Dwhin and Rex, they had helped her escape from the institution. That night they had asked her if she had a family she wanted them to take her to, and without hesitation she said no. She told them to take her wherever they were going and that she wanted to help free other U.P.s too. She joined their revolutionary work and never looked back.

Working at the receiving center fed a part of her soul that had died at that east-facing window. Welcoming new U.P.s to Southing was a kind of tenderness she had never known. She felt for the Arrivals, traveling all that way from Earth as tiny babies, so far from where they came from, so full of questions. She knew what it was like to live with that kind of longing always at the back of your heart. But she also knew Southing was a far better experience than they would ever have had if they had been kept on Earth. She knew the other side, and it was impossible to tell them.

. . .

> Dear U.P.s,
> If you are reading this, you have survived too and we are waiting for you. Somehow, you have survived the soldiers' return to Southing. We never wanted to leave, but it was the only way. We couldn't stay; we had to leave to try and find a way to return. Southing was our home and one day it will be again.

There is no time left. The soldiers are coming and I fear we will not make it through this final battle. Tomorrow we leave for the other side of Hollow, towards the edge of the red sky in the hopes of finding other U.P.s, in hopes of surviving. It is our last attempt to save Southing and the world we have built here, the world the Perfects want to destroy.

My name is Ona and I am writing this to you from inside Southing. I am an Arrival and have lived in Southing all my life, from the moment I landed on Hollow as a baby sent from Earth, until tomorrow morning when I will leave for the first time.

I have been raised by the Earlies, who have taken me in, raised me and taught me everything I know. They are the architects of Southing and what it has come to be. They were all part of the last great revolution on Earth and were brought to Hollow as a punishment, as a last resort.

They have told me of their time on Earth and the glory days of the revolution when they thought they had won and the people finally seized the government, Perfects and UnPerfects working side by side for liberation. Wild tells of her chair rolling next to Jean's long strides, escaping the soldiers, taking each turn and alley in unison, moving with the wind and rain, instead of against it. And the quick backlash, when the revolution was broken and fell. When the New Regime took hold after just a week and forced the U.P.s into the camps, it killed them one by one before finally sending those still alive here.

They will never tell you this history, but I want you to know how the Earlies came to Hollow and built Southing into a land we could finally call our own. Free from the Perfects and Earth. I want you to know the magnificence of Rex as she swings and glides, twisting and turning on her crutches with such grace and strength. I want you to feel the tenderness of Seva's heart, the determination of West and the warmth of Al Dwhin's smile.

Our history is all we have and the Perfects will work to erase it. Southing was never meant to be, and it must live on, it must never be forgotten. We will return here one day.

If the Perfects come and all is lost, remember these names: Rex, Wild, Seva, Jay Lu, Prolt, Al Dwhin, Nuroh, and West.

Follow the edge of the red sky and look for us. We will keep our eyes to the horizon for you.

We will find each other and build Southing anew,
Ona

ላሊበላ ፥ አለም ከ
7ብርኤል ቴዎድሮ

GABRIEL TEODROS

ላሊበላ: la·li·be·la
(noun)
1. Town in northern Ethiopia famous for its eleven monolithic rock-cut buildings (how they were built is unknown).
2. *(Amharic)* Given name meaning "even the bees recognize its sovereignty."

Addis Ababa, Ethiopia, Present Day
THE KEY WAS HIDDEN IN PLAIN SIGHT. IN TWISTED METAL AND SHAPES within shapes. In fractals and complex geometric patterns people just accepted as religious symbolism. They called it a cross, but it was no crucifix. The truth was buried generations deep and kept there by nothing but a common belief. Most people wore a variation of it around their neck. Some had it sewn into fabric. Like the history of all humanity, it was buried in Ethiopia under nothing but a thin layer of dust.

His appearance started as a tiny piece of metal that appeared in the rubble on the side of a road. Insignificant, barely noticeable. The metal multiplied itself and then multiplied itself again, growing in the same pattern of what people would then recognize as a Meskel. Soon it stood upright, and it grew taller and taller as a light bled through every opening in the pattern. When it was tall enough for him to pass through, an old man appeared from the light, holding the cross. When he was fully present, the light was gone. He seemed out of time, wearing all white the way a monk would.

Cars sped by, people walked past, and donkeys carrying wood moved about, seemingly oblivious to a human that had just appeared out of thin air.

"You can't expect us to wait forever!" a young man yelled at the elder in the overcrowded Addis Ababa traffic. "Move on, or get out of my way!"

Gebre Mesqel Lalibela had had quite the journey and was understandably shaken up. In his time, Ethiopian technology allowed his people to build computers, teleportation devices, starships, and even a spaceport in the highlands of Roha. There people lived in buildings on top of buildings that were all carved from a single rock. There were many people he loved whom he'd had to say goodbye to as they went on trips to distant galaxies, knowing he might never see them again. Yet nothing he had seen then compared to the chaos surrounding him now. In this new Capital of the country he had ruled over eight hundred years earlier, what he saw made him wish that time machines had never been invented.

The air now smelled like black pepper and the sky was covered by smoke that didn't move, making it hard for him to breathe. The streets were crowded with vehicles that coughed up this poison, and with people and animals, and he couldn't see how they all fit together. There were huge palaces, and there were people crawling and even sleeping on the busy street.

He leaned on the cross like it was the only thing holding him up, and he thought, "How have we become so close and so distant at the exact same time?"

መስቀል: mes·kel
(noun)
1. (Ge'ez) Processional cross used in church services, as prayer sticks,

for exorcisms, and in time travel, of four basic styles with hundreds of variations.

Roha Highlands, 1141 EC (AD 1148)

Lalibela's mother had often spoken of a swarm of bees that had surrounded him just after she gave birth. Her heart had stopped for a moment, thinking her baby would be stung to death, but the swarm, although blanketing her child, had mysteriously left him untouched. This was a signal to her that Lalibela was not hers alone. He would do great things. He would even lead the country. The bees had recognized his sovereignty.

The burden of being leader was placed upon him before he even knew how to walk. Lalibela grew up between the pressure of his parents and the jealousy of extended family members and his older siblings, which was like another swarm of bees surrounding him. He often wanted to run away, and when he was old enough he did, as much as he could. Roha at the time overlooked a forest. It was like beachfront property over an ocean of treetops. Lalibela loved to submerge himself in the trees, observing and learning from nature all around him. As a child he was captivated by the complexity of what seemed at the surface to be simple things. Patterns in spider webs. Roots of trees that grew above the Earth. Neither his imagination nor his body could be contained. Not by anyone's tradition, expectations, or beliefs.

He was the youngest child and his mother's favorite son, whether she would admit it or not. His imagination was a threat to the establishment, and, aside from his mother, the royal family despised him for it. He wasn't motivated by power, even when it was what his mother wanted him to have. Out of jealousy, when Lalibela's older brother Kedus Harbe inherited the throne, one of his first acts as king was to secretly have Lalibela poisoned.

It was an herbal potion that came with a plate of shiro, and instead of killing Lalibela it put him to sleep for three days. The visions and dreams he had during that time would come to define his life even more than the bees had.

Close to death, Lalibela was transported through space and time. His spirit traveled light years to other worlds, where he saw technology that hadn't been invented yet and Ethiopians who were taking care of multiple planets. He saw faces of people he had never met, from parts of Ethiopia he had never seen, and everywhere he went he was with an eclectic group of farmers, scientists, and artists. They seemed to him to be family he had never met, and with them he felt like he could fly. From the stars, he traveled back to the Roha highlands overlooking that ocean of treetops, but things were different now, and there was a magnetic focus on the volcanic rock underneath his birthplace. He saw the spaceport that would be built there, carved into the mountain, with waterways connecting every building. It was a new foundation, and as such it would be called Addis Yerusalem.

When Lalibela finally awoke, he was in a room with only his mother by his side.

"Gebiye, you keep talking in your sleep. What is it you see?"

"Emaye. I've seen what I must do. It's like three heavens just opened up and became one. In the stars, on the earth, and within ourselves."

"My son has died and come back to life!" his mother wept.

He never bothered explaining more of his dreams to her or even blaming his brother for this near-death journey. He didn't want to get in another fight, and he still didn't want to be the leader his mother wanted him to be, the leader his brother feared. He just needed to build what he saw and find the people he had seen in those visions. It was as if he had never known why he was alive until he almost died.

መንኮራኩር : män·ko·ra·kur
(noun)
1. *(Geʽez)* Spaceship.

ARBA MINCH, 1159 EC (AD 1166)

Lalibela learned the true beauty of his culture by spending time on a farm in the south. He was undercover, starting to grow a beard, and no one recognized him as a member of the royal family. The kindness of strangers in this part of the country both broke and strengthened his heart on a daily basis. He was invited to eat in the homes of people who barely had anything, who offered him everything they had and took it as an insult if he refused. He realized that being raised as royalty had isolated him from the experience of having true friends.

The farmers he stayed with were beekeepers as well, which he took as a sign that he must be on the right path. From the farmers he learned how to work the land, and from the bees he learned how to use the stars and the curve of the earth as a guide. Every day felt like seven, and he had never felt so alive. His best friend during this time was the farmer's daughter Kibra. She made trips selling food at the market on a regular basis, and she had become an expert mathematician. In her spare time she experimented with inventing new tools.

"Why are you always following me to the market?" Kibra asked with a half-smile one day. "Don't you have something better to do?"

"Anything I could be doing would be better with you," Lalibela responded without hesitation, "But if you want me to go, I'll go."

"No, I want you to stay."

Kibra was the first person with whom Lalibela shared all his visions and dreams, and in time the visions blossomed and became their dream together. He was the first person who ever challenged her. She was the first person to fully see him. She was much smarter, but he had more ambition. Somehow they made a perfect team. And they were completely in love.

The young couple spent most of the next decade with their hands in the dirt, honey in their tea, experimenting and traveling throughout the Ethiopian countryside. Compared to his upbringing in Roha, everything was so new. He looked at the world as if he was seeing it for the first time, and this helped Kibra see things differently too. Together they unlocked potential in one another. They worked hard and played harder, until the work felt like play.

Everything in the villages was shared, from food and other resources to labor. If just one person yielded a good crop, no one went hungry. The idea of just having a single occupation was foreign. A farmer with a science lab in a *gojo* who also happened to be an expert *krar* player was a very common thing. Everyone sang and played music. The simple but rare combination of people following their passions, innovating and learning from the arts, science, and nature, fed into an isolated Ethiopian renaissance, completely self-contained. While Crusaders were violently expanding from Europe and Saladin was defending Egypt and pushing back, Ethiopia turned inward and grew in a way that took them all the way to the stars.

Every technological leap during this period started in a small village or on a farm. Kibra worked with a group of craftspeople, masons, and beekeepers to develop the first computer. She taught them a system of complex multiplication that she was able to do in her head, which became the foundation of the coding system their computers were based on. She worked with Lalibela to assemble materials based on beehives. Soon what they created was able to function as a calculator, predict weather, and replicate itself.

Kibra and Lalibela's relationship was like a quiet nucleus in the center of this renaissance. It wasn't Lalibela or Kibra alone that made anything happen. It was the connection they shared that transformed each of them as well as everyone they interacted with. They believed in each other's dreams enough to make what seemed at first impossible completely real.

Roha Highlands, 1174 EC (AD 1181)

Fifteen years later, when Lalibela finally returned from the countryside to Roha, it was not to claim the throne. It was only to propose the idea of building a spaceport. As sure as bees are vital to life on Earth as pollinators, Lalibela thought outside of the planet and dreamed of pollinating the stars. He arrived with Kibra and a whole community of friends who had become family.

Lalibela's mother shed tears of joy when her son returned, and all of Roha had a celebration. It was her joy that kept him safe. His brother Kedus feared that Lalibela had come to take his place as king, and that night he ordered one of his guards to cut Lalibela's throat while he slept. What Kedus didn't know was that this guard had grown especially fond of Lalibela's mother and was happy to see her ecstatic and full of joy. He couldn't stand to be the one to take away her joy, so that night the guard cut Kedus Harbe's throat instead.

A day of celebration was followed by a time of mourning, and no one ever knew why or by whom Kedus Harbe was murdered in the middle of the night. The only one who truly mourned was his mother, as he was as ruthless to the masses as he was to his own brother.

Lalibela was then offered the throne, but he didn't want it. His mother tried to pressure him, but it had no effect. A conversation with Kibra was the only thing that could change his mind.

"If you take the throne, you won't have to do things the way they've been done before," Kibra reasoned, "Ethiopia needs a new kind of leadership. The kind that isn't power-hungry."

"I agree that Ethiopia needs a new kind of leadership, but how do we center the needs of the farmers here in the capitol?" Lalibela questioned. "Before I ran away and met you, I never even saw what really made this country what it is."

"That perspective you have now is why this moment is important. And the fact that you don't want to dominate is another reason I fell in love with you. You won't be alone here anymore," she reassured him.

"So you'll still marry me?" Lalibela asked.

"How is this even a question in your mind?" Kibra smirked.

With new leadership and an influx of newcomers from the countryside, the energy in Roha grew electric. The people believed Lalibela traveled with angels since the people he came with were able to do things they had seen no human do. Even now, eight hundred years later, people still say the spaceport in Roha was built at night by angels. They will say it was built by angels before they will say it was anything but a church. The spaceport was built by regular people inspired to create something for more than themselves, and that creative spirit has always had a way of keeping people up at night. They built machines that cut through rock like butter, and eleven structures formed a launchpad for starships that was loosely based on the mechanics of lily pads and frogs.

Lalibela and Kibra led Ethiopia together, never losing touch with the countryside. The capitol was transformed inside and out. There were more than a few villages with aspirations to see the heavens, and people traveled from as far as West Africa and India to take flight from the Roha spaceport. The country was flourishing, and Roha became a cosmopolitan center.

"Let's go see the future," Lalibela proposed to Kibra one day. "If we are to have children, I want to see the world their great-great-great-grandchildren are to inherit."

"Why not?" Kibra chuckled, amused by her partner's spontaneity. "How about the year 3000?"

Ethiopian engineering by this time had gotten to a microscopic level, and again based on a bee's perception farmers and scientists had found a way to slip through the very fabric of time. It started when they realized that bees could perceive movements at one three-hundredth of a second versus human's perception at one-fiftieth. Once they developed instruments that could perceive movements and navigate as fast as bees, it wasn't as complicated to fine-tune things even further. Soon they found pockets in space at a submicroscopic level where matter appeared and disappeared, seemingly at random. After they realized that simply observing these anomalies was actually changing how they occurred, they were able to communicate with the pockets and, little by little, slip right through the space-time continuum. Time travel was always possible, and is actually always happening, but in Ethiopia most people just use it to make the good moments last longer.

ራእይ : ra'·əy
(noun)
1. *(Amharic)* Vision.
2. Revelation.

Gondar, Year 3000

"Have you ever heard those stories of when we were people?" a young dragon asked the other, while dancing in flight and playing catch with a ball of fire. "They say we were creative. Even all the ruins below us were structures that we built, and we used to live inside of them. Now we only destroy. Destroy just so it can be rebuilt someday when we become human again."

"*If* our descendants ever become human again," the other dragon interjected.

The air felt like an oven. The sky was black, and small fires were everywhere, burning all that was left of what could have been a city. The whole world looked like the inside of a volcano.

A blue light emerged, and the air rippled as Lalibela and Kibra stepped through a space pocket. A hot wind rushed across their faces as they looked up to see several enormous creatures descending from the sky. Dragons landed all around them, shadows dancing over green scales and piercing eyes. One dragon stepped front and center, crouched down to a human level, and spoke in a voice both calm and massive.

"Human time travelers. Welcome. Earth is now our home. We were here before your reign on the planet and we rose again after."

"After?" Lalibela trembled.

"We have studied your ruins and the stories you left behind. It is apparent to us that humanity did not have to end its time on Earth in the way that it did."

"I don't understand. What happened? Where are we? Is this Ethiopia?" Kibra asked.

"This is what you left. If you wish to prolong your existence on the planet, you must begin to understand that you, all humans, and all life on Earth are inextricably linked. You are all one organism. Even us now. You are a part of us and we are a part of you. There is no separation."

"That makes sense to me, scientifically speaking," Lalibela agreed.

The dragon's nostrils flared. "Yes, time travelers always say they understand. Your ego is a problem. As a species, the stories you left tell of division and hierarchy. You constantly fought wars with each other while exploiting resources you knew would make the planet inhospitable for generations to come. You must act on what you say you understand if you wish to travel back to this time and see what your people could have done. The atmosphere isn't safe for you now. It is clear to us that something went horribly wrong for you in the twenty-first century."

"Why are you helping us?" Kibra asked, visibly frightened.

"You are the children of dragons, and we are what you will eventually become. There is no more time for you here. Go back and get what you lost."

The other dragons, who hadn't said a word, suddenly exhaled in unison, and a ring of fire surrounded the two time travelers. They had no choice but to step through another space pocket into the past, immediately.

Roha Highlands, 1180 EC (1187 AD)

"Lalibela, I think our most important work is here, in the present," Kibra reasoned. The immensity of what she had seen convinced her that time travel was useless.

Lalibela's childhood habit of running away to explore was kicking in again. "But you heard that dragon. You saw their world. We can do something! We have to go to the twenty-first century."

"Then go if you must. I'll still be here when you return. I don't want you to go, but I don't want to hold you somewhere you don't want to be either." Her heart ached, but she meant it.

Lalibela's first trips to the future were brief, but they became longer. The time he was gone from the present was time that he really missed. He could never go back exactly to the moment he'd left. Kibra eventually gave birth to a son, Yetbarak, who grew up knowing more stories of his father than the actual person. Lalibela became a wanderer in time, so obsessed with this idea of saving the future that he never saw what it was causing him to lose. Kibra raised their son, led the country, and completed the most extensive construction project Roha had ever seen. The love between Lalibela and Kibra never diminished, even as the distance between them increased. Lalibela existed in all time and no time, while the world continued on its path. Slowly, pieces were lost, drifting like petals on water. In a few generations, all Kibra and Lalibela had built was remembered only as religious folklore.

Addis Ababa, Present Day

Lalibela still didn't know exactly what to say or who to say it to. Even as a king, he looked at the palaces and knew true power wasn't there. He wandered the noisy streets and felt desperation in his bones. A need to touch earth and feel water, but deeper still was a need to tell people what he knew. Every now and then someone would ask for his blessing, but most just saw him as a crazy old man. History may have regarded him as a saint, but alone he was no hero.

On this day, a young girl saw Lalibela emerge from a space pocket in a busy Addis Ababa street. The girl stared at the man who had appeared from nowhere. He turned, and she saw his face.

"Gashe, I know you," she said out loud, voice trembling. "I thought you were only a legend," she said softly, as she moved closer toward him.

Lalibela looked down at her sadly. She was very thin and wore a T-shirt with an image of Thomas Sankara and the words "Invent the future" written in Amharic: መጻፊትን መፍጠር. She had a hungry look in her eyes, but he also saw determination.

Then she boldly reached out a hand to grab his. A burst of blue light filled the air around them.

"This is strange," Lalibela murmured. "I have not felt this for centuries. Not since my people remembered how to slip through time. I have traveled on my own for so long, trying to make things right. But I am not strong enough. Perhaps, multiplied by two—"

The girl stared up at him without speaking. Minutes stretched, the light spiraled, and Lalibela's heart sank. She does not understand, he thought. It was a mistake.

"Well," she said impatiently. "Are you going to show me how to move through time, or do I have to figure it out on my own?"

Lalibela smiled at her, a bright star in the midst of so much chaos. Her fire reminded him of one that burned now in the distant past.

"Let me tell you a story," Lalibela said. He held the girl's hand, and together they walked out of time.

LITTLE BROWN MOUSE

TUNDE OLANIRAN

A LITTLE AFTER THREE IN THE MORNING, THOMAS BURST OUT OF THE house into the cool night air and down the front steps toward the quiet suburban street. Tripping on the last step, he fell painfully onto his right shoulder and elbow, rolled onto his back, and then tumbled, gasping and wincing, into the grass by the curb. His thoughts ran incoherently and his muscles tensed, expecting violence, feeling animalistic fear. He felt like a little brown mouse.

• • •

When he was about eleven, almost twelve years ago, Thomas had caught a mouse in the attic, trapping it under a shoebox as it zoomed out from under a box spring he had moved. Instead of killing it right away or letting it loose outside, he dumped the mouse into a plastic food container in the kitchen then sealed the container with a lid. The mouse pawed the walls of its makeshift prison frantically. Thomas stood at the sink, opened the lid just enough to fit the faucet inside, and turned on the water, watching the container fill up with the mouse trapped inside. He looked into the mouse's dark eyes, watched its struggle to escape. Death came for the little brown mouse, but Thomas didn't feel a sense of control—or much of anything. He just watched the mouse float.

• • •

Now he looked up from the ground, gasping like a little brown mouse, dark eyes staring wide at the door of his house.

Nothing. Five fast beats of his heart. Nothing.

His heart beat faster. Nothing. A sliver of iridescence in the black, there it was. A nightmare unhinging itself from behind his eyelids and stepping over the scuffed wooden threshold of the mahogany front door. Thomas couldn't move or speak. His teeth ground together. The sliver fanned into an arc as it came closer.

"What is it? What is it?"

Thomas's nightmare spoke to him from beneath her veil. Her eyes were beautiful and terrible, and he knew they would see him no matter where he ran or hid. Red and gold layers moved like water, and she floated toward him. The fan of long, shimmering spines atop her head grazed the doorway, trembling delicately.

"What is it?" she repeated.

The woman was suddenly upon him, hands tightly gripping Thomas's head, her thumbs pressed against his temples. A wave of heat radiated through his body, remembering his nightmare, the liquid filling his lungs, foaming out of his mouth. His eyes squeezed open and shut, and he wondered how reality could betray him. Thomas felt the dirt under his head soften as they both sank slowly into the ground. The woman looked down at him peacefully as Thomas realized that this was his death.

"Tommy, what are you doing out here?" It was not the woman's voice. Whose voice was that? Thomas opened his eyes to see Ange staring down at him. Her expression was perplexed, faintly irritated. Her car was still running in the driveway, the idling engine and faint thudding bass from her radio breaking the silence.

"Tommy! What is going on? What are you doing?"

He wasn't dead. His body was aboveground. The strange woman was gone. Had she ever been there? Thomas still felt her pressure on his face. His mouth worked silently, his ragged breathing slowed in Ange's protective presence. Though his body warned that the partition between nightmare and waking life had fallen, Ange's firm gaze made him clumsily put them back up, a tin shanty roof against the elements, against his experience. That's what Thomas did best: push things away, ignore them, deny them. He refused his sister's extended hand and rose from the lawn. Patches of grass torn from the ground scattered as his clenched fist opened. The air now felt cold, chilling the sweat on his face and neck.

"Leave me alone, Ange."

Thomas turned toward their house and carefully climbed the steps. Years ago, he'd played and hidden beneath them, protected by their sturdy wood. Now they creaked and bowed under his weight. The foundation was missing large chunks of its beige and gray brick. The entire house seemed smaller, old, and darker. He hesitated at the door, and Ange shoved past him, reaching under the lampshade on the foyer table and flooding the doorway with light. Thomas held his breath and looked over his shoulder, afraid he'd see the woman again. Ange stared at him.

"Will you close the door? It's freezing." Ange's tone had lost even a faint trace of concern. She looked at him like she did when they were younger and his episodes would consume her days, when time would stop because of Tommy and his problems. He knew that she blamed him for their mother's death. He knew because he blamed himself. It was his fault. Everything was always his fault. He and Ange had been close when they were very young, but leading up to the accident, his episodes made it impossible for them to connect. He wanted, more than anything, to talk with her like they used to do before she became popular, with all of her friends and secret late-night phone calls with boys and—

"Wait. What is that? Tommy, what happened?" Ange was still staring at him, and now her brows furrowed as she took a step closer.

"On your face—"

Thomas turned to look in the foyer mirror. Below his eye was a mark, some kind of stain. An iridescent blue stain, chalky and dried. Thomas recognized the color from his nightmares, from choking on the liquid as it rose from his throat like bile and blood. An unnatural color.

"Nothing," he mumbled, "it's nothing. Forget it."

Wiping the smudge away, he slammed the door shut and locked it, neglecting to use his sleeve as a barrier between his skin and the handle. As he touched it, foreign memories forced their way into his mind. Ange's friends at Shad's Bar downtown, drinking and laughing and shouting over the music, reaching for Thomas's hand and dragging him onto the dance floor. No, those weren't his friends.

And that was not him, that was Ange. That was Ange's night—and Ange's *mind.*

Thomas swallowed hard, stepped back from the door, and ran upstairs past Ange. The shock of his nightmare, how real it felt, was distracting him from his usual focus, his careful control of these problems. Thomas felt safe enough with Ange home to pretend that *she* was a hallucination.

• • •

After the death of the little brown mouse, something had changed for Thomas, or inside Thomas, or in the world around Thomas—he wasn't sure which. It was just different. He'd read books about extrasensory perception, but they did nothing to explain what he was experiencing. The world got silent for Thomas. He could still hear, and people still spoke, but that sense of space (or lack thereof) shifted. He stopped needing to tune people or things out. They simply seemed silent, no matter the sound. Until he touched them.

The first time the world exploded, he was eating dinner with Mom and Ange at his sister's favorite pizza place for her birthday. The most mundane, ridiculous thing: passing a glass of water. When it reached his hands from the server's tray, a burning knife buried itself into the back of Thomas's head. He was in three, four places, filled with strangers doing things to him, saying things to him that he couldn't understand. His mouth foamed and his arm stiffened, flinging the glass across the table. It shattered on the floor. Mom jumped up and tried to hold him still while he spasmed. At her touch, Thomas was suddenly looking into the mirror of their downstairs bathroom while his mother's reflection carefully applied mascara and then picked pills from the dark blue sweater she was wearing for Ange's birthday dinner.

My son Tommy what is happening is he dying oh my god call 911 call 911!

"Call an ambulance!" Thomas and Mom screamed in unison. In the ambulance, a needle jabbed into his arm and the explosion cracked and fizzled, pushing Thomas into sleep.

For a long time after that, sleep was when this terrible new world stopped. Thomas knew that no matter how many voices he heard in his head or how many memories forced their way into his own, sleeping would make it end for a precious few hours. He kept others from touching him or his belongings, kept their thoughts from flooding his brain and sending him into an episode of seizure followed by catatonia.

Emergency room doctors eventually referred him to a psych ward, where drugs flowed. Benzodiazepines for catatonia, antipsychotics for schizophrenia, and mood stabilizers for bipolar disorder. Mom didn't want it, but what could she do? She wasn't a professional, just Mom. To doctors and therapists and friendly Miss Brooks who came to their house one day and asked Thomas questions alone with him in his bedroom she was just a single mother, maybe not smart enough to use birth control or have a job with better insurance. They knew what they knew and trusted other doctors and other therapists and other Miss Brookses more than they trusted her. Thomas could never conceive of a scenario where the truth would keep him from being permanently institutionalized. Since the glass of water and until the accident, Thomas's mind and free will belonged to other people, to strangers.

• • •

The upstairs hallway was dark, and Ange's noises from the kitchen downstairs gave Thomas the courage to walk into the hallway and reach the light switch. His bedroom door was open still. Just minutes had passed, but the nightmare was already a distant memory. The world was quiet, and he was grateful for that right now. He needed a bath. He wanted to float in the water, no, go beneath the surface and disappear. Next to bed, the bathtub was the best place for him. Submerged in water he felt like the little brown mouse, except he knew what water meant and felt like. He never fought it, he floated, the lip of water clinging to his cheeks.

Thomas went to the bathroom, closing the door behind him. After starting the water, he quickly peeled off his jeans, T-shirt, and underwear. He normally took a bath in the dark to try to further disconnect, but tonight was not a night for darkness. He needed to see clearly into the corners of the bathroom, the hallway, his bedroom. Rushing hot water released steam into the air, coating the windows, walls, and mirror. Thomas took a deep breath and slid into the tub, lowered his head back to submerge his ears.

He just wanted to forget the accident. He wanted to forget the little brown mouse, forget hurting Ange when he wouldn't even let her hug him at Mom's funeral. Then she'd called him a monster for not letting anyone touch him. At that point they hadn't had an actual conversation in almost a year. His body was the monster, not him.

Thomas reached up to turn off the faucet. The water pooled into his ears, and he floated in silence. The bathtub felt endlessly deep.

What is it?

Thomas's eyes snapped back open when he heard her voice. His vision was cloudy, and he realized that the air above the water was frozen. A milky layer of water trapped him in the tub. Instinctively he pushed against it, which thrust him deeper into the water. Not water, though. It had been replaced with the blue liquid which now rushed to fill his lungs. Thomas coughed, and it splattered from his mouth onto the frozen air above him.

What is it? Her voice whispered next to him.

He screamed and pushed away from the sound, slamming his shoulder against the side of the tub, thrashing and kicking at the solid layer trapping him.

You know we always gotta leave something behind.

Thomas couldn't breathe. The blue liquid in his throat and nostrils was thickening. Now he was little brown mouse that didn't understand what was happening was inevitable, that he couldn't escape. For the first time, Thomas understood little brown mouse's struggle. No struggle feels futile to the one struggling. He had fantasized about trading places with the mouse, but now he didn't want that. He just wanted to be alive, pawing at the lid even as something watched him, knowing the outcome. And this was drowning. This was drowning. His limbs slowed their movement.

"Tommy? Are you okay?" Ange's voice had concern creeping back in as she banged on the bathroom door with her open palm.

"Tommy! I'm coming, I'm right here!" She sounded just like Mom.

Ange slammed her body into the door, forcing it open. Once she entered the room, Thomas could move and breathe again. He lurched forward and gripped the sides of the bathtub, his breaths ragged and broken, greedy for air.

"Jesus, Tommy. Are you all right?"

Ange took a step back as Thomas climbed out of the tub and unsteadily approached her. He knew it would be painful to touch someone, but he didn't care. He hugged his sister, his wet naked body shamelessly exposed and pressed against her. Thomas clenched his jaw, preparing to keep Ange's thoughts at bay.

There were none. Wait. None. His hands gripping too much fabric, Thomas opened his eyes. In the steam-streaked mirror, he saw himself hugging the woman, her trembling spines reaching for the ceiling.

You made it out, little brown mouse.

Thomas's throat tightened in fear, his eyes pressed shut. He felt his nakedness now. His grip loosened, and he lurched back, sucking in too much air. Her face, always hidden before in shadow, was fully visible. It wasn't terrible. Her face was serene and plain, round with large eyes and calm lips. The tub faucet was dripping.

"What do you want?" Thomas's voice was a raspy whisper. Did he really want to know?

She smiled. *Little brown mouse. You know me.* Her voice was in his head, but it wasn't a voice. It was his thoughts, but they weren't his thoughts. His eyes grazed the towel rack, but the idea of being wrapped in a towel didn't make him feel less exposed.

"Are you—?" She frowned, suddenly looking more human. *Stop speaking. I'm here.* Thomas swallowed, then closed his eyes.

Are you real? Is this real?

I'm real, little brown mouse. I have been waiting for you to see me.

Stop calling me that. My name is Tommy.

You don't think you deserve that. I'm calling you what you call yourself.

I just want you to leave me alone.

You've been alone. That's over. We have too much to do.

What do you want?

I want you to look at me. Little brown mouse, I know you think you're alone, but we're the same. We don't have to be alone.

She took a step toward Thomas.

We aren't alone. We are hundreds. I've been waiting for you to be open enough to talk with me. For some reason, you responded to fear, to the idea of dying. You were open to it, and it made you open to me.

Thomas wiped damp hair from his forehead. *You aren't here? Where are you?*

I'm here. Just a here that's to the side. We all live here. It's a place we half-discovered, half-built. We're preparing, learning, unlearning.

I don't understand.

You think the life you've been leading is some kind of punishment for your mother's death, but it's not. You are here to help us change the future. I need you to come with me, but it's dangerous if you don't want to live. Where I'd take you is a lot like here, where our thoughts have power. Only there, because of your abilities, the power is much stronger.

A faint humming, and the lights flickered and dimmed in the bathroom. The woman reached out her hand.

For this to work, you have to be calm. I know you're afraid. Everyone is afraid. But your fear will keep you from shifting to there from here.

Thomas clenched and opened his hands, trying to steady his breathing. This had to be a psychotic break, some insanity. *If I come with you, will I come back?*

We have to come back. You always leave something behind. This is the first step.

This moment felt like it was stretching back in time. Her hand was reaching into the past, through the darkness of the early morning. It reached through the shattered window of the gold Cavalier, past Mom's hair, caked with the same blood that was smeared across the windshield. It touched Thomas's heaving shoulder, traveled down to loosen his grip on his mother's limp right arm. He let go of Mom's arm and his guilt unfurled. An intense light shone through the cracked windshield, past the jutting tree branch that had abruptly ended Thomas's argument with his mother, broken the connection he'd somehow forced her to create when he grabbed her arm.

Thomas reached out and took the woman's hand. Insanity. The water was still.

Get in.

I'm going to die, aren't I?

I know you want to, but you have too much to do.

Thomas stared at her hard. Her face was expressionless: no lines, no movement. He wasn't completely sure that he no longer wanted to die, but he felt ambivalent enough to see what would happen if he didn't fight whatever came next. He stepped into the tub and allowed her hand to rest on his back as he lowered himself down. The water begin to boil, but it still felt cool. He wasn't afraid. He wanted to reach the end of whatever this was, to look back from the other side. His hands pressed against the sides of the tub, and he waited. Suddenly she pulled him up and held his face in her hands.

"We're here."

Thomas was still in the bathroom, in the bathtub. In his home. The woman was wearing a long gray dress, her headdress gone, her hair short and curly, a shiny black.

"Nothing happened."

The woman just smiled. "You're here."

"What are you talking about? This is my house. We didn't go anywhere." He looked down at her clothes, then up at her mouth. "You're talking."

"I wasn't really there. I was here. I can use my voice here."

Thomas stood up again and stepped out of the tub, which was now completely dry. The woman took a step back as he turned to face the bathroom mirror. He squinted at his face, leaning closer to examine something strange, a flash of ice blue cutting across his left eye, which was usually deep brown. Thomas turned his head from left to right, watching the sliver of blue vanish and reappear.

The woman smiled. "That's one physical manifestation of your abilities." Her voice was a rich, calm rasp. "You'll see more as we work together."

He looked down and saw simple, earth-toned shoes on his feet. He was dressed in a loose white shirt and gray pants. His body felt charged. Not tense and raw like before, but humming, tingling.

"What is the work? I still don't understand."

"The work is you. The reason you lived in so much pain is because you weren't meant to survive. There were many of us who have been looking for you, hoping that you were somehow alive. This is hard to explain, but someone from the—from *our* future put you there, expecting you to die with your mother. I brought you here because you are one of only a few people who can help stop something from happening that eventually kills almost everyone that—"

"Wait," Thomas cut her off. "This still sounds—I don't even know. Can you just start with where we are? Where these clothes came from, where the water went, where my sister is?"

"One of your abilities is to travel between pockets of reality. We are in a universe that is on the periphery of dozens of worlds. Pretty soon you'll be able to not only see into all those pockets, but step in and out of them."

For several seconds, Thomas just stared at her. Her expression was patient, half-illuminated on the side facing the window. The light from the shuttered glass seemed bright. Not sunlight but too strong for the middle of the night, even if it was from street lights. The woman watched Thomas as he walked over and opened the blinds. There was his street. No cars, which was strange, but everything else was there. The big tree he read under, the McCray's dented mailbox. Thomas looked up and gasped. There were five moons in the sky. He snapped the blinds shut and stared at the ground for several seconds with his back to her. Then slowly he turned to face her.

"Tell me what I'm meant to do."

SANFORD AND SUN

DAWOLU JABARI ANDERSON

Scene 1

Lamont and Rollo with their three visiting guests from out of town walk through the door.

Pause for audience applause.

LAMONT: Sistas, that was one baaaaad show!

ROLLO: Told you, Jack, three celestial bodies in perfect alignment with each other: the sun, the moon, and q star.

LAMONT: Right on!

Lamont and Rollo give each other congratulatory fives.

Mild laughter.

CHINA: Thank you, bruthas. Like we said before, "It's our invitation for you to be of our space world."

LAMONT: But dig, you all say you're not professional dancers, but what you're doing is just as good as any dance choreography I've ever seen.

ETHIOPIA: Thanks for the compliment, but think of it as *kata* in *karate.* They are choreographed movements, dance movements, but the actual application is for self-defense. Well, we're stellar cartographers. My profession is astrobiology. China and Jette are stellar astrophysicists. The application of our fieldwork becomes choreographed configurations. So they are dance moves in the sense that kata employs a series of dance moves but more specifically they are ancient ceremonial movements charting the constellations or star chart rituals.

JETTE: These rituals unlock inner space chambers, unlocking us from conformity, so later for the stars and bars, dig? We salvage the stars as we liberate sistas and bruthas from their cultural bars.

Applause.

CHINA: Basically, it breaks you out of your House Negro training. [*laughter*]

ROLLO: Yeah, what if your audience is all white?

ETHIOPIA: Then we break'm out of their house Anglo training. [*laughter*]

ROLLO: Star chart rituals, that's solid.

ETHIOPIA: Dig, brutha, you have to internalize the stars and planets. *SPI* stands for *Stars and Planets Internal.* Take that *spi* and place it at the beginning of *ritual,* 'cause everything we do is spiritual. The spiritual obtainment is through the performance of ritual. To perform a ritual is to internalize patterns and cycles of celestial bodies that unlock our inner space.

LAMONT: So why not do these rituals anytime? Why only do it to music?

ETHIOPIA: Our sun emits vibrations just as the other billions of stars do. We are a billion-year-old species made of stardust. If the sun's composition is vibratory, then so are we. The sun rises in the east, so we face east.

LAMONT: That's some heavy stuff. How 'bout we chart some constellations as I place some vibrations in rotation? [*laughter*]

JETTE: We call nights like this Saturn.

LAMONT: Saturn?

JETTE: Dig. It's a Saturday night for the records to turn! [*laughter*]

LAMONT: Right on! Look here, this is not exactly the Taj Mahal when it comes to space but, Rollo, if you help me slide this couch over we can have a bit more "get down" space.

FRED, *walking out the kitchen, eating crackers:* Yeah, but it's my Taj Mahal, and if any of my treasures end up in Rollo's pocket, Ali Baba is going to find himself a thief short. [*applause and laughter*]

LAMONT: Awww, Pop, what are you doing here?

FRED: I got home early.

LAMONT: I can see that! I mean, I thought you were going to catch the late feature with Grady.

FRED: We did, son. It started off real good. *The Wolfman Meets the Creature from the Black Lagoon* [*laughter*]—it was supposed to be the scariest movie of the year, but I couldn't make myself stay and finish it.

LAMONT: Don't tell me it was too scary for Fright Film Fanatic Fred.

FRED: No, that's just it, son. See, I've become immune to all kinds of fear after years of overexposure to your Aunt Esther's radioactive face [*laughter*]—so we left early.

LAMONT: Look, Pop, we're trying to get educated by some heavy sistas. You can't go over to Grady's place to watch TV or something?

FRED: The picture on Grady's TV roll too much.

LAMONT: What? You were just over there yesterday watching the baseball game.

FRED: Yeah, but the picture rolled so much, we couldn't tell if Doc Ellis was trying to pitch the ball or bowl it. [*laughter*]

LAMONT: Ha ha. Very funny.

FRED: Look here, why don't you introduce me to your lovely friends?

LAMONT, *reluctantly*: Sistas, this is my father. Pop this is China, Jette, and Ethiopia.

FRED: That's Fred G. Sanford.

CHINA: It's a pleasure to meet you, Mr. Sanford.

ETHIOPIA: I detect some heavy wit in this house.

FRED: Oh, that'll be the "wit" I had in the leftovers.

ETHIOPIA: Leftovers?

FRED: Yeah, salt bacon wit' collards, oxtails wit' mash potatoes, and fried okra wit' hog snout. [*laughter*]

LAMONT, *with a smirk*: Pop.

FRED: I know, I know. I'm only kidding. It's good to meet you, ladies.

LAMONT: Say, Pop, they're here to perform with the jazz musician Sun Ra at the Watts Towers. China, Jette, and Ethiopia are all a part of his Arkestra.

FRED: Arkestra?

LAMONT: Yeah. Dig, Pop, an ark and an orchestra as one. Music that takes people high up to the outer reaches of new gardens.

FRED: I don't think it's the music that's getting them high. It's probably something growing in those new gardens. [*laughter*] Sun Raw might be *Sun Rotten.* [*laughter*]

JETTE: No, Mr. Sanford. It's *Sun Ra.* It's part of our heritage. Ra is the sun god in African Egyptian culture. Surely you know of the pyramids and the ancient Egyptian mummies.

FRED: All I know is the ghetto and the ancient Watts auntie named Aunt Esther. [*laughter*]

LAMONT: Would you stop it? Just stop it! You're hopeless. You always have to go and make fun of things you don't understand. You don't know anything about African culture.

FRED: Are you kiddin'? I'm the one that tried to get you to watch the late night picture the other night on Africa.

LAMONT: *The African Queen* starring Humphrey Bogart does not count, Pop. [*laughter*]

JETTE: Mr. Sanford, why don't you come down to our show tomorrow and check it out for yourself?

ETHIOPIA: Yeah, that's a great idea.

LAMONT: Ohhh no! That's a bad idea.

FRED, *with a pitiful frown:* Maybe my son is right. An old man like me with a bad heart condition would just get in the way.

ETHIOPIA: Lamont, this is your father. Mr. Sanford, we are giving you a personal invitation. Come on, Lamont, it's only right.

LAMONT: I can dig it, but my father's nature is to sabotage everything. He can't stand to see anything go right. Even when he drives he only makes left turns. [*laughter*]

JETTE: Lamont, everybody is invited to the space ways—

FRED: Yeah, Dummy, "the space ways." [*laughter*]

JETTE: And everybody is an instrument in this vast cosmos—

FRED: That's right, "cosmos." [*light laughter*]

JETTE: And each of us have a part to play in it.

FRED: Everybody's an instrument with a part to play, you big dummy. [*laughter*]

LAMONT: With all the hot air you blow, you're perfect for the woodwind section. [*laughter*]

FRED, *holding up his fists*: How would you like a "do" and a "re" across the lips by "mi," leaving you to B flat? [*laughter*]

CHINA: On the outside you two may appear to be disharmonious but in actuality you all are rhythmically in sync. A little fine-tuning is all that's needed.

FRED: That's why I always sing when coordinating the office space. [*Lamont rolls his eyes.*] [*laughter*] It brings peace in the home.

CHINA: Mr. Sanford, you can sing?

FRED: Like a bird.

LAMONT: Yeah, a strangled one. [*laughter*] [*Fred scowls*]

CHINA: Why don't you sing something for us, Mr. Sanford! [*Jette and Ethiopia concur.*]

FRED: All right, then. [*Gestures to Lamont.*] Back up, dummy.

If I didn't care
more than words can say
If I didn't care
would I feel this way.

Laughter and applause; commercial break.

FRED: You know, I think I would like to meet Solar Rays.

LAMONT: That's "Sun Ra!" [*laughter*]

ETHIOPIA: Right on, Mr. Sanford! I know you two will hit it off. Look, it's getting late and we have to get back to our group.

ROLLO: I'll take you sistas back.

China, Ethiopia, and Jette each give Fred a peck on the cheek.

JETTE: So we'll be seeing you tomorrow, Mr. Sanford?

FRED, smiling: I'll be there.

CHINA: The show starts around five. Bye, Mr. Sanford.

FRED, waves to them: Bye-bye, girls.

The five o'clock whistle didn't blow.
The whistle is broke and whadda'ya know?
If somebody don't find out what's wrong
Oh my pop'll be workin' all night long.

Applause.

Fred closes the door while Lamont looks at him in disapproval.

FRED, singing: Oh, who's gonna fix the whistle? Won't somebody fix the whistle?

Fred finishes his cracker, pushes out a weak whistle, blows cracker bits on Lamont.

LAMONT: You better not mess this up, that's all I got to say. Is there anything here to eat? I'm starving.

FRED: Just some leftovers I was warming up before you came.

LAMONT, opening a pot on the stove top: Wheeeew! What is that in the pot? It smells horrible!

FRED: I told you it was leftovers.

LAMONT: We didn't have this last night. We had collards, beef roast, and dinner rolls.

FRED: Yeah, but the night before that we had neck bones, cornbread, string beans, and sweet potatoes, and before that we had smothered pork chops, black-eyed peas, oxtails, and Rice-A-Roni.

LAMONT: So?

FRED: So, leftovers. [*laughter*]

LAMONT: You mean to tell me you mixed together all the food from this entire week?

FRED: Yeah. I call it "sweet smothered black-ox collards and string beef-o-Roni chops." [*laughter*]

LAMONT: Yeah, and if you eat that you're going to be "graveyard-dirt smothered Fred-o-Roni." [*laughter*] You're impossible. I'm going out to eat something that has one name to it.

FRED: Good. More for me. [*laughter*]

Scene 2
Fred walks down the stairs; Lamont looks in the mirror, putting on cologne.

LAMONT, *admiring himself and his dashiki*: Ha! When you got it, you got it.

FRED: And by the smell of it, you should be quarantined before someone else gets it. [*laughter*] What's that stuff you stinking the whole house up with?

LAMONT: Well, for your information, it's what's happening. It's a new cologne all the uptown dudes are wearing.

FRED: More like uptown fumigators. [*laughter*] Why you getting ready to leave so early anyway?

LAMONT: Rollo and I are going to help out with stage setup. You might as well head up there with us since you're going to be going there anyway.

FRED, *rubbing his stomach*: I got a bit of stomachache from last night's meal. I'll have to pass.

LAMONT: You mean pass out. I can't believe you pulled a stupid stunt like that. You have one foot in the grave and the other foot on a banana peel. [laughter] Pop, our bodies aren't made for eating pig, long ones or short ones. That's why we think like slaves, 'cause we still eat and live like slaves.

FRED: Well, I ain't no slave. I like to eat good food.

LAMONT: Pig snout, oxtails, pork chops? That's slave food. How are you ever going to vibrate on a spiritual frequency?

FRED: I don't want to vibrate on spiritual frequencies. That's why I always stay home for Super Bowl Sunday and watch it on VHF frequencies. [*laughter*]

LAMONT: Dig yourself, Pop. I'm talking frequencies of consciousness, not television. I'm talking transcendental experiences. Talking to you is like talking to a rusty bucket of sand.

FRED, *holding up a fist*: Watch your mouth or you'll be having a hands-in-dental experience. [*laughter*]

LAMONT: Never mind. I'm through with this conversation.

FRED, *looking bewildered*: What's that?

LAMONT: Forget about it. You'll only have some smart remark to make.

FRED: No I won't. I think it's perfectly normal to walk around in a Zulu picnic blanket. [*laughter*]

LAMONT, *looking fed up*: You only show how ignorant you are of the dashiki.

FRED: Die chic? Not in that. You'd be dying ugly. [*laughter*]

LAMONT: I give up.

There's a knock at the door.

LAMONT: That must be Rollo. [*opening the door*] Hey, Rollo.

ROLLO: What's happenin', Lamont? You ready?

LAMONT: Yeah, step in. Let me run upstairs and get my jacket.

ROLLO: What's happenin', Pops? What's the word?

FRED: The word was *abracadabra*, but you still here. So I have to figure out a new one. [*laughter*]

ROLLO: Aw, Pops. Man, you cold.

FRED: If I stand next to your jewelry I'm not. [*laughter*]

ROLLO: You got it all wrong, Jack. This ain't stolen. I paid for this. Cold hard cash.

FRED: You mean you'll pay for it in cold hard time. [*laughter*]

ROLLO: Aw, Pops. Every time I come around you always got some gag.

FRED: And you always got someone tied up and gagged, you crook. [*laughter*]

Rollo waves his hand dismissively.

LAMONT: All right, I'm ready. Let's split.

ROLLO: Solid.

LAMONT: Later, Pops.

ROLLO, *teasingly:* Later, Pops.

FRED, *mumbling, biting lip, clenching fist:* I'll later you, you ol'—

As Fred almost makes it to the couch, there's a knock at the door again; he goes and opens the door.

GRADY, *walking in:* Hey, Fred. I just saw Larry and Rothko walking off.

Laughter.

FRED: That's Lamont and Rollo.

GRADY: Oh yeah.

FRED: Come on in, Grady.

Both have a seat; Fred groans a bit.

GRADY: What's wrong with you Fred? You look like you half dead.

FRED: I think I got some stomach trouble from last night's supper. It could be the big one. The big one might be trying to sneak up on me from my stomach this time. [*laughter*]

GRADY: You don't have a bad stiffness in your back, do you?

FRED: Yeah, right between my shoulder blades.

GRADY: Do you feel a slight shortness in breath when you bend over?

FRED, *worriedly*: Yeah. Yeah, I do.

Grady slowly shakes his head.

FRED, *worried*: What? What is it, Grady?

GRADY: You remember that cousin of mine that was in real estate?

FRED: Yeah, yeah.

GRADY: Well, you have the same symptoms he had. He went to see one of those doctors that cure all your ailments with natural herbs, plants, and stuff.

Grady sits shaking his head as Fred waits for him to continue.

FRED: Well don't just sit there like a dummy. What combinations of plants did he take for it?

GRADY: A funeral wreath. [*laughter*] Now he's beneath the real estate. [*laughter*]

FRED: Grady, you're supposed to be my friend. Whatchu go and say something depressing like that for?

GRADY: I'm sorry, Fred, I wasn't thinking.

FRED: Why don't you go find someone else to depress. They ought to call you "Gray Cloud" Grady.

GRADY: I'm sorry, Fred, I was just trying to help. But you can't keep on eating like that. It'll kill you. They say more people die from their food related sickness than homicides.

FRED: That's the same stuff Lamont always saying. You all don't know what you're talking about. "Cut out the pork, cut out the cigarettes, cut out the wine." How's someone going to look eating healthy their whole life, then on their deathbed they die of nothing? [*laughter*]

GRADY: You do have a point, Fred. I had another cousin that cut out all pork and wine from his diet. He was perfectly healthy. He ate nothing but vegetables, and, wouldn't you know it, it turned out vegetables took him to his grave.

FRED: See, that's my point exactly.

GRADY: Yeah, one day he was crossing the street and got hit by a produce truck. [*laughter*] [*Fred scowls at Grady.*] Well, I have to get going. See ya, Fred.

FRED: All right. See ya, Grady.

Fred walks Grady to the door; on his way back to the couch, he sees a Sun Ra album Lamont left on a counter.

FRED: One of Lamont's albums. Hmmm [*reading the title,* Sun Ra: Nuits de la Fondation Maeght], Sun Ra: Nutes de la fondashun ... mate? [*light laughter*] Let me see what this sounds like. [*Fred places disk on the record player. The music begins to pulsate.*] I guess it wouldn't hurt to kick my feet up a bit. Well, I guess it wouldn't hurt to take a little nap so I can be well rested for the show. [*Fred drifts off to sleep.*]

Hours later, a knocking at the door.

FRED, slowly waking up: All right, all right, I'm coming.

Fred opens the door and a person with a huge ibis head mask of the Egyptian god Thoth walks in.

FRED, backing up clenching his chest: Oh, no! [*laughter*] Ohhhh! It's Rodan! [*roaring laughter*] He finished eating Tokyo, Japan, now he wants Watts, California! [*laughter*] Oh, Elizabeth! Elizabeth, I'm coming to join you, honey! This time Polly wanna nigga! [*laughter*]

Sun Ra steps through the door dressed in elaborate ancient ceremonial garb.

SUN RA: Mr. Sanford? [*pause for applause*] Mr. Sanford, are you all right?

FRED, coming out of shock: Ohhhhh. Huh? What?

SUN RA, coming to Fred's aid: Are you all right, Mr. Sanford?

FRED, looking up and down at Sun Ra's clothing: Am I all right? A black Liberace and Yul Brynner in a Big Bird mask are standing in my living room. Do I look all right? [*laughter*] Who are you?

SUN RA, *spreading his arms*: I—am Sun Ra.

FRED, *scanning Sun Ra from head to toe*: You. Are. Sun Ra?

SUN RA: I apologize if I startled you.

FRED: The way you're dressed, you'd startle Monty Hall. [*laughter*]

SUN RA, *shaking his head in amusement*: These space suits are signature clothes worn by your great ancestors both on Earth and on Saturn.

FRED: And all this time I thought junkies were only on Earth [*laughter*].

SUN RA: Mr. Sanford, all catalysts at one time or another were criticized for their eccentric ideas.

FRED: Well, those cattle lists probably had the wrong type of cattle. [*laughter*] They probably started off like you trying to herd bird people instead of cows. [*laughter*]

SUN RA, *chuckling*: You don't understand, Mr. Sanford. I'm just going to have to show you. As the ambassador of the intergalactic federation, please accompany me on a journey to the diamonds in the sky. [*He gestures*]

FRED, *grabbing his baseball bat*: You see this Louisville slugger? It's known for its batting average on the diamond on the ground. [*Roaring laughter*] If you don't—

A strange pulsating sound coming from outside interrupts.

FRED: What's that sound?

SUN RA: Those are the natural minors of vibro-ion accelerator engines.

FRED, *going to the door*: Engines?

Fred looks out the door and sees a spaceship.

FRED, clutching his chest again: What [*gulping*] is that?

SUN RA: I told you, Mr. Sanford, I'm an ambassador from the inter-galactic federation of outer space.

SUN RA, singing:

Hereby
our invitation
we do invite you
be of my space world.

FRED, falling into a hypnotic state as Sun Ra's entourage escorts him into the ship: Be of your space world?

SUN RA: Rhythmic equations...

FRED: Rhythmic equations...

SUN RA: Enlightenment is my tomorrow...

FRED: Enlightenment is my tomorrow...

SUN RA: Has no plane of sorrow...

FRED: Has no plane of sorrow...

SUN RA: Be of my space world.

FRED: Be of my space world.

Scene 3
FRED: Where am I? What is this place?

SUN RA: You are riding sacred sounds, the sounds of enlightenment by way of strange mathematics and rhythmic equations.

FRED: Sounds of what-ment? Wh-what you mean, "riding sounds of enlightenment"? [*laughter*]

SUN RA: You are flying in a spacecraft propelled by the depths of wisdom upon vibratory star patterns. Enlightenment enables us to defy the oppressive weight of ignorance.

FRED: You mean we're in the air?

SUN RA: We're in space.

FRED: Put! Me! Down! [*laughter*]

SUN RA: Down, Mr. Sanford? In the vastness of space, down is relative. It's only when earth lies beneath your feet that "up and down" has any significance.

FRED: Oooh! [*Fred stumbles back clutching his chest*] Oh no! This is the biggest one yet! You hear that, Elizabeth? I'm with a junky from Jupiter and I don't know if I'm coming to join you, honey! I can't tell which way is up! Oooh! [*laughter*]

SUN RA: You are perfectly safe, Mr. Sanford. Everything is as it should be.

FRED: Listen, are you for real?

SUN RA: I'm not real, I'm just like you. You don't exist in your society. If you did, your people would not be seeking equal rights.

FRED: Oh, yeah? Try driving through Beverly Hills at night and see if you don't exist to the police [*laughter*]. You'll end up being nonexistent. [*laughter*]

SUN RA: That's just my point, Mr. Sanford. See, your existence is that insignificant. If you were real, you'd have some status amongst the nations of the world. So we're both myths. I do not come to you as reality. I come to you as myth because that's what black people are: myths.

FRED: This is all crazy. It has to be a dream. That's it, I'm dreaming. It was that food I had last night. That has to be it.

SUN RA: I came from a dream that the black man dreamt long ago. I'm actually a presence sent to you by your ancestors. I understand why this is difficult for you to comprehend. Your entire life you have been veiled from the fiery truth of enlightenment. You believe the extent of your existence is the role of an ex slave, an Afro-American. But what were you before that?

FRED: A bald-headed African? [*laughter*]

SUN RA, *smiling with amusement*: Please try to stay focused, brother Sanford. You see, you have both an outer space and an inner space to explore. One should never exceed the other. Inner development prepares you spiritually, while external works help society. When you abandon either, you suffer the consequences of subjugation. This is why you become dependent and beg for jobs from the system. This is why you beg them for rights.

FRED: We don't beg. We deserve those rights.

SUN RA: To deserve means you are "worthy of." Whoever determines you to be worthy of something wields the power to administer judgment. You have to define your own worth, not empower someone else to decide that. Coltrane determined his worth. Garvey determined his worth. You've only made a partial journey from the inner space of the womb to the outer space or outcasts of society. Your new inner space is the inner city. Control that and explore the outer world beyond your country.

FRED: Couldn't you tell me that without showing up as the ghost of Kwanzaa past? [*laughter*]

SUN RA: You had to obtain this through vibrations, through rhythmic equations. You are an instrument, brother Sanford, and I treat everybody as such. We all have a part to play in this vast Arkestra.

The engine changes frequencies.

FRED: What was that noise?

SUN RA: Not noise, music. Look out the porthole. We've arrived at the Black Sanctuary. As soon as we land we can go to the gardens to nourish our spirits.

FRED: Just so we're clear about things. When you say "nourish our spirits" in this garden, are you talking about picking and eating or rollin' and tokin'? [*laughter*]

SUN RA, laughing: Picking and eating, Mr. Sanford. Knowledge expands through the rigorous discipline of science, not through mind-altering stimulants. We haven't time for that. The intellect is sacred, and in our tradition we guard it.

FRED: Yeah, well, in our tradition if you're caught with that you will end up being guarded while doing time. [*laughter and applause*]

As Sun Ra and Fred nourish their spirits, rollicking frenzied polyrhythms are heard

FRED: What's that knocking sound, that beating going on in my head?

SUN RA: Inner percussion, Mr. Sanford. Vibrations are in you. Bare the tones of life. Be a baritone. The sharps and the flats, the ups and downs. Electrify!

FRED and SUN RA, singing:

The sound of joy is enlightenment
The space fire truth is enlightenment
Space fire
sometimes it's music
strange mathematic
s'rhythmic equations
The sound of thought is enlightenment
the magic light of tomorrow
Backwards
out of the sadness
forward and onward
others of gladness
Enlightenment is my tomorrow
it has no planes of sorrow
Hereby,
my invitation
I do invite you
be of my space world
This song is sound of enlightenment
the fiery truth of enlightenment
vibrations
sent from the space world
is of the cosmic
starring dimensions
Enlightenment is my tomorrow
it has no planes of sorrow
Hereby
my invitation
I do invite you
be of my space world
Hereby
my invitation
I do invite you
be of my space world.

FRED, *singing in his sleep*: Hereby our invitation, we do invite you—

SUN RA, *touching Fred on his shoulder:* Mr. Sanford. Mr. Sanford.

FRED, *coming out of sleep:* Huh? What? Who? [*Seeing Sun Ra standing above him, he gives a hard swallow.*]

SUN RA, *touching Fred on his shoulder:* Mr. Sanford, you were singing to the record in your sleep. I cut it off.

FRED: You. How did we get back so fast? Where's Lamont?

SUN RA: Back from where, Mr. Sanford? And Lamont, China, Jette, and Ethiopia are following right behind. He told me to come on inside the house and meet you. I was knocking at the door. You didn't really answer, you just started singing.

FRED: So it was all just a dream?

SUN RA: I suppose so. We missed you at the show so when our set was over, I insisted on still meeting you.

FRED: So you don't want me to take you to my leader or anything? Even though he's kind of tied up with some tapes. [*laughter and applause*]

SUN RA, *light laugh:* No, Mr. Sanford, I don't need to see your leader.

Lamont walks in the door with China, Jette, Ethiopia, and Rollo.

CHINA: Oh, hey, Mr. Sanford. I see you two have met.

SUN RA: Yeah, but I think I gave him a bit of a fright at first.

LAMONT: Let me guess: my pops had one of his routine heart attacks? [*laughter*]

FRED: As a matter of fact, no. It's just that Sun Ra had these two giant birds, and we all got on this space— Oh, forget it. It was just a dream anyway.

Final Scene
Fred and Lamont are sitting as Fred relaxes, finishing a drink.

LAMONT: Well, Pop, it was good having Sun Ra at the house.

FRED: Yes it was, son.

LAMONT: Oh, yeah, almost forgot: Sun Ra told me to tell you that perhaps someday we can ride rhythmic equations and all meet up at the Black Sanctuary. [*Fred spits out his drink.*] He said you would understand what he was talking about. [*laughter*]

FRED, swallowing, his hand to his chest: Black Sanctuary?

Fred looks at Lamont in shock and Lamont gestures confusion.

Credit music comes in.

RUNWAY BLACKOUT

TARA BETTS

THERIANTHROPES. THAT'S TECHNICALLY WHAT THEY CALLED THEM, BUT they weren't just throwbacks to Circe or Skin-walkers. They were the replacements for the supermodel. No more worries about weight complaints, skin discoloration, or scars. In fact sometimes, an entire magazine only required one model for all of the issue's glossy pages.

Where did it start, you ask? Well, as people started to date more interracially, whatever that means, different genes started popping up. Not just dark-skinned people with green eyes or white-looking people with Afros or albinos with features like elegant African masks and almond-shaped eyes. It wasn't those surface changes that mattered anymore. It was the genetic traits that no one expected, bigger than illnesses like sickle cell, Tay-Sachs, or Tourette's. There were the secrets that people had managed to hide from their children and spouses and had started to fade out, but the splicing of gene pools somehow revived these traits—traits of shape shifting.

This generation of therianthropes was playful. They weren't only changing into birds, cats, or their scarier cousins, lycanthropes, prowling through horror movie history as werewolves. They started appearing in kindergartens across the country at the beginning of the twenty-first century. Their teachers would often discover them changing in the corner into the twins of their playmates or shrinking down to beige rabbits to rapidly twitch their noses at class pets. No one knew what to do except try to make the children feel welcome. Some people just pretended they didn't see it for fear of being labeled insane. Some parents got to know their children's high jinks. There was sitting in on classes for friends during their free periods at school and even eavesdropping like a fly on the wall. But there were no angry mobs and burning torches. These tykes weren't carted off to secret laboratories.

As those children grew up, they had children of their own, but the thing that usually made them stand out was their unusual beauty. Therianthropes radiated with healthy hair, glowing skin, perfect teeth, and shapely, muscled bodies.

It seemed to be little surprise that many of them went on to become models without the trappings of drugs, anorexia, bulimia, aging, weight gain, or attitudes shaped by diva pretenses. They looked at modeling like a regular job, had children, read books, and went grocery shopping like everyone else because they could easily slip into disguise. Now the myth was that it became progressively more difficult for them to return to their original form, whatever it was. However, whatever their original form was, all therianthropes shared one common trait: they all had black ancestry. Because of this, they felt more comfortable in that type of body than any other. Grace Jones, Denzel Washington, Jay-Z, Oprah, Dorothy Dandridge, Eddie Murphy—you name it, as long as some vestiges of the melanin were intact.

I worked for the highest-paid model among the therianthropes who dominated the modeling industry. Her name was Voile.

When Voile came along everything changed, and everything eventually went back to the way of old—models starving themselves and sabotaging other young women who wanted to walk down the catwalks.

Voile had been on the cover of every magazine, including *Vogue* (even the Italian and French editions), *Harper's Bazaar*, *Glamour*, *Elle*, *Essence*, *Marie Claire*, and *Nylon*. At one point, Voile even posed for *KING* and *Smooth* magazines, and toy stores carried dolls with Voile's likeness.

I came across old press photos for those dolls when I was cleaning out my attic recently. I still have so many files, photos, and articles about Voile after years of working for her. Usually people grow to resent being an assistant, because they are treated subserviently, even less than human. It wasn't that way with Voile. She knew well the dangers of treating anyone as less than human. On shoots, she made sure they provided two meals, one for her and one for me. She always said "please" and "thank you." She never barked at me or flung papers at me. "Dawn, what do you think of this?" was her favorite question to ask me, raising her left eyebrow. Then I knew she was up to some sort of plot. She'd ask me what I wanted to do when I left here, because I was too talented to stay. She was traveling constantly, and a perpetual flow of people called, emailed, and wrote to her, so I sorted through her mail, logged calls, and filtered all the messages.

When she was home, she was fond of green tea and watching documentaries, surrounded by stacks of books like small piers among the sea of pillows in so many colors—orange, purple, brown, yellow. Curls of smoke snaked from sandalwood incense toward the sunlight of her half-opened curtains. Voile would look out of the window or stare intently at a documentary about Jamaica, Africa, or historical figures across the globe. Sometimes, if I caught her during a pivotal scene, I'd see her shake her head and sigh.

Whether she was working or not, Voile always stayed black, even if her shade or shape changed. When she wasn't shooting, she wore her hair as silver as razors. The streaks throughout it changed color frequently, whether she morphed it into an Afro, dreadlocks, or bone straight. Teenage girls were dying their hair white to imitate the silver and adding a streak. When Voile first heard about this, I remember her insisting, "This is just one way to see me. There are so many ways to see ourselves and see each other."

It was this kind of aphorism that made her agency more and more nervous. Her agent Liz thought she was losing her mind or going militant. Voile simply said she was lifting the curtain on what she always thought. No one was saying what was the problem. The magazines were still requesting and using therianthropes as blonde, blue-eyed models, even though there were fewer and fewer people who looked like that all. Voile kept insisting that people should look more like themselves, an act people deny and cringe away from to this day. Voile was one of the few therianthropes who refused to change her color.

Voile often threw gatherings for therianthropes at her New York penthouse. The warm evenings filled with laughter, tinkling glasses, and the comforting murmur of fountains. I'd check the guest list, catering, decorations, the night's musicians or DJs, book cabs for departing guests.

The parties were always festive and bright, but one spring evening Voile seemed more serious than usual. This night differed from all the rest. Voile hosted the largest gathering she'd ever held. She stood at the center of the loft-size living room and chimed against her glass to call everyone's attention:

> You're probably all wondering why I brought
> you all here tonight. What makes tonight so
> special, so distinct from all our other gatherings:
> I have a proposal, or a challenge, rather, to issue
> to every one of us in this room. I've heard of the
> exploitations and degradations we endure on these
> seemingly endless shoots: the racial slurs, and even
> the groping from those who seem to think therian-
> thropes are nothing more than moldable clay. We
> have more dignity than that. We have to assert our
> claim as human beings who warrant some respect.
> I say we remain our true selves, our beautiful
> selves, the selves most comfortable for our bodies.
> I propose we avoid shape shifting and taxing our
> physical endurance. I propose each of us stay black,
> a sort of going on strike, if you will.

The clicking of heels toward the door by some of the party's attendants was not lost on Voile. She kept talking, as I checked off the names of guests who stayed. She had known some of them would leave.

Some of those who remained lobbed questions at her:

"How do you think we'll make money when our ability to shape-shift is our greatest asset?"

"What about the benefits that some of us earn in spite of the occasional discriminatory moment?"

"What if I like looking however I want on a particular day?"

"What's wrong with not wanting to be black?"

It was when she heard that last question that she seethed:

> I cannot even count how many of you have
> come here crying to my door or called me com-
> plaining about your mistreatment. Vivian, what

about the time you had to leave the shoot because
the photographer said he wanted to "walk inside
your skin"? Malik, what about the time the director
asked if you could change the size of anything on
your body? Georgie, how many magazines have had
you take on the shape of every damn living thing
in an entire issue? They may have paid you all well,
but believe me: they are making far, far more! I
think it's time we show the industry what a blackout on the runway can look like.

Some of the guests looked intently into their wineglasses and shifted their feet. None of them wanted to speak, but finally Malik asked
what week.

"Fashion Week, of course. Fashion Week!"

A few more people walked away, uncomfortable with risking the
paychecks that had made them rich, but the majority stayed. Even as
they felt indigestion from the fruit, whole-grain crackers, and cheese
mixing with their own dissent, they knew Voile was right.

Fashion Week was one month away. Finally it was decided: everyone would arrive in gloves, trench coats, hats, sunglasses, and especially their black skins.

. . .

Bryant Park bristled with camera flashes, and excited throngs huddled behind velvet ropes. The enormous tent housing the runways
and seating areas made it seem like a royal entourage had set up camp
in midtown Manhattan. Night came and the models began arriving.
Trench coats filed in, while some of the early therianthropes began
shedding layers, too heavy for the summer warmth amplified by the
incandescent lights.

When it became clearer that there would be no shape shifting
tonight, the uproar began. Hair stylists complained that they could
not do certain types of hair. The makeup artists had no color palettes
to flatter the models' dark skins. Even designers flapped about their
lines long having been deemed NUDS—Non-Urban Dictates—since

black people couldn't wear or afford these clothes anyway. Like many other fashion events in the past, they had planned for a much whiter night. All the backstage staff complained until the therianthropes threatened to leave outright. Every single one of the catty comments was silenced, and no one changed to a shade lighter than a paper bag.

When the staff finally acquiesced, the models had just enough time to coordinate their looks. When they began their struts down the catwalk, the applause thundered across the tent and outside toward Forty-Second Street. The flashes brightened more than usual. And the gasps and murmurs grew louder as the audience realized it wasn't a conceptual presentation for one line.

Every single model in one of the biggest fashion shows in the world was black. The attendees, fashionistas, and industry heads were used to a few black models—maybe one or two in each line, or even an occasional black designer—but this unending parade of black models was stunning.

The designers tried not to panic. They just pretended it was part of the plan. They knew this Fashion Week would generate more publicity for all their collections, even though the reviewers were already mumbling about reverse racism. Some of heads of clothing lines were mumbling behind closed doors about drops in sales because their clothes would seem less "universal," whatever that meant.

The models walked elegantly, fierce and flawless, feeling for the first time that their careers were a little less zoo-like, and the camera clicks sounded less like locks being bolted. Some of them channeled Beverly Johnson, Donyale Luna, Alek Wek, Naomi Campbell, Tyra Banks, Iman, Tyson Beckford, Lupita Nyong'o, and even a young Nichelle Nichols to make a sort of shape-shifting homage to models and beauties who came before therianthropes dominated the industry. The press ate it up, with front-page coverage, but the majority of the models themselves were silent for days, weeks, and some even months after.

Voile, however, didn't wait long at all. She thought the blackout had made a clear point. She visited her agency two days later, after she'd waited in vain for her phone to ring. Her tension climbed as the elevator doors opened on her floor, and then she was shocked to see the office completely vacant. No staff, no phones, no desks, just a few scraps of paper and a couple of abandoned cubicles. Most of the other agencies shut down too and reconstituted themselves under new names in an attempt to avoid arguments with the press and clients who ran multimillion-dollar fashion lines. Contracts were not renewed for therianthropes. Political pundits railed against the mutant freaks that had taken jobs from "classically beautiful people," and some demanded that laws represent the rights of people who did not have the unfair advantage of shape shifting. When non-therianthrope women saw an opening to reenter modeling, they hoped the sentiment around Fashion Week would get them a foot back in the door.

Voile had thought that her plan would show everyone how vibrant, vital, and necessary therianthropes were in their natural form. What she witnessed, and not just from her silent phone and appointment book scored with cancellations, told her otherwise. Most of her peers stopped speaking to her. Some of the therianthropes created completely new identities, so no one knew they could change, and continued modeling. Others started entirely new careers.

Fortunately Voile had paid for her penthouse and established investments for herself. She knew beauty always ebbed with time. There was never a made-for-TV movie, a documentary, or a tell-all book recounting her story. She had been the highest-paid therianthrope model of all time, and she faded from the pages of history, except for a one page spread in *Essence* that came and went.

Eventually Voile had to let me go just to cut down on expenses. There wasn't much for me to do any more. She gave me six months' severance pay and a generous bonus. Still, it was a painful parting for me—I had loved working for her. She had a good sense of humor, she was generous with my salary, and she'd provided anything I needed to get the job done. Voile had always trusted my abilities, and I know she was committed to taking a stand. I wanted her stand to impact this industry, but her courage did not protect her career.

She called me into her library, an immaculate nook with books alphabetized by the authors' last names. She'd had this room dusted every day, even if it was just by me with a damp paper towel delicately polishing leaves and shelves. This room was sacred to her. I never understood where she found the time to read with her nonstop schedule, but I knew she had read almost every book lining the walls. She sat, surrounded by plump jade plants and regal snake plants.

You know my name's not Voile, right? Voile's the French word for "veil." My great-great-great-grandmother was named Crown because she was the first child born to her parents after slavery. She was able to shift before she was two years old. Their little princess had a power that people insisted was made up by storytellers.

It took our family some time to figure out that this "skill" kept skipping a generation. My parents named me after that distant grandmother who was only a legend to me. My family knew I had this skill quite early in life. They watched me turn into rabbits, butterflies, a mirror image of another child. I was the only person in my house who could shift, and they were patient with me.

I assumed a French name because the fashion world is fascinated with two cities—New York, and above all others, Paris. Besides, a crown or veil— they are both worn on your head to elicit an effect. So when I became a model, so many people just insisted I was a therianthropic diva because I didn't jump at every request to change my appearance. People insisted I was too demanding when I said that being who I am, being black, was not enough. They wanted me to be exotic, versatile, more than black, better than black. They didn't make the connection between this brown skin or silver hair that my ancestors shared with me.

That said, she pressed a copy of *The Souls of Black Folk* by W. E. B. DuBois into my hands, saying, "Most of all, I haven't met anyone in the fashion world who's read this book. I want you to have it."

The book was battered and worn, like it had been read again and again. It was inscribed by Voile's mother, Vermona Washington, "to a young Crown." And that night I read it in its entirety.

One passage from DuBois was underlined in faint pencil, and I think Voile had wanted me to find it:

Then it dawned upon me with a certain sudden-
ness that I was different from the others; or like,
mayhap, in heart and life and longing, but shut out
from their world by a vast veil. I had thereafter no
desire to tear down that veil, to creep through; I
held all beyond it in common contempt, and lived
above it in a region of blue sky and great wandering
shadows. That sky was bluest when I could beat my
mates at examination-time, or beat them at a foot-
race, or even beat their stringy heads. Alas, with the
years all this fine contempt began to fade; for the
worlds I longed for, and all their dazzling opportunities, were theirs, not mine. But they should not
keep these prizes, I said; some, all, I would wrest
from them.

KAFKA'S LAST LAUGH

VAGABOND

THE PROTESTERS BARRICADED THE ENTRANCE TO THE NEW YORK Stock Exchange, effectively silencing the opening bell of trading for the day. The riot police lined up in formation. The protesters stepped forward with locked arms, creating a front line of defense. More riot police marched in from the north on New Street with shields and batons. The protesters stood their ground, shouting their demands. Some of them shouted because the lack of a voice had been building in them, some because their patience had finally run out, some simply because they found that the sound from their throats converted fear into courage.

A white-shirted cop with a captain's hat barked orders through a megaphone in an attempt to disperse the crowd. "According to PA-TRIOT Act IV this action is not in compliance with the Representational Grievance Clause 7 Section 1, which states that it is illegal to have more than 123 protesters at any protest. It is also not in compliance with Representational Grievance Clause 8 Section 1, which states that all protests must have gathering permits from the state to take place. This action is also in violation of Representational Grievance Clause 9 Section 1, which states that all protest must take place within predetermined free speech assembly zones."

The protesters snarled and booed and threw empty water bottles at the captain and his bullhorn. In the thick of them, Resister Fernandez, a young Puerto Rican woman dressed in black, pushed her way to the front line, then scanned the area, looking for possible escape routes, but there was no way out. The police had them boxed in from the east on Nassau Street and the west on Broadway, and now cops advanced from the south on New Street. The irony of having one's back up against Wall Street was not lost on her.

A heady cocktail of memory, pride, adrenaline, and conviction gave her a surge of courage when she realized that she had been a part of the last rebellion where protesters broke out of the "free speech assembly zones," two years earlier. It had been after the election of Jenna Bush in Dallas, the G16 protests of 2022. She had spent years searching—in meetings and collective houses, at radical bookstores and anarchist community spaces, in the streets at demonstrations—for a way to find the system's fatal flaw and exploit it. Resister wasn't sure that she was going to find it protesting here on Wall Street, the very epicenter of the capitalist technocracy, but she was frustrated and it felt good to be out in the street again going toe to toe.

The energy broke like a brick through a window. On the front line between protesters and police, Resister threw her shoulder into a police shield as she tried to get a better foothold. She managed to get a good stance, and she lunged forward. The cop lost his footing. She immediately pushed into his shield again. This time the cop went over on his ass, and she came down on top of him, the shield wedged between them.

Another cop wielding a baton yanked her off the shield and dragged her into more open ground. Two protesters broke out of the mass of bodies and snatched her left arm. For a moment, she felt like a rag doll being fought over by siblings. One protester let her go and reached around to shove the cop in the chest. When he toppled, Resister was able to break free, but she tripped on a protester who was sprawled on the ground. She scrambled to get up, but now the cop was on her. She looked up just in time to see his club rushing toward her face. Excruciating pain exploded behind her eyes, and everything went white and numb.

• • •

Unconsciousness was ripped away from her as cold water flooded down her throat. She gagged and choked, struggling for air. It was a hell of a way to wake up. Her interrogators had a talent for stopping just before you felt like your lungs were going to burst. They gave her a few minutes to compose herself, then pulled her hair back, and the water came rushing in again. When they weren't pouring cold water into her mouth and nose, the exhaustion of fighting to breathe settled into her muscles, and her body went limp.

In her mind, she had it all figured out. Instead of using the adrenaline kick to breathe, she would use it to break her bonds and then bash their brains in. But her body would not cooperate with her thoughts. It was locked in an instinctual survival mode. The adrenaline only came with the water.

Resister's chin rested on her collarbone as she spit up water. She watched a shadow on the floor, without the strength to brace herself for the right hook heading for her jaw. She knew it would bring momentary oblivion, and at this point she welcomed that.

. . .

When she woke again she was in a hospital bed. Her head was bandaged, as were her ribs.

A man sat by the bed. When he saw that she was awake, he leaned in. She could smell the breath mint he had in his mouth, noticed his hair was thinning. He was probably in his early forties but his haggard face made him seem older. He looked like someone trying to juggle chainsaws.

"Good. You're awake. I'm your court-appointed public defender. I have a meeting in fifteen minutes, so I'll have to go through this quickly. If you have any questions please save them till the end."

He paused. Seeing that she had enough intelligence to remain silent, he nodded and continued. "You've been in the hospital for three days. Your trial would have been tomorrow but I took the plea deal they offered. I couldn't speak with you about it; the doctors said it was best for you to be sedated for a few days."

The lawyer glanced down at his watch. Resister could see the clock counting down in his eyes.

"I tried to move the trial to a date when you could be present, but the judge felt pressure, both politically and from the media, to wrap up as many of these Wall Street Riot trials as soon as he could.

"You were charged with 680 counts of seditious conspiracy to overthrow legitimate business interests; terrorism; and assault of six police officers. I pleaded you down to a mandatory three-year sentence for aggravated organized protest."

Resister involuntarily sucked in a deep breath of air as the lawyer continued.

"Seeing as you were charged with 680 counts of seditious conspiracy to overthrow legitimate business interests and no one who has ever been charged with even just one has ever beat it, I took what they were offering." Defensiveness tinged the lawyer's tone.

She sat up, her head buzzing. She wanted to ask him something, bur her mind was so sluggish she didn't know what it was.

She heard a thin electronic beeping. The lawyer hit a button on his watch and got up. "And that's time. I guess I didn't have time for questions. It's all here in the file. If you still have questions, I'll be back in a week. You can try and call this number," he said, handing her a business card, "though because of your charges, PATRIOT Act VII only allows a monitored phone call every two weeks. That's based on charges, not convictions. Take care and stay out of trouble."

She flipped throughout the trial transcript, read the charges written in Orwellian doublespeak. Everything felt surreal. She wondered if she was stuck in a nightmare. Her head throbbed and her vision blurred.

When she got to the report of the Wall Street protest, which was at least four times as long as the trial transcript, a strange feeling came over her. She wasn't sure what it was. It began deep within her bowels and rolled up into her throat. It began in short spasms just above her groin and moved up her diaphragm, into her chest, then rolled into her shoulders. It bubbled up into her throat uncontrollably, and finally it spilled from her lips as she erupted into laughter. She couldn't stop laughing, and she didn't want to. Lying in a hospital bed, looking at a mandatory three-year sentence after surviving a near death experience, she felt a freedom she had never even dared to imagine. The three other patients stared at her curiously, searching for a clue as to the source of her mirth. The laughter moved across the room, spreading like an airborne contagion. They too began to laugh.

Two nurses stuck their head into the room and were taken aback by the scene: four patients, bandaged and wrapped in flimsy hospital gowns, all laughing uncontrollably. The nurses looked around, searching for the catalyst, but they couldn't find any. After a few moments standing in curious wonder, they began to smile—and then to laugh.

Resister threw her legal papers in the air, chortling as she watched gravity do its thing. A doctor entered the room, surveying the scene. He quickly called for orderlies, then grabbed a syringe filled with a sedative. He seemed to instinctively know that the virus began with Resister and commanded the orderlies to hold her down. For some reason, the doctor and the orderlies seemed immune to the laughter, as if they had been inoculated against it.

The orderlies grabbed her, and now, like a switch had been flipped, she was in a rage, flailing, screaming obscenities. They struggled to hold her. As quickly as the laughter and joy had come, it was drained from the room.

The doctor injected her and a few moments later her consciousness slipped away like the laughter.

• • •

Resister sat across from an intake officer on her first day at Sunny Day Prison, Incorporated.

"My name is Ms. Selas," the officer said coldly, overemphasizing the "Ms." "After a rigid and thorough psychological evaluation, you've been selected to be a part of a special program known as Corrective Retail Operation Confinement—CROC. You may have heard of this program being referred to as Prison Malls. It's a new initiative in prison reform partially funded by some of the largest retailers in the world—Walmart, Target, Bloomingdale's, Dillard's, Macy's, The Gap, Banana Republic, Abercrombie & Fitch, American Eagle—in partnership with psychologists, neuro-market researchers, criminologists, and penologists. The goal is to explore the link between prisoners and free-market capitalism."

Ms. Selas's contempt for Resister was almost like a third party in the room. "A recent study found prisoners such as yourself have no respect for capitalism, and that is the source of your criminal behavior. The best way to rehabilitate you and others like you is to develop a healthy respect for capitalism. In doing so, you'll channel all your desires and energies through capitalism. If you can learn to place the proper value on your desires through capitalism and use it as a moral compass, you could be cured of your criminal tendencies."

Not being one to let an opportunity to question authority pass her by, Resister asked, "What if I don't want to participate in CROC? What if I just want to do straight time?"

"Your attorney didn't tell you?" Ms. Selas tried to hide her smugness but failed.

"Tell me what?"

"Oh, that's right, you weren't at your own trial. CROC is a part of your plea deal." Ms. Selas didn't even try to hide the self-satisfaction that comes with working on behalf of authoritarianism. "It's three years of CROC or eight years straight time—co-ed of course."

Resister sat in stunned silence.

Ms. Selas continued. "You'll be paid a prison wage."

"And what is that?"

"Fifty percent reduction of one-tenth of the federally set minimum wage, minus 360 percent of taxes paid by the median household."

Resister's head was spinning. "What does that actually mean?"

Ms. Selas pulled out a calculator, even though she knew the answer very well. "That averages 0.7 cents an hour."

"What? Is that legal?"

"Of course. We have to offset the cost of extra security measures."

"So no one has protested this?" Resister asked.

"Oh, there was a short-lived backlash by those who were employed by these retailers," Ms. Selas said dismissively, "but since they were not unionized and lacked organizational skills, that resistance was drowned out rather quickly by retailers promising cheaper prices with the new 'prison hire' initiative."

"Wait. You said I was psychologically evaluated and found to be a candidate for CROC? When did that happen?"

"During your trial."

"But I wasn't there."

"You didn't need to be. You were protesting against capitalism on Wall Street. It's obvious you're a perfect candidate for CROC."

"But it was also a part of my lawyer's plea deal? Which one was it?"

"Both."

Resister wanted to argue but didn't know where to begin. She was lost, and the irony of it all sent her further down the rabbit hole.

Ms. Selas pushed a button on her desk, and two correction officers came in. One of them grabbed Resister's arms. Resister was caught completely off guard when the other seized her jaw and held her head up.

Ms. Selas barely looked up from her tablet. "These officers are here to administer your daily dose of Contentina."

They squirted a tingling aerosol blast into her nose.

"You think you could have warned me?" Resister yelled.

Ms. Selas ignored the question. "Contentina is a nano drug used to monitor and transmit information such as body temperature, eye dilation, adrenaline, oxygen intake, and heart rate. It works by attaching itself to the nervous system. It allows inmates to be tracked through GPS by Prison Mall security monitors with applications that run on mobile devices. I'm mandated by the Prisoners Rights Act of 2017 to inform you that Contentina will also transmit corrective electroshock signals to the nervous system if it's deemed that your behavior is working against your rehabilitation."

Ms. Selas's tone was mechanical and routine. Clearly she had given this speech many times before. She was completely oblivious to the horror written on Resister's face.

"It's been designed and set to your height, weight, BMI, and blood type. You're being assigned to serve out your work sentence at Galleria Prison Mall, at the Nordstrom perfume counter."

Resister felt herself begin to float out of her own body. Was she a character in Kafka novel? A Terry Gilliam film? Could this really be her life? Ms. Selas prattled on, as Resister pulled so far back out of the situation that she felt she was watching herself in a movie. What did her comrade Beaumont call moments like this? Dialectic displacement. She had never really understood before what that was. But there was definitely a sense of dialectic displacement as she felt everything from some far-off place.

"I don't like perfume" was all Resister could think to say.

"You'll get used to it."

• • •

During Resister's first week of working at the perfume counter, she complained to Prison Retail Management, requesting reassignment. The chief neuro-marketer officer at the Galleria felt that it would help in her capitalist rehabilitation for her to overcome her nausea at the smell of perfume. Resister had never been around so much perfume for so long, and it irritated her to no end, which was reflected in her customer service. Her exasperated attitude with customers led to a lot of coercive electroshock jolts to her nervous system. She felt a constant queasy uneasiness in her stomach, but she didn't know if it was from the perfume or the electroshock. She went to see the prison doctor, who conferred with the chief neuro-marketer. They concurred that what she was feeling was a physical side affect of her social rehabilitation.

Resister finally managed to find out how to make a formal complaint and filled out the paperwork, in quadruplicate, against the warden of the mall, asking officially for transfer to a different position. When she turned in the paperwork, she was told that it would be two weeks before her complaint would be heard.

Due to her continuous nausea, she had a complete lack of appetite. The upside of this was all the friendships she'd made by sharing her meager rations in the food court with the other retail prisoners.

"You know, there's a really simple solution to your problem," said Slinky as he grabbed her synthetic milk substitute and took a swig. Slinky had been arrested for making guerrilla political videos in the park without the proper permits. He'd already done more than two years.

"What's that?" she replied.

"Stop fighting it."

Resister just stared at him.

"Look," Slinky said, his words flavored with his father's Jamaican accent. "Just give in to the nausea. Allow it to affect you fully. You'll be reassigned in no time, I guarantee it."

The next day, Resister took Slinky's advice. She let the nausea take over and vomited three times before noon. She thought of those as practice runs; she was learning to gauge how long it took. The next time she made sure to vomit on a customer.

The perfume counter manager sent her back to the prison doctor immediately, and the prison doctor sent her back to her prison dorm cell. The perfume counter manager then complained to Prison Retail Management, and the next day Resister was selling shoes.

Three weeks later, the judgment on her request for reassignment came in. She and the other retail prisoners on her shift were unwinding in the common area, like they did every night before lights out. One of the guards handed a sheet of paper to her as he walked by. At first, Resister was confused—she wasn't even sure what it was. As she read, she realized it was a denial for the request to be transferred she had put in five weeks ago, that was supposed to have been answered three weeks ago. It informed her that she had to stay in the perfume department and that there would be no possibility of reassignment for at least another year.

She looked down at the work nametag she had taken off a few minutes before, which, in addition her name, read "Shoe Department."

Suddenly Resister began to laugh. Realizing that she found absolute and absurd elation in the incompetence of the system, which gave her hope that there was a way out of all this, she laughed and laughed uncontrollably. The other prisoners asked her what was so funny, but she couldn't answer. The laughter made her knees weak and she fell to the floor. The other prisoners looked down at her, and smiles broke out on their faces—and then they too began laughing. A virus of joy spread across the common area of the prison dorm. Resister held up the mall warden's denial. One of the prisoners took it and read it out loud. Well, he started to, but one by one laughter took each of them until finally the prisoner reading collapsed mid-sentence, guffawing.

Through tears of laughter, Resister looked around and saw the others laughing, and she realized she'd found a way out. Laughter liberated them from the search for logic within the illogical. It validated for them what they had known all along—that the system was a joke. They laughed because the key to their freedom was always within them. The absurd simplicity of it all was just too much for them to contain, even if they didn't fully grasp it at the moment.

Prison dorm cell security forces were perplexed at the riot of laughter that had prisoners wriggling on the floor. They called in the prison doctor, a nano security biology officer, and the chief neuro-marketer. The nano security biology officer activated a fail-safe riot program in the Contentina, but it seemed to have no effect. Endorphins produced by the laughter blocked Contentina's effect.

None of the prison staff knew what to do at that point. This only served as more fodder for the prisoners' howling. Out of sheer desperation, the guards dragged them one by one back to their cells. All the while the convicts laughed at the guards.

The warden called an emergency meeting of Prison Mall officials. There was a flaw in Contentina. Something needed to be done. If it got out that endorphins from laughter blocked the electroshock of Contentina, they would lose control of the prisoners.

An hour later, Resister sat on the cell floor, her back against the wall, still chuckling quietly to herself. She was already planning how to grow this resistance of hilarity beyond their cellblock, how to not only break herself out but as many of the other prisoners as she could. Then it struck her. She had removed herself from thought processes that kept her from imagining turning the world upside down. The more she thought about how warped and surreal the world had become, the more she found an absurd humor in its flaws.

Then the most dangerous thought rushed out of the depths of her subconscious: as long as you could find a way to laugh at the madness, they couldn't reach you. And if they couldn't reach you, then they couldn't beat you. This laughter at the absurdity of it all brought the mad reckless optimism every revolution needs. This wasn't just a threat to the prison. It was a threat to everything. Laughter was the means by which everything could change.

22XX: ONE-SHOT

JELANI WILSON

FUCK MY SNOOZE ALARM. FUCK SCHOOL. FUCK THE GUY DATING Delia Darlington. And fuck my life.

That's pretty much what I think every morning I wake up these
days. You guessed it. I'm a jaded teenage manchild with a chip on my
shoulder. The name's Sasha Sangare. That's the kind of name you end
up with when you got a Russian mom and a Malian dad.

Who's Delia? We'll get to her later. It's a long story. You don't want
to make me late for class, do you?

I'm a sophomore at the Institute, in case you didn't know. From
the name you'd think it was a shining citadel on a hill. It's actually
inside a terraformed dome on the desolate moon of Phobos orbiting
Mars, nestled inside the Stickney Crater, spinning round and round
above yet another planet for humanity to run into the ground.

The Institute was built by the AFIP (Armed Forces of the Inner
Planets), which makes us all tools for the military, even though students don't classify as enlisted. I shouldn't complain, though. There
are still kids starving, or forced to be slaves and soldiers, or who at
least never got the chance to test into exclusive Martian high schools
for kids too smart for their own good.

That's my excuse for being at the bottom of my class, by the way.
My parents didn't like it either.

If it wasn't time for my nanomechanics class, I'd give you the campus tour. Just don't let the bright, sunny day fool you. It's a holo-
graphic sky projected on the inside of the dome. The cumulous clouds
glitch every once in a while.

Anyway, Prof. Tsai is giving summations of final projects today.

Apparently, the scoring committee saw one project, more of a breakthrough really, that blew them all away.

Bet you can't guess whose that is.

"Sasha!"

All right, so I'm exaggerating, but it's good, okay?

Oh, and that tall, husky kid with the spiked black hair calling my name? That's Herb. We tested in together. Been best friends ever since. We swore to never tell each other our scores. That's our bond. Weird, I know.

Anyway, no time for a chat. We just give each other the nod amid the flocks of students switching classes. He's got astrophysics now. He looks nervous as shit, jaw clenched, trying not to sweat.

The sliding doors to the building nearly close on me as my scrawny ass squeaks through. The halls empty; everyone files into class. The bell goes off right as I make it through the doorway of room 108B.

But Prof. Tsai isn't there.

Instead some straight-razored zealot in an infantry uniform stands in front of the class, looking like he came out of a twenty-first-century propaganda poster. Only difference is he's been surgically reconstructed into an automaton, complete with rubbery, synthetic skin, flat cybernetic lenses for eyes, and some intensive psychological programming.

Everyone is silent as I take a seat and dock my data drive.

"Now that everyone is here," the corporal says in a stern voice, "I have an emergency announcement to make. I expect complete silence, and there will be no questions. Understood?"

No one answers.

"Good. Perhaps you're as smart as they say."

The corporal grimaces before beginning to read aloud from a handheld datapod. "Due to violations of academic and research codes, Professor Thomas Tsai has been terminated from his position, effective immediately. Due to indications of student involvement, all students are hereby ordered to surrender their data drives and report to their residence halls for room searches. Any student who fails to comply will be placed under immediate arrest."

But we're just kids. We don't even know what Prof. Tsai supposedly did.

"Any non-compliance will be met with subjugating force. Keep in mind, your tracking implants *are* active. Class is hereby dismissed," the corporal concludes, cutting off the faint murmur moving across the room as a dozen soldiers in riot gear file in and march between the aisles, confiscating data drives.

I barely dare to glance up when the faceless soldier in a helmet pulls the slim silicon card from the flat-screen data module of my workstation. I just hope I deleted those *Venus Girls* holos Herb sent me after I found out Delia has a boyfriend. Just the image of her majestic, dark, oval face and dense brown eyes peering at me in my mind makes my heart gush.

I just wish she wasn't all the way out on Europa. And that I could stop thinking about her.

Man, I'm hopeless.

The soldiers line everyone up as the corporal barks names. I rise up as my name is called and take my place with the twenty-five other kids in my class who are already waiting obediently in formation. Matching my name to my face, the corporal gives me an especially sour look as our room assignments are cross-checked.

We are all marched out into the hallway. It occurs to me how much of a prison this school really is. Every now and then, something like this happens. Like at the beginning of first term when we were all forced to wear tracking implants. All the conditioning to obey authority kicks in and you try to defy, but you follow orders anyway. Just like everybody else.

But this is different. Prof. Tsai is the faculty member I work with the most, and there's no way he's guilty of whatever it is they say. Or *don't* say.

"Psst! Sasha!" a voice whispers from behind the automat.

"Herb?"

"Shh! Come on. Hide!"

He drags me down before I can move, and I crouch with him behind the bushes as everyone leaves me behind.

"What the fuck is going on?" he whispers.

"How the hell should I know?"

"Well, why'd you ping me this message?" he asks, holding up the disc-shaped orb of his datapod:

Help. Something very bad happening. Will be
walking past automat with class. Help me hide in
the bushes. Will explain later. Go now.

What the hell? "I didn't write that."
"Then who did?"
I shrug. "I don't know, but something fucked up is going on. Prof.
Tsai has been charged with some kind of 'research violation' and I'm
supposed to be getting my room searched or risk 'subjugating force.'"
I peek over the top of the bushes and watch, somehow relieved
that I didn't make it back to Moravec Hall. Another unit of soldiers
is posted around the mirrored plastiglass building. Herb clasps my
shoulder as he steals a glance.
His cybernetic eyes whirr. "With my prosthetic vision, I can get a
better look."
PING! PING! PING!
Let's hope no one heard that. Strange, the soldiers didn't confiscate
handhelds. I look down:

What are you waiting for? They will use the tracking implant in your arm to locate you. Get below
ground. The corporal wants to weaponize your
project. Hurry!

My project?
"Herb," I say, trying to keep my cool. "We gotta move."
"Wait. Everyone is being gathered in the common area."
"No, it's time. Believe me."
I show him the message.
He follows me to the glitchy window well behind us that Milton
Maxwell showed me when I first came to campus. I was so depressed
when he graduated last year. We used it to sneak in for extra rations at
night. Who else would know it was here?
I punch in the override code on the side panel like he taught me,
and the window spreads open like parting curtains of glass alloy. This
is also where I hid extra samples in case I needed more evidence for
my project.

Refrigerated vapor floats out from the frigid interior as we slide down through the window and land in the automat's frozen storage unit. Herb and I use the light from our datapods to see in the darkness. He keeps his light trained on the door while I scurry to the back corner, searching behind suspended animation crates for my pressurized lockbox.

"Shit," I mutter.

Where the fuck did I put that thing?

The only answer I get is the clank and hiss of the freezer door coming open.

"Looking for this, are you?"

Jumping back if only to catch up to my own skin, I press my back to the wall as a cloudburst of vapor pours in, followed by a darkened figure. I swing the light of my datapod over to expose his face, but the corporal doesn't flinch. His flat cheeks look paler than before. His eyes cycle and whirr, dilating with prosthetic vision like Herb's. He extends his hand as if to reach his fingers through my face, holding me in his gaze.

There is no disdain like there was in the classroom. Just cold curiosity, as if he's wondering how I'll sound when he breaks me.

"Professor Tsai did his best to destroy your work, but he didn't know you'd already submitted your abstract to the Scoring Committee," the corporal remarks, striding through the beam of frosted light from my datapod. "I found it curious that surveillance feeds showed you coming here every few nights. That's how I found this. Organelle samples you kept for yourself. Only question now is whether to keep or kill you."

Eyes shifting, he makes his choice and snaps his attention to Herb. Stumbling backward, Herb throws his hands up as the corporal trains a heavy slug pistol at his forehead. The corporal doesn't fire. Backing toward the door, he chuckles and makes his exit. "I have what I need, so I might as well leave. You, on the other hand, can either go back out the way you came and turn yourselves in—or you can freeze to death in here. Your choice."

The door slams and locks. It echoes like a cell door. The reverberation dies as Herb and I are left alone in the frozen dark with only the dim lights of our datapods. Herb points his straight at me.

"T-t-t-tell me," he demands, voice shivering. "No more secrets. What *was* that project you were working on, Sasha?"

"We'll freeze to death if I explain it all," I tell him, though I'd prefer to die in here than face the corporal again. "But it's basically an interface of nanomachines and chromosomes at the subatomic level. Perfect human-cybernetic fusion. I got desperate and 'borrowed' from some old abstracts I found in the Librarium. I cleaned up some random errata in the calculations and when it worked, I just went with it."

His eyes narrow. "How could you test something like that?"

On myself. How else? He's already thinking it. He just can't believe I'd do it. He looks at me like he doesn't recognize me. Like I'm not the person he thought I was.

Maybe I'm not. Maybe I got too desperate. Maybe I went too far trying to prove I'm as smart as everybody else. Maybe I went too far to get Delia to like me. It was more than that, though.

It's about what it means to be an extraterrestrial human.

People like me who live in space are loaded with cybernetic implants. They protect us from the muscle atrophy, bone density loss, and radiation endemic to life in space or on other planets. They allow us to survive, but they are also a means of control for the corporate and government sponsors who paid for them.

I'm tired of being an investment. Human capital. So I decided to try programming myself.

But that doesn't matter right now. Herb and I are going to die if I don't do something.

"I'm sorry, Herb," I murmur as the cold sinks its teeth into my earlobes. "I didn't want any of this to happen. I know it's all my fault. But I'm going to get us out of this. I promise you that."

"H-h-h-how?" he chatters.

"With this," I answer, rolling up my sleeve to reveal the tracking implant on the back of my right wrist shaped like a metallic starfish grafted to my skin.

The sensor in the center fades in and out with dim blue light.

"I'm going to show you what I discovered, Herb," I say. "Even though the tissue samples I extracted from myself are in that lockbox, my body has begun replicating nanomachines on its own—in specialized organelles in my cells. And they are able to sync with my implant. They can use body heat to energize."

Herb swallows. "And what does that mean?"

"That I can do this," I answer, brandishing my tracking implant as I press down the two nodes nearest my wrist, causing the sensor to blare into a vibrant azure.

This is the capability the corporal wants to weaponize.

My hand grows hot from the inside out and a power surge spears up my arm. I try to let go of the nodes but my fingers won't move, locked into place as they complete the circuit.

The power surge concentrates in my tracking implant and projects into a dense beam of blue energy blasting from the sensor into the door, disintegrating the plasteel alloy. The blue light forces my eyes closed as Herb takes cover behind me and a high-pitched harmonic screams through the air.

The light fades and then so does the sound. The beam disappears, splintering into dissolving threads of energy. All that's left of the door is a pool of coagulated steel. All else is silent except for the fading sizzle of my fried-out tracking implant.

I should probably be dead right now.

Instead, my mouth just tastes like metal. My mind and body feel like separated magnets. The connection is still there, but they are floating apart. I can't say what kind of energy I emitted for sure, but it reminds me of something in that old research I plagiarized.

Cyberbionic plasma.

"Sasha?" Herb is shaking my shoulders. "You okay?"

"Pretty much. Unfortunately that was a one-shot deal."

Good thing, too. Not sure I could survive another blast.

"Then let's get the fuck outta here," he says, deadly serious.

He grabs my arm and takes off out the door, leaping over the melted steel that is just starting to cool. The corridor is more shadow than walls or floor. Pipelines course around us, dingy, brown, and cold. I glance back for some idea of where we're going and see a bunch of soldiers who, of course, start chasing us.

PING! PING! PING!

I look at my handheld:

> Hurry to the hangar bay. What's taking you so
> long?

"Uh, Herb."

My handheld says that the message is coming from him.

"I know! Got the same message. Mine says it's from you again," he shouts, showing me on his handheld as he shoves me into an elevator and hits the button a few thousand times. The doors close before the soldiers can reach us and as we move down, the magnets of my mind and body come back together again.

"I think I've figured it out," he explains as we catch our breath. "I bet Professor Tsai is sending these pings."

As if to applaud, the elevator chimes and the doors open to, you guessed it, a hangar bay lit only by auxiliary lights along the ceiling. The elevator doors close as soon as we step out, and the elevator heads back up.

Which means the soldiers will be right behind us.

"We gotta hide," I whisper, leading the way past cargo canisters and vacuum crates like I have an inkling where the hell I'm going.

"Look! A shuttle," Herb points.

The elevator dings behind us as we duck and run for the gull-class transport shuttle. The gangplank is down. Only good thing that's happened since my snooze alarm went off late. The elevator doors open and a squadron of six soldiers led by our dear corporal emerges as Herb and I scramble under the wing as quietly as we can.

"We gotta get onboard," he murmurs as the soldiers sweep the docking bay with flashlights affixed to their assault rifles. "And somehow not get spotted."

Before either of us can even begin to figure out how the hell to do that, an abrasive klaxon goes off.

"WARNING! WARNING! LAUNCH SEQUENCE INITIATED," the operating system kindly advises. "REPEAT: LAUNCH SEQUENCE INITIATED. FULL DECOMPRESSION IN 36.5 SECONDS."

Herb makes his move and runs for the gangplank. I follow as the soldiers rush to the control station to override the launch sequence.

"That's my ship!" I hear the corporal sputter.

Ha ha, asshole.

Herb and I try not to laugh as the hatchway closes behind us and the engines spin up. We make our way up to the front of the shuttle, trying to stay in the shadows. The door to the cockpit is open and we peek inside for a look at whoever is flying this thing. I half-expect it to be the corporal as the pilot chair spins towards us.

"Professor Tsai?" Herb blinks.

Prof. Tsai looks the same as he did when we first met him as part of the admissions committee. The same long, stringy salt and pepper hair in a loose ponytail, the same droopy eyes, and the same leathery, unshaven face.

Only now he's wearing a gray, skin-tight space suit, minus the helmet. His face is bruised and battered but a fierce will smolders in his blackened eyes.

"Looks like the corporal underestimated us," Prof. Tsai observes, offering the chair at the navigator's display and the communication screen. "You two should probably have a seat."

The hangar door slides open with a lumbering screech of steel and the hangar bay decompresses. The magnetic clamp locking the shuttle to the metal floor fizzles and releases, as the engines whir into a rising whine and Prof. Tsai steers out into an infinite sea of space.

"I hope those soldiers made it to the elevator," he says.

I look back, but Phobos is already behind us, a barren floating rock shaped like a peanut. The terradome built on its surface has already rotated away. The desolate, rusted planet behind it looms like an ominous eye of orange fire, ever-watching.

"I apologize for destroying your project, Sasha. I was trying to keep you from being tangled up in all of this."

"You *were* sending the messages?"

Prof. Tsai nods and engages the thrusters. "Not to brag, but I also disabled the school's tracking system, neural net, and defense grid."

"So where are we going?" Herb asks as we buckle in.

"The Academy at Europa," he answers. "That should keep us beyond the reach of the AFIP at least for a while. My old research assistant Milton Maxwell adjuncts there now."

I blink. "Milton? I know Milton. He taught me how to get extra food from the automat!"

Herb looks at me. "You don't think—"

"*He* could be Delia's new boyfriend?" I blurt, imagining the worst possible scenario.

Prof. Tsai gives me a puzzled look. "Delia?"

"Genius next door he never confessed his love to," Herb summarizes.

"It's a long story," I sigh as we jettison off to the reaches of the Outer Planets.

It'll take two weeks to get there. Plenty of time to mull over all the ramifications of defying the AFIP and running away from school. The only good news is that I might get to see Delia again.

Oh, and that I'm still alive and all.

Am I hopeless or what?

MANHUNTERS

KALAMU YA SALAAM

"Is there anything else, Mauve? Do you want to amend your debriefing report in any way?"

"No, Elder Umoja. That's it. It stands as reported," I say as I code off the computer and sit up straight with my legs crossed, satisfied that my statement from three weeks ago is accurate. Typing with one hand has been slow-going, but I am proud of myself. I have proofread and corrected my report without anyone's assistance.

"Good. You will have two months' down time before your next detail assignment."

"But I'm healed enough to function," I insist. "I could—"

"Two months, Mauve." Elder Umoja speaks with an unmistakable finality.

"Yes, Elder," I reply quickly. We sit in silence for a moment. Elder Umoja's silver-gray locks flow down almost to her waist. She wears glasses—why? The lenses do not appear to be very thick. She probably could have chosen laser surgery. But even through her glasses the warmth of her brown eyes is clear. Although she is stern of tone and often brusque in her mannerisms, she radiates a calming influence. Like floating in the bath pool on a warm evening, her aura makes you want to linger in her presence.

Her gaze is strong. I blink before asking, "And my hearing? Any word?"

"You will be heard before your next assignment. Have you made a decision?" Elder Umoja asks, referring to whether I want to be present and speak, or be present and simply observe. If I speak well, I have a good chance to get fully exonerated, but I also risk being dismissed from the compound. If I do not speak, I will remain in the compound regardless of the results of the hearing, but I risk the elders putting restrictions on me, such as not allowing me to escalate. Over ten years of effort comes down to a choice between speaking or remaining silent.

At some point, life is not about decisions but rather about faith. I just have to trust that the elders will understand me. Certainly they have trained me well. What else can I do? I know I made mistakes. Elder Umjoa is awaiting my reply.

"I trust the elders to de—"

"You are responsible for your life. You are responsible for your decisions. We elders can only assist you on whatever path you have chosen. Your life is your life."

"Being here is my life. I will listen to the leadership. I have nothing to say."

"So getting impregnated means more to you than honor?"

"The hearing is not about my honor. The hearing is about whether I acted according to warrior code and whether I intentionally or unintentionally risked the security of the compound by my actions. Everyone knows I am honorable." I pause to collect my ping-ponging emotions. "And, yes, I really want to be pregnant."

"We appreciate your honesty." Elder Umoja beams a tight-lipped smile toward me. Her mouth is small, as are the rest of her facile features, but she is compact and sturdy rather than slight and delicate. Her skin is smooth ebony, and her voice is clear, untarnished by time. She is very economical in her movements, never hurrying, never a wasted motion. Plus she is unerring in noticing details. She misses nothing.

I would have to be a fool to think I could fool any of the elders or conceal my true feelings from them, especially Elder Umoja, who has a sixth sense when people are trying to conceal something from her.

"Thank you, Elder Umoja."

"That is all."

"Yes, Elder."

I rise quickly from the low stool, salute, and start to leave the one-room hut that serves as headquarters. There is only one large table that doubles as desk, workspace, and stand for the communications module: a linkcomputer, laserkeyboard, and talkChip base. The cpu must be under the table or somewhere else. The walls are bare wood. HQ is not used much. I am going into my fifth year here and this is only my second time in this room. There is nothing to indicate that anyone works here on a daily basis.

Elder Umoja turns her attention to other matters. She checks off an item in her duty book and speaks without looking up at me. "Mauve, we hope that you will dance tonight."

"If I'm strong enough to walk during the day, surely I'll be strong enough to dance at night."

Elder Umoja smiles wryly. "Good. We look forward to enjoying your movements. That is all," she says, her attention still focused on her duty book. She said "we" rather than "I." Have the elders been discussing my case? What am I saying? Of course, they have discussed my case. My thwarting of Cobalt's escape attempt has been the major issue of the compound. Over the five-year period I have been here, I do not remember anything else of this magnitude happening. "Mauve, you may go."

Even though the domed ceiling is seven feet high, I crouch slightly while stepping briskly out of the hut into the courtyard in front of HQ. It has been a month since the incident, and I am anxious to know when my hearing will happen. But nothing specific was said, and now I stand in the sunshine, eighty degree sunbeams bathing my brown body. I curl and uncurl my toes in the warm dust.

As I look around the compound, I give thanks: I am alive. I stretch my arms fully extended above my hairless head. I wiggle the fingers on my right hand and slowly shape my left hand into a claw. Tense, release, tense, release. My fingers barely move. I can't close the hand. In fact, I can barely curl my fingers. It doesn't hurt, it's just scarred and deformed. At my last physical therapy session, Elder Ujamaa suggested that my hand may only come up to 60 percent functional.

"Mauve, there's good news and bad news." I remember her speaking in her distinctive high-pitched, fast voice.

"Tell me the bad. I can handle the good any time it happens."

Elder Ujamaa gently encased my bandaged left hand in both of her own. "Your hand will be at best only 50 or 60 percent functional."

"It's good to have a hand, and I'll work to get it up to 75 percent. Nothing less."

"Warrior Mauve," she had replied with a quick smile, unable to fully conceal her admiration for my attitude. Elder Ujamaa is just about the same height I am, but she is much heavier, maybe even twenty kilos heavier. Her thick, solid black dreadlocks are pulled to the back of her head and tied with a green ribbon. Elder Ujamaa does not seem to age much. Maybe she stays young and healthy because she is one of the best dancers in the compound. Plus, as a healer she probably knows the best dietary and exercise regimen to maintain sparkling health. On a few occasions I have seen her jogging. The first time I was surprised by how strongly she ran. Since she has been caring for my hand, I have had the opportunity to talk with her almost daily for the last month.

As I recall our conversation about the mending of my hand, I flex and relax my left hand once again and then start walking back to my quarters on the far edge of the compound.

The compound spreads out in a small, secluded valley midway up a mountain range. I have no idea what the mountain is called. We usually just say "the mountain." There's a waterfall that turns into a stream that runs through the compound, out through the wooded area surrounding us, and then down a rocky slope over a kilometer high. There's only one ground entrance on the smaller side of our pear-shaped thirty-square-kilometer canyon. The entrance is accessible only by a steep, narrow path that is not accessible to wheeled vehicles. Militarily, the compound is an almost impregnable fort, especially with our scanners and sentinels on the peaks above us.

HQ is close to the mountainside, as are the other three areas: the assembly area, living quarters, and the cheddo quarters. Each area is walled and connected by paths that run in an arc around the wide side of the valley. The walls are really only wooden fences. HQ is between the living quarters and the assembly area, with the cheddo quarters beyond the assembly area. The stream runs around the living quarters on two sides before heading out to the woods. The stream, together with the four areas, is enclosed by an electronic fence equipped with sensors and lasers. There are only two safe gates: one on a visible path leading to the assembly area and the other through woods near the stream.

Once the shield goes up, there is no way into the general compound area. The lasers reach half a kilometer above us and are strong enough to knock down the mountain piece by piece. We all feel safe inside the compound and relatively safe in the surrounding woods.

Most of the time when we rise, we jog over to the assembly area and take the path that goes around rather than the path that goes through HQ area. We seldom visit the cheddo area unless we have a client meeting.

Client meeting. That's what got me in this mess in the first place.

I look up as I pass the longhouse. Dinner will be soon. Our diet is heavy on legumes, grains, soups, and vegetables, with abundant fruit (though limited in range) that we are able to grow. Everyone has a prescribed vitamin and mineral supplement based on individual chemical profile. The food is food, but more than the food there is the conversation and the singing we do at meal times. The competition between squads to come up with the best step-and-song lines. With Azure and Persia as drummers, our squad is always the strongest.

We warriors are divided into four squads of ten members each, an escalating squad matched with a new squad. We assemble, exercise, work, study, and dance together. Azure and Hyacinth are on meal duty this week. They wave as I walk pass the longhouse. I wave back.

I have remained isolated on the east wing of the living quarters in a hut of my own, totally out of contact with the cheddos and most of the other women. Because I have been pulled out of the daily routine and given a special therapy routine, I usually do not encounter many others.

It is the fifth day of my period and the heaviest flow is over.

I am tired of doing nothing. I work in the garden early in the mornings, do two hours of therapy, and then the rest of the day I usually read, study, and exercise. Usually in the late afternoon I have warrior thought classes with Elder Imani. I look forward to them, but I am bored with everything else. No, I'm not bored. I'm anxious. I want it all to be over. I want to know if I will be impregnated. I want to know what my next assignment is. I hate all of these uncertainties hanging over my head.

As I turn the corner of the courtyard wall and enter the personal quarters, I see Elder Imani sitting on a mat outside my space. My breath leaves me. I stop. The hearing can't be now. Elder Umoja just asked me for my decision. How could they assemble so quickly?

Elder Imani rises as I approach. "Mauve, it is a good time for a hearing. Are you ready?"

I am too dumbstruck to say anything. I simply nod my head yes and fall into step beside Elder Imani as he strides past me headed back in the direction from which I have just come. He is considerably taller than I am. My skin tone is a shade lighter than his, but we have similar builds, oblong faces, elongated ears, and long necks. Plus we both have lanky strides. We walk in silence, but my head is full of voices debating whether I have taken the right course in not speaking. Warrior training prepares you to confront most everything except a hearing.

I look over at Elder Imani. He is only fifty-seven and is the youngest of the elders. But he has a reputation of being the most serious and the most somber. I have only danced with him once. He is a strong dancer, although neither as fluid as Elder Ujamaa nor as impressive as Elder Kujichagulia. Elder Imani always seems so self-contained, so self-assured. He radiates confidence on the one hand but on the other he has a way of knocking you off balance with his soft-spoken but deeply probing questions. I wish he would question me now so I can get a feel for what is happening, but his face remains emotionless and he does not return my look as we walk back to HQ.

I have so many questions. I have never had a hearing before. I want to break this thick silence surrounding us as we trek toward the assembly area, but I can think of nothing to say that does not give away what I am: tense and apprehensive. I roll my head from side to side trying to loosen my neck muscles. I clear my throat. Twice. I would whistle, but I can't. I never learned how. I hum while I work. I am humming. It's an old song. Something by Coltrane, I think. A mournful song.

As we pass the longhouse, I glance over there, but no one is outside. Without thinking about where everyone is, I return my focus to the nothingness of space before me. I remember another long walk.

I was a child in detention. They say that it appeared I had cheated—my score was perfect and according to my social profile I was not supposed to be that smart. So they had jailed me until my appeal time. I stood in the middle of the cell, my arms folded. I said nothing to anyone.

When they called my name over the speaker and said that my mother had come to get me, I acted like I didn't hear anything until two policemen came. It costs more work points to stay in than to get out. "School cheating" bail was high, but jail rent was higher. So I was doubly glad to go, but I never let on how relieved I was. I wanted to leave the holding room, but I didn't want to face my mother. My eyes were shut as I walked through the steel door into the waiting area. My mother was there when I opened my eyes. Standing. Waiting. We walked out of the station after I mumbled my way through the paperwork. I remember my mother signing for my release. Even now, I can clearly hear the scratch of the stylus on the computer screen where she signed. A hard tapping as she dotted an "i" and crossed two "t's." Poilette 437-70-8530.

"The name is not necessary. All we need is the number." So they said.

She signed her name anyway. I knew she would. When she finished she looked them in the eye. Two of the officers were like us.

"That's all. You can go."

My mother moved toward the door with long strides and waited for the trip switch to buzz. As it did, she palmed the ID-plate. Then we waited for the computer scan to ID-check her palm impression. After a few seconds, a green exit light flashed on. The door slid back. We walked through.

All the way home in the tube we said nothing. Nothing. It was so hard. Nothing had ever been so hard. Forty-eight minutes of nothing was hard. I kept fighting back tears. I pressed my forehead to the window. We were sitting close together, my mother and I, but we were not touching. All the way home. Nothing. She said nothing. She looked straight ahead. I said nothing, my face against the window. All the way home.

And then the long walk from the tube to our place. Just like I'm walking now. A long walk. Elder Imani says nothing. My mother said nothing. I say nothing.

I know I have done nothing wrong. Well, it's not so much that I have done nothing wrong, because there is always something wrong, but at least I am sure that I have meant to do nothing wrong. I have tried my best. Which, at moments like this, may or may not mean anything.

You try your best and nobody speaks to you.

I had done so well on that test. I had everything right. And the teacher insisted that my getting everything right was wrong. But then if you didn't get everything right on the test you didn't have a chance to advance to city entrance level.

We had walked home in silence. When we got inside, my mother took off her stoic face. "Catherine, I cannot keep you. You are no longer a child. I cannot keep you."

"Mama, my mama, my mama. Mama, Mama. I. Mama. I know. I know. I know. Mama. I know."

"Tomorrow, one of us must go to work."

"I know, Mama. Mama. Mama. I know."

"Next they will put you online."

"I know."

"If you run. They will get me."

"I know."

"If you go to work, it will kill you."

"I know."

"If I go to work—" her voice faltered. "I . . . cannot work."

"I. Mama. I know."

We were standing the whole time. Just like I am standing now, outside HQ. Waiting for a hearing. Waiting for a future I don't control but which has so much control over me.

"Catherine," is all she said. I heard each syllable softly explode into the silence. Cathhh. Haaaa. Rinnnnn.

"Mama. Mama. It is okay. It is okay. It. Is okay. Okay? It really is. Okay."

"Look." She peels out of the plastic jumpsuit. "Look." Her locator patch is red.

"Look." She points to the maroon glow beneath the skin on her left thigh. I look down and then look up at her naked torso. She gave up wearing a bra long ago. She stopped wearing anything but a jumpsuit. My mama's smell is so strong. We do not have enough points to visit the baths more than once a week. So we wait for rain. We stink. We stand it.

My mother reaches out to me and pulls me close to her. Her musky odor is so strong. I'm sure I smell too, but she folds me in a huge embrace. "Catherine. Remember I have a name."

"Yes, Mama."

"Say my name."

"Poilette. Poilette. Poilette." We are standing and holding each other. I will always see that moment. The moment I realized that I was on my own. I had to run. My mama was sending me away. My mama was paying with her life for me to run.

At that moment I was frozen into a stiff column of flesh. And then she spoke very, very softly, almost so low I did not hear her. I felt her breath against my ear stronger than I heard the sound of what she said. I could feel her lips move, her arms tighten around me when she said, "Go. Run."

I stood there for several seconds trying to avoid the finality of what I had been told to do, trying to understand how was it possible to thank her for my life. With so little time left. Before I could say anything to her, she said a benediction into the hair on my head. "And may you find some god to shelter your soul."

May I find some god.

Many years later I would have a name for this moment. The religious folk call it epiphany, the moment of realization. What I realized at that moment was not god but rather where god came from. God is one answer to our need to explain ourselves, to make sense of ourselves. But the moment you just accept yourself, then no explanation is needed, and god is everything together and nothing in particular. But that was later. At that moment—my mother holding me and urging me to run, not telling me where to run, and knowing that she would die after she would not account for my absence—at that moment I had to believe in something, so I believed that god was life. The urge to live is god.

In some really deep way, her sacrifice was not a death wish but a life wish. My mother's sacrifice was designed to pass life on.

We didn't say anything else all night.

I am called back to the present when I feel an arm around my shoulder. Elder Imani embraces me. The cotton of his blue tunic is very soft.

"Mauve, you are a good warrior. But you need to improve your dancing. Let us face this together."

Before I can ask what dancing has to do with my hearing, Elder Imani draws back from the embrace, takes my hand, and we walk into HQ.

• • •

"Mauve took off her TalkChip. She broke contact while outside the compound. That is a violation," Elder Ujamaa comments as she uses a remote to scroll through my debriefing report, which is flashed on a screen large enough to be read from ten meters away.

"Yes." Elder Imani stands and replies with a sardonic tone that implies "And so what?" It was like he was asking a question instead of responding to an assertion.

"Mauve had no way to know the shield was not raised for a full minute after the alarm."

"If she had had her TalkChip on, she would have heard the instructions." Elder Jamaa is speaking softly, slowly, emotionless.

Elder Jamaa has pinned me with that. Elder Imani pauses before answering her charge. At first it seems as if he is going to concede I was wrong. "Elder Jamaa, you are talking instructions and code. Let us talk reality. The reality is that Cobalt was going to run, and if Mauve had not been with him, he would, at the very least, have made contact with the guerrilla forces."

As Elder Imani pauses, Elder Jamaa starts to speak, but Elder Imani continues. "Where was Indigo at this time? She was outside the compound. What was she doing? We did not know at the time. Where was Mauve? Outside the compound. What was she doing? Mauve was with Cobalt. We later learn that Indigo makes contact with a guerrilla who has a tracking dog. Let us suppose that Mauve followed instructions but Cobalt did not cooperate." Elder Imani looks at Cobalt briefly and then continues, "What then?"

Cobalt, who is sitting by himself on the ground near Elder Umoja, looks down. This hearing is the first time I have seen Cobalt since the incident.

Elder Umoja sits as Elder Imani sums up, "I think we are fortunate. We lost one warrior who had betrayed us. We repelled a guerrilla extraction attempt. We retained a cheddo."

"True, that is the end result. But this hearing is to determine whether Mauve violated code."

"Yes, on one level. But for the good of our community, Elder Uja-maa, shouldn't this hearing also be to determine what we as a compound should do with Mauve, with Cobalt, and with ourselves after we have assessed the reality of what happened? Shouldn't we be here to heal rather than solely to punish? What if we punish Mauve but do not address our problems? They will recur. And next time, we might not be so lucky as to have a warrior taking a one-on-one interest in a cheddo." A fleeting smile flits across Elder Imani's face. There is a murmur of what I hope is concurrence from some of the elders.

As if in agreement with Elder Imani, Elder Umoja stands and ad-dresses the full assembly. "Does anyone else wish to speak?"

"Yes," someone says from behind me. I turn around. Turquoise steps forward. I had become so wrapped up in the elders, I forgot that the whole compound was present. When Elder Imani and I had en-tered HQ to begin the hearing, the other six elders were inside. They went over my report and told me that I would be examined in front of the whole compound.

"Mauve, do you wish to change your mind and speak?"

"No, Elder Umoja. I stand by my original decision."

"Good. Let us go to the assembly area." The elders walked out of HQ in order: The elegant and beautiful leader Umoja. Kujichagulia, chunky and fierce, a fierce competitor who trains us in martial arts and has never been bested by a student, never. His sense of humor ranges from wry irony to near sadistic sarcasm, but all of his angles are balanced by an uncompromising sense of loyalty and protectiveness. Ujima—this is my first time seeing her, and I am not sure what to make of this robust and muscular, dark brown woman who obviously was a tremendous warrior. Ujamaa, whom I have come to think of as the older sister I never had. Nia, the most eloquent speaker I have ever heard—she greeted us when we first arrived and immediately incul-cated into us a sense of mission and dedication to duty. Kuumba, who is an incredible drummer and also a trickster. He frequently pops into our ideology sessions, asking trick questions and challenging us to outwit him. Finally Imani. If there is any man in the world of whom I can honestly and unashamedly say this, I say of Elder Imani, "He is the man I love."

Elder Imani held my hand as we fell in at the rear of the procession and briskly walked the half kilometer to the assembly area where the elders sat in a small semicircle on stools and where I stood near Elder Imani facing the other elders. The thirteen cheddos sat on the ground about five meters away, facing the elders. The four warrior squads were assembled behind the cheddos.

Now I stand facing ebony-hued Turquoise, Indigo's twin sister.

"I agree with Elder Imani. I want us to heal." Almost in slow motion, Turquoise strides over to Cobalt. "Cobalt, you talked to my sister all the time. She would smile whenever your name was mentioned. But her emotions were not safe in your hands. I do not know what you really felt for her. I know she would have done anything for you. I know that she *did the undoable for you*. She betrayed everything she believed in so that she could believe in you." Turquoise looks at Cobalt for a long time. Cobalt is both visibly frightened and fascinated with Turquoise's movements, demeanor, and emotional intensity as she carefully chooses her words.

When Turquoise pauses momentarily, no one says anything. Our silence highlights the rustle of leaves as a breeze shakes the treetops.

Cobalt looks like he is about to say something. He opens his mouth and then closes it.

Death is still fresh in my heart. I almost hate Cobalt, but he is a cheddo, a man. What more could I expect than that he would think of himself before thinking of others. Yet I had to face the undeniable strength of my own desire to one-on-one with him. Looking at him now, his head slumped down into his hands, I want nothing more to do with him.

"We say we are a family," Turquoise turns, sweeping her extended arm about her to indicate all of us. "We say we are committed to revolution, to the future, to dedicating our lives to our people. And then something like this happens. And it is hard to know what to believe."

With her arms outspread, Elder Umoja walks directly over to Turquoise and hugs her. "Work it out. Let it out. Speak your feelings, your thoughts."

"Why do we let these men mess up our lives so much? Indigo was strong and beautiful, but she just—she . . . if only we could have babies without these men, then we could live our lives in peace."

"Some babies grow up to be men." Elder Umoja speaks loud enough for everyone to hear, while she holds Turquoise in a strong embrace. In a gesture of maternal care, Elder Umjoa places her left hand firmly atop Turquoise's head and pulls Turquoise's face into the hollow of her neck. After briefly resting her head, Turquoise pulls back abruptly.

"I would give all the males to the people," Turquoise spat out.

Turquoise was right. Why do we let these men mess up our lives?

Elder Umoja is undeterred by Turquoise's temporary bitterness. She pulls Turquoise close again and gently rubs her cheek back and forth in a soothing motion. "Who are you really angry with, Turquoise: Cobalt for seducing Indigo? Mauve for killing Indigo? Or all of us women who love men?"

Elder Umoja reminded me of my mother. I could hear Poilette counseling me. "Catherine, if you study and work and study, and study and pass the entrance exam, there is the possibility that you could go live in the city. That you would find a place for yourself among the citizens instead of out here in the subcity just barely existing."

My mother had always believed that the meritocracy would work. That if you applied yourself you could make perfect scores and get admitted to the city.

My mother would hold me and whisper into my ear, "Never forget, there is nothing in the subcity for you. The men are sterile and the women are barren. These men will do nothing but bring you disease and grief."

Once I had been foolish enough to ask her why, if men only brought grief, did she have me? If men were sterile, how could she have had me? And she had answered me with a hug, just like Elder Umjoa was hugging Turquoise.

"I had you because I never gave up trying to become pregnant. I knew that I could. And I knew that there was a man somewhere whose sperm was still virile. So I lay with so many different men. Catherine, I do not know who your father is. I had you because I was selfish. That's all. But I love you. I owe you my life. Without you I would have been nothing."

"Mama, Mama. Not true. Not true. You could never be nothing." My desperate reply kept circling in my head.

Turquoise suddenly draws away from Elder Umoja. "I am angry with myself. I knew Indigo was going to run, and I did, well, I mean I felt that she was going to run, and I didn't do anything to stop her because—because, well because I believed that if running away would make her happy she had a right to be happy. And that's wrong."

"It's never wrong to be true to yourself," Elder Imani responds quickly. Though not loud, his voice nevertheless startles me. "The problem is, once we commit ourselves to a path in the company of others, we should keep our word." I feel like Elder Imani is talking to me rather than to Turquoise. For some reason, I believe Elder Imani is probing at my internal and unspoken fears.

"But what if things turn out different from anything you expected?" I hear myself asking.

"A blade of grass may blow this way and that, but an oak tree must be firm. If you volunteer to be an oak, you must be firm," Elder Imani says calmly, looking at Turquoise but obviously speaking to me.

"But a big enough wind will blow even an oak tree to the ground," I speak up defiantly. I am talking about myself, but Turquoise answers as though I was talking about Indigo.

"No, this was not a big wind. Indigo wanted to be with Cobalt more than she wanted to keep her warrior vows." Turquoise points at Cobalt as she speaks. "If Cobalt had asked Mauve to run, what would have happened?"

Elder Imani chuckles quietly. "There are some women men don't mess with. Mauve is one such woman. Believe me, I am a man. I know."

Everyone I look at seems to be shyly smiling, but no one says anything.

Finally Turquoise turns to face Cobalt. "It's time to heal. Cobalt, I forgive you," she says, standing in front of him, her arms wide open, inviting an embrace. He rises slowly. She steps into his assent and hugs him tightly before he is fully upright.

"We all have our weaknesses. Unfortunately for my sister, your weakness and her weakness were twins."

Cobalt says nothing. He is visibly shaking. Turquoise steps back after kissing him on both cheeks, first right and then left. "You used her," Turquoise intones, without any bitterness in her voice. Cobalt looks down. Turquoise raises his face with her hand cupped beneath his chin. "But that was only possible because she wanted to be happy more than she wanted our people to survive."

"I'm s—" Turquoise puts her fingers to his lips before he can complete his words.

"I forgive you."

Turquoise turns and faces me. There is calm in her face. She looks like my mother did. The calmness of finality, I think. The calmness of having decided and successfully facing a hard truth.

Turquoise walks slowly toward me. "Mauve, you killed my sister."

Turquoise's words pull me to a standing position. I am strong enough to take her hate. I am strong enough to take her anger. I am strong enough to accept what I have done. Indigo was a traitor. Traitors must die. Now, as I stand before a traitor's sister, I steel myself to bear the weight of whatever is to come. Indigo's sister is walking to me. She stands before me.

Her arms are not out.

My mother just stood there before me like that. Just like that.

Work killed her. I killed her. One of us, me or my mother, had to work.

Turquoise, if you hate me, I will understand.

"My sister betrayed our compound. Betrayed us all. Betrayed me. That was the hardest part for me." Turquoise's breathing is labored. But she does not stop talking. Slowly talking. Her words take so long to come out. Each syllable seems to take an hour. I killed her sister. I killed my mother.

I want our people to live, and so far all I do is kill. I killed the extractor. I killed Indigo. I killed Poilette. Never forget my name, Poilette's last request to a daughter she dies for.

"I—"

I have succeeded in killing. I have failed at living. If I die tonight, who will mourn that I am gone? Whose life depends on me? Mama. Mama. I.

"Can—"

I never wanted to be what I have become. I had no choice but to become a killer so that others might live.

"Mauve, I can forgive you."

Turquoise, why?

Turquoise opens her arms to me. I cannot move. Turquoise steps closer to me. I cannot move. I want somebody to tell me this life is over. These hard choices that are not choices.

"Mauve, I forgive you. Please embrace me."

Turquoise stands with her arms open before me. I cannot move. I do not feel a need to be forgiven even though I have killed so many people. I cannot move. I will not play along. I will not lift my arms. I cannot take even one false step that I do not believe. I am sure that what I do is what I should do, regardless of how it seems to others. I grind my teeth like I always do when I am forced to do the difficult.

"I dance before you." Turquoise bends into a semicrouch, her compact dark brown body undulating from shoulder to hip, her arms outstretched. Her small breasts with thick dark aureoles surrounding her nipples are arched outward as she thrusts and contracts. She probably does not even need a halter when she runs. Every time she raises her arms the small, curly tufts of hair in her armpits peek out. Two dense, short, glistening, jet-black patches.

Turquoise has exquisite thighs, thick and muscular. Her calves are also thick, but her feet are small. Dust rises softly as she stamps her feet on the earth and implores, "Dance with me please? I need your dance. Dance with me? I dance before you."

I do not move. I cannot move.

Turquoise is crying. Her eyes are almond-shaped but big as peach pits. Tears fall with each step. She sings and dances. In a slow circle she moves. Holds herself erect and then bends before me, a graceful bow. Her hips move. Her feet lift on the beats in her voice. She is singing. Singing. And dancing.

I cannot cry.

Maybe I would feel better if I could cry.

There is a hole in me where a well of feelings should be. An endless hole. Deep but with nothing inside but more nothing in the spot where tears should be. What is wrong with me? Turquoise wants to forgive me. Why can't I let her? Why can't I pretend? Why must I always be so true to my beliefs?

I have learned to survive how others feel about me. I have learned to survive without feelings of need.

"Indigo betrayed us," I hear myself saying. "I need no forgiveness for protecting the compound." The warrior me is speaking. The only person I truly trust.

"My sister is dead. Who will love me now?"

. . .

"Mauve, I have news for you."

It has been almost a week since the hearing. After I refused to embrace Turquoise, the elders continued reviewing my case and dismissed us without announcing a decision. I know the verdict is due within seven days. Is this the news?

"You have an assignment," Elder Imani says casually.

I stop walking. I smile. I feel the tension release from my body. I crouch down and circle slowly in a dance. Chanting to myself, but out loud. *Oh-yea, oh-yea, oh-yea.* The fact that I have an assignment means that I am still a warrior, still part of the society, still eligible to escalate. I will still be able to have a baby. *Oh-yea, oh-yea, oh-yea.*

"You need to improve your dancing," he says with a straight face.

"Is that my assignment?"

"Yes and no. We elders have decided that what would be best for the compound is for you and Turquoise—"

"Turquoise. What does she have—"

"Please do not interrupt me when I am giving a directive."

"I'm sorry."

"You must learn to dance with Turquoise. The compound will be healed when Mauve and Turquoise are able to live together. You are the senior warrior so you must bend to receive her."

My mind reels. What does this all mean? Will she live with me? Will I have to move in with her? What? Do the elders expect us to become lovers? What?

I am confused by this assignment. I did not expect anything like this. "When will this begin?"

"Turquoise already knows." We are about to turn into my area. Elder Imani stops. "Mauve, you are a great warrior. We ask greatness of you. We receive greatness from you. You are deeply appreciated."

"So what are you saying?"

"I'm saying I will see you tomorrow. This is as far as I am going. Be well." Elder Imani salutes me.

I return his salute. I am so confused that I almost mumble the salutation, "*A luta continua.*" Does he mean Turquoise is waiting for me now? Waiting for me to come home? To her? How long is this supposed to go on? Whose idea was this? Questions, questions, and more questions flood through my consciousness.

I turn the corner. Turquoise is sitting patiently waiting for me. Her backpack of personal items rests next to her. And something next to the backpack. A drum. I stop. Speechless. Our eyes lock. Neither of us smiles. This will not be easy.

AFTERMATH

(EXCERPT)[1]

LEVAR BURTON

DR. RENE REYNOLDS HAD SPENT YEARS MAPPING THE NEURAL NET works of the human brain, using everything from nuclear magnetic resonance scanners to high-speed computers that recorded the firing order of each individual neuron. Working closely with computer designers and electronic engineers she had developed the Neuro-Enhancer. The device repeated neuron firing orders, but at an increased rate, sending tiny electrical impulses shooting through the hundreds of electrodes lining the inside of a copper headband.

She had been looking for a cure for Parkinson's disease, which slowly destroys a tiny section of the human brain called the substantia nigra. It is the substantia nigra that supplies the neurotransmitter dopamine to a larger area in the center of the brain, called the striatum, which controls movement and motor skills of the human body. As dopamine supplies to the striatum dry up, movements slow and become erratic, eventually grinding to a complete halt. Although Parkinson's disease is not usually fatal, many of those afflicted die from injuries suffered in falls. Others end up needing wheelchairs to move, or unable to even speak.

After only a few weeks of testing with the Neuro-Enhancer, Rene noticed a remarkable transformation begin to take place in her patients. In almost every case the uncontrollable tremors of hands and legs, characteristics of the disease, were completely eliminated. Motor skills and muscle strength also returned. In less than three

1   Slightly edited excerpt from the novel *Aftermath* (New York: Aspect, 1997).

months, 90 percent of her patients were again walking and talking normally.

Excited over the prospect that she might have actually found a cure for Parkinson's, Rene was absolutely stunned when she discovered that treatment with the Neuro-Enhancer also resulted in the elimination of chronic pain, an increase in memory, and, probably the most important of all, the complete regression of cancer cells within the body. The regression did not stop when treatments were halted but continued until the cancer was completely eliminated.

With 65 percent of Caucasians suffering from skin cancer due to a depleted ozone layer, and with the steady increase in the reported number of cases of carcinoma, leukemia, lymphoma, and sarcoma in the general population, the country was on the brink of a major health collapse. Since the Neuro-Enhancer had proven effective in the battle against all types of cancer, it could just be the invention of the century.

Adjusting the metal bands on Mrs. McDaniel's head, Rene inserted a pair of coded micro CDs, containing neuron firing patterns, into the Neuro-Enhancer microcomputer. If the visiting scientists had come to see a show, they were going to be disappointed. There really wasn't anything to see. No flashing lights or fireworks, no lightning bolts coming out of the sky like in the old Frankenstein movies, nothing but a mild hum and the readout of the instrument gauges to show that the device was even working. Nor was the healing visible to the eye. Cuts did not vanish with the wave of a wand. Tumors and infections did not run screaming from the body. The healing that occurred took days and weeks, not minutes and hours.

Rene flipped a switch on the computer console. On the wall behind her a projection scene lit up, displaying the readouts of Irene McDaniels's pulse, blood pressure, EKG, and bio-rhythm. She flipped another switch and a video movie appeared next to the readouts. The video showed Mrs. McDaniels as she was eight weeks ago, suffering from the advanced stages of Parkinson's disease, barely able to walk or get out of a wheelchair, unable to feed herself or even speak clearly. Rene allowed the video to play uninterrupted for a minute, then turned to face her audience.

"Welcome, doctors. I'm glad that you could be here today. Thank you for coming." She picked up a small laser pointer and switched it on, aiming the tiny red dot of light at the screen. "The lady in the video is Mrs. Irene McDaniels; she is a patient of mine. These pictures were taken a little over two months ago. As you can see, Mrs. McDaniels suffered from Parkinson's disease. Like many who are afflicted, she was no longer able to move about without the aid of a wheelchair. Nor could she feed herself or engage in normal conversation. Prior to coming to the institute, she had been treated by several other doctors in the Atlanta area with a variety of different medicines, including levodopa. Unfortunately, what little relief the drugs provided proved to be only temporary."

Rene fast-forwarded the film. The image of Irene McDaniels jerked and shook like a high priestess in a strange voodoo ritual. Rene slowed the action. "This footage was taken a little over two weeks ago."

The video showed Irene sitting at a table, writing a letter. Gone were the herky-jerky movements of her hands and head. Gone too was the unsmiling, unblinking facial expression, typical of those who suffered from the disease. The last section of the video, taken a few days ago, showed Mrs. McDaniels working on a backyard garden, pulling weeds, planting flowers, and performing a host of tasks that should have been impossible for someone with Parkinson's. Rene looked away from the video screen to study the reactions of those in the room, amused at the stunned expressions on the faces of the visiting scientists.

"Bullshit. It's a hoax," someone in the back row whispered, loud enough to be heard. "The woman in the video is an actress."

Rene stopped the video and shook her head. "I promise you that Irene McDaniels is no actress. If you look in the folders you will find complete medical reports from four of Atlanta's top doctors. If Mrs. McDaniels is an actress, then she's good enough to fool all of them. She's also talented enough to fake blood tests, X-rays and lab work. And as you can see by the reports, not only has she been cured of Parkinson's disease, she has also been cured of colon cancer. Even the melanoma on her arms and the back of her neck have disappeared."

She paused to allow the information to sink in. Several doctors flipped through the folders given to them, reading the day-by-day progress of five of Rene's patients. The others stared intently at the charts displayed on the projection screen.

In the back row sat a large Caucasian man, powerfully built, his face and arms covered with a patchwork of dark brown skin grafts. Rene recognized the man, having seen his picture in numerous scientific journals. He was Dr. Randall Sinclair, one of the nation's foremost authorities on the treatment of skin cancer. Dr. Sinclair made worldwide headlines three years ago when he invented "skin fusion," a process of grafting skin from African Americans and other dark-skinned ethnic groups onto Caucasians in order to increase skin pigmentation to stop the spread of skin cancer. The process was often effective, but it was very expensive and only the very wealthy could afford it.

The Neuro-Enhancer, on the other hand, was affordable and would be available to everyone. It was a cheap cure-all for the masses. With so many poor and dispossessed people dying from lack of even minimal health care, the Enhancer would go a long way toward bringing the country back together. If Rene never did another thing in her life, the Neuro-Enhancer would have made her existence meaningful.

. . .

Rene lay on the ground, gasping for breath. She wanted to close her eyes and make the world go away, but the men wouldn't let her. They grabbed Rene by the arms and dragged her to her feet, marching her back across the field in the direction of the truck.

She moved in a white-hot haze of pain. Overheated from running, her body felt like a blazing furnace. Sweat poured down her face and into her eyes, blinding her, ran salty and stinging into the cut on her back. The muscles in her legs quivered with fatigue, her feet stumbled as she was dragged along.

Rene turned her head and looked at the men who held her, wondering what evil they had in store for her. The men were dressed alike, each wearing combat boots and white coveralls that were splattered with what looked like dried blood. Heavy leather belts encircled their waists, from which hung large, curved hunting knives. The handles of the knives, as well as their sheaths, were also stained with crimson splotches.

They arrived back at the truck, the driver waiting with rifle in hand. Rene voiced a plea for water, but her request was ignored. Instead the driver trained his rifle on her as the other two men searched her, confiscating the stun gun and pocketknife. She was then dragged around to the back of the truck and forced to kneel while one of the men opened up the trailer's double doors.

Shaken from the ordeal, and about to pass out from heat exhaustion, she was staring at the ground when the trailer's doors were unlocked and opened. Her thoughts as unfocused as her gaze, Rene didn't look up until she heard a moan of pain similar to the one heard before. She looked up—and screamed.

Inside the narrow trailer were at least sixty men, women and children—all African American—packed together so tightly there was barely enough room to sit down, let alone move around. There was no air-conditioning in the trailer, no windows or vents of any kind. The air that spilled out when the doors were opened was stifling hot and reeked with the odors of urine, vomit, and death.

Rene screamed again as the two men hauled her to her feet. She tried to fight back, but she no longer had the strength to resist and could only groan in despair as she was bodily lifted aboard the trailer and forced to sit with her back against a large wooden crate. An iron manacle was clamped around her left ankle. A length of chain fastened the manacle to an iron ring on the trailer's wall. She turned her head and saw other rings, other chains, hundreds of them.

Rene stared in disbelief at the manacle fastened around her ankle. She was a prisoner again, and this time there would be no escaping. She wanted to scream, wanted to attack the men who stole her freedom, but she was unable to gather the strength needed to mount such an assault. Her body, weak from physical exertion and fright, refused to obey even her simplest commands. She could only sit there and watch as the ring of iron snapped in place, feeling a numbing cold seep slowly into her back.

Cold? It was definitely not cold in the trailer. Rivulets of sweat poured down her face as a testimony to the stifling heat. Not only was there no air-conditioning, there were no fans, not even a window.

But Rene still felt a chill. It came from the wooden crate her back rested against, a crate that was refreshingly cool in the unbearable heat of the trailer. Curious. She turned her head and looked into the crate, seeking the source of the coldness. What she saw chilled her all right—chilled her to the bone.

Inside the crate were steaming blocks of sterile ice and layer upon layer of human skin, black and bloody, carefully peeled from the body of some poor victim. Resting on top of the skin was a small plastic container filled with blood. Floating in the blood were two human livers and a kidney.

Rene stared at the contents of the crate and then at the bloody clothing and knives of the two white men, her mind reeling with horror as she realized what they were.

Skinners! Dear God, they're Skinners!

Climbing down out of the trailer, the Skinners stepped back and slammed the doors closed, casting Dr. Rene Reynolds into the darkness of hell.

• • •

He had come all the way from Atlanta, drawn to a woman he did not know, following a voice that he could not explain. Though the voice was now silent, he still felt a tingling in the very fibers of his being, like the caress of invisible fingers along the inside of his spine. He could still feel her.

But where?

Leon focused his attention on the closest of the buildings but felt nothing to make him believe she was in that one. He studied the second building. Again nothing. He concentrated on the third livestock building for a minute and was about to pass over it, when something touched him. Call it a feeling, a hunch, the voice of his consciousness, whatever, he was certain the woman he sought was somewhere inside the third building.

Waiting until the area was temporarily free of guards, Leon moved closer to the fence. A quick check for transformers and insulators turned up negative. The fence was not electrified, but it was topped with three strands of razor wire that would rip him to shreds if he attempted to climb over it. Even if he wore protective clothing, which he didn't, there was still the danger of being seen as he climbed the fence. Such an unwelcome intrusion would probably be greeted with a hail of gunfire. So if he couldn't climb over the fence, he would have to crawl under it.

Leon moved along the fence until he found a natural depression in the ground. He looked to be sure no guards were in the area, and then he tore away the weeds and began digging handfuls of dirt from under the bottom of the fence. Luckily, the ground was soft from years of farming so it only took a few minutes to scoop a hole large enough to squeeze beneath the fence. Checking again for guards, he crawled under.

The light on the top of the pole was positioned in such a way that it reflected of the side of the third building. There were no shadows on the side of the building that faced him, no place to hide if a guard happened to wander by. Once he stepped into the open, Leon would be exposed until he made it inside the third building. And if the door happened to be locked he was doomed, for there would not be time to retrace his steps back to the safety of the shadows before another guard showed up.

Here goes nothing. Mystery lady, I hope you're in there.

Leon pulled the .45 from his belt and switched off the safety. He took one final look around and sprinted toward the third building. He reached it without being seen, but he wasn't out of danger yet. Framed against the brightly lit wall, he hurried to the end of the building and peeked around the corner. No one was between him and the door. He made a run for it.

He had just reached the door when he heard voices approaching from the other side of the building. Someone was coming!

There was no time to make it back to the safety of the shadows along the second building. He didn't even have time to make it to the corner. The voices came closer. Two men. Any second they would appear from around the opposite corner. He was caught!

Terror nearly tore a scream from Leon's lips. He clenched his teeth, cutting the cry off in his throat. He grabbed the handle of the door and twisted.

Please open . . . please open . . . please.

The handle turned; the door was unlocked. Frantic, he pushed open the door and slipped inside, closing it behind him.

He stood in the semidarkness facing the door, afraid to move, afraid to even breathe. He was certain that he was caught. Someone must have heard him when he closed the door, nearly slamming it. He waited for the handle to turn, waited for the guards to enter after him to investigate the cause of the noise. He would kill the first man who stepped through the door and likely be killed by the second. He faced the door, waiting for his death.

But to his surprise the men kept walking. He heard their footsteps and snippets of their conversation as they passed the door, and then they were gone.

Leon's legs trembled so badly it took a tremendous effort just to remain standing. He wanted to sit down but didn't. Instead he stood motionless, taking deep breaths to steady his nerves and slow his racing heart. He couldn't believe that he hadn't been caught. Either he was terribly lucky, or the guards were terribly inefficient. Maybe they were just overconfident in their own security. Whatever the reason, he was grateful. His composure somewhat recovered, Leon lowered his gun and turned around, shocked by what he saw.

Oh, my God.

The interior of the building lay cloaked in shadows, lit only by two amber light bulbs at opposite ends. Still, it was not dark enough to hide the horrors that lay before him. Once a home for horses and cattle, the livestock building now housed people. Lots of people. About a hundred men, women and children—most of them black—were scattered along the length of the building's interior. Half-naked, dressed in filthy rags, they were shackled and chained to the walls like slave ship cargo. Some of them slept on the dirt floor, their bodies cushioned by only a thin layer of straw; others sat around in silence, their backs to the wall, appearing to be almost oblivious to their plight. Leon stared at the prisoners, sickened by the sight.

Slaves! Oh, dear God, they're slaves!

He remembered images he had seen in history books, black-and-white photographs that captured the suffering of his ancestors. But these were no photographs; the people were real. Slavery had again reared its ugly head in America.

Horrified, Leon moved through the building, carefully stepping over and around the people in his way. Some of the ones who were awake turned their heads in his direction, but most looked off into space with glassy, wide-eyed stares. He had seen such stares before, on the streets of Atlanta, among those who lived their lives in the haze of drugs and alcohol.

No wonder the guards are so careless. There's nothing to guard. Prisoners who have been drugged and chained are no threat, no threat at all.

He was almost to the end of the building, when he felt a familiar tingling at the nape of his neck. Turning, he noticed a woman watching him with keen interest.

Leon felt his breath catch. Even in the shadows there was no mistaking her. She was the woman from the alley, the one whose voice had led him here. He had found her.

Rene must have recognized him too, for her eyes widened in surprise.

FIRE ON THE MOUNTAIN

(EXCERPT)[1]

TERRY BISSON

Yasmin Abraham Martin Odinga drove across the border at noon. The man and woman at the station looked at her Nova African plates and Sea Islands University sticker and waved her on through without even asking for papers. Yasmin figured she was probably the first stranger they had seen all morning. Laurel Gap was not a busy crossing, and most of the traffic, from the looks of the road and the trucks and the area, was church picnickers and relatives home for Sunday visits—all known to them. Mostly white folks on either side of the border through here. Mostly older. Even socialist mountains give up their young to the cities.

An hour later Yasmin was in the valley, heading north, with the high, straight, timbered wall of the Blue Ridge to her right, clothed in its October reds and golds. She scanned the radio back and forth between country on A.M. and sacred on A.X., ignoring the talk shows, enjoying the high silvery singing. There was no danger of running across the Mars news, not on a Sunday morning here in what Leon had often impatiently but always affectionately called "the Holy Land." She eased on up to 90, 100, 120, enjoying the smooth power of the big Egyptian car. She had a 200-klick run down the valley to Staunton, and she couldn't shake the uncomfortable feeling that she was late.

She was looking forward to seeing her mother-in-law, Pearl. She was and she wasn't looking forward to seeing her daughter, Harriet.

1   Slightly edited excerpt from *Fire on the Mountain* (Oakland: PM Press, 2009).

She had something to tell them both, but it wasn't for them she was late. It was for the old man. She patted the ancient black leather doctor's bag beside her on the seat. In it were her great-grandfather's papers, which she was taking to Harper's Ferry to be read on the hundredth anniversary of John Brown's attack, fifty years after they were written, according to the old doctor's very precise instructions. Except that it was October and she was three months late. She had been asked to stay an extra month in Africa to finish the Olduvai Project; a month had turned into three, and she had missed the Fourth of July Centennial. A fax had been sent to the museum director, but it wasn't the same. Now she was bringing the original, according to the old man's will, in the stiff old pill-smelling doctor's bag that had held them for the thirty-six years since he had died (the year she was born), hoping maybe that it would make it up to him.

It's hard to know how to please the dead.

Near Roanoke she was slowed, then stopped, by buffalo. There was no hurrying the great herds that paced the continent's grassy corridors, east to west; they always had the right-of-way across highways and even borders. These were heading south and west toward Cumberland Gap, where even the mountains would stand aside to let them pass.

There was more traffic on toward Staunton: dairy tankers deadheading home for the weekend, vans of early apple pickers from Quebec and Canada, Sunday go-to-meeting buses—even a few cars, mostly little inertial hummers. Things were changing since the Second Revolutionary War. She heard more singing and reached over to scan the radio up, but it was the Atlanta-Baltimore airship, the silver-and-orange *John Brown*, motoring grandly past in the lee of the mountain; it sounded so joyful that Yasmin raced it for a few klicks before falling back and letting it go, worrying about potholes. The roads in the U.S.S.A. were still un-rebuilt, wide but rough, straight and shabby, like the long, low, worn-out mountains themselves. Appalachia, on either side of the border, was a well-worn part of the world.

• • •

I am Dr. Abraham. When you read this, in 1959, what I have to say will be illuminated by the light of history or perhaps obscured by the mists of time. Decide for yourself. I write as an old man (it is 1909), but I experienced these events as a boy. I was ignorant and profoundly so, for I was not only a n'African and doubly a slave (for no child is free) but an unlettered twelve-year-old unaware even of how unaware I was: of how vast was the world that awaited my knowing. There was only beginning to stir within me that eagerness, my enemies would say greed, for knowledge that has since guided, my enemies would say misled, my exact half century of steps thereafter. Fifty years ago today, in 1859, I was barely beginning to hunger and I knew not what I hungered for, for hunger was the natural state of affairs in the Shenandoah. Whatever the bourgeois historians tell us, and they are still among us, some in Party garb; whatever lies they might polish and toss, the slave South was a poor land. P-o-o-r. Great-grandson, do you even know what poor means fifty years in the future, In your day of socialism, electricity, nitrogen-fed catfish, world peace, and mules so smart they would talk, if mules had anything in particular to say to us humans? In 1859 kids in Virginia and Caroline (called Carolina before Independence) didn't grow up, half of them—of us, I mean, of "colored," which is what we were beginning to call ourselves, forgetting that we were Africans at all. We thought Africa was where the old folks went when they died, and why not? That was what the old folks told us. The Shenandoah Valley was poor even for the whites, for it had the slavery without the cotton. There were plenty of what people called "poor whites." Nobody ever said "poor colored"; that went without saying, like cold snow or wet rain. Ignorance was the unshakable standard. The average man or woman, black or white, was as unlettered as a fencepost and about as ashamed of the deficiency. I could, in fact, read (this was my sworn secret from all but Mama and Cricket, for Mama had "learned me" my letters in the hope that someone, somehow, someday might teach me to do what she couldn't — combine them into words). And she was right, the trick was done by a tinker from Lebanon who was laid up in our livery stable in the winter of '57 while he healed his bone-sick horse. I had to bite my tongue whenever my master (for I was as owned as the Arab's horse), Joachim Deihl, gave up on a medicine label in frustration. But a "colored" boy reading was not to be tolerated even by a relatively tolerant Pennsylvania German like Deihl. Yes, I fought with John Brown. Old Captain

John Brown, and Tubman, too. In fact, I helped bury the Old Man, as I will tell. I could show you his grave, but we swore an oath, six of us, six thousand of us, so I won't. If General Tubman is the Mother of Our Country and Frederick Douglass the Father, our Dixie Bolivar, then bloody old Shenandoah Brown, the scourge of Kansas, the avenging angel of Osawatomie and the Swamp of the Swan, the terror of the Blue Ridge, is some kind of Godfather. Blood may be thicker than water, but politics is thicker than either, great-grandson, and I loved the old man. I count myself as much his kin as any of his actual sons, that brave abolitionist family band who were the boldest of all his soldiers, willing even at times to stand up to their captain, a thing which I saw no one (except Kagi) ever do. No, I never rode into battle with Captain John Brown, for he was too old and I was too young; he was as old as I am now, and I was as young as your own child, if you have one. But I fetched him his potboiled chicory-cut coffee on many a frosty morning while he and Tubman consulted with Green and stern Kagi. Then I watched him while he watched them ride off to war; then he would sit by the fire reading his Bible and his Mazzini while his coffee got cold, while I helped Doc Hunter make his rounds, but always keeping one eye on the Old Man as Doc ordered.

Many a frosty morning. Fifty years ago.

The backs of my hands on this typewriter tell me that I'm sixty-two now, an old man myself, but I was fourteen on those frosty wartime mountain mornings, sixteen when he died, and twelve when it all started on the Fourth of July, 1859, and it wasn't frosty that morning.

• • •

Staunton was getting to be a big town. The three-county Red Star of the South Dairy Co-op and the smaller poultry- and catfish-processing plants were gradually luring the last of the small farmers down from the hills and even a few of their children home from the Northern cities. The square ponds and dairies and the hillside orchards and flatland wheat stations up and down the valley were prospering. Yasmin only came to Virginia once a year, and even though she knew it was backward of her, she resented the changes that came with peace, socialism, and reconstruction: the new buildings, the treeless burbs, the smooth, metalled streets. Staunton wasn't her hometown, it was Leon's, and she resented the change because he had never lived to see them, because they marked with architectural precision how long it had been since his spectacular, world-famous death. Five trips. Twenty seasons. Three new growstone overpasses. He was, this early autumn afternoon, four new morning schools, a hundred houses, and one new stadium dead.

It was ungenerous, Yasmin knew. After decades of underdevelopment and years of civil war, the U.S.A., now the U.S.S.A., deserved a little prosperity. Leon, especially, would have wanted it. Leon, who had always loved his countrymen, even from exile. Leon, who had always welcomed the new.

Pearl, Leon's old-fashioned mother, lived near the center of town in the neat, tiny "rep" house that had been built ninety five years ago for her grandfather: part of the reparations for the n'Africans who had elected to stay north of the border, in the U.S.A., after the Independence War. Whether they had moved south to Nova Africa or not, all black people had been covered in the settlement. The little frame house was perfectly painted and trimmed. Pearl shared it with another widow, also in her sixties, "a white lady, deaf as a post but a church member," according to Pearl.

Pearl had been expecting her daughter-in-law since noon; she came to the screen door with flour on her hands and tears in her eyes. Yasmin always made her ring-mother cry, then usually cried herself, once a year like a short, welcome rainy season.

But this year was different, and even though Yasmin looked for them, her own tears wouldn't come.

Harriet was at the center, Pearl said—working on Sunday, was that what socialism was all about?—come on in. Not that Harriet would ever even consider going to church; she was like her daddy that way, God rest his soul, sit down. This was the week for the Mars landing, and Pearl found it hard to listen to on the radio until they had their feet on the ground, if ground was what they called it there, even though she wished them well and prayed for them every night. God didn't care what planet you were on; have some iced tea. Or even if you weren't on one at all. Sugar? So Pearl hoped Yasmin didn't mind if the radio was off.

Yasmin didn't mind. She sat at the kitchen table and sipped that unchanging-as-the-mountains sweet Virginia iced tea that she had never been able to bring herself to tell Pearl she couldn't stand, listening to Pearl talk while she rolled out pie dough for the social at the church. *What would God and Jesus do without their pies?* Yasmin wondered. They would neither of them ever have to find out. War, slavery, revolution, civil war, socialist reconstruction: nothing slacked the flow of chess, apple, pecan, and banana cream pies from the Appalachians. Pearl gave Yasmin the bowl to lick as if to remind her that, even at thirty-six, her boy's girl was still a kid to her.

Yasmin loved the little woman with her seamed glowing face, tiny mahogany hands ghosted with flour, white hair like a veil, tied up; loved her in that way women never get to love their own mothers because there is not enough unsaid, and too much said, between them.

Still. She decided not to tell Pearl her news. She would tell Harriet first. That was only fair.

The house felt stuffy and, as always, too filled with junk. Walking through the tiny rooms, Yasmin found the usual holograms of Douglass, Tubman, and Jesus oppressive; the familiar P.A.S.A. cosmonaut photo, with Leon mugging at the end of the row, had finally stopped tearing at her heart and now only tugged at it like a child pulling a sleeve.

She clicked on the vid and, at the sight of stars, as quickly clicked it off.

She decided to get her gifts out of the car.

Back in the kitchen, she helped Pearl tidy up and explained that she was only staying for the night. She had to leave first thing in the morning to take her great-grandfather's papers to Harper's Ferry, as specified in his will. Yes, she would be back to watch the Mars landing. Promise. Meanwhile, this was for Pearl. And she gave her ring-mother a helping basket from Arusha, showing her how it would grow or shrink, shaping itself to fit whatever was put into it.

"Wait till Katie Dee sees this," Pearl said. "She's deaf as a post, but she loves baskets."

"I didn't forget her. I brought her a scarf," Yasmin said, realizing even as she said it that it was scarves, not baskets, that her ring-mother loved. Why did she always get the little things backward? "But wait till you see what I brought Harriet." She patted the flat little box on the table, not even aware that she was listening for them until she heard the clatter of feet on the porch, shouted good-byes, and Harriet burst through the door. Twelve last summer, still all legs and hands and feet. Bearing in her face like an undimmed ancient treasure her daddy's goddamn big brown eyes.

• • •

On the Fourth of July, 1859, I was with old Deihl, winding up the Boonesborough Pike north of the Potomac, carrying a load of cedar posts to a cattleman in trade for a horse that was said to be lamed, but healed, but testy. Deihl owned a livery stable and speculated in "bad" horses. It was just before dawn on the Fourth of July. It wasn't our Independence Day then, great-grandson, like it is now, it was only theirs; but even "colored" boys like firecrackers, and I was busy figuring where I could get a few later that day. Old Deihl was snoring on the wagon seat as we passed a line of men in single file walking south, toward Harper's Ferry. They were all wrapped in cloaks, unusual for even a cool July morning, under which I caught—for a twelve-year-old misses nothing—the gleam of guns. At first I thought they were slave catchers, with which the Shenandoah was well supplied in those days, but several were Africans like myself; also, there was something strange about a crew so big. I counted thirty. In the back walked an old man in a slightly comical peaked hat with ear flaps, stranger still on a July morn; and beside him, in a long wool scarf, a n'African woman carrying a tow sack by the neck like a chicken, only swinging slow and heavy, as if it had gold inside. All of the men who filed by looked away nervously as they passed, except one, who smiled shyly and saluted me with two fingers. It's that little sad salute that I remember, after these fifty years. Though he seemed like a man to me then, at twelve, he was probably only a boy himself, maybe seventeen. He was white; I figure he was one of those who died, maybe gentle Coppoc or wild young Will Leeman; and I think he knew in his heart, for I am convinced boys know these things better than men, that he was marching off to die, and marching anyway—for what did he salute in me that morning, a skinny n'African kid on a jolting wagon seat: a brotherly soul? I was and still am at sixty-two. Maybe he was saying good-bye to all the things boys love: the things the rest of us take a whole lifetime saying good-bye to. But he went resolutely on, as they all did. Old Kate, Deihl's fifty-dollar wagon mule (he'd bought her for five) plodded steadily on up the pike, laying a rich, plunderous mule fart every hundred steps. Deihl snored on, put to sleep by them, as always. I've often thought that if I could have figured out a way to bottle mule farts and sell them back in the hills to old men, I could have stayed out of medicine altogether (and made several doctors I could mention happy, as well as myself, but that's another story). The woman, of course, was Tubman, with her big Allen & Thurber's .41 revolver, the very one that's in the Independence Museum in Charleston today. The old man was Brown in his Kansas war hat, given to him by a chief of the Ottawas, I forget his name. The rifles were all Sharps, as the Virginia militia was to find out the hard way. For though they were outnumbered, Brown's men had better weapons than any of the enemy they were to face over the next few years. At least in the beginning.

• • •

How do you tell your ring-mother you're pregnant? Especially when her son's been dead five years. Especially when his name happens to be on the damn vid every day. Especially when you're not married again. And don't want to be. And she's a Jubilation Baptist. And.

Yasmin would worry about it later, on the way back south to Nova Africa, after Harper's Ferry.

After telling Harriet.

They sat up not very late, the three of them, and talked of very little. Pearl was so uncurious about Africa that Yasmin wondered if she suspected something had happened there. Harriet went on and on about school. She had come to spend the usual month in Virginia with her granny; she had ended up starting school when her mother had been delayed two extra months in Dar es Salaam.

Yasmin's fingers were hungry to braid her daughter's hair, but Harriet had cut it almost too short, in the Merican style. So instead, she gave her her present. Excitedly, Harriet unwrapped the box and opened it. An icy little silver fog came out. Inside the box, nestled in sky blue moss, was a pair of slippers, as soft and formless as tiny gray clouds, but with thick cream-colored soles.

Pearl oohed and aahed, but Harriet looked puzzled.

"They're called living shoes," Yasmin said, "They're like the basket, only they change color and everything, and they never wear out. It's a new thing. They'll fit perfectly after a few days."

"Like yours?"

"No, these are just regular shoes." Yasmin held up one foot, clothed in a golden brown African high-top of soft leather that shimmered like oil on water. "Yours are special, honey. The living shoes are something new, just developed; you can't even buy them yet. The Olduvai team helped get this pair from Kili especially for you. To apologize for keeping me over."

Harriet thought this over. *So are they from you or them?* she wondered. She picked up one slipper; it was warm and cold at the same time and felt creepy. They looked like house slippers.

Why couldn't her mother have brought her beautiful shoes, like her own?

"The only thing is, they're like earrings," Yasmin said, kneeling down to slip the shoe on her daughter's foot. "Once you put them on, you have to leave them on for a week."

"A week?"

After Harriet went to bed, Yasmin sat up, brooding. "Don't be discouraged," Pearl said. "The child has missed you. Plus, even though she doesn't say it, all this Mars business troubles her too. Be patient with her.

"Now come over here, child, and let me fix your hair."

. . .

Harriet got up early so that she could walk to school with her friends one last time. It felt funny to want and not want something at the same time. She wanted to get home to Nova Africa, but she would miss her friends here in the U.S. She waited with the girls on the street in front of the school, hoping the bell would ring, hoping it wouldn't. The new shoes looked like house slippers with thick soles.

"Harriet, did you hurt your foot?" Betty Ann asked.

"My mother brought me these from Africa," Harriet said. "They're living shoes, so I can't take them off for a week. They're like earrings."

"They look nice," Lila said, trying to be nice.

"They don't look like earrings to me," Elizabeth said.

"They gave my granny shoes like that in the hospital," said Betty Ann. "And then she died."

"Oh, wow," the girls all said. Harriet's mother pulled up to the curb in her long university car, too early. The girls were used to the little inertial hummers, and the university's Egyptian sedan was twenty feet long. Its great hydrogen engine rumbled impressively. Harriet didn't tell them they were driving it because her mother was afraid to fly.

Yasmin watched from the car while the girls traded hugs and whispers and promises to write and shell rings—all but Harriet and one other, white girls; all in the current (apparently worldwide) teenage uniform of madras and rows of earrings in the Indian fashion. No boys yet. If Yasmin remembered correctly, they lurked in the background at this age, in clumps, indistinguishable like trees.

The precious living shoes she had brought her daughter looked shapeless and drab next to the cheap, bright, folded-over high-tops the Merican girls were wearing. Yasmin watched as Harriet tried to hide her feet. Well, what did they know about shoes out here in the boondocks?

"What's this?" Harried said, opening the car door and eyeing the doctor's bag on the front seat.

"This is your great-great-grandfather," Yasmin said. "Let's put him in the back seat. He won't mind. He's only twelve, anyway."

It was good to hear the child laugh. On the way down to the valley, Yasmin suggested to Harriet that after dropping off her great-great-grandfather's papers at the museum in Harper's Ferry, maybe they should spend the night. "It'll give us some time to hang out together before we head back to Charleston and work and school. I can tell you all about Africa."

Harriet liked the idea. She reached back and opened the bag. It had a funny pill smell.

"I knew great-granddaddy fought with Brown," she said. "I didn't know there were any secrets."

"Brown and Tubman," Yasmin corrected. Why was it always just

Brown? "And it was great-great. And he didn't actually fight with them. And I didn't say secret papers. The story is the same one you've heard all your life in bits and pieces. He just wanted the original to be in the museum. This is the actual paper that he wrote fifty years ago, in 1909. It's like a little piece of himself he wanted buried there."

"Creepy." Harriet closed the bag.

"Oh, Harriet! Anyway, I couldn't take it on the Fourth, since the dig wasn't finished yet, and—what with one thing and another, I was held up in Dar. . . ."

There it was. Yasmin smiled secretly, feeling the little fire in her belly. At this stage it came and went at its own pleasure, but when it came it was very nice. "So we're going now," she finished. "You and I."

"There was a big celebration on the Fourth," Harriet said. "I watched it on vid."

"Aren't you going to ask me about Africa?" Yasmin said, searching for a way to begin to tell her the good news. How do you tell your daughter you're pregnant? Especially when her father's never been buried? Especially when. . . .

"Why didn't you ask me?" Harriet said.

"Ask you what?"

"Ask me to go. I could have taken the papers to Harper's Ferry. Then they would have been there for the Fourth."

Yasmin was embarrassed. It had never occurred to her.

"I'm his relative too. I was here the whole time."

The *Martin Delaney* motored past, but Yasmin didn't race it this time. The high whine of the differential plasma motors sounded complaining, not joyful. She searched her belly, but the little fire was gone.

• • •

The airship looked like an ice cream sandwich, with the ice-blue superconductor honeycomb, trailing mist, sandwiched between the dark cargo hull below and the excursion decks above. While Harriet watched, the honeycomb blinked rapidly: the ship was making a course correction, and it existed and didn't almost simultaneously for a few seconds. Then all was steady again. Weighing slightly less than nothing, and with slightly more than infinite mass, it sailed north-ward as unperturbed as a planet in its orbit.

Harriet waved two fingers enviously as the ship glided way. From up there the world was beautiful. There was nothing to see from the ground but catfish ponds and wheat fields and country towns, one after another, as interesting as fence posts.

She punched on the radio, double-clicking on the news, then dou-ble-clicking again on Mars. Until her mother gave her that look.

"It's not that I'm not interested, honey," Yasmin said. "We'll be back at your grandmother's to watch the landing. I don't want her watching it alone. I just don't want to exactly hear the play-by-play until then, you understand?

"Sure."

• • •

Two hours later, they were in Charles Town. Yasmin turned east at the courthouse toward Harper's Ferry. The road ran straight between well-kept farms, some still private. The wheat was still waiting for the international combine teams, working their way north from Nova Africa; but a few local hydrogen-powered corn pickers were out, their unmuffled internal-combustion engines rattling and snorting. Yasmin saw a green-gabled house at least a hundred years old and started to point it out to Harriet, thinking it was the very one in the story in the doctor's bag in the backseat, Green Gables. But no, hadn't that one burned? Besides, Harriet was asleep.

The shoes did look plain. There was something you were supposed to do with living shoes, to train them, but Yasmin couldn't remember what it was. She sighed. Her reunion with her daughter was not off to a very good start. Oh well, things could only get better. Ahead, the Blue Ridge, blue only from the east, was red and gold. Neatly tucked under it at the gap was Harper's Ferry, where the Independence War began.

• • •

By noon I had unloaded the fence posts while Deihl dickered and spat in Low German with the owner, and we started back with the new horse tied to the wagon; he was indeed a skittery character. His name was Caesar, which I spelled in my mind, "Sees Her," for I had not yet formed that acquaintance with the classics which was to enrich my later years, and will I hope yours as well, great-grandson. The owner, a breakaway Amish, said he had bought the horse lamed from two Tidewater gentlemen passing through; it made a Southern horse nervous, he joked, to live so close to the Mason-Dixon line, which ran, he said, at the very bottom of the field in which we stood. He pointed out the fence row. Sees Her munched hay out of the wagon bed as we headed back south, and Deihl unwrapped the sausage biscuits Mama had sent with us. Deihl was stingy with words, but he shared a pull of cider from the jug he kept under the seat; he was no respecter of youth in the matter of drink, but who was in those days? I lay out in the back of the wagon with my head under the seat out of the sun and went to sleep. Deihl went to sleep driving, and unless I miss my guess Kate went to sleep pulling, which mules can do. I was dreaming of soldiers, perhaps influenced by the little band I'd seen before dawn; or perhaps my second wife was right when she said I had the second sight; or perhaps the Amish was right and Sees Her smelled abolition; certainly he was to live the rest of his life surrounded by the smell: the horse woke me up whickering nervously. I sat up and heard popping that I thought at first was Fourth of July firecrackers. We were on the Maryland side of the Potomac, near Sandy Hook. The railroad bridge to the west was burning, or at least smoking mightily. A train was stopped on the Virginia side, leaking steam, and men with rifles were swarming all over it. Every once in a while one of them let off a shot toward the sky. A soldier watching from the riverbank rode into town with us. Deihl didn't waste words asking what had happened because he knew we'd be told with no prompting. The town had been attacked by an army of a hundred abolitionists, the soldier said. He'd been sent with a detachment from Charles Town to guard the railroad bridge, but too late. The mayor, who was pretty universally liked, was dead, and so was a free black man named Hayward, who worked for the railroad. The soldier though it was a great irony that a free "nigger" had been shot, since the attackers were "abs." The papers were to make much of this also; but since almost half the population of the Ferry was n'African, and almost half of that free, or what passed for free in those days, I don't know how it could have been otherwise. George Washington's grandson and a score of other Virginians had been killed, the soldier said. He had a chaw the size of a goiter and spat into the wagon straw, and I kept expecting Deihl to straighten him out, but he didn't. Coming past the end of the railroad bridge, we saw that the tracks had been spiked and two of the bridge pilings knocked over by a blast. The railroad workers were standing around looking either puzzled or disgusted, and one of them joined us for a ride across the wagon bridge into town. He'd been drinking freely. He spat into the hay too, and still Deihl said nothing. I remember watching him spit uncorrected and thinking: what's this world coming to? Sees Her was tossing his head and whickering, but Kate was steady. In the town the hotel and several other buildings were still smoldering. There was a wild, scary smoke smell: the smell all of us in Virginia were to come in the next few years to recognize as the smell of war. There was no fighting, but armed men were all over the streets looking fierce, bored, and uneasy at the same time. I felt my black face shining provocatively and would have not hidden it but damped its blackness down if I could. The railroad men and the soldier both said "Kansas Brown" was behind the raid, as if the name had deep significance. White folks made much of Brown, though I had never heard his name nor had any of the slaves until that day, when he became more famous among us than Moses at one stroke, and not as "Kansas" or "Osawatomie" Brown but as Shenandoah Brown. The railroad man told how the hotel had been torched and in the confusion Brown and his men had retreated across the Shenandoah into the Loudon Heights, which is what we called the Blue Ridge there. They had fast-firing breech-loading Sharps rifles. Once in the laurel thickets, who would follow them? "Not the Virginny milisshy," the soldier said, laughing. "They're at the tavern a-soaking their wounds in gov'mint whiskey." I will attempt no more dialect. The railroad man seemed to take the soldier's words for an insult and sulked and spat, wordless from there on. The soldier's cut was not altogether true, anyway, I found out later: four of the "Virginias" had been killed in the fighting before falling back, all upon one another. I felt a deep, harmonious excitement stealing over me, though I did not at the time truly understand the events or what they meant. Who did, Merican or n'African?

HOMING INSTINCT

DANI MCCLAIN

"GREEDY" IS THE WORD THAT COMES TO MIND. AS THE ANNOUNCE-
ment's meaning sunk in, I got greedy for the 70 degree days in the
middle of February and the way sunlight bounces off the leaves of jade
green succulents no matter what time of year. How the air—even in
the middle of downtown Oakland—smells like flowers (yes, and weed
and sometimes urine). The options always presenting themselves: look
toward the hills and see yellows and browns and the promise of a place
where the wind blows a little less; or look toward the bay and see it
glistening like a sheet of light, dotted with sails and bits of sky

I got greedy for things that likely wouldn't be around much longer
anyway.

As I listened to Breslow speak, my mind wandered to the parties at
the New Parish and, before that, Oasis, places where old Stevie Wonder jams and Chaka Khan remixes brought back memories of childhood. The Malcolm X Jazz Festival in East Oakland and the Ashby
flea market, the same people always turning up at all the same places.

When EO 3735 came down, I got nostalgic for the things around
me. It should have made the decision easy, but it didn't. Paloma, on
the other hand, knew immediately.

"I'm staying here," she told me just moments after the press conference at which the executive order was announced. Because the situation
was so dire, the president had said, everyone would have ninety days to
reposition themselves. That was the word she had used: *reposition*.

"They couldn't even put it to a vote?" I said to Paloma, realizing
that this would be the only conversation that mattered for the fore-
seeable future.

"Why? So the people who still believe all that snow proves the climate isn't changing can get on TV? If it had gone through Congress, we'd have to listen to their ignorant rants get equal time with the scientists and the people who won't let their fear override what's in plain sight."

We'd watched the speech together and talked it over from every angle we could think of once the president had answered her final question and walked offstage and away from the press corps.

"I'm glad Breslow just went ahead and said, 'Here's what's up: figure out where you want to be and get there. And quit all this jumping on planes, trains, and automobiles all the time like your presence is so desperately needed at this meeting and that conference and this family reunion and that weekend getaway.'"

Paloma was from Chicago but she knew her home was Oakland. It didn't feel so cut and dry to me.

• • •

I walked home thinking that if the Breslow administration were smart, it would hire Paloma to do a series of PSAs. For the print ads, it could just be her face, serious and resolute, eyes staring straight ahead. The caption in bold, block text would read, "COMMIT." For the online and broadcast versions, it could be her voice saying something like, "When you move"—and the phrase would hang in the air while you watched quick takes from footage of the latest disasters: a shot from the Outer Banks of North Carolina when they still existed, the wind whipping giant waves into the cottages and splintering their stilts to shreds—"you prove"—and now the stampede on the Venetian Causeway during the Miami Beach exodus—"that you don't get it." The now iconic images of people swimming in the streets of New Orleans would fill the screen as Paloma said, her voice heavy with disappointment and judgment, "You still don't get it."

Playing off of people's fear, their memories of the disasters no one even bothered calling "natural" anymore, was key here. The relationships between water and land, between humans and the weather, *had* changed dramatically. And, yes, it was long overdue for a political leader to demand that people stop living in the fantasy of the infinite.

But this change, this new emergency rule that mandated that people lock themselves into a location, was replacing the fantasy of the infinite with the fantasy that immobility would bring safety. The new lie around which people were to orient their lives was the possibility of buffering one's self from the chaos and destruction that had come to define the times.

The first questions at the press conference had, surprisingly, been the right ones:

What happens if people decide not to register their location in the database?

Aren't you creating the conditions for a black market in travel?

Won't the people who need food and shelter sell their mile allotments to people who can afford and want them?

Aren't you making mobility a luxury item?

And then came the expected ones:

Isn't travel expression? Isn't this a violation of the First Amendment?

Will the government take over the airlines, the high-speed trains? Will all transport be socialized?

Breslow had delivered her answers with a calm and diplomacy that made phrases explode in my mind like popcorn kernels in hot oil. "sex for sky miles," "rooftop heliports." I remembered reading about dog collars that sent a shock when the animal got too close to an invisible fence. What would be the logistics of this new boundary? In the absence of knowing, my mind ran wild: women would be selling their bodies to get a flight to a dying parent's bedside. The people who marched around in knee breeches and three-cornered hats screaming about the founders would pull their usual publicity stunts, protesting EO 3735 for all the wrong reasons. But would they resist? Would anyone? Why refuse to register and be shipped off to an up- or out-state federal penitentiary, the fate Breslow had said resisters would meet? By the time I got to my apartment, I'd decided that anyone who went that route was a fool. Why refuse if it meant having someone else choose home for you?

• • •

The next day, the administration announced its title for the mandate: Operation HOMES (Honoring Our Most Enduring Settings).

A secondary goal of this thing was to get people to move away from the coasts, the places the oceans reclaimed for themselves more and more each year. There would be financial incentives for people who chose to leave the Gulf Coast and parts of California and the Eastern seaboard. They would get "sky miles" (the government had jacked the phrase from the airlines) added to their allotments.

Commentators had already found a way to turn this into a political debate, as if various Republican and Democratic perspectives were relevant as people scrambled to make personal decisions. I took a break from following the commentators and the presentations and called my mom back east.

We danced around it for as long as we could, talking instead about what this pundit had said about the policy and what that news report had revealed about how it would be enforced. We touched on the high points from the coverage—the man who had broken down crying as he recounted that his wife had told him in no uncertain terms that she and the kids would be moving to Virginia to be close to her family and that he could do what he liked, the Wisconsinite who stood thigh-deep in snow declaring that she was a seventh-generation Badger and those goddamn Floridians better not flood her pristine state. Well, the news had bleeped out one word, but you could see it forming on her blue lips.

Finally my mother asked the obvious: "What do you think you'll do?"

She had always accepted my wanderlust. More than accepted, she'd financed it at the start and encouraged it once I wanted her blessings more than her money. And though it had meant we hadn't lived in the same state for more than a decade, she had settled into the rhythms: I would be home a week in the summer and a week at Christmas, and Mom would travel west so we could spend time together at Thanksgiving, and another week together in the spring. A month total. One out of twelve. That's what we had together. The new law capped all oil-dependent travel at twenty miles per month. So it would take either one of us ten years of sacrificing all other car or plane trips to save up the miles needed to close the distance between California and Ohio.

I knew she was thinking it, so I went ahead and said it: say I had a child. Say it happened this year. You would be able to meet your grandchild when she or he was what, nine? And that's if I chose to make my birthplace my first destination. What if I wanted to go someplace else? Take the child to some part of the ocean that was warm and calm enough to swim in? Or to another country, to see how other people lived? When would we see each other again, and how would it feel when we finally did?

People in Washington weren't talking about this new law like it was a temporary measure. When it was discussed, there was never an expiration date attached. It was the new way. It was the new scaffolding for our lives.

"What do you think you'll do?" she asked.

I took a deep breath and fought the urge to hold it. "What would you like me to do?"

She chuckled. "I know better than that, missy. What do you want? Hasn't that always been what I told you to figure out first?"

"Yep. Sure has been." Now silence was heavy in the exchange. "I haven't figured it out yet. Yesterday I told myself I had a week to decide. So that's what I'm taking."

"Did you make your pros and cons lists?"

I laughed, thankful for the constancy of my mother's belief that logic and the length of one list measured against another could solve any problem the world threw at you.

"Yes, ma'am. I'm just starting them," I said, but of course I didn't plan to. I already knew everything that would go into a column making a case for staying in Oakland. The list would confirm my fears that I was an individualist to the bone, that I had turned into someone who placed personal comfort and loose camaraderie above the bonds of blood and going—instinctively, without the need to think it through—where family needs you and you know you need them.

If I couldn't be safe—and I couldn't, no one could—I should face the chaos shoulder to shoulder with the people whose love and care I'd been able to count on for decades, right? And I should pick the place where those people were concentrated, yes? The answers should have been obvious, and I'd always thought that when push came to shove, I'd know what to do. But they weren't and I didn't.

• • •

Some people were angry drunks or got sloppy and far too certain of their own wit or brilliance after too many glasses of wine. Paloma got spiritual. Or rather, a little liquor made her willing to talk about ideas she usually kept close to the vest, ideas that could easily be used against her by anyone looking to paint a picture of the Bay Area as home to a set of loopy, half-serious seekers who stayed high on positive thinking and law of attraction bromides.

We were at Tony's apartment, and I washed the dinner dishes and listened. The first sign was that Paloma had used the word "transformative" at least three times in a handful of sentences as she spoke to the group that had gathered to pretend their lives weren't about to radically change. Similar indicators followed. Paloma, who had been my bestie for more than a decade, first referenced "the universe" as the source of her strength in the midst of EO 3735 talk, then thanked "the most high" for keeping her grounded.

A petite, intense woman named Robin spoke. "You need to be thanking President Breslow. She's about to keep you grounded for real."

I smiled and looked away from the sink and toward the table where my friends sat.

"Go ahead, laugh," Paloma said, her face relaxed as she set down her wine glass. "Y'all know about that river flowing fast these days. It's so great and swift that some will be afraid. They will try to hold onto the shore. They'll feel like they are being torn apart, and they will suffer greatly." The lilt dropped from her voice as she said with a wink, "That's not you, is it Rob? 'Cause I don't want to be the one that has to come pry your hands off that shore, girl. I really don't."

Robin raised her eyebrows and shook her head slowly. "Nope. That's not me. I know the river has its destination. Now go ahead. Finish preaching, Reverend Doctor."

Tony jumped in instead, continuing the lines. "But we all know we must let go of the shore, push off toward the middle of the river, keep our eyes open, and our heads above the water."

I sat down at the table, drying my hands on the front of my jeans. "See who is there with us and celebrate," Tony added.

It was just something that had gotten shared around. A message attributed to the old holders of an even older wisdom in a place none of us had ever been, somewhere in Arizona with a vowel-heavy name where Native people had decided to advise anyone who'd listen on how to live. It was very likely the Internet ramblings of some Berkeley hippie who honestly believed "Hopi elders" had asked him to communicate on their behalf. But Paloma had been taken by its pointed questions—"Where are you living? What are you doing? What are your relationships? Where is your water?"—the message's urgency and the way it seemed to point a path toward accepting and making sense of a nonsensical and ever-changing world. She had painted some of the words in black block letters on a huge canvas and decorated the remaining space with images of pregnant women, gardens in bloom, children dancing, and a pack of wolves howling together at the moon. When Paloma had mounted it on a wall in her living room, we all praised her artistry, but I admit I rolled my eyes a bit at the Earth Mama archetypes.

That night in Tony's kitchen, I realized the message had lodged itself in our minds, finding a place to settle amidst the cynicism, fear, and doubt.

• • •

Later that night, I dreamed that the sky was red and the air smelled like burnt oranges—tangy and smoky in a way that made my mouth water and my eyes tear up. I knew I was on a long and likely futile walk eastward, with no maps or sense of direction other than the knowledge that I was walking away from the ocean and toward a place called Nevada, followed by a stretch called Utah, followed by an obstacle course called Colorado, followed by an expanse called Nebraska and on and on. I walked toward the hills and eventually through the Caldecott Tunnel, and after that I knew nothing other than that I was passing the towns where men had tested open carry laws in Starbucks, so bold in their love for the Second Amendment that they brandished their guns like shiny new toys. I looked up at the sky and knew that it was always some shade of red or orange now, everywhere. I knew that to the west, in the direction I had come from, redwoods were dying, toppling over on each other with loud, disastrous sounds like a chorus of whips cracking at once. And to the east, in the direction I was headed, great lakes were drying into exaggerated puddles. I stood still and felt a cold prickling move like a wave through my body. I knew that feeling. It was my body accepting some hard truth before my mind was ready to. The sensation was there as I woke up, and with it a clear string of words echoing in my head: "not a place to live, but a way of living."

• • •

My body traveled its normal paths the next day, but my attention was elsewhere. In the shower I wondered who I could trust. Paloma? My cousin whose libertarian leanings sometimes brought us to the same conclusions? Were there others whose minds had already landed here (there had to be), and, if so, how would I find them? How would we find each other, and what would we do once we did? Walking the blocks to the BART station I considered what I might need and how I could possibly prepare. I had my idée fixe—that phrase stuck in my head and pulled me forward. Toward what and how, I had no idea.

Without warning, my thoughts ran full speed into a wall of fear that left me paralyzed, nervous about having peeked through this door that was opening. Some part of my consciousness, deputized by the Breslow administration, kicked the door shut, admonished me for even thinking that path was a possibility. I muttered a silent apology to the watcher within and shrank back from the risk, the threat of punishment. And that's how I remained until I found myself that afternoon ostensibly typing an email to my boss but unconsciously straining to remember all I could about Fred Korematsu. Assata Shakur. Others who had hidden, escaped, run, resisted.

By the time I was home again that evening, I was clear. Sure, the law was right to urge people to think about where the land could actually sustain them. But geography was not destiny. Nowhere was safe and nothing was infinite, and to impose a law predicated on an outdated belief in stability was immoral. I would not obey an immoral law. Instead, I decided to let go of the shore, the nostalgia, the need for certainty. I thought of Tony, Robin, and the others, my family in Ohio, people I knew all over the country. Who among them would refuse to register and what would they do once they did? When I pushed off toward the middle of the river—if I could keep my eyes open and my head above the water—who would I see there in the torrent?

[HILDREN WHO FLY

LEAH LAKSHMI PIEPZNA-SAMARASINHA

For Kumari Indigo Frances Piepzna-Samarasinha

KUNJU, YOUR MOM SAID SHE KNEW YOU WANTED TO BE BORN. SHE DIDN'T want you to be abused, but some things, they don't change, or they don't change enough. That's where you came in.

Kumari wakes up and watches her breath. The shack is made out of a thin layer of reclaimed cedar, rainbow layers of old wool sweaters staple-gunned to the inside of the walls to keep out the chill. Oakland in November 2032 is warmer than it used to be but still colder than anyone wants to admit, hot planet be damned, and East Bay folks still remain in denial that it is not always summer here because we live in California. She swings her legs off the side of the mattress, stands up and stretches. Reaches for some old black and pink ASICS and bends over to lace them up. They were her mom's. This was her mother's shack. Her mother died last year.

She pushes the double door open, steps out into a dew-wet, shaggy back garden. Fucking endless kale, sunflowers crisping in November, dry grass with lush roots above raised beds above the lead. Walks to the gate, then breaks into a run.

It was hard for the ancestors to think of dissociation as positive. Back in the day when Amma was around, back when she was a riot grrl sulky teenager in the nineties (the nineties!), everyone was still ashamed. They didn't even have words yet. Like disassociation? That's that thing that makes it so you can't feel it when you fuck? So you look at your leg and go that's my leg? What does that mean, it's my leg? Just some hunk of meat down there. *Back when her mom was a kid-kid, they didn't even have those zines, those whispers, and folded pieces of paper. They had solid bodies of rage and trauma that never had a chance to be whisper-shouted out. Just got passed on.*

Amma was Generation One on the big butcher paper on the wall of the U.S. Social Forum 2010. You, kids, you are Generation Two.

Kumari pushes the gate open and starts trotting down Stuart Street. When the ocean rose, it stopped right at Sacramento, and, inshallah, the sea dikes and barriers and marvelous human-engineered ecosystems stay working, it means they are three short blocks from the beach. To run next to earth and sky and water, the smell of salt and oil, hunks of highway 80 poking up through the sea. The sharks that glint, come inland from the Farrallons, the ones that lived through nuclear warheads dropped and left for fifty years by a Navy sub. When she hits the crumbling street, its ruined gas station and liquor store, its gardens, she turns right and breaks into a faster run. She is late. Two blocks of crumbling pier ahead, her fam are waiting.

What happens when you are raped early and young? When your amygdala and cerebral cortex are still forming? When your lizard brain and limbic system are raw and open, still governing your body's choices? Instinct, smell, and memory. What happens when your pussy and cock are touched in a way that maybe breaks open that third eye into a canal you can escape through?

They call it the opening.

"Your Amma was a child of Oya, you know," Luis uncle said once, a couple months ago. They were sitting at the old dining room table in front of the janky ancestral altar, nonworking gas fireplace, and the "open hearted: love freely, love fearlessly" poster Kiran aunty made tacked above it. Ze stirred hir coffee at the old kitchen table. Hir eyes a galaxy, streaked with aging Fishnet shadow from a 2015 vintage Urban Decay palate. Lavender magenta over taupe golden streaks to the brow bone.

This table was old when Amma got it, when she moved into the house at thirty-four. She kicked the table. "I know. She used to say it all the time: 'Am I too old to roll my eyes?' Didn't she ever think it was culturally appropriative or something? Since she was Sri Lankan and white, not African?"

Luis gave an elegant shrug, looking away and sipping. "It was easier to get into orisha than to find some kind of diasporic Dravidian Hindu temple that was queer positive. She was always respectful of Kali, but she found some Luisah Teish book at the Buck-a-Book Barn in Worcester when she was ten, and she and Oya, they always had an affinity. She was a daughter of Oya and a Taurus. She'd always said that it was like being cosmically topped by the goddess all the time. 'No, wait, stop, mama! No more change! I've figured out the Method!' And Oya would put her hand on her hip and slap her around a little more, send her spinning. Whirling skirt don't play."

"I know all that."

Luis looked at her over the plate. "So when are you going to do something with it? You're her daughter."

Go up.

Your mom did all those somatics and trauma weekend intensives in the Bay in the early 2000s, back before so much horrible, back when friends of hers still had that exotic thing called jobs. The workshops that left you tender and spent, ripped open and new. Back when life was still on that cusp of bougie organizer. Broke but organic honey fig lavender ice cream in Rockridge and shit on your EBT. Back before more horrible things than you could imagine happened. Nuclear warheads going off under Antarctica, no salmon for a decade and a half, the beautiful, raging, dead ocean. You did all those courses and what you knew a little bit of in the women's therapy collective of El Cerrito in 2010— feeling warmth in your belly like tiger lilies smeared with yellow pollen from love and safety and sex, the stank meat-locker chill of cold blood when you leave through your left armpit—you know how to do it when you want to now. You close your eyes and envision those tiger lilies in your belly, the wet smell of that pond in Princeton, Massachusetts, nature sanctuary 1995, that secret Detroit river fold where you took your lover summer of 2012, yes, at the Allied Media Conference, sticky mango yellow tube top over browning humid skin, how happy you always were at that confluence of river bend, Rust Belt city, and revolutionary holiday. You can call those memories and you come rushing back, but you can also call them up, go deep inside the gut, and then spiral out through the ladder of your breath. All those years post you know how to leave your body. Now go up.

The Piepznas, the long-lost Ukrainian roots of Kumari's family, have always been psychic when it comes to heartbreak and disaster. Great-great-grandma Pat woke up in the middle of the night and walked down to where the pilot light had gone out and the gas was leaking in 1975 Watertown, Massachusetts, and turned it off before it could kill her daughter and husband. Screamed and threw her arm in front of her husband just before the pickup-driving drunk barreled out of the hidden driveway and would've killed them all. Amma knew when she was about to get dumped via text message in the middle of her fifteenth underfunded queer and trans people of color art tour, 8 a.m. in Los Angeles. Told a lover she dallied with one fall that he would hurt his new lover badly in the fourth month, that the lover would move to New York and break his heart in the ninth month. She waited to see if you would get the gift.

Kumari, she can't see everything, but she can see some things.

There's a whole grip of kids sitting on the pier, cross-legged, waiting. Some wear filter masks; some wear nothing. There are jagged blocks of ex-highway stone and pavement, all tore up.

A lot fell apart. Some people are lucky and live in places that are too toxic to be valuable, but not enough to kill you. Not yet.

All the parents are dead. Mostly. Plutonium leaking. Bombs set off. A weakened ozone shield. The highest concentration of all the cooperative economics and passive solar and transformative justice healing circles in the world can only do so much. War and plague and all those translucent immune systems. All those 2000s thirty-year-olds, they got sick in their forties. Died in their late fifties after a lot of community acupuncture.

The parents died, but left them this.

They nod and circle. Grasp hands. Close eyes. Length, width, depth. Go down. Root. Breathe.

They don't have a lot left, in these zones. Akwesasane, Detroit, the remnants of the East Bay, the fractured necklace of outposts, the care webs, were almost destroyed when everything was almost destroyed. They have backyards. Each other. Big bags of hoarded grains in the pantries. Mushrooms for toxins and tinctures out of looted vodka. What they have always had. And they have this. This is what is working, more than guns or negotiation, to win the war that is left.

Amma, thank you for teaching me.

Kumari closes her eyes, and her spirit leaves her body like all those years ago, but on purpose this time. All the way out her right foot. She can see it trickle out, on purpose. Not gray dead meat. Orange tiger lilies, smeared pollen. She is on the ceiling of the sky, watching. It is so effortless, delicious. She can taste the colors her spirit hovers in. The tongue tip of that lavender cloud, the ways all the colors taste and smell when there are no words to bind them. She can feel it. Then she moves.

It's corny, right? The spirit plane. But really, it's just familiar. The place you go every night when you dream. The place you go when you get on your knees, to that rickety little fruit crate altar, all splintery with cloth from a thrift store called Courage My Love in Kensington Market, Toronto, and an assembly of brown girl, corner-store botanica saints and novelties.

She feels them too. Not alone. The difference with this one is that no one is alone. Some were raped. Some were just taught how to do this. Maybe the weakened ozone shield, the radiation, all the planet's open trauma, has been birthed in them too. It is so much easier than it used to be to come out the top of the forehead.

There are still kids being raped. There are still prisons, functioning in the middle of the gaping maw of utter disaster. There are still bombs being made.

This is what they have.

Back in 2010, Morgan aunty wrote that article for Amma's book, about telling a story that was still being written. It is. Still being written.

Cleveland? Someone thinks or feels toward her. She experiences it as peacock feathers, azure breath, the ghost of a word.

Yes, she feels back. Lavender simple pulse of yes from breastbone. They move.

STAR WARS AND THE AMERICAN IMAGINATION

MUMIA ABU-JAMAL

WHEN *STAR WARS* PREMIERED, IN 1977, IT SWEPT THE NATION LIKE A fever.

Lines circled blocks, and before long it was more than a movie—it was a craze.

TV commercials hawked wares emblazoned with *Star Wars* figures, available from McDonald's—"Get yours now!"

Before all was said and done, the movie grossed nearly half a billion dollars That's "billion"—with a "b."

I was, however, out of the loop.

In 1977, I was in my twenty-third year of life, and the targeted demographic was preteen and teen, rather than post-teen.

Besides, I was more of a *Star Trek* guy (and it didn't hurt that one of the stars of the Trekkie universe was a Black beauty who blazed the screen like a dark, luscious comet every time she appeared).[1] That said, I watched with fascination as the lines grew, and other film companies tried to copy the moneymaking magic of the *Star Wars* franchise (they usually failed miserably, however).

Why did *Star Wars* strike such a deep and jangling nerve? Why did it become a craze, one that seemed to surprise everyone—critics, the movie's executives, all, it seemed, except producer George Lucas?

The nation had just recently been forced to submit to a seemingly uncivilized (as in low-tech) enemy, and it faced the generational rebellion of the '60s.

---

1   To the uninitiated, the author here refers to actress Nichelle Nichols, who performed as Lt. Uhura of the *Trek* bridge crew —Eds.

Vietnam syndrome permeated the entire culture, not just the political elites.

The younger were virtually uniformly antiwar in their orientation, and a counterculture was sweeping the nation, changing dress, hairstyles, sexual mores, food consumption, and the way national minorities were perceived and perceived themselves.

In short, the land was in the midst of a cultural and political rebellion, sparked, in large part, by resistance to an unpopular war.

An American president (R. M. Nixon) had recently resigned several months after his vice president, and some of his top aides (including Attorney General John Mitchell) were sent to prison, the human detritus of the Watergate scandal.

In this context, why would a movie, even one set in another world, find appeal when the heroes were a ragtag bunch of rebels, decidedly low-tech, fighting against a fearsome, militarily invincible empire?

Part of the success of *Star Wars* was its undeniable youth appeal, yet there must be deeper reasons for its cultural resonance.

America, the Empire, didn't like its role (at least among its young). It wanted to reimagine itself as the ragtag band, fighting against great odds, against an evil empire.

It imagined itself as it wanted to be, as it had claimed to be in its infancy against a cruel and despotic king in the late eighteenth century.

It reshaped itself into the rebels, not the imperial overlords.

It shaped itself as oppressed, fighting for freedom.

But America, like every nation, has its ages of psychosis. It has fits of indecision and periods of self-delusion.

Consider how presidents spoke movingly of "freedom from tyranny" while personally holding hundreds of men, women, and children in slavery.

Or imagine Jefferson, the Sage of Monticello, who was the father of half-Black children, at the same moment as he wrote, in his only book *Notes on the State of Virginia*, that Black people were essentially nonhuman, a species related to the orangutan. (Does this mean that he saw himself as being into bestiality? Or did this mean he really thought his children were, well, half monkey?).

Americans, like any people, are subject to delusions.

Was this fascination with *Star Wars* and the national identification with the rebels one of them?

For generations, Americans have declined to define themselves as imperialists. That's what our enemies called us. That wasn't what we called ourselves.

We were for freedom. We were for self-determination. We were good. We were white (mostly).

We were Luke Skywalker, not Darth Vader, and definitely not the cruel, warped emperor!

Yet aficionados of the *Star Wars* saga know that Luke and Darth were, after all, intimately related.

Darth's infamous line at their light saber battle has become a cultural byword: "I am your father, Luke!"

It is a measure of Lucas's genius that he scripts that moment of self-realization, of self-discovery and revelation.

In the grisly aftermath of a war that tore millions from the face of Asia, all to cover for the corporate exploitation of Vietnam's bauxite and other natural resources, the imperial shock trooper, the imperial, metallic death's hand, was father to the rebel.

They were, in fact, more than related.

In truth, they were one.

That is the meaning of *Star Wars*: we *were* rebels; we *are* Empire.

And like all rebellious children, we were but going through a phase.

We are getting ready for adulthood, after we sowed a few wild oats.

Once grown, we put on our imperial uniform, and bowed to the Empire.

"It is your destiny."

Right? Unless—

THE ONLY LASTING TRUTH

THE THEME OF CHANGE IN THE WORKS OF OCTAVIA E. BUTLER[1]

TANANARIVE DUE

"I'm a 46-year-old writer who can remember being
a 10-year-old writer and who expects someday to be an
80-year-old writer. I'm also comfortably asocial—a hermit in
the middle of Los Angeles—a pessimist if I'm not careful, a
feminist, a Black, a former Baptist, an oil-and-water combination of ambition, laziness, insecurity, certainty, and drive."

—Octavia E. Butler, "About the Author,"
Mind of My Mind

If I SQUINT MY EYES JUST RIGHT, I CAN ALMOST SEE HER RIGHT HERE
in this room. An aspiring writer like all of you—a gangly giant who'd
been six feet tall since she was fifteen after a growth spurt that horrified her, probably sitting in the back row, so shy that you'd have to
move your head closer to hear her speak, because she would cover her
mouth with her hand.

That's how pioneering science fiction legend Harlan Ellison remembers Octavia Estelle Butler when he met her in 1970, the year
he introduced her to the Clarion Science Fiction & Fantasy Writers
workshop—and the rest is history.

---

1   Slightly edited transcript of a lecture given at Antioch University Los Angeles,
    December 2010.

Octavia was dyslexic, the only child of a housekeeper, whose father died when she was a baby. She grew up in poverty. Seeking escape from the constraints of her life when she was twelve, Octavia started watching a movie called *Devil Girls From Mars*, and she had the epiphany so many of us have experienced: "Hell, I can write better than that!"

Thank goodness for bad science fiction movies.

In her novel *Parable of the Sower*, and in other works, Octavia writes about characters who are "empaths" or suffer from "hyper-empathy"—a condition that forces them to suffer the pain of others, often to paralysis. As a writer who suffered from depression in addition to physical challenges, Octavia did not have to stretch her imagination too far to imagine the plight of characters like Lauren Olamina.

"I can remember getting very upset over things that weren't upsetting to anyone else," she told Terry Gross in a 1993 interview on NPR's *Fresh Air*. "Most kids empathize too much at some point in their lives and are forced to grow out of it. My character [Olamina] is a person who can't grow out of it."

And Octavia never grew out of her own brand of hyper-empathy. Like Ellison, her mentor, Octavia was deeply offended by the societal ills she saw around her: poverty, racism, political oppression, and disregard for our natural environment.

She loved this planet, but her vision stretched far beyond it. Not only was the premise of the Earthseed religion her character created in her *Parable* series pointing toward a destiny in the stars, Butler's personal email address included *Butler8Star*, which I see as her own private commitment to her vision of a different place. A new place.

A change from everything we have known.

• • •

What is *speculative fiction*? This umbrella term refers to science fiction, fantasy, and horror—the fiction of fantastic scenarios and world-building. *The Passage* by Justin Cronin is speculative fiction, for example, depicting a world that is not quite our own, and creatures that don't exist in the world as we know it. H.P. Lovecraft. Edgar Allen Poe. Kurt Vonnegut. George Orwell. Ursula K. Le Guin. Stephen King. All well-known authors of speculative fiction.

Speculative fiction by black authors enjoyed a surge of interest at the end of the twentieth century. If you'd like to see a sampling of speculative short stories by black authors, check out the *Dark Matter: A Century of Speculative Fiction From the African Diaspora* and *Dark Matter II: Reading the Bones* anthologies, published in 2000 and 2004 respectively, edited by Sheree Renée Thomas. These anthologies include work from authors as disparate as Butler and W. E. B. Du-Bois—who wrote his own post-apocalyptic story at the turn of the century as a way to examine issues of race.

Like Butler, DuBois—a cofounder of the NAACP, an early vocal advocate for civil rights and a crusader against lynching—uses a science fiction premise in his 1920 short story "The Comet" in the hope of planting the seeds of change in his present.

Walter Mosley declares in a compilation of transcripts from the National Black Writers Conference at New York's Medgar Evers College, entitled *Meditations and Ascensions: Black Writers on Writing* (2008): "The only form of fiction that I know of that is truly revolutionary is science fiction and speculative fiction. . . . Not only is it revolutionary to mean to say it overthrows a way of thinking; it also puts pressure on you to figure out, what are you going to do now that you're here?"

I first met Octavia Butler at a speculative fiction conference at Clark Atlanta University in the spring of 1997, "The African-American Fantastic Imagination: Explorations in Science Fiction, Fantasy & Horror." At the time, I had published only one book, *The Between*, a novel of alternate realities that had been favorably reviewed in the *New York Times*. On the basis of my entry in the field as an author of speculative fiction, Clark sent an invitation to my publisher that was tied up for months before it finally made it to me.

I didn't know all of the authors invited, but I knew Octavia Butler and Steven Barnes by reputation. Butler was an author whom a white male writer friend in college had told me I *had* to read, and I knew Barnes from his television work on *The Outer Limits*. Other attendees were the pioneering writer Samuel R. Delany and Jewelle Gomez.

Octavia was gracious and pleasant, having learned to shed much of the shyness of her earlier years in her public interactions. As Steven Barnes—who would later become my husband—said of Octavia in an interview in *Crisis* in May 2006: "She definitely learned how to relate to the public more fluidly and openly as she became aware of the way the public saw her. The science fiction field was never as open to her as the feminist and black female readers were. They opened her up and set her free."

Octavia, like all of us, was glad to have found a literary home. The participants of that conference posed for a photo together that was later published in *Locus* magazine—and in 2000, when Steve and I visited Octavia's home near Seattle to interview her for a magazine story (and a long visit in her kitchen, where she gave us lentil soup and fresh bread)—I noticed that photo of all of us posing at Clark Atlanta framed on her wall.

"My other family," Octavia told us warmly.

Steve had known Octavia for twenty years—she never drove, so he used to give her rides and exchange dinner invitations with her early in her writing life—but I primarily saw her at conferences during a bubble of time when we felt like a "community" of black speculative fiction writers. Octavia returned to that notion of family in March 2003 at a Howard University conference entitled "New Frontiers: Blacks in Science Fiction." Steve and I appeared with Butler and acclaimed fantasist Nalo Hopkinson.

"I think there is something very interesting about the four of us sitting here," Octavia said. "Okay, we're all black writers, three of us are female, but I think if you gave all four of us a single topic, you'd come up with four very, very different books. I think it's neat the way we bounce off of each other when we're talking, and it might be the same when we're writing. I'm not trying to write like Steve, or he like me or whatever, but somehow it helps that they're here."[2]

If black speculative fiction authors are a family, Octavia was our matriarch. In 2006, three years later, we felt like we'd lost our family.

Octavia's death forced us all to remember the primary Earthseed tenet that powers Lauren Olamina's belief system in *Parable of the Sower*: the only lasting truth is change.

• • •

2   Quoted in Gregory Jerome Hampton, *Changing Bodies in the Fiction of Octavia Butler: Slaves, Aliens, and Vampires* (New York: Lexington Books, 2014), 141.

Octavia was not, perhaps, a stereotypical revolutionary.

I saw her in disagreements but never heated arguments, never heard her raise her voice, and the only weapon she raised was her pen.

But she truly was revolutionary—entering the science fiction field, which was overwhelmingly white and male, and becoming the first science fiction writer, black or white, male or female, to win the noted MacArthur "Genius Grant" in 1995.

As an aside, Butler, like many writers, had fame without fortune—so the MacArthur award gave her an unprecedented opportunity to have more financial control of her life. She bought a house and was so struck by the experience that she recalled for me and Steve that she couldn't believe it.

At the time we spoke with her in 2000, the huge change in her life represented by the grant was finding its way to her muse: "My character in this novel receives a gift that is a really major gift," she told us.[3] "She's so powerful that I had to invent some Kryptonite for her. But I didn't know how she would handle it until I looked back on the MacArthur. I need her to handle it and stay sane. I don't need her to go nuts, especially since I'm using my life and those years. . . . All of a sudden, I was given something I absolutely never expected and barely realized existed. . . . I didn't really accept it until I began to see some evidence of it."

Sadly—though Octavia described at length during that interview work involving her character who wins a gift and memories of a charismatic older woman who boarded at her mother's house when she was young—I never again heard her speak about that novel.

Unbeknownst to me at the time, Octavia suffered from debilitating bouts of depression, and her medication made it very difficult to write. When the fog lifted, the last book she published was *Fledgling*, her own interpretation of vampire mythology—in which a race of vampires is trying to build immunity to daylight by increasing the melanin in their skin.

Vampires written only the way Octavia could.

Fledgling, Butler's last novel, encompassed many of the same themes that ran like a beacon, or perhaps a plea, through her short stories and twelve novels, which she published over thirty years—between 1976 and 2006.

3   Interview in *American Visions* magazine, October 2000, 27.

As I observed in *American Visions* magazine in 2000: "Whether Butler writes about the struggles within a society of telepaths (*Patternmaster*, Doubleday, 1976), a contemporary black woman whisked back in time to the antebellum South (*Kindred*, Doubleday, 1979), an alien species intent on splicing itself genetically with our own (*Dawn*, Warner Books, 1987) or the creation of a new religion to help prevent a near-future America from coming apart at the seams (*Parable of the Sower*, Four Walls/Eight Windows), her work is a prism through which she examines ills in American society."

Octavia began publishing in the mid-1970s, toward the end of the powerful student protest and Black Power movements of the 1960s and early 1970s, tied to civil rights and calls against the Vietnam War. Just as an example, at my alma mater, Northwestern University, in May of 1968, students occupied the Bursar's Office to demand higher black enrollment, scholarships, housing, and a Black Studies program.

In the aftermath of this highly charged political environment, Butler published her first novel, *Patternmaster*, where humans are subjugated by a race of telepaths all tied to a central powerful telepath known as the Patternmaster. Humans are chattel and playthings. The novel focuses on the pitfalls of a hierarchical society, another theme Butler raises again and again—particularly in her novel *Dawn*, where her aliens tell us that the hierarchical tendencies of our species will be our downfall.

At the time it was published, Butler's themes of dominance and resistance didn't resonate with her black detractors, who thought she was writing about the Struggle—at least the struggle as they saw it.

Ironically, nearly all of Butler's fiction is about the Struggle, especially as it relates to the quest for change—either depicting change in the world of her fiction, or advocating for change in her creation of dystopian societies that feel eerily like ours.

In traditional science fiction, according to Robert Heinlein, there are three lines of thought that drive writers:

"What if—" [What if we built a colony on Mars?]

"If only—" [If only we could fix past mistakes by traveling through time.]

And "If this goes on—"

"If this goes on" is where much of Octavia's fiction dwells, and it is the theme of her novels *Parable of the Sower* and *Parable of the Talents*.

Butler was a thorough researcher, with a library in her home, and was well known for making research trips—including a trip to the Peruvian rainforest, where I believe she grew quite ill. She had an excellent understanding of the sciences, but Octavia was a social scientist first and foremost.

My husband Steve recalls many conversations with Octavia where she held his feet to the fire for not having strong enough political views—she was well informed about the issues of the day and dreamed a better world.

Her dreams came to life in her work.

To quote Gregory Jerome Hampton, an assistant professor in African American literature at Howard University, in his well-researched book *Changing Bodies in the Fiction of Octavia Butler: Slaves, Aliens and Vampires*: "For Butler, the highest goal of humanity is survival by any means necessary, but mainly by accepting difference and acknowledging the inevitability and omnipotence of CHANGE."

These ideas of accepting difference and the inevitability of change are dramatically examined in Butler's *Lilith's Brood*, also known as the Xenogenesis series. As Hampton points out, Butler likely drew the character name Lilith from Hebrew mythology. Lilith, reputed to be the first wife of Adam, ran away because she refused to be subservient. She was cursed to see her children die, the first woman to defy the laws of man.

Lilith's Brood is a trilogy of novels: *Dawn* (1987), *Adulthood Rites* (1988), and *Imago* (1989), set in the aftermath of nuclear destruction on Earth that has claimed an overwhelming percentage of the human population.

This series represents some of the most biologically based of Butler's science fiction, introducing her alien species, the Oankali. The Oankali have three genders—male, female and the Ooloi, who are neither male nor female but "lie between partners, gather and recombine genetic material, and inseminate the female to produce offspring. The main Ooloi organ, the yashi, contains genetic information about every living thing. Ooloi can cure anything with a single touch."[4]

---

4   "Butler, Octavia; *Imago*," Literature Annotations, Literature, Arts and Medicine Database, NYU School of Medicine, http://litmed.med.nyu.edu/Annotation?action=view&annid=222.

Males and females are controlled by the Ooloi, who release pheromones to influence them. In the first novel, *Dawn*, the Oankali set out to colonize Earth with human hybrids. In the final book, *Imago*, Lilith's child Jadahs serves as the catalyst for blending human and Oankali cultures, representing a new day and the promise of more lasting change.

This vision of genetic splicing, alterations and recombination—and the struggle between disparate groups to make peace and create change for the sake of the collective—is the heartbeat of Octavia's work.

As an aside, I'll point out that even as she tried to create images of evolution, Butler's work was still bound to the realities of the real world. Although Butler describes the lead character in *Dawn* as Black, my 1987 paperback cover of *Dawn* features two white women on the cover. (Ah, book marketing!)

Change is a slow, arduous business.

The first time I read *Parable of the Sower*, I could only read four or five pages in a sitting—the gritty, unforgiving world of Lauren Olamina's Robledo was too tough to take in bigger doses: a world where a family's only safety is in walled-in communities under constant surveillance, where the world outside is overrun with scavengers, rapists, and killers.

By the time I read the last line of the book, I was sobbing, struck by the actual parable of the sower that Butler quotes on the final page.

A sower went out to sow his seed;
And as he sowed, some fell by the
Way side; and it was trodden down.
And the fowls of the air devoured
It. And some fell upon a rock; and
As soon as it was sprung up, it
Withered away because it lacked
Moisture. And some fell among
Thorns; and the thorns sprang up
With it, and choked it.

And others
Fell on good ground, and sprang up,

And bore fruit an hundredfold.

The words hit me like a gunshot. (And how interesting that a novel about the creation of a new religion ends up right back in the lap of the King James Bible.)

In some ways, this parable may sum up the artist's view—or perhaps Octavia's view—of the impact of our work in larger society and Octavia's hopes for her work in particular.

We are artists. Some of us are out in the world more than others—and I'm always so moved by the field studies and work outside of the purely creative realm that so many Antioch students hold dear. I myself was raised by civil rights activists. My mother spent forty-nine days in jail for sitting in at a Tallahassee, Florida, Woolworth lunch counter in 1960—so I have grown up with a sense that, like the activists told Octavia in the 1970s, I am somehow shirking my social duties by holing myself up in a room to make up stuff.

Yet we hope that the work we create is the planting of a seed. And most of the seeds we plant will have no impact beyond entertainment—if that. But one, perhaps one, might actually help change the world. The Quran, after all, is a poem. And the miracles of Jesus were merely an oral history—hardly the underpinnings of a powerful world religion—before the authors of the Gospels wrote the story.

Parable of the Sower is a book that quite literally sets out to change the world by forcing readers to consider what a powerful force change really is.

As both a reader and probably especially as a writer, what struck me most about this novel was the way the story actually forced me to become stronger, or else I wouldn't be able to keep on reading. So, yes, while I cringed through some of the frankness and violence of the rape and murder running rampant in the society she depicts, I felt uplifted by both the sliver of hope offered in the parable itself and by the transformative aspects of the story that touched me in such a personal way. It was one of the few times I'd felt that the ending of a novel took my breath away.

In *Parable of the Sower*, a teenaged protagonist, Lauren Olamina, creates her own spiritual doctrine to help order the chaos of the near-future world Butler depicts. She calls her musings "Earthseed:

The Books of the Living," and its primary belief system is that God is change. Butler sprinkles excerpts from the fictitious Books of the Living throughout the chapters as we follow Olamina and her newly gathered disciples across a nightmare-scape.

Perhaps Butler's most oft-quoted words are the following passage:

All that you touch,
You Change

All that you Change,
Changes you.

The only lasting truth
Is Change.

God is Change.

I've often wondered since Octavia's death what she would have thought of Barack Obama's successful presidential election bid promising hope and change.

In *Parable of the Sower*, rather than depicting genetic splicing to create a new species, the change Butler calls for is in attitude and the interpretation of events around us. Attitudes are in need of change to prevent the dystopia in our book, moving away from a class system— again, the hierarchy—of rich, poor, haves, and have nots. In the world of *Parable*, a college professor can still get work, but all jobs are hard to come by, and getting to work can be a life-or-death matter. The rich are squirreled away in high-security compounds, the poor live in squalor and violence on virtually unprotected streets, and the middle class—much like now—must fend for itself, in constant flux between the dream of safety at a higher income or the threat of chaos if they lose their homes and neighborhoods.

Moving also away from racism: although it is set in the near future, beginning in the year 2024, Octavia's vision for our future is far from postracial. Mixed couples catch hell on the roads, and the characters in this book, as in her earlier works, are often themselves a combination of ethnicities. Protagonist Lauren Olamina's black father is married to a Mexican-American woman, for example, and the core of her discipleship is made up of ethnically blended families or couples.

But Butler's plea—and Lauren Olamina's—goes beyond the traditional remedies to social ills that we've seen embraced by our own politicians.

Earthseed calls for a change in the way we view ourselves, our world, and our God.

God is Power —
Infinite,
Irresistible,
Inexorable,
Indifferent.
And yet, God is Pliable—
Trickster,
Teacher,
Chaos,
Clay.
God exists to be shaped.
God is change.

Perhaps Lauren Olamina's (and Butler's) greatest challenge is to convince her potential followers that she is describing a valid belief system.

An excerpt from the book starts with a skeptical character, Travis.

> "I still can't see change or entropy as God."
> "Then show me a more pervasive power than change," [Lauren Olamina] said. "It isn't just entropy. God is more complex than that. Human behavior alone should teach you that much. And there's still more complexity when you're dealing with several things at once—as you always are. There are all kinds of changes in the universe."
> He shook his head. "Maybe, but nobody's going to worship them."
> "I hope not," I said. "Earthseed deals with

ongoing reality, not with supernatural authority
figures. Worship is no good without action. With
action, it's only useful if it steadies you, focuses
your efforts, eases your mind."

To Butler, action to create change is the highest imperative. She re-
visits that idea in another Earthseed verse: "Belief initiates and guides
action—or it does nothing."

I can't help believing that if Octavia were alive to witness our mort-
gage crisis unfolding and the ongoing debate over health care, she
would think she was seeing the pages of her novel coming to life. Several families crowded in a single home because of the inability to find
work and a system of de facto slavery by companies that hire workers
at pitiful wages in exchange for food, shelter, and safety.

I can guarantee you that no part of Octavia would be surprised.

What is, in fact, most horrifying about reading *Parable of the Sower*
is that the world of this novel DOES feel so much like our own.

Identity, Community and Change in Octavia E. Butler

Much in the way that Barack Obama's blended ethnicity helped
pave his way to the White House, Octavia Butler's work often points
to the blending of ethnicities and species as a portal to the future.

As Gregory Jerome Hampton points out in chapter six of *Changing Bodies in the Work of Octavia Butler*, "The blurring or mixing of
character identities in Butler's fiction is facilitated by migration over
land or through space. To be identified as a hybrid in Butler's fiction
is, often times, synonymous with becoming a survivor and a signifier
of the future."

This idea is very clear in Octavia's last novel, *Fledgling*, where, as a
sometimes horror writer, I was personally thrilled to see Octavia ven-
turing into the realm of the vampire novel. It was Octavia's first novel
in seven years after a terrible bout of writer's block due to medications
and illness—and the last she would write.

But naturally, Octavia isn't simply going to write a vampire novel
as we have come to understand them.

Octavia herself was somewhat dismissive of *Fledgling*. I got the
first call from her in a long time in the summer of 2005, when she

asked me to read *Fledgling* for a blurb, and she sounded so embarrassed about the book that I assured her, "I'm sure it's brilliant!" Butler seemed to go out of her way to insist to me that no, actually, it was not.

I only mention this to point out that we all face insecurities about our work, and Octavia was no different. But as I said in my blurb—which, incidentally, never appeared on the book cover—I considered *Fledgling* to be "vintage Octavia Butler." There is no mistaking the author and her favorite thematic preoccupations, including the call for change.

As in *Parable of the Sower*, the protagonist in *Fledgling* represents youthfulness—although she is chronologically in her fifties, the protagonist has the appearance of a ten- or eleven-year-old girl. This girl, named Shori, has also suffered a memory loss, so part of her quest in the story is to discover herself and her history—as all young people must.

In *Fledgling*, the telepathic ties Butler first introduced in *Patternmaster* emerge in a different form. This time, Shori gains control over a band of followers by biting them and feeding from them—which creates strong loyalty and mutual satisfaction and pleasure.

There is again the pattern of hierarchy—Butler's race of vampires holds domination over mortals—but Shori, like the character of Mary introduced in *Mind of My Mind*, the second of her *Patternist* series, feels a deep sense of responsibility for the mortals in her "family." Just as Mary needed to feed from the power of weaker telepaths to gain strength, Shori must have seven or eight "symbionts" in her circle to maintain her feeding.

Shori hails from a race called the Ina, who form the basis of all vampire myth. Like the Bram Stoker variety of vampire, they are saddled with the vampire's burden: an inability to come out during daylight.

In other words, Butler's vampires are also forced to live in darkness. The first line of the novel, in fact, is: "I awoke to darkness."

Shori is badly burned, naked, and hungry. Over the course of the novel, Shori learns that she is the result of a genetic manipulation—partially human to give the Ina more melanin, so they can venture out in daylight, thereby redefining their concepts of who and what they are. But she is a target of her own people, who are offended by her existence and consider her a mutant.

Once again, Butler points to change through blending, urging us to learn to accept those differences between us.

• • •

Doro, a central figure in Butler's Patternist series, is a genetic fluke. He alone has the ability to shift his essence from one body to the next—making him a very dangerous telepathic vampire. In order to survive, he must feed from his offspring.

But simultaneously, over four thousand years he has conducted a carefully controlled breeding program to preserve telepathic and other gifts in a scattered population of very psychologically unstable descendants. His ultimate quest is to find a "latent"—as his subjects are called when they have potential but have not yet made the painful transition into their abilities—who can emerge as the most powerful since him.

This novel signals a fundamental change. For the first time, there is a telepathic pattern that ties the telepaths to a central figure, the beginning of normalcy and a new day for the beleaguered "latent" population struggling to master their gifts instead of being mastered by them.

The creator of that pattern is a character named, not surprisingly, Mary.

In holding so many others to her telepathic breasts, Mary is the ultimate mother figure. But as is often the case in Butler's work, there is also moral ambiguity. As with the vampires in *Fledgling*, Mary has intractable power over the others in her Pattern, so although there are benefits to her mental prison (for example, more control over their gifts, combined strength), a prison is still a prison.

Mary overtakes the amoral Doro—who lived with no concern for anyone but himself and his genetic research—and signals a new day.

But clearly even the new day is fraught with potential pitfalls.

He or she who holds ultimate power also holds ultimate power for abuse.

As Butler wrote in "Earthseed: Books of the Living" in *Parable of the Sower*:

Any Change may bear seeds of benefit.
Seek them out.
Any Change may bear seeds of harm. Beware.
God is infinitely malleable.
God is Change.

• • •

Butler's seminal novel *Kindred*, perhaps the most-read of her work, offers readers a unique glimpse into the antebellum slavery period in the South by introducing a black female character, Dana, who is whisked back from the present—or, in this case, 1976—through time because of an unconscious summoning of a child ancestor who is drowning.

At least that's how they first meet. Over the course of the novel, Dana will find herself unexpectedly transported back several times and will herself suffer the indignities of slavery.

The theme of change is persistent in the reading of *Kindred*, even if it is not as clearly delineated as the focus of a religion, as it is in *Parable of the Sower*.

There is also a through-the-looking-glass aspect of *Kindred* that invites the reader to undergo a psychological shift, or transformation, as the moral complexity of Dana's predicament—and, thus, the moral predicament of all of the players in the Old South—becomes more and more apparent.

Kindred, with its contemporary setting in Southern California, invites the reader to reflect on change from the opening pages. Like many of Butler's characters, Dana is in an interracial relationship with a white man, this one named Kevin. Even readers who overlook the significance of an interracial relationship in a nation where such relationships were once considered illegal, the social changes entailed in this relationship become much more obvious when Kevin too travels back in time with Dana.

Suddenly the white man who was one's husband and soul mate is forced to play the part of a slave master when he tries to protect her in the thick of slavery in Maryland's Eastern Shore.

Unbeknownst to him, Dana is being summoned by a child, Rufus Weylan, whom we later learn is Dana's ancestor.

But here's the quandary: this helpless young child Dana finds drowning in the river is going to grow up to rape a black woman who began as his childhood friend—which is how Dana's genetic line begins.

As Dana is forced back to the South several times, she sees the changes in Rufus, from young child to an arrogant, violent grown man she would rather kill than save. But how can she? If she kills Rufus—or prevents the rape of her black female ancestor—she will never be born.

This, of course, is the moral dilemma all blacks face in their examination of our past in slavery—and, to me, represents one of the most brilliant acts of literary sleight of hand on Octavia's part. After generations of heartache and discrimination, Black Americans as a collective are also among the most powerful and affluent Blacks in the world. We too were ultimately the beneficiaries of slavery.

So *Kindred* not only recounts a horrible tale of violence, slavery, torture and rape—subjects Octavia is never shy with—it also invites the reader to change his or her perspective on the moral lines dividing whites and blacks when the subject of slavery is examined.

The intricate social webs between the racial groups during the practice of slavery have never been purely black and white. For example, slaves who had opportunities to run away did not—most slaves did not run away—and not simply out of fear of capture or lack of opportunities. In many cases, the reason not to run was much simpler: they didn't want to leave their families and loved ones. And, yes, others did not venture to run because of fear of the unknown. Or, no matter how uncomfortable the notion, there was, at times, genuine affection for slave masters, a kind of systemic Stockholm Syndrome that those of us who haven't experienced slavery will never understand.

My father—who is our family genealogist—delighted me through childhood with his story about how a group of my relatives in Indiana, freed Blacks, set up their own thriving community; it thrived so much, in fact, that neighboring white farmers grew jealous and attacked them. This is a familiar story, as in a massacre in Rosewood, Florida, but this story had a very different ending. Instead of politely dying as they were expected, these black settlers raced to a round house. With the women loading rifles, men shooting from the windows or wielding axes in the doorway, they actually fought their white attackers off. And instead of being burned to the ground, lynched, or thrown in jail, the blacks were resettled by the governor, with their own tract of land called Lyles Station, which exists to this day.

My father's story is one of empowerment. There is an element of victimhood—the black settlers are treated unfairly—and victimhood carries its own sense of moral elevation, in a pinch. But beyond victimhood the story also represents a rare moment of empowerment, which to me, as a child, was far more satisfying than victimhood. If I had been descended from the settlers of Rosewood, I would have felt pride in them too—but there is far more pride in the notion of fighting back and being victorious.

Well, recently my father gave me a story from our lineage that left a very different moral taste in my mouth. One of his cousins was teasing him after recently learning that he is descended from a slave owner in the Carolinas.

Why is that news? Because this slave owner was not white—he was Black.

Bye-bye, moral superiority. While I might be able to rationalize how rare black slave owners were, they did, in fact, exist. I'd known this before, but to have a black slave owner in your own family line—through marriage, I understand—is a different matter. Slavery was not entirely an issue of race, even if race was the primary component. In my mind, my family story is no longer simply an issue of black and white.

Which brings me to the brilliant transformation I think Octavia calls upon from all of her readers of *Kindred*: Dana is a victim, yes. She is transported through time against her will. Her female forebear was victimized and raped by the slavery system. Yet Butler forces us to reflect on Dana's culpability in not helping to prevent the rape—killing the dragon while he's young—and thus erasing her own family line. She is a caregiver to both Alice, the black victim, and Rufus, the slave master.

Dana finally kills Rufus when *she* feels threatened by rape, but all of her education, knowledge, and savvy still can't prevent what happened. That is, she can't prevent the tragedy of her future conception.

Dana and Kevin say quite often that they can't change history—but the reader is left with the niggling notion that, well, actually, Dana *could* have changed history. But despite the horrors and heartache to Alice, her Black female forebear, Dana and Rufus were sucked into a very odd, codependent dynamic not dissimilar from power dynamics in Butler's Patternist and Xenogenesis novels—that resulted in no change to history at all.

Except for the physical changes to Dana.

As Hampton points out in *Changing Bodies*, the transformation in *Kindred* is a physical one for Dana—as symbolized by her permanent injury she sustains during her time travel: she loses her arm, literally sacrificing her flesh as a cost for the experience and the memory.

• • •

One Sunday morning in February 2006, when a magazine reporter emailed me to say she'd heard Octavia Butler had died, I didn't want to believe it. I saw nothing in the news or on the Web.

I called Octavia's home number and listened with a pounding heart as her phone rang. Once. Twice. Three times. I delighted for just a bare instant when the ringing stopped and I heard her voice. On her answering machine. Already distant, clearly a recording.

Steve and I called Harlan Ellison—who had discovered Octavia so many years ago—and he later called us back to confirm her death.

So many times since then, I've thought of the other times I had called her—never enough, it turns out—when I tried to make our conversations brief, never able to fight the certainty that I was pulling her away from a stream of brilliant thoughts. Once she apologized for the loud music playing in the background. It turned out that Octavia, like me, enjoyed listening to music while she wrote. How many times did I hesitate to dial her number simply because I didn't want to disturb her?

She was fighting a cold when I saw her in Seattle at the "Black to the Future" science fiction conference in June 2004, when she was happy to meet our new baby, Jason, but she didn't want to give him germs. She was sick again when I saw her in New York for the Yari Yari Pamberi International Conference of Literature by Women of African Ancestry in October that same year.

I cautioned her to be careful about too much travel. Subsequently, I have learned that Octavia was far more ill than I knew.

Like most people, I cannot say that I knew Octavia well. But in the too-brief time I knew her, I saw many sides of her. Her fierce disappointment with humankind's worse habits. Her girlish side. Her goddess side. Her insecure side.

The Christmas before she died, we sent Octavia a photo of our son, Jason, on Santa's lap and said we hoped she was feeling better. Octavia could not have been feeling well when she sent out her own cards that year, but hers were always among the first to arrive. She wrote to us: "Have a creative, prosperous New Year down there in California where it's WAY too warm."

I must call her soon, I thought many times. *I must call Octavia. But what if she is writing?*

OUTRO

ADRIENNE MAREE BROWN

WE HOLD SO MANY WORLDS INSIDE US. SO MANY FUTURES. IT IS OUR radical responsibility to share these worlds, to plant them in the soil of our society as seeds for the type of justice we want and need. It has been beautiful to gather these stories, collaboratively edit them, and begin to understand not just the challenges we face or the enemies we need to transform, but the abundance of imagination we in the social justice realm hold, and must cultivate.

We see ourselves as part of a growing wave of folks connecting science fiction (or what we're calling *visionary fiction*) with social justice. Science fiction is the perfect "exploring ground," as it gives us the opportunity to play with different outcomes and strategies before we have to deal with the real-world costs.

In the process of hearing and working these stories, we developed tools, frameworks, and principles that would help us to bring the work off of the page and into our lives. We wanted to end this anthology with an offering of three of these tools. The first is visionary fiction, which Walidah spoke about in the introduction. The elements of visionary fiction are that it: explores current social issues through the lens of sci-fi; is conscious of identity and intersecting identities; centers those who have been marginalized; is aware of power inequalities; is realistic and hard but hopeful; shows change from the bottom up rather than the top down; highlights that change is collective; and is not neutral—its purpose is social change and societal transformation. The stories we tell can either reflect the society we are a part of or transform it. If we want to bring new worlds into existence, then we need to challenge the narratives that uphold current power dynamics and patterns.

We call upon science fiction, fantasy, horror, magical realism, myth, and everything in between as we create and teach visionary fiction.

The second tool is emergent strategy. A strategy is a set of plans toward an action. Emergence is the way complex systems and patterns emerge from a series of relatively simple interactions. Instead of linear, hierarchical, outcome-oriented strategies and strategic plans that can't adapt to changing conditions, we need ways of strategizing together based on understanding and respecting change. So far, the elements of emergent strategy are that it is intentional, interdependent and relational, adaptive, resilient because it is decentralized, fractal, uses transformative justice, and creates more possibilities. One of the ways we've been reading Octavia Butler's work is as case studies of emergent strategy. In sessions with local communities, we're introducing people to the framework and asking them to assess which elements of emergent strategy might be most necessary to their local work and supporting them in generating strategies together.

One aspect of emergent strategy is that there is no waste—we are encouraged to see everything around us as a resource. Butler's book *Parable of the Sower* follows the main character Olamina, a young Black woman who lives in a slightly dystopic future in a gated community. She carries a radically different vision for the purpose of humanity than her Christian family. She believes our "destiny is to take root among the stars," to see Earth as a womb rather than a permanent home. She calls her beliefs Earthseed, and she cultivates Earthseed as she matures in the tiny and dangerous container of her home. The essence of emergent strategy can be found in the central tenet of Olamina's Earthseed: "All that you touch, you change. All that you change, changes you. The only lasting truth is change." Olamina begins studying the skills needed to survive outside of the walls and packs a survival bag. When the community is attacked and the walls fall, she finds herself on the outside with her bag, her knowledge, and her dreams. She finds people along the way, other survivors willing to dream with her new forms of community, adapting constantly to ever-changing conditions. Exploring these and other examples from Butler's work—in addition to studying other aspects of emergence— creates a solid foundation for changing the way we strategize on our path to justice.

Finally, we have our collective science-fiction/visionary fiction writing workshops. Our premise is that if we want worlds that work for more of us, we have to have more of us involved in the visioning process. One of the ways we perpetuate individualism is by ideating alone, literally coming up with ideas in solitude and then competing to bring them to life. Our workshops are designed to encourage collaborative ideation. Together we identify issues that are relevant to the local community and build a world in which to explore the issue and possible solutions.

In each workshop, we start out by asking ourselves what in our community needs vision, with the idea that we can apply our collective ideation to it like a healing salve.

We identify lead characters—often pairs or groups of lead characters to disrupt the solitary hero narrative—and we intentionally move those voices that are often marginalized in our society to the center of the world-building.

We then build the setting, identifying where we are in time, creating a geography and conditions, naming any shared assumptions we have, and determining what the major conflict will be in that world. What is the change our characters seek? Who else is seeking change?

Once these elements are laid out, we send people off to spend time writing their stories in this shared world. So far, no matter how much time we give people, they are still writing when the timer goes off. The imagination just needs a little nudge to run wild.

The writers come back together to read their work and affirm each other for being part of such a collective act of genius. Each time, participants are surprised and inspired by the ways others interpret and experiment in the world. We believe that this experience helps grow the capacity to truly vision and implement together.

We are touring the country, sharing these tools for communities to use in their own local work. What we continue to experience are the kinds of groundbreaking conversations that transform how people view their present lives and work.

ACKNOWLEDGMENTS

THE BIRTH PROCESS FOR THIS ANTHOLOGY HAS BEEN A LENGTHY ONE, and there have been countless writing and ideating doulas who helped us come to this point. We unfortunately don't have the space to list everyone by name, but know you are now and always part of the Brood.

Octavia's Brood thank yous:
John Jennings for a cover design that exceeded even our intergalactic dreams. Sheree Renée Thomas, who went above and beyond in her role as adviser, for her insight and guidance. All of the contributors for their commitment to this visionary process. AK Press and Charles and Zach, Chris Dodge for such an amazing copy-editing job! The Institute for Anarchist Studies and Lara and Paul Messersmith-Glavin and Cindy Milstein. Jordan Flaherty and *Left Turn Magazine* and everyone who contributed and supported the Visionary Fiction section of the magazine. Everyone doing Octavia Butler Emergent Strategy sessions/groups across the country. Max Rameau for the wonderful website. Mumia for writing and recording his essay. The Allied Media Conference for incubating this project, and continual support. Everyone who worked on *Octavia Butler Strategic Reader* and *The Transformative Justice Reader.* Tananarive Due for her mentorship. Steven Barnes, Kiese Laymon, Jen Angel, Jeff Chang. Camilo Mejia, Seth Mulliken, Richard Ejire, Sage Crump, Ronica Mukerjee, Ibrahim Abdul Matin, Wild Dandelions, Bryonn Bain, Bernard Collins. Ayana Jamieson, Moya Baily and the Octavia E. Butler Legacy Network. Soraya Jean-Louis McElroy. Jonathan Cunningham and the Experience Music Project. Luzviminda Carpenter and Uzuri Productions. Invincible and Gabriel Teodros for donating music for our indiegogo campaign. Sham-e-ali for donating poetry

to the indiegogo campaign. Copperwire for their visionary music partially born out of the Brood. Warsan Shire. Lynnee Denise. Jeff Perlstein and Solespace, Moon Palace Books, Ancestry Books, Wildseeds NOLA. Nisi Shawl, Samuel Delany, Nalo Hopkinson, NK Jemisin. *ColorLines, Red Door Project, The Skanner, Racialicious, Hooded Utilitarian, Bitch Media*. Carl Brandon Society for existing and their ongoing important work. South End Press. Everyone who supported the indiegogo campaign in any and every way, anyone who has attended an event.

Oppressed people fighting for justice and liberation worldwide.

To our ancestors, for dreaming us up and bending reality to create us. May we carry that legacy into the far future.

Walidah's thank yous:

Mom, Kakamia Jahad Imarisha, Sundiata Acoli, David Gilbert, Bayla, Turiya, my god kids Elijah and EKela, Petey, John Joo, Kodey, Hasan Shakur (RIP), Ian Head, Leah Yacoub Halperin, TARDIS Collective past present and future members, Rivas and Alegre, Joseph Austin, Kiwi Illafonte, Daniel Hunter, Noah Prince, Khalil Edwards, Hasan Salaam, Fayemi, Aishah Shahidah Simmons, Amara Perez, Stephan Herrera, Dan Berger, Claude Marks and the Freedom Archives, Kristian Williams, Larry Colton, Matthew Shenoda.

adrienne's thank yous:

Jane, Jerry, April and Autumn Brown, Sam Conway, Finn, Siobhan, Mairead, Brad, Summer, Bran, and the rest of my family. Papa, Grandma Brown, the baby, Charity Hicks, David Blair and the rest of my ancestors. Lynnee Bonner. Kat Aaron, Grace Lee Boggs, Janine De Novais, Tananarive Due, dream hampton, Shea Howell, Shane Jones, Ife Kilimanjaro, Jenny Lee, Dani McClain, Mike Medow, Evans Richardson, Sofia Santana, Adriana and Diallo and Auset Shabazz, Sterling Toles, Jodie Tonita, Ill Weaver and all my beloveds. Allied Media Projects and Generative Somatics (Team B!), Denise Perry and BOLD and the movements that shaped and radicalized me. Kresge Literary Arts Fellowship and Knight Arts Challenge. Detroit—the people and the place.

We also ran a crowdfunding campaign to raise the funds that would bring this book into the world. The supportive response overwhelmed us, more than doubling our goal. We think every single person who donated whether it was $1 or $1,000, is part of this collective dreaming process, and so we want to list everyone who shared their name with their contribution here:

Aaron Brown, amber yada, Aleena Jack, Amanda Garces, Eva Agudelo, Oliver Hayes, Allyse Heartwell, Alice Eastman, Anushka Jagdeo, Alex Leclerc, Alison Abrcu-Garcia, aly d., Arun Mathur, Amelia Cates, Amy McKie, Blaine Vogt, Anh Phan, andrea marcos, Anne Watanabe, Antoinette Poindexter, Annika Fagerlind, April Cunningham, Andy Allen, Deb Burgard, Abram S Himelstein, Ayana A. H. Jamieson, beth gutelius, Bethany Jacobs, Christopher Lee, Brian Frank, Cara Graninger, Casey Carmody, Caroline Picker, Carolyn Williams, Cayden Mak, C. Oberholtzer, Celia Alario, cesar maxit, Chani Geigle-Teller, Benjamin Chapman, Alicia Garza, Choya Adkison-Stevens, Christopher Leinonen, Christopher Hamann, Carmela Feigenbaum, Nicole Ricket, Courtney Martin, Silas Woodsmith, Damon Constantinides, Jonathan Urquhart, Daniel Stalter, Darby Hickey, Diana D. Duarte, Deborah Schwartz, didier deshommes, Diana Sands, Kenny Rose, Danielle, praveen sinha, Drew Herzig, Todd Graham, Nick Ackerley, Eie Irons, Elizabeth Franke, Elizabeth S. Q. Goodman, Ellen Shull, Deva Kyle, Erica McGillivray, Emily Croft, Emily Wong, Esperanza Tervalon-Daumont, Marlo J. DeMauro, fayemi shakur, Kate Bell, Fiona Ning Cheuk, Jonel Daphnis, J. K. Riviere, Gan Golan, Greg Buckland, Beth Boose, Cree Boyechko, Carol Squires, Dona Gomez, Geoffrey Blanchette, Gretjen Clausing, Greg Stromire, Jeff Gundy, Gillian Andrews, Guy Schaff, Heather Martin, Heidi Guenin, holly hessinger, Ian Rhodewalt, Davida ingram, jessica firsow, Kelley Meister, Irit Reinheimer, Maggie Block, Jon Berger, Laura Valentine, Kenyeda Adams, Jasmin Thana, Jazmin Smith, John O'Brian, jean Catherine steinberg, Jeanelle Wittcke, Jeanne Burns, eliana machuca, Jenn Welna, Jere Martin, Jeremy G. Kahn, Jess Daniel, Jessica Lee, Jesse Freeston, Jessica Rosenberg, karen blanco, John Lodder, Jody Rutherford, John Hardenbergh, John H. Joo, Jonah S Boyarin, Joshua C Burnett, Joshua Kahn Russell, Jeremy Weyl, Judy Hatcher, Julia Haverstock-Wagner, J. Nelson, Julian Rodriguez-Drix, Julia K.

Perini, Kai Lynch, Emi Kane, Kari Koch, Kate Weck, Kirsten Anderson, Keara Purvis, Kelly Jennings, Ken Green, Katrina E Schaffer, K. L. Davis, KellyAnne Mifflin, Kristen Westfall, Kristie McKinley, Kay Shaw, Kyem Brown, Kimberly Murray, Rosana Cruz, Jocelyne Houghton, Adam Haley, Jennifer Armas, Laura Fletcher, Lauren Bacon, Lauren Ressler, Laurel Hoyt, Leland Baxter-Neal, Otts Bolisay, Lindsay Baltus, Liz Burgess, Liz Carlin, Elizabeth Fussell, Lily Cavanagh, Laurie Stevens, Julia Santo, Alexander Cotton, Jocelyn Burrell, Lars Ingebrigtsen, Lydia Ondrusek, Margot Weiss, Marie Choi, Martin Eve, Martyn Pepperell, Sine Hwang Jensen, Megan Obrien, Meghan McCarron, Melissa Getreu, Mary Ganster, michael erwin, Mary Gillmor-Kahn, Minal Hajratwala, Michael Eaves, MaPo Kinnord-Payton, Moira OKeeffe, Morgan Payne, Anjali Taneja, Moya Bailey, Maura Pavalow, mary miratrix, Kristine Maitland, Martha Wells Wilson, Monique Walton, Nick Murphy, Nadia Alexis, Naomi Sobel, Kathryn Wawer, Nicholas Javier, Nitika Raj, Nadia Mohamed, Jessica Lin, eric reece, Dani Jordan, Joe overton, Kenji Liu, Patti Powell, Patrick Evans, Bruce Poinsette, Soli Johnson, suzanna foretich, Rachel Miller, Maryse Mitchell-Brody, Josh Wilson, Rebecca Lundberg, Belia Saavedra, Rosa Squillacote, Aaron Rosenblum, Rossella De Leon, Roxanne Lawson, Roy Perez, Renee Perry, Asmara Ruth Afework, Ryan Li Dahlstrom, Sara Ryan, Sage Crump, Samirah Raheem, Sara Brodzinsky, Sarah Insel, Sean Parson, Myrna Morales, Katie Seitz, Lauren Smith, jeffrey severe, Sarah Grafman, Damon Siefert, Sienna Morris, Scott Macklin, Selamawit Misgano, Jean Carmichael, Manish Vaidya, Soya Jung, Julianne Gale, Marcus Tenaglia, Adam Purcell, Stu Marvel, Social Justice Fund, Suzanne Fischer, Christina Springer, Sami Wannell, Tamara Lynne, tash shatz, Kit Lorraine Stuber, Jenny Montoya Tansey, Djibril al-Ayad, Tom Andes, Tanuja Jagernauth, Tiffani, Anthony T. Teel, Todd Cooley, Amanda Torres, Tree Bressen, Jen-Mei Wu, Victoria Donnelly, Vicki Capalbo, Thomas Walker, Robert Karimi, Ashley Whitfield, William Chalmers, scott winn, Lynn Brown, Kristin Ming, shanti diane, Yashna Padamsee, Katherine Aaron, Yuki Kidokoro, Zachary Sandfield, Jordan, Zakaria Mohamed, Zefyr Scott, Zanetta BH.

BIOS

Walidah Imarisha

Walidah Imarisha is a writer, organizer, educator, and spoken word artist. Author of the poetry book *Scars/Stars* (Drapetomedia Press), her nonfiction exploration of crime, prisons, and redemption will be published by AK Press and the IAS in 2016. She was also one of the editors of *Another World Is Possible* (Subway Press), the first 9/11 anthology. Her work has appeared in many publications, including *Total Chaos: The Art and Aesthetics of Hip Hop, Letters from Young Activists, Word Warriors: 35 Women Leaders in the Spoken Word Revolution, The Quotable Rebel, Life During Wartime: Resisting Counterinsurgency, Joe Strummer: Punk Rock Warlord,* and *Near Kin: A Collection of Words and Art Inspired by Octavia Estelle Butler.* One of the cofounders and first editor of political hip-hop publication *AWOL Magazine,* Walidah also helped found the Human Rights Coalition, a Pennsylvania organization led by prisoners' families and former prisoners. Walidah directed the 2005 Katrina documentary *Finding Common Ground in New Orleans.* She has taught in Portland State University's Black Studies Department and Oregon State University's Women Gender Sexuality Studies Department.

adrienne maree brown

adrienne maree brown is a writer, science fiction scholar, love and pleasure activist, facilitator, healer, and doula living in Detroit. In 2014 she was part of the inaugural Speculative Fiction Workshop at Voices of Our Nation. In 2013 she was awarded the Kresge Literary Arts Fellowship, and received a Knight Arts Challenge Award to run a series of Octavia Butler–based science-fiction writing salons in Detroit (detroitscifigenerator.wordpress.com). Learning from her eighteen years of movement facilitation and participation, she approaches Butler's work through the lens of emergent strategy: complexity born of simple interactions, aligned with nature, rooted in relationship, resilience, and embracing adaptability and change. adrienne has helped to launch a loose network that is growing Octavia Butler– and emergent strategy– related work with and for people interested in approaching speculative fiction from a social justice framework. adrienne centers emergent strategy in her facilitation work, and believes that changing how we create and strategize will change the way we exist. She is also on a teaching and healing path with Generative Somatics and Black Organizing for Leadership and Dignity (BOLD). She documents her awe and learning at adriennemareebrown.net/blog.

CONTRIBUTORS

Alexis Pauline Gumbs

Alexis Pauline Gumbs is a queer black troublemaker, a black feminist love evangelist, an Afro-Caribbean grandchild, a prayer-poet priestess, and a time-traveling space cadet who lives and loves in Durham, North Carolina. Alexis is the founder of the Eternal Summer of the Black Feminist Mind local and intergalactic community school and a cofounder of the Mobile Homecoming Project, an experiential archive amplifying generations of queer black brilliance. Alexis was the first scholar to research the Audre Lorde papers at Spelman College, the June Jordan papers at Harvard University, and the Lucille Clifton papers at Emory University while earning her PhD in English, African and African American Studies, and Women and Gender Studies from Duke University. And her mother is a Trekkie.

Alixa Garcia

Alixa Garcia is cofounder and artistic director of Climbing PoeTree, an internationally renowned activist, multimedia theater, and spoken-word duo out of Brooklyn, New York. She has facilitated workshops and performed in hundreds of venues, from Harvard

University to New York City jails on Rikers Island. Garcia has presented alongside such powerhouses as Angela Davis, Alicia Keys, and Alice Walker. Her work has appeared in dozens of literary journals and magazines, including *ArtForum* and *ColorLines*. Her visual art has been featured on large-scale walls in New York City, Cuba, and Jamaica, as well as in galleries and museums, including the Smithsonian, and the African American Museum in Philadelphia. She was the recipient of the Global Arts Fund/Astrea Visual Artist Grant, 2013–14, and won the best director award at the Reel Sistah Film Festival, New York City, 2008, for *Unnatural Disasters and a Great Shift in Universal Consciousness*. Through multiple artistic media, this multidisciplinary artist is on a mission to overcome destruction with creativity.

Autumn Brown

Autumn Brown is a mother, community organizer, theologian, artist, and facilitator. She is the Interim Executive Director of RECLAIM! and serves on the board of directors of the Common Fire Foundation. She has facilitated organizational and strategic development with community-based and movement organizations and trained hundreds of community organizers in consensus process, facilitation, and resisting racism. A graduate of Sarah Lawrence College, she has also completed specialized study in theology at Oxford University and the General Theological Seminary of New York. She is a recipient of the 2009 Next Generation of Leadership Fellowship through the Center for Whole Communities and the 2010 Creative Community Leadership Institute Fellowship through Intermedia Arts. She currently lives in Avon, Minnesota, with her partner, children, dog, and wildlife.

Bao Phi

Bao Phi has been a performance poet since 1991. A two-time Minnesota Grand Slam champion and a National Poetry Slam finalist, Bao Phi has appeared on HBO's *Russell Simmons Presents Def Poetry*, and a poem of his appeared in the *2006 Best American Poetry* anthology. His first collection of poems, *Sông | Sing*, was published by Coffee House Press in 2011 to critical acclaim. He has been a *City Pages* and *Star Tribune* artist of the year.

Dawolu Jabari Anderson

Dawolu Jabari Anderson lives and works in Houston. He studied fine arts at Texas Southern University and the University of Houston and completed residencies at Lawndale Art Center in Houston, and Skowhegan School of Paint and Sculpture in Skowhegan, Maine. Selected solo exhibitions include *Dawolu Jabari Anderson: Black Film,* Glassell School of Art, Museum of Fine Arts Houston, and *The Birth of a Nation—Yo! Bumrush the Show: Works by Dawolu Jabari Anderson,* Arts League Houston. Selected group exhibitions include the *Whitney Biennial 2006: Day for Night* at the Whitney Museum of American Art, New York; *System Error: Work is a Force that Gives Us Meaning,* (2007), Palazzo delle Papesse, Siena, Italy; and *Who Goliards? Artists at the Turn of the Century,* (2004), University Museum, Texas Southern University.

Dani McClain

Dani McClain is a journalist living in Oakland, California. Her reporting and writing have been published in *The Nation, ColorLines, Guernica,* and *Al Jazeera America.*

David F. Walker

David F. Walker is an award-winning journalist, filmmaker, educator, comic book writer, and author. His publication *BadAzz MoFo* became internationally known as the indispensable resource guide to black films of the seventies, and he is coauthor of the book *Reflections on Blaxploitation: Actors and Directors Speak* (Scarecrow, 2009). His other work includes the young adult series *The Adventures of Darius Logan,* as well as comic book series *Number 13* (Dark Horse Comics) and *The Army of Dr. Moreau* (Monkeybrain Comics).

Gabriel Teodros

To know that another world is possible and to bring it to life through music: this has always been the mission of emcee Gabriel Teodros. He first made a mark in the Pacific Northwest with the group Abyssinian Creole and reached an international audience with his critically acclaimed solo debut *Lovework.* He has since set stages on fire across the United States, Canada, and Mexico, as well as in

Ethiopia. The year 2012 saw two more acclaimed albums: the solo release *Colored People's Time Machine* and CopperWire's *Earthbound*, a hip-hop space opera set in the year 2089 that Teodros recorded with fellow Ethiopian-American artists Meklit Hadero and Burntface. In 2014 Teodros released *Children of the Dragon* with Washington DC–based producer AirMe, followed by *Evidence of Things Not Seen* with New Zealand–based producer SoulChef. For more information, see www.gabrielteodros.com.

Kalamu ya Salaam

New Orleans–based writer, filmmaker, and educator Kalamu ya Salaam is a senior staff member of Students at the Center, a writing program in the New Orleans public schools. Kalamu is the moderator of *neo•griot*, an information blog for black writers and supporters of our literature worldwide. Kalamu can be reached at kalamu@mac.com.

Jelani Wilson

Jelani Wilson lives and writes in Jersey with his kick-ass family. If he's not voraciously reading, watching cartoons, or practicing rapper hands, he's off somewhere training in jiu jitsu or subverting authority. He promises to start posting his fiction along with mercifully brief musings and sociopolitical commentary at pageswithoutpaper.com, but on the real we'll believe it when we see it.

Leah Lakshmi Piepzna-Samarasinha

Leah Lakshmi Piepzna-Samarasinha is a queer mixed Sri Lankan writer, performer, educator, and healer. The author of the Lambda Award-winning *Love Cake and Consensual Genocide*, she is also the coeditor, with Ching-In Chen and Jai Dulani, of *The Revolution Starts at Home: Confronting Intimate Violence in Activist Communities*. She is the cofounder of Mangos With Chili, and a lead artist with Sins Invalid. She has organized around issues of transformative justice, disability justice, and radical teaching and learning for twenty years. Her next book of poetry, *Bodymap*, and memoir, *Dirty River*, are forthcoming. For more info, see www.brownstargirl.org.

LeVar Burton

LeVar Burton is an actor, presenter, director, producer, and author. He published his science fiction book *Aftermath* (Aspect Press) in 1997. Burton is best known for his roles as Kunta Kinte in the 1977 award-winning ABC television miniseries *Roots* and as Lt. Commander Geordi La Forge in *Star Trek: The Next Generation*. He was the host and executive producer of the long-running PBS children's series *Reading Rainbow*, which ran for twenty-three years, garnering over two hundred broadcast awards, including a Peabody Award and twenty-six Emmy Awards. Burton and his company RRKIDZ re-imagined *Reading Rainbow* as an iPad app in 2012, which became the number one educational app within thirty-six hours of its debut. In 2014, Burton ran a successful Kickstarter campaign to bring *Reading Rainbow* back as a Web-based show with free access available for schools in need.

Mia Mingus

Mia Mingus is a community organizer, writer, and educator working for disability justice and prison abolition via transformative justice and community accountability. She identifies as a queer physically disabled Korean woman transracial and transnational adoptee. She works for community, interdependency, and a home for all of us, not just some of us, and longs for a world where disabled children can live free of violence, with dignity and love. As her work for liberation evolves and deepens, her roots remain firmly planted in ending sexual violence. She works locally to build and support responses to child sexual abuse that do not rely on the state (i.e., police, prisons, the criminal legal system) with the Bay Area Transformative Justice Collective. Her writings can be found at leavingevidence.wordpress.com. This is her first foray into writing fiction.

Morrigan Phillips

Morrigan Phillips is an organizer, writer, Hufflepuff, and social worker living in Boston. Over the years, she has been a campaign and direct action organizer to thwart the forces of globalization. She currently works in the HIV/AIDS community in Boston, building networks of peer support and community-based programs to combat rising rates of infection. As a part of the Beautiful Trouble trainers network, Morrigan gets out and about doing direct action training. She is particularly enamored with creating and facilitating trainings that merge the power of imagined worlds with time-honored direct action training tools to find new and exacting avenues for radical change in the realms of climate justice, health access, public transportation, and more.

Mumia Abu-Jamal

Mumia Abu-Jamal is an award winning journalist who chronicles the human condition. He was a resident of Pennsylvania's death row for twenty-nine years and is currently incarcerated at SCI Mahoney. Written from his solitary confinement cell, his essays have reached a worldwide audience. His books *Live from Death Row*, *Death Blossoms: Reflections From a Prisoner of Conscience*, *All Things Censored*, *Faith of Our Fathers: An Examination of the Spiritual Life of African and African-American People*, *We Want Freedom: A Life in the Black Panther Party*, *Jailhouse Lawyers: Prisoners Defending Prisoners v. the U.S.A*, and *The Classroom and the Cell: Conversations on Black Life in America* (with scholar Marc Lamont Hill) have sold hundreds of thousands of copies and been translated into nine languages. Mumia Abu-Jamal was in his youth a Trekkie and has read and loved sci-fi from Asimov to Herbert and Butler to Bisson. Forthcoming: *Writing on the Wall: Selected Prison Writings of Mumia Abu-Jamal*.

Sheree Renée Thomas

Sheree Renée Thomas writes in Tennessee between a river and a pyramid. She is the author of *Shotgun Lullabies: Stories & Poems* (Aqueduct Press) and editor of *Dark Matter: A Century of Speculative Fiction From the African Diaspora* and *Dark Matter: Reading the Bones*, winners of the 2001 and 2005 World Fantasy Awards, respectively. A Clarion West '99 grad, Sheree has served as a juror of the Speculative Fiction Foundation, the Carl Brandon Society, and the Tiptree Awards. Her own writing received honorable mention in *The Year's Best Fantasy & Horror* (16th and 17th eds.) and was nominated for a Pushcart Prize and two Rhysling Awards. Read her work in *Eleven, Eleven*; *Strange Horizons*; *Mythic Delirium*; *storySouth*; *Callaloo*; *Meridians*; *Obsidian*; *Harpur Palate*; *The Moment of Change: Feminist*

Speculative Poetry; *80! Memories & Reflections on Ursula K. Le Guin*; *Mojo: Conjure Stories*; *Hurricane Blues*; *Bum Rush the Page*; *The Ringing Ear*; *Mythic 2*; and *So Long Been Dreaming: Postcolonial Science Fiction and Fantasy*.

Tananarive Due

Tananarive Due is the former Cosby Chair in the Humanities at Spelman College. She teaches in the creative writing MFA program at Antioch University Los Angeles. The American Book Award winner and NAACP Image Award recipient is the author of twelve novels and a civil rights memoir. She recently received a Lifetime Achievement Award in the Fine Arts from the Congressional Black Caucus Foundation, and in 2008 she won the Carl Brandon Society Kindred Award. Due and her husband/collaborator Steven Barnes wrote and coproduced a short film, *Danger Word*, based on their novel *Devil's Wake*, which was nominated for best short narrative film at the Pan African Film Festival and BronzeLens Film Festival. A leading voice in Black speculative fiction, Due's first short story collection, *Ghost Summer and Other Stories*, will be published in the summer of 2015 by Prime Books. She lives in Southern California with Steven Barnes and their son Jason.

Tara Betts

Tara Betts is the author of *Arc & Hue* and the libretto/chapbook *THE GREATEST! A Tribute to Muhammad Ali*. Tara earned her PhD in English and creative writing at SUNY Binghamton University. Her poems appear in *Near Kin: A Collection of Words and Art Inspired by Octavia Estelle Butler* and several other anthologies. Her writings have appeared in *Black Scholar*, *Essence*, *Black Renaissance/Renaissance Noire*, *Callaloo*, *Xavier Review*, *Mosaic* magazine, and *Sounding Out!*, a journal in sound studies. For more info: www.tarabetts.net.

Terry Bisson

Terry Bisson is a science fiction writer who lives in Oakland. He has also written biographies of Nat Turner and Mumia Abu-Jamal. His latest novel, *Any Day Now* (Overlook Press, 2012) is an alternate history of 1968.

Tunde Olaniran

Tunde Olaniran is a community-focused entertainer and educator specializing in the areas of gender, sexual equality, and sexual health and awareness. A long-time community activist and recording artist based in Flint, Michigan, he excels in merging arts programming and events with social issues–based learning workshops as a way to present new ideas and viewpoints to a diverse audience. He holds a master's degree in nonprofit administration from the University of Michigan-Flint and is the manager of outreach for Planned Parenthood Mid and South Michigan.

Vagabond

Born in Brooklyn to a Jamaican father and Puerto Rican mother, Vagabond's interest in art led him to become an artist, writer, and filmmaker. He studied fine and commercial art at a specialized high school in New York City and went on to study film at the School of Visual Arts. He dropped out of school to work with Spike Lee on *Do The Right Thing* and has worked in the film industry since then. He's worked in the Puerto Rican independence movement since 1997 and has organized rallies, protests, and marches and created murals, pamphlets, and agitprop with the artist collective he helped found, the RICANSTRUCTION Netwerk. His work has been featured in *Blu Magazine*, *AWOL*, *SALVO*, *Centro*, *Left Turn*, and *Liberator Magazine*. His first feature film *Machetero* is about the ongoing struggle for Puerto Rican independence and has won awards in South Africa, Wales, England, Thailand, Ireland, and New York.

* * *

Institute for Anarchist Studies

The Institute for Anarchist Studies (IAS), a nonprofit foundation established in 1996, aims to support the development of anarchism by creating spaces for independent, politically engaged scholarship that explores social domination and reconstructive visions of a free society. All IAS projects strive to encourage public intellectuals and collective self-reflection within revolutionary and/or movement contexts.

To this end, the IAS awards grants twice a year to radical writers and translators worldwide and has funded nearly a hundred projects over the years by authors from numerous countries, including Argentina, Lebanon, Canada, Chile, Ireland, Nigeria, Germany, South Africa, and the United States. It also publishes the journal *Perspectives on Anarchist Theory* and the Lexicon pamphlet series, organizes anarchist theory tracks and other events, offers the Mutual Aid Speakers List, and collaborates with AK Press on a book series. The IAS is part of a larger movement seeking to create a nonhierarchical society. It is internally democratic and works in solidarity with people around the globe who share its values. The IAS is completely supported by donations from anarchists and other anti-authoritarians—like you—and their projects, with any contributions exclusively funding grants and paying IAS operating expenses. For more information or to contribute to the work of the IAS, see www.anarchist-studies.org.

AK Press

AK Press is a worker-run collective that publishes and distributes radical books, visual and audio media, and other material. We're small: a dozen people who work long hours for short money because we believe in what we do. We're anarchists, which is reflected both in the books we provide and the way we organize our business. Decisions at AK Press are made collectively, from what we publish to what we distribute to how we structure our labor. All the work, from sweeping floors to answering phones, is shared. When the telemarketers call and ask who's in charge, the answer is: everyone. Our goal isn't profit (although we do have to pay the rent). Our goal is supplying radical words and images to as many people as possible. The books and other media we distribute are published by independent presses, not the corporate giants. We make them widely available to help you make positive (or, hell, revolutionary) changes in the world. For more information on AK Press, or to place an order, see www.akpress.org.

INSTITUTE FOR ANARCHIST STUDIES

THE IAS, A NONPROFIT FOUNDATION ESTABLISHED IN 1996, AIMS TO support the development of anarchism by creating spaces for independent, politically engaged scholarship that explores social domination and reconstructive visions of a free society. All IAS projects strive to encourage public intellectuals and collective self-reflection within revolutionary and/or movement contexts. To this end, the IAS awards grants twice a year to radical writers and translators worldwide, and has funded some eighty projects over the years by authors from numerous countries, including Argentina, Lebanon, Canada, Chile, Ireland, Nigeria, Germany, South Africa, and the United States. It also publishes the online and print journal *Perspectives on Anarchist Theory*, organizes the Renewing the Anarchist Tradition conference, offers the Mutual Aid Speakers List, and collaborates on this book series, among other projects. The IAS is part of a larger movement seeking to create a nonhierarchical society. It is internally democratic and works in solidarity with people around the globe who share its values. The IAS is completely supported by donations from anarchists and other antiauthoritarians—like you—and/or their projects, with any contributions exclusively funding grants and IAS operating expenses; for more information or to contribute to the work of the IAS, see http://www.anarchiststudies.org/.

Support **AK Press!**

AK Press is one of the world's largest and most productive anarchist publishing houses. We're entirely worker-run & democratically managed. We operate without a corporate structure—no boss, no managers, no bullshit. We publish close to twenty books every year, and distribute thousands of other titles published by other like-minded independent presses from around the globe.

The Friends of AK program is a way that you can directly contribute to the continued existence of AK Press, and ensure that we're able to keep publishing great books just like this one! Friends pay $25 a month directly into our publishing account ($30 for Canada, $35 for international), and receive a copy of every book AK Press publishes for the duration of their membership! Friends also receive a discount on anything they order from our website or buy at a table: 50% on AK titles, and 20% on everything else. We've also added a new Friends of AK ebook program: $15 a month gets you an electronic copy of every book we publish for the duration of your membership. Combine it with a print subscription, too!

There's great stuff in the works—so sign up now to become a Friend of AK Press, and let the presses roll!

Won't you be our friend? Email friendsofak@akpress.org for more info, or visit the Friends of AK Press website: www.akpress.org/programs/friendsofak